A Walk on Broken Glass
Elisabeth, Empress of Austria

A Walk on Broken Glass

Elisabeth, Empress of Austria

a novel by

Gloria M. Allan

Revised Edition

GRANVILLE ISLAND
PUBLISHING

Copyright © 2014 Gloria M. Allan

Library and Archives Canada Cataloguing in Publication

Allan, Gloria M., author
    A walk on broken glass: Elisabeth, Empress of Austria: a novel / by Gloria M. Allan. — Revised edition.

Issued in print and electronic formats.
ISBN 978-1-926991-79-5 (paperback).—ISBN 978-1-926991-80-1 (pdf)

    1. Elisabeth, Empress, consort of Franz Joseph I, Emperor of Austria, 1837–1898—Fiction. I. Title.

PS8601.L42783W34 2015   C813'.6   C2015-906669-7
                                                C2015-906670-0

Editors: Bookmark: Editing & Indexing
Copy editors: Renate Preuss and Kyle Hawke
Proofreader: Neall Calvert
Cover and text designer: Omar Gallegos
Cover image: *Kaiserin Elisabeth mit offenem Haar* by Franz Xaver Winterhalter
Used with permission of Kunsthistorisches Museum Wien

Some of the characters are fictional and others are based on the author's perceptions from numerous history books.

Granville Island Publishing Ltd.
212 – 1656 Duranleau St.
Vancouver, BC, Canada V6H 3S4

604-688-0320 / 1-877-688-0320
info@granvilleislandpublishing.com
www.granvilleislandpublishing.com

To my beloved grandchildren
Ashley, Ryan, Tyla, Erin and Seana.
Where there is will, there is a way.

Our inner strength comes from the seeds sprinkled at birth. The nourishment of our childhood forms the blossoms of our maturity.

Contents

Part 1 — Hope and Betrayal

Part 2 — Love and Tragedy

Lineage of Elisabeth and Franz Josef

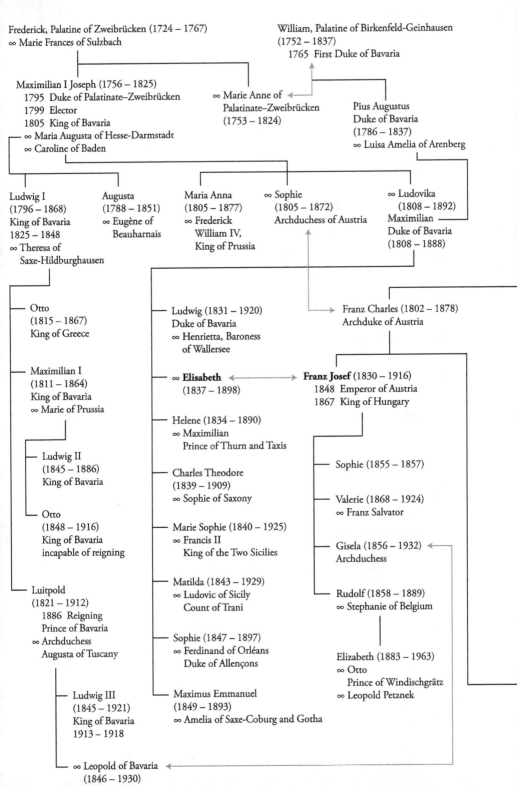

Franz Stephan of Lorraine (1708 – 1765)
1745 King of the Holy Roman Empire (until his death)
∞ Maria Theresa (1717 – 1780)
1740 Archduchess of Austria, Holy Roman Empress, and
Queen of Hungary and Bohemia (until her death)

Leopold (1747 – 1792)
1765 Grand Duke of Tuscany
1790 Emperor (until his death)
∞ Maria Luisa of Bourbon
Spanish Infanta

Josef II (1741 – 1790)
1765 Emperor (until his death)
∞ Isabella of Parma
∞ Maria Josepha
of Bavaria

Ferdinand Charles
(1754 – 1806)
∞ Maria Beatrice
d'Este

Maria Christina
(1742 – 1798)
∞ Albert of
Saxe-Teschen

Maria Amalia
(1746 – 1804)
∞ Ferdinand
of Parma

Maria Carolina
(1752 – 1814)
∞ Ferdinand of
Naples and Sicily

Marie Antoinette
(1755 – 1793)
∞ Louis XVI
of France

Franz II (1768 – 1825)
Emperor 1792 – 1806
Emperor of Austria 1804 – 1835
∞ Elizabeth Wilhelma of Württemberg
∞ Maria Theresa of Naples and Sicily
∞ Maria Ludovica d'Este
∞ Caroline Augusta of Bavaria

Ferdinand (1769 – 1824)
1790, Grand Duke
of Tuscany

Charles (1771 – 1847)
Field-marshal
Duke of Teschen
∞ Henrietta of Nassau-Weilburg

Josef (1776 – 1847)
Palatine of Hungary

John (1782 – 1859)
Regent of the Empire
∞ Anna Plochel

Rainer (1783 – 1853)
∞ Elizabeth of
Savoy-Carignano

Rudolf (1788 – 1831)
Cardinal

Ferdinand (1793 – 1875)
Emperor of Austria
1835 – 1848
∞ Maria Anna of Sardinia

Marie Louise (1791 – 1847)
∞ Emperor Napoleon I
∞ Adam of Neipperg

Leopoldine (1797 – 1826)
∞ Pedro I
Emperor of Brazil

Marie Clementine (1798 – 1881)
∞ Leopold of Salerno

Caroline (1801 – 1832)
∞ Frederick Augustus
King of Saxony

Franz Ferdinand (1863 – 1914)
1889 Succesor to the throne
∞ Sophie Chotek
Duchess of Hohenberg

Otto (1865 – 1906)
∞ Maria Josefa of Saxony

Charles Ludwig (1833 – 1896)
∞ Margaret of Saxony
∞ Annunciata of Sicily
∞ Teresa of Braganza

Maximilian Eugene
(1895 – 1952)

Maria Anna (1835 – 1840)

Ludwig Victor (1842 – 1919)

Maria Annunciata
(1876 – 1961)

Charles (1887 – 1922)
Last Emperor of Austria and last
King of Hungary 1916 – 1918
∞ Zita of Bourbon Parma

Ferdinand Maximilian (1832 – 1867)
1864 Emperor of Mexico (until his death)
∞ Charlotte of Belgium

Elizabeth Amalia (1878 – 1960)
∞ Alois of Liechtenstein

Prologue
September 17, 1898, Vienna

The mourners were gone. The Capuchin Church was dark except for candles flickering here and there. Black velvet draped the walls and black curtains covered the entrances. Down the aisle and up the altar steps ran a long black carpet. A gold candelabra with six candles illuminated a large cross set in a golden tapestry hanging from the towering altar. Below it lay a coffin surrounded by flowers. A lone figure huddled at its side. His sobs echoed through the silence, reverberating against the stone walls.

On the coffin lay a jewelled crown, resting in Maréchal Niel roses. In a gilded frame below it were the words:

> Elisabeth
> Empress of Austria
> Queen of Hungary
> Princess of Bavaria

On a cushion lay a black fan, a pair of white gloves, an umbrella and a gold-framed picture of a parrot.

At the foot of the coffin, in a bed of pink chrysanthemums, a meticulously-embroidered silk wreath from the Prince and Princess of Wales read:

Though taken long before your time
Thy saintly soul now flows
Where tears are wiped from every eye,
And sorrow is unknown.

The figure struggled to his feet. He gripped the casket. His body trembled. He let his head rest on the casket. He closed his eyes and groaned. His tears poured. He covered the casket with kisses. Then he lifted his head and stared into the hollow blackness.

Franz Joseph, Emperor of Austria, cried into the silence.

"If only I had shown her how much I loved her."

Part 1
Hope and Betrayal
1853–1860

Elisabeth

Bavaria, 1853

1

It was a bright spring morning. Birds chirped among the forest trees and sailed across the skies in rhythmic swoops, as if phantom musicians churned the air. Elisabeth dashed along the mountain trail, her spirits soaring. Her world was changing. She felt more like seventeen than fifteen since Count Richard had come into her life.

She jumped over rocks and sidestepped protruding roots, trying to keep up with her father, Max, trudging ahead on the trail leading to Kramer Ridge, high in the Bavarian Alps. It was the most challenging climb they had done. The sun was warm, the breeze soft. Her heart sang.

She stopped and inhaled the cool alpine air. She loved Possi, short for Possenhofen, her summer home on the Starnberger See which wound through the Eton Valley with tiny villages nestled on its shore. She loved the snow-trimmed peaks reaching into the sky and the green plateaus stretching along their ledges. She loved galloping through the forests on her pony Punch and singing with the birds.

Winters in Munich were just too dull. Snowball fights with the neighbouring children were her only real fun. Of course, the royal noses flared in disgust — it was hardly appropriate behaviour for a royal princess. Elisabeth smiled and ignored them. She never thought of herself as a royal princess. And it didn't bother her that Possi, with ivy growing up its exterior and the odd cow munching in the gardens, was more like a farmhouse than like the surrounding mansions of the aristocrats. Her father bragged that at least its four turrets gave it prestige.

She gathered up her skirts and continued on. The forest enclosed her in a chapel of greenery. Huge hanging boughs full of tiny chirping birds displayed their new birth of leaves. Ferns and wildflowers grew everywhere. She stopped again, closing her eyes, letting the quietness filter through her. Only nature strummed the tunes.

There was nothing more fun than swinging on the huge branches with the peasant children from the nearby villages who were her best friends, especially Allie. On the windiest days, she and Allie swayed back and forth in the treetops. She'd close her eyes and let the breeze caress her. It was as if she had arrived at the gates of Heaven. Allie hoped to be a trapeze performer in front of crowds of people, which was why she loved swinging in the trees. Not Sisi, as her family called her. Sisi hated crowds. That's why she loved the forest.

She shared all her secrets with Allie, told her about Count Richard. Allie was in love with a young village man who worked in a garment factory, so she understood.

Eating at Allie's little cottage was more fun than any royal banquet. The cottage was rustic and cozy, there was always a warm fire, and her mother and father clowned around like happy children. Allie's mother made the best cabbage strudel, with flour and eggs layered with hot lard. Elisabeth's mouth watered just thinking about it.

Of course, the neighbouring royals could not hold back their sneers. "Elisabeth is a disgrace to her society. She acts more like a peasant than a royal. She is a Wittelsbach," they snorted. "The Wittelsbachs have ruled Bavaria for over five hundred years, and her uncle, King Ludwig, sits on the throne in Munich. She is royalty, and she eats in the peasants' cottages." Their cigars almost flew from their vibrating fingers.

Elisabeth's mother, Ludovika, told her about their sneers, a shadow clouding her face. Sisi knew her mother was perturbed. But not her — the last thing she cared about was royalty.

She loved dancing at the village carnivals, with her father strumming his zither like a madman and her own feet flying just as fast. Max often joked, "If we weren't royalty we'd be circus performers." That would bring her a smile. Of course, the royals thought him the devil himself.

When she held out her apron to catch coins from the local peasants, the villagers clapped with laughter, the aristocrats went into stunned shock and her mother fled to her home in shame. Elisabeth couldn't hold back her smile, though she did her best to hide it from her mother.

She knew her mother was stressed, maybe a little *over*stressed. Her mother wanted to be a part of elite society — her rightful place, really, but she was rarely invited into their homes and Max, never. That did not bother him. Nor did it bother him that the aristocrats referred to Possi as an ongoing circus. Elisabeth had to admit it really was.

Most times, her mother sailed through the family chaos with a placid smile, in a kind of mystical daze, even when tripping over the guinea pigs, rabbits and snoring dogs who lay on the frayed Aubusson carpets or watching Elisabeth and her three brothers and four sisters churning up the lawns and the rose gardens with their ponies. Elisabeth's pony, Punch, was the wildest one, as long as you didn't count Elisabeth herself. Still, there were times when Ludovika's face hardened into tight lines and her smile disappeared. That's when her headaches came. She'd vanish into her room, slam the door shut and pound on her piano until the walls seemed to vibrate. Then out she'd come again, with her complacent smile back on, tripping over dogs, the children's screams sending her eyes to the ceiling.

The aristocrats shunned them in Munich as well. If they were invited to the royal salons, which hardly ever occurred, Elisabeth never went if she could help it. Her mother told her it would teach her a little etiquette. That kind of etiquette Elisabeth could do without. Their disdainful looks and their sarcastic jabs filtering through their cigar smoke were just too much.

Elisabeth knew it was mainly her father's liberal ideas and crazy antics that kept the royal noses tilted skyward and the tongues wagging. He created as much gossip as Lola Montez, the 'black witch' who swept into Munich with her raven hair hanging to her heels, a trail of scandals and broken hearts across Europe in her wake. When Lola descended upon the old king, Elisabeth's uncle Ludwig, he was so smitten with love it almost toppled the Bavarian throne.

"He's no different than any other man," Ludovika had scoffed.

Lola created havoc, putting forth her views and disrupting politics. Cabinet ministers fell and new rules shattered the court. Caroline Augusta, the Dowager Empress of Austria, offered her two thousand guilders if she would leave Bavaria. Elisabeth and her older sister Helene — whom the family called 'Néné' — quivered with barely concealed mirth. When the old king dried Lola's indignant tears by making her a countess and a canoness of the Order of St. Theresa, their mirth turned into giggles. The court went into disgusted shock.

The people rioted that winter and Elisabeth and her family fled to Possi. The people regained their sanity, the old king fled to Italy to mend his broken heart and Lola was escorted to the frontier. That was their first Christmas in Possi and their most wonderful ever. Especially Christmas Eve.

The snowdrifts were piled to the tops of the windows that night, when her father bellowed from outside.

"Come out, come out. Every one of you!"

It scared them half to death. Dropping everything, they ran for their coats, certain that rioters were invading. Even Elisabeth's baby sister, little Sophie, came running. Ludovika scooped Sophie up in her arms to keep the other children from tumbling over her.

"Quick, quick! Get in!" her father yelled.

He hurried them into a large sleigh, tucking blankets around them right up to their chins. The horses were stamping their hooves in the snow, eager to be off. The driver released the reins and cracked his whip and the sleigh tore into the forest.

"What's wrong?" Helene wondered aloud. The sleigh had slowed to a snail's pace, winding through snow-cushioned boughs of evergreens standing silent and mysterious as they passed.

"There is nothing wrong, Néné," her father assured her. "I wanted you to see the forest on a winter night when the new-fallen snow forms a world of mystical stillness and magical beauty."

No one spoke — not not even little Sophie. They gazed in silence.

That evening, the peasant families came to Possi. They danced the night away, whirling to the wild gypsy music emanating from her father's zither. The ladies raced down the wide halls that were lined with Christmas trees and through the drawing room, their colourful skirts flying, their husbands following, their children trying to keep up. Sisi's brothers and sisters flew too, swinging and swaying in wild rhythm. Ludovika, forgetting the snobby royals, had just as much fun tossing little Sophie up into the air and catching her.

Those moments Elisabeth never forgot. Many times, years later when despair filled her world, she would close her eyes and let that beautiful warmth fill her soul. She would still almost smell the pine logs burning, the sweet fragrance of apples and roasting chestnuts, the wonderful cakes studded with candied fruit and the big bowls of punch.

"Sisi! Hurry, hurry!"

Her father's cry jarred her back to reality, to the mountain trail. She almost tripped on her skirts as she dashed after him. It was hard going as the rocks and roots had taken over the trail. Her mind was racing too, with thoughts of Count Richard.

She had not told her father about Count Richard, although she was sure he would like him — he was like the man hiking ahead of her. She had not told her mother, either. Max always joked that her mother's main concern was to find a royal prince or an emperor for her daughters. It was not easy with all the chaos that went on in their lives. Count Richard was not royalty, so she was not quite sure what her mother would say.

Her sister Néné would not like him; Elisabeth was sure of that. Néné liked the royals. She used to chase around with the children but, since turning seventeen, she had changed. It was as if she had stepped into another world. She paraded around as if she had wings on her feet, continually fluffing her hair in the mirror. Her mother said Néné's hair was the colour of the autumn sun. People always remarked about her mysterious eyes, and the scent of her perfume followed her everywhere. Elisabeth hated perfume. Still, she had to admit that her sister was far more beautiful than she. And though she was taking more time in front of a mirror since Count Richard, it was still not as much as Néné.

Oh, well, she thought as she quickened her pace to catch up with her father, *if Néné wants an emperor, she has to be beautiful.* The last thing Elisabeth wanted was an emperor. She thought of Count Richard. A warm feeling went through her. She would marry for love.

Elisabeth knew all about love. She kept romantic novels well-hidden beneath her bed, knowing full well that Bavarian princesses were not allowed to read romantic novels.

"They might infect your mind with false ideas," her mother would say. "Love is not always in a princess's destiny."

"And why shouldn't there be love?" Elisabeth would lash out.

Her mother's eyes would take on a veiled look and she would change the subject.

Rounding a bend, Elisabeth stopped suddenly. There was her father, his feet planted solidly on the ground, gazing up at Kramer Ridge. Her heart swelled. *No matter what the Munich royals think about my papa,* she thought, *to me he is magical.*

He had shown her a world she would never have found on her own. He showed her the wonders of nature, the beauty of the seasons, silence and solitude. He had shown her the splendour of sunsets, the mystical depth of the stars. He had shown her the simplicities of the world so often hidden in the complexities of life.

She rushed to his side and slipped her hand through his arm, hugging it.

"It won't be easy," Max said, giving her a hesitant glance.

She looked at Kramer Ridge towering above them, and smiled.

"I can do it. Let's go, Papa." Tightening her hand on his arm, she added tenderly, "And I love you."

Then she took off, with her arms flying as fast as her feet.

Max dashed after her. *With that determination, the world will be hers*, he thought. At least he hoped it would be. But in his heart there was fear.

It was a long climb before they dug their toes into tiny crevices and pulled themselves up by plant roots onto the ledge. Once there, they collapsed in exhaustion, gasping for air. Their faces glowed.

"We did it, Papa."

Elisabeth pulled the red-checkered kerchief from her head. Her chestnut-coloured braids tumbled to her shoulders.

"Yes, we did it."

Max dropped his knapsack to the ground. He was a tall man with broad shoulders and a dark beard that matched the hair curling around his neck. He had a gentle but rugged face, with large cheekbones and woolly eyebrows. Elisabeth knew he had a charm the ladies couldn't resist, even the aristocratic ladies. Though they tried not to show it, their sparkling eyes and half-hidden smiles gave it away.

Tired and triumphant, they gazed around in awe at the mountains still high above them. A cool mist surrounded them and wisps of soft clouds cradled the high peaks. Patches of snow lingered here and there and clumps of grass sprouted in the brilliant green of new birth. Yellow and red wildflowers were everywhere. Below them lay the Eton Valley, with its green fields and tiny villages.

"Look at Starnberger See. It is like a tiny saucer," Elisabeth announced. "And Possi is like a dollhouse."

"It is beautiful."

Max was beaming, but more for their mutual passion for the wilderness and nature. These were memories that would never fade.

"This was a big climb for a little girl," he said affectionately.

"Oh, Papa. I'm not a little girl," she shot back. "I'm fifteen now."

Her eyes twinkled, her face rosy.

Her father was momentarily struck by her beauty — the pudginess of her face was gone, her features were now fine and delicate. Sisi was beautiful. His eyes shifted down. Beneath her woollen vest, her body was blooming. He turned away. The beauty around them faded. His little Sisi was growing up. She was on the edge of womanhood and he had not noticed.

A cloud caught the sun. A breeze brushed his face.

Time flies like shooting stars right before our eyes, he thought, staring into space. *And it never slows, not even in paradise.*

For the first time, he questioned his sentiments.

Was Ludovika right that day recently when her anger had set the table shaking?

She was usually a gentle woman, with remnants of her youthful beauty still lingering in the contours of her face. That day, there had been nothing gentle about her — her beauty had been framed with rage. She had banged her fists on the table, repeating the latest slur that raced through the royal salons.

"'It would be surprising if any of Duke Max's children, especially that wild Elisabeth, ever achieves a suitable marriage.' And they are right," Ludovika had cried as she pounded harder. "Sisi is wild and undisciplined. She must be brought from the wilderness of the hills. The shepherd children cannot be her constant companions — she is royalty! She must be prepared for her place in her own society. She must be taught the etiquette of the royal court. It is our only hope of finding her a suitable marriage."

"Sisi is a child of nature, and she is still young," Max had shot back. "Don't take her precious childhood and crush her in the artificial glitter of the imperial salons. That would stifle her." The clouds still swirled around the peaks above them, but the breeze had assumed a sharper bite.

Had Ludovika been right?

They were both Wittelsbachs, Ludovika from the royal branch and he from the landowner's branch of the family tree. Ludovika's father, Maximilian, king of Bavaria, had made him a duke so that Ludovika would be a duchess. Still, he was free from any court responsibilities. He lived his life as he wished, tossing aside all royal pomp and providing the salons with lively gossip. The court royals never had it so good.

Max fancied himself a writer, an actor, a musician — whatever he wanted to be. His children howled with laughter when he dressed up as King Arthur to preside over a drama club of fellow knights. He frequented the local taverns, enjoyed the company of the common people. He invited them into his home for a meal. Not one royal salon in Munich would let him through its door, and he did not give a hoot.

But Sisi? Was he doing her justice?

He turned and watched her arranging yellow and red flowers in her hands. He looked away and stared out at the valley below. He could not hide Sisi forever in the magic of nature, in the simplicity of childhood. The unrelenting march of time was shifting the innocence of her youth into the uncertainty of adulthood.

I can live my life as I please, he thought, *but she is a princess from the royal house of Wittelsbach. No matter how uncomfortable it might be, she must take her rightful place in the superficial aristocratic society into which she was born.*

Elisabeth jumped up, her eyes twinkling.

"Papa, I have something to tell you."

"Is it something that will enhance this day even more?" he asked, trying to be lighthearted again.

"Yes, yes." Her eyes were dancing. "Papa, I'm in love."

"In love?" His eyebrows knitted together tighter than his voice. "In love with what? A horse? A puppy? A rabbit? With what?"

"Oh, Papa," she giggled. "A young man."

"A young man?" His words shot out like a flying cannonball.

"Yes. A young man." Her laughter rippled. "And don't look so shocked. After all, I am fifteen, and people do find me attractive."

His shock made him see reality. Royal princesses did not marry for love. They were merely pawns destined for political matches with the royal families of Europe. He dug his fingers into his palms.

"Does your mother know?" he blurted out.

Her eyes widened at his expression.

"Of course not, Papa. I haven't told anyone else. Only Allie and Maria."

Her sister Maria was three years younger than Elisabeth. They were very close. They raced their ponies through forests and built hideaway castles deep in the woods. Maria performed on a horse in Max's circuses almost as well as Elisabeth.

"Who is this young man?" Max's voice shook.

"Oh, you know him well. And I know you like him." Her sparkle was back, her feet danced. "Count Richard."

"Count Richard?" Again, his words shot out. "Is that the young man with the long blond hair and that floppy green hunter's hat that he never takes off?"

"Yes, yes. That's him!" She clapped her hands together.

Max sighed in relief. He knew the young Count Richard all right. He was tall and gangly, a little clumsy, and always had a big affectionate smile. He was a poor bourgeois who considered himself an actor, as Max did. In fact, he was part of the dinner club Max presided over in his King Arthur garb. He would be easy to dislodge. One flick of Max's finger and he would be gone. His calmness returned.

"How long has this been going on?"

He was a little afraid to know.

"It's not really going on, Papa. He comes to all your circuses, and we smile at each other. He told me I'm a very skillful rider, better than he. He slips me notes. He says he loves me and will never love another. Then he says crazy things, like he's not good enough for me, that he is not royalty," she smiled. "As if that mattered."

Then her smile disappeared. What was wrong with her father? His face was solemn.

"He is right, my little one. He cannot be for you. He is not of royal blood."

"But Papa," she cried. "It makes no difference. You have said that many times. Class is not important. You have told me that."

He was nodding. How easy the words were to say, and how rational and justified they seemed. But not in this real world could they be realized. Ludovika would never allow Sisi to marry Count Richard. He knew that. He also knew he could not allow such a match either. He put his arm around her shoulder.

"Come, Sisi. Let's start down. You know how quickly it can close in up here."

Elisabeth stared a moment at her father. This was not what she had expected, but his expression told her it was not the time to argue.

"Yes, Papa." She flashed him a look that pained his heart. "I'll race you down."

She picked up her knapsack, tucked the flowers carefully inside, wrapped her kerchief around her head and bounced down the trail ahead of him. It was much easier going down.

As she hopped over rocks and roots, her excitement grew. In two weeks it would be circus day at Possi and Count Richard would be there. This time, she promised herself, she would take his hand and not let him escape for the rest of the afternoon. And — she glanced back at her father trudging along, his face pulled together like his knapsack — she would tell Count Richard that her Papa knew.

Fate raced at her side with unrelenting claws. It was the year 1853, the year her life would change forever.

2

Children screaming widly as they bounced on Possi's couches with flying arms sent Ludovika fleeing into her tiny salon, her haven of escape. She collapsed on her settee, kicked off her shoes and placed a cold cloth on her head. At that moment, a courier arrived with a letter from her sister Sophie, the Archduchess of Austria.

Ignoring the courier, Ludovika ripped open the envelope. She read Sophie's letter, and then read it again, and then a third time. The children's laughter filtered through the walls, along with an occasional scream. It didn't faze her. The courier bowed his way out. Her eyes remained on the letter in her trembling hands.

"I can't believe it!" she exclaimed. "Sophie wants Néné, Sisi and me to come to Bad Ischl for a visit."

Sophie had written: 'It is the only time that poor overworked Franz can snatch a few weeks of holiday. It will give Néné and Franz a chance to meet in a quiet atmosphere.'

Ludovika let out an excited screech and jumped from the settee, almost stumbling over her shoes. She paced around the room, her thoughts spinning. Franz Joseph, Sophie's son, was the emperor of the great Austrian Habsburg Empire — and the most sought-after bachelor in all Europe.

Five years earlier, with Néné and Sisi, she had visited Sophie in Bad Ischl, the Habsburgs' summer residence in upper Austria. The Habsburgs had fled there when Vienna verged on a revolution that threatened the Austrian Empire. Even with all that turmoil, Sophie had raved about fourteen-year-old Néné's beauty. She had even suggested that, with the proper training, Néné might make a very suitable empress. Ludovika was sure that Sophie had Franz in mind, as he would one day be the emperor.

That day had come sooner than expected.

The revolution peaked, Emperor Ferdinand resigned and Franz Joseph replaced him. Now, a contented populace lived under his rule, though Ludovika had heard rumours that Sophie was the power behind the throne.

After that visit, no further word had come from Sophie. The French instructor and the dance master Ludovika had hired to enhance Néné's social graces were gone. Possi had fallen back into its usual disarray and she had dismissed all hopes of Néné marrying the Emperor of Austria, especially as rumours of his charm with the ladies swept Europe.

Ludovika read the letter again.

"Oh my God!" she cried out, the Lord's name exploding from her tongue as never before.

Franz's younger brother, Charles Ludwig, would also be there. He was just two years older than Sisi. She remembered his eyes had been full of amusement as he followed Sisi around, often giving her little gifts of candy.

"Oh my God." This time it was a whisper.

Was Sophie suggesting a match between Sisi and Charles Ludwig? She raced to the window and pushed open the shutters. The battering wind in her face had no effect on her escalating thoughts. Perhaps, she dared to think, there would be a prince for Sisi. Her sons she didn't worry about, as they were guaranteed commissions in the Imperial Army, but each time she gave birth to a girl, her biggest pain was for her daughter's future.

Ludovika's five sisters had married reigning princes, kings or emperors. Not like her. And all resided in prestigious royal courts. Though they were known as the 'Five Sisters of Woe' — five women with broken hearts — it did not lessen Ludovika's resentment. She envied, sometimes bitterly, their royal marriages and their prestigious stature, especially when the Munich royals rebuffed her with vague smiles and superior glances. She tried to calm herself with thoughts that it didn't matter, that her children were her world. And they were. But there were also many times when their screams and rowdy manoeuvres triggered a hasty exit to her own room.

Then Ludovika would let the memories of a springtime in Spain to fill her mind. She would close her eyes and let the tears pour out.

She had been young and beautiful that spring, so they'd said, more beautiful than any of her five sisters. She was seventeen, dancing a festive evening away in a Spanish palace, when a young man had caught her eye from across the room. Through the crowd he'd come, his eyes never leaving her face. He'd stopped before her, his smile wide, and made a sweeping bow.

"I have never seen anyone as lovely as you," he had said.

They'd walked in the palace gardens, among blossoming trees and chirping birds seeking mates. Prince Miguel of Portugal had laid his heart at her feet.

But it had been a time when smaller empires were struggling to retain their sovereignty.

"Marriage is a tool to enhance and secure the power of a country," her father had informed her. "Prince Miguel is of no benefit to us."

Her father did what he thought best; it was the way of the times. Her hope of a marriage for love was shattered.

Remembering now, as she often did, Ludovika looked up at the bare ceiling and let her tears come again. She had been cheated of her destiny, for Prince Miguel became King of Portugal while she had married a duke who couldn't decide whether he was an actor, a musician or a writer. So she had committed herself to ensuring that her daughters did not also end up on a lower rung of society.

Ludovika caught her breath. Sisi, endowed as she was with her father's eccentric temperament, was her greatest challenge. Her latest attempt, in Saxony, to work out a match between Sisi and Prince George, the heir to the throne, had been a disaster. The young prince had never tired of following Sisi around with amused smiles as she performed her usual antics, like galloping bareback through the woods without a guide. However, the old king had a face of stone. In his farewell letter, he wrote: 'Elisabeth is attractive but she does not have a single pretty feature. She is very animated, but she is also somewhat flighty and unpredictable. We feel she is unsuitable.'

It had not bothered Sisi. She had been amused and responded, "Prince George can't even ride a horse properly."

Now Ludovika clasped Sophie's letter to her chest. Her heart pounded. Perhaps a miracle. An emperor for Néné, and maybe, just maybe, a royal Habsburg prince for Sisi.

"Oh my God."

This time, the words shot out of Ludovika with fervour. She charged from the room so fast she forgot to put on her shoes.

Ludovika stumbled over a snoozing dog as she ran into Possi's salon. The sweeping windows in the rustic, pine-panelled room gathered the last rays of the sunlight.

"Mama," Helene exclaimed, "you look like you have witnessed a miracle!"

"Read this letter I have just received," Ludovika exclaimed, thrusting it into Helene's hand.

Helene read it slowly, her placid expression unchanging. Ludovika's impatience took over.

"You know what she's suggesting?"

Helene was a closed, reserved person, often keeping her feelings so hidden it was hard to know what was in her mind. This time, her complacency sent Ludovika into a jittery crisis.

"Yes, that I meet Franz Joseph," Helene answered with a tone of indifference.

"And you are not excited?" Ludovika's query almost rattled the beamed ceiling.

Helene's face tightened. She sat silently.

"I'm more in doubt than excited," she said, finally.

She flung the letter on the table and looked painfully at her mother.

"Oh, Mama. He would never consider me to be his empress."

Ludovika fell to her knees and took Helene's hands.

"Push those negative thoughts from your mind," she said. "You are very beautiful. The Munich aristocrats rave about your beauty. You are intelligent. You have poise. Do not cast shadows on yourself and do not for one minute forget that you are a Bavarian princess."

Helene thought about the days at Bad Ischl a few years earlier. She remembered Franz strutting around in an imperial uniform, his body so stiff and straight she had wondered if he was real.

"Mama," she said almost desperately, "that summer in Bad Ischl, I was not impressed with him, nor was he with me. In fact, I doubt he even noticed me. His eyes would pass over me as if I were invisible. He spent all his time with his adjutant, Count Grünne, a gangling snob who couldn't even remember my name. And all they did was babble on about military manoeuvres."

"Néné," her mother said, "that was five years ago. You have changed and so has he. You've heard the glowing rumours about him."

Helene sniffed. She had heard them all right. His romantic escapades were the talk of Europe. There was never a shortage of female charm, with coquettish smiles full of promises. According to gossip, no beautiful woman, regardless of her social standing, escaped his eye or his desires. They said he was dashingly attractive, a magnificent ballroom dancer. They also said he was eloquent and charming — but that she could not imagine.

Helene strode to the window. The sun was taking its last peek, the sky had an orange hue and the mountaintops glittered in gold. She turned back to her mother.

"Why would he want me when every eligible princess and countess from every country in Europe and England is falling at his feet?"

"Néné," Ludovika said, "don't be pessimistic. I know our exposure in society has been limited, but we are Wittelsbachs and we must stand proudly with our inheritance. Now — " She jumped up, excitement growing, " — we have three months to make you irresistible. We can do it. We'll show all those sanctimonious aristocrats in Munich. We'll show all Europe. And when we get through, Franz will not be able to resist you. You'll see."

Helene stared at her mother. Could she be right? She felt a touch of excitement. She turned back to the orange sky, and smiled.

"I can't waste a moment," Ludovika said, rushing out the door.

Within minutes, she was at her desk pulling out writing paper. *Three months.* The French lessons must resume; the dance master must be brought back. Dresses, hats, shoes, dressmakers. Her heart pounded. Never had she felt such excitement. Then she remembered Sisi. *I must ask my nephew the king to remove Count Richard to another part of the country until Sisi regains her senses,* she thought. Maximilian had taken the throne when old King Ludwig had abdicated, his heart still broken by Lola Montez.

Excitement raced across Bavaria like a river in a raging storm. All Munich was abuzz with the talk of a possible match between Helene and the Emperor of Austria. The royals' voices almost rattled the chandeliers: "Can Ludovika pull this off?"

Ludovika and Helene were suddenly stars — the royal ladies now could not get enough of them. They buzzed around them like bees over honey. They hosted sumptuous banquets and balls. Ludovika loved every minute. She had forgotten how lavish it could be. Even Max was invited — of course, he never went. Neither did Elisabeth if she could help it. Her mother kept reminding her of Charles Ludwig, and how she could do with a little polish. But she didn't want that kind of polish and Charles Ludwig had not replaced Count Richard in her affections, even if he was a royal prince. She was counting the hours until circus day.

Ludovika and Helene revelled in the attention. Ludovika's inferiority sailed off into infinity and her headaches disappeared.

Helene, to her own surprise, enjoyed it all too — it was like a roller-coaster ride. She skillfully mastered the engaging smiles and the shallow conversational ways of the aristocrats. She discovered that it didn't matter what you said as long as you smiled and used syrupy words. No one listened anyway, unless it was gossip. She smiled graciously at the royals who raved about her beauty. She loved the new dresses, and the makeup was more fun than she'd ever imagined. She never tired of standing in front of a mirror. Often, alone in her room, mesmerizing thoughts drifted in: perhaps the dashing young emperor might fall at her feet with love and she would love him. With a glow of excitement, a soft smile and misty eyes, she would gaze out at the stars until she fell asleep.

3

When circus day at last arrived, Possi positively vibrated with excitement — but not because of the circus. Everyone was busy fussing over Helene's wardrobe. Dressmakers were everywhere. A French governess had arrived and everyone, including the youngest children, practised their French phrases. Everyone except, of course, Duke Max. A dance master elegantly swept Helene around the drawing room and everyone, this time including Duke Max, was swaying and humming Viennese waltzes. Little Sophie wobbled around on her unstable legs, having just as much fun.

"But the circus will go on, emperor or no emperor!" Duke Max proclaimed. "Nothing will deter that!"

Chairs were set up and boxes arranged. The local shepherd families with their bouncing children, all dressed in colourful costumes, covered almost every blade of grass on Possi's lawns. Music sailed from fiddlers' bows and everyone walked with a musical lilt.

Not one aristocrat attended. They stayed behind their massive gates, plugged their ears and wondered why Ludovika would allow such a disgusting display, especially with the rumour circulating that the Emperor of Austria was eyeing her daughter.

Elisabeth dressed with particular care on circus day and was out early, smiling to all. Her smile widened at praises for her new hunting hat with its large golden feathers, the latest English style. However, her anxiety was surfacing. There was no Count Richard.

She performed her riding feats without a flaw, never missing a jump. Her father had taught her skillfully. There were oohs and aahs. People rose to their feet, hands clapping.

Still, there was no Count Richard sitting in the front row, clapping the loudest.

Elisabeth pushed through the crowds, searching. Clowns with laughing faces did flips, music blared and people reached out to her with congratulations. She sidestepped dogs and children, struggling to keep her hat balanced on her head.

Still there was no Count Richard.

She found her father conversing with some village men.

"Papa," she called, interrupting, "have you seen Count Richard?"

He had not, and he excused himself abruptly, turning back to his friends.

That was when she knew she would never see Count Richard again. She knew it. It had been in her father's eyes that day on the mountain. It was there in his eyes again today.

She raced back through the crowds. Everyone saw her tears. Some reached out to her in sympathy but she brushed them aside. She locked herself in her room for two whole nights and days. Her mother didn't knock. Helene didn't knock. Only the younger children knocked.

The Viennese waltzes never stopped echoing through the walls. When the third sun had dipped beneath the horizon and all hope was gone, she buried her sorrow in one last tribute to Richard.

> Richard, alas there is no more.
> The bells toll,
> The moonlight whispers to thee
> How much I love thee.
> Never shall I see thee again.

She hid the note in the bottom of her dresser. She dried her tears and went out into the chaos of Possi. She did not speak of Count Richard again, not to Maria, not to Allie, not to anyone.

"Sisi," Ludovika called.

She pulled her into the drawing room, dodging dressmakers pinning hems and adjusting sleeves, while Helene smiled patiently.

"We have a new dress for you for — the ball at Bad Ischl."

"A ball?"

Elisabeth had never been to a ball. And a new dress? A smile ventured forth.

When her mother flashed the white and rose gown before her, Elisabeth gasped. She could not believe her eyes.

"Is that for me?"

"Yes, for you," her mother said, eyes twinkling.

Elisabeth took the dress and held it in front of her. She whirled around in front of the mirror.

"It's beautiful. Beautiful!"

Count Richard fled her mind.

"And it wouldn't do you any harm to learn a few dance steps," her mother said with an impish grin.

"Who would dance with me?" Elisabeth sang out, still swirling with the dress in front of the mirror.

"Don't forget, Charles Ludwig will be there."

"Charles Ludwig." Elisabeth came to an abrupt stop. "I had forgotten."

She remembered Bad Ischl, her eyes sparkling.

"He was a little strange and skinny, but he always gave me little gifts of fruit and chocolates."

"Sounds like him," Ludovika laughed.

Back Elisabeth turned, eyeing herself in the mirror, whirling around. *Charles Ludwig*, she mused. She stopped.

"Mama," she said coyly, "I should learn some dance steps and maybe do something different with my hair, like Néné."

Ludovika's eyes glowed. She looked up at the ceiling. *Maybe, just maybe*, she prayed, *it might work out.*

As the day of the journey to Bad Ischl drew closer, Elisabeth's excitement grew along with her curiosity. What would Charles Ludwig be like now?

4

Far away in Vienna, Franz Joseph pondered his mother's latest dictum: he must take a wife. She had also decided who it would be. He knew, as he gazed out the window with a grim heart and growing apprehension, there was no going back when his mother, Archduchess Sophie, made up her mind.

Franz Joseph's penchant for conquering young ladies had grown to enormous proportions — but his time was running out.

Franz Joseph

1

Sophie, Franz's mother, had been nineteen when she arrived in Vienna, a disillusioned bride with a dull and complacent husband. He was square-faced, with dark bobbed hair. His eyes were gentle and often floated in a mystical glow. He had only two interests in life: chasing with the hounds and siring an heir.

The announcement of her marriage had come like a blow from the devil. Her father, King Maximilian of Bavaria, proudly informed her that the Archduke Franz Charles of Austria — the second son of Emperor Franz II — would be her husband and Vienna would be her place of residence. His face had beamed, and her shock had not put a dent in his exuberance.

"It is a dynastic union between two of the greatest families of Europe," he'd anounced ecstatically " — The Habsburgs and the Wittelsbachs."

Sophie had covered her face in despair. Her youth had been destroyed. Though Franz Charles told quirky jokes that made her laugh, he was the last man she would have chosen.

"Smile, my dear Sophie, smile," Maximilian had said. "The old Emperor Franz has promised that his epileptic oldest son Ferdinand will not succeed him. The throne will pass to Franz

Charles, and you, my dear, will be the empress of the Habsburg Empire, the greatest dynasty in modern history."

And it was. It covered almost the whole of Europe. It had begun five hundred years before with a single family, the Habsburgs, in the lush green valleys of the Danube River, that flowed through Alsace and Switzerland. While other countries used war to acquire their vast lands, the Habsburgs also used marriages and treaties. Germans, Serbs, Poles, Italians, Hungarians, Slovaks, Romanians, Croats, Czechs and one hundred thousand gypsies were living under their rule.

Maximilian's chest had swelled.

"And you, dear Sophie, will be empress over forty million people."

His beaming smile could not have stretched a further notch.

He did not tell her that Rudolf, Count of Habsburg, began the marriage tradition in 1273 by sacrificing his daughter Mechtild to the semi-barbarian Louis the Stern of Bavaria for his help in acquiring the lands of Bohemia. Or that Louis had beheaded his first wife.

Sophie had stared at him through blinding tears.

"I don't want to be an empress," she'd cried. "I want to marry for love."

But love was not part of a dynastic union. Though Maximilian loved his daughter dearly, his country took priority.

So Vienna became Sophie's home. And Vienna, the city of dreams, the gayest in all Europe, captured her with a joyous revelation she could never have imagined.

And love came into her life.

Vienna, once a tiny fishing village on the Danube River, had become the royal residence of the Habsburgs and was now a city of magnificent palaces with baroque façades, winding staircases and gold-trimmed murals on the walls and across the towering ceilings. Streams flowed through the gardens, and fountains of exotic statues and mythical figures illustrated the city's medieval past.

It was a city that had grown from its people's triumph over misery and gloom. In 1679, the plague had filled Vienna with headstones — seventy-six thousand people perished. In 1683, the Turkish siege had left bodies heaped high and the city in ashes. Only St. Stephen's Cathedral had been left standing.

The people had yearned with their hearts and souls for beauty, joy and gaiety. Artisans and musicians, in turn, had flocked to the city. The music of Mozart, Beethoven, Haydn, Schubert and the Strausses swept through the air and dancing was everywhere. The first coffee houses in the world appeared, all serving Turkish coffee.

Dancing had become Sophie's passion, but Franz Charles did not know a waltz from a minuet. To keep Sophie happy and to free him from that responsibility, he provided her with an escort, Franz, the young Duke of Reichstadt. Franz had curly black hair and melancholy eyes that lit up like drops of sunlight whenever Sophie appeared.

The duke's mother was the old Emperor Franz II's daughter, Maria Louise. When the great Napoleon had stamped across the borders of Austria, the emperor had flung Maria Louise into the arms of the Corsican adventurer for political advantage. Maria Louise had smiled when she told Franz her favourite story.

"I was only seventeen when I travelled alone to France to marry a man I had never seen, who had a reputation that terrified an army. He hated dogs and I was not permitted to take my little dog, Sprit, with me. But," she explained, "Napoleon did fall in love with me. He even engaged a dance master to teach him the Viennese waltzes."

Victory had soon deserted Napoleon, and he wilted away in prison on Elba Island. But Franz still carried in his heart a secret pride for his father and a dream that, one day, he would overcome his father's defeat and rule France. Franz's dream stayed buried and he and Sophie danced the winters away.

No one danced like the Viennese. The people danced in the streets to barrel organs, in the cafés, in their homes. As they walked down the streets, there was always a little lilt in their stride, as if they were humming the waltz tunes. The children had waltzes blaring across their playgrounds as they chased each other in games. When winter darkness descended upon Vienna and the streets blanketed in snow, and ice spread up the Danube, it triggered the first of five hundred seasonal balls held throughout the city.

The dancers whirled like spinning tops, from ten in the evening to seven in the morning, each couple trying to outdo the other. They danced in hotels, in theatre foyers, in the museums. They danced in ballrooms with gilded mirrors and in magnificent dining rooms. There was always a room set aside for the unexpected arrival of a newborn, where the Strauss waltzes filtered in.

Johann Strauss had been Sophie's favourite. He would saw on his violin, his black shaggy hair whipping around like a madman's. His passion, his fire would send her body whirling like a top, almost out of control. He would work himself into such a frenzy that his limbs seemed not to belong to him. Sophie and Franz would fly and sway like wild tree branches in a hurricane.

"Strauss ignites the wicked devils in our bodies," Sophie would say to Franz, as they spun around with glittering eyes, their hearts entwined. It would be the closest to love Sophie would ever come.

The outside world viewed Vienna as the gayest city in all Europe, but it was a gold-encrusted blanket covering the people's growing frustrations. Foreign newspapers were not allowed in and spies were everywhere to ensure loyalty to the emperor, considered to be chosen by God. The people were required to live like well-disciplined children beneath the thumb of the emperor and to respect his wishes as a child does his father's. Though they were well taken care of with housing and employment, citizens had few freedoms. They had no say in politics, though the growing nationalistic movements throughout Europe were creeping in.

They drowned their frustrations in beer and wine and danced the nights away to the music flying from the ballrooms, the sidewalk cafés and the fiddlers who lined the streets. And no one in the world felt sorry for them.

Sophie was a little concerned by what she might inherit. The tyrannical Chancellor Metternich was a threat, the power behind the throne. Still, the dance floor had been her first love and Sophie hardly missed a night of dancing.

On August 25th, 1830, after five years of marriage and three miscarriages, in the Napoleon room of the Schönbrunn Palace — the room where Mozart had performed his first recital and, reputedly, gleefully jumped into the arms of Empress Maria Theresa — Sophie's son Franz took his first breath.

Church bells pealed, guns thundered the royal salute and people went wild in the streets. The old emperor, Franz II, had raised himself out of his chair when he heard the cries of the newborn and the excited cheers of "It's a boy! It's a boy!" He'd gone to the window and looked out. Intermarriages had for generations tainted the blood of the royal families, and he thought, *Please keep the tainted blood of the Wittelsbachs from bringing disaster to this newborn.*

Fate deemed otherwise.

Franz, the young Duke of Reichstadt, was swept from this earth by consumption. Sophie's dancing ended and love disappeared from her life. Many times, in the quietness of her room, her tears took over. The old emperor had departed soon after, but Sophie did not become the Empress of Austria, as her marriage had promised.

Metternich, the devious Imperial Chancellor, had not trusted her. He knew Sophie's husband had no desire to rule and that she, his strong-willed wife, would influence her husband and be, in effect, the ruler. To protect his own career, Metternich skillfully manipulated the epileptic Ferdinand onto the throne.

But Sophie had certainly not wallowed in despair. Her ambition took over and she'd made sure that her son followed her stoic example.

Franz had been six years old when she quashed his fantasies and stole his childhood. She'd lifted the soldier's helmet from his blond curls and put her hands on his tiny shoulders.

"My son," she'd proclaimed, "these hands will groom you into a great emperor."

"I don't want to be an emperor!" he'd pouted. "I just want to be a soldier."

Soldiers stood on guard everywhere in the palace — they were his heroes. He could say 'Attention!' before he could say 'Papa.'

His childish play ended and his life became a preparation for the throne. At age eight, he spent nineteen hours a week in study; at age eleven, thirty-seven hours; and by age fifteen, fifty-five hours.

From his infancy, he'd stood in awe of his mother. Although she had stolen his childhood, he worshipped her. He never questioned her, following her every whim. That is, until Elisabeth would come into his life.

Even so, the military remained his passion.

And the opposite sex? He was surprised how his mother turned a blind eye when rumours proclaimed that his mentor, Count Karl Grünne, arranged romantic liaisons for him. He was more surprised that the ladies found him equally as charming as he found them.

Sophie had sealed her ambitions. One day, she would rule at her son Franz's side with the power of an empress.

2

In February 1848, carnival time in Vienna, the celebrations had seemed more brilliant and more rollicking than ever. The ballrooms were crowded night after night. Meyerbeer had been there for his *A Silesian Encampment*, performed at the opera, and

Jenny Lind was more dazzling than ever as Vielke. University students, in their joyous reactions to Jenny's rapturous songs, had taken the place of her horses and pulled her carriage through the cheering crowds.

But rumblings from the outside world crept into the bustling streets of Vienna.

Like the spring sun sneaking out from behind a winter cloud, the people had raised their heads and opened their eyes. Vienna, the city of dreams, had begun to unravel at the seams. The aristocrats had secured their gates with extra locks and Sophie had shivered in fear.

It had begun with whispers in the coffee houses where the intellectuals gathered. It had even seeped into the homes of the bourgeoisie. It had crept through the streets, where the music had dropped an octave lower, and down the dark alleys where the rats resided as permanent guests. On a grey March morning in 1848, the revolution had ignited. Franz had been seventeen. It would take his youth and change his life forever.

A body of students had filed into the Herrengasse. Their faces were grave and determined, their hopes fired by the wild, free spirits of the revolutions sweeping across Europe from France, they had stopped, momentarily fearful and uncertain.

Adolf Fischhof, crowded in among the strained bodies, had fingered his beard as he looked at the faces around him. He was a young Hungarian doctor incensed by the crushing discipline enforced on the people. Usually shy and quiet, his patience had reached an end.

"Gentlemen," he'd called, raising his arms, "listen to me!"

Faces had turned towards him. A slow agitation had stirred the ranks. In minutes he'd been hoisted up on restless shoulders. His face had been white and strained, but his voice was determined.

"We have no freedom of speech, no freedom of the press. We have no constitution. No foreign books or publications, especially those from French authors, are allowed for fear they might influence us with new ideas. *And what do we do about it? . . .*"

He'd ended with a roar, shaking his fists to the sky.

Like small pellets of rain, scattered cries had risen. Then, like the burst of a summer storm, the students, who moments before had stood placid and unsure, had exploded with frantic arms and screaming voices.

"Down with Metternich!"

"Down with his tyrannical régime!"

"We want freedoms!"

"We want a constitution!"

On towards the Hofburg Palace they'd marched, shouting, charging through the streets and into the stores and offices.

"A constitution! A constitution! Down with Metternich!"

Their cries incited the startled onlookers, pulling from their minds their buried grievances, and they raced to join the marchers. Stores were hastily locked.

Nationalists from Italy, Budapest, Prague and Kraków had run through the streets, shouting. Some workers, complaining of working conditions and the hovels in which they lived, joined the revolt. Chaos exploded. Passion swept away all reason. The gates of the inner city were battered down, gunsmith shops were plundered, shots echoed through the streets. Gas lamps were torn down, pipes uprooted and buildings sent up in flames. The music had come to a stop when street musicians joined the march.

The students had pounded on the palace gates, determined to force their way in. Soldiers had waved swords, fighting to bar their entrance as they climbed the gates. The commander of the garrison, Matuaschek, had charged into the mob on horseback, firing his pistol in the air and shouting.

"Disperse! Disperse or you will be sorry!"

Fresh explosions of fury ignited. Stones, blocks of wood, pots and pans were thrown at the soldiers. A gigantic man stepped up and seized the commander's horse.

"You are the one who will be sorry!" he'd bellowed, and struck the commander with a blow so violent he fell dead on the spot.

The patrol fled back to the palace and the crowds pounded harder on the iron gates until they tumbled down.

The roar of the angry mob had reached into the Hofburg.

Hand in hand, Sophie and young Franz had stood helpless with terror.

When darkness came and burning flames draped the sky in a smoky orange haze, Franz, shocked by a citizenry seeming to have gone mad, had watched fragile old Emperor Ferdinand stumble across the marble floor of the Hofburg's reception hall, cringing in fear of the rioters. The revolutionaries who'd fought their way into the palace then pushed him into the chair at the black-lacquered desk and jabbed a quill pen into his hand. They'd loomed over him like vultures.

The glow of city fires had sent flickering shadows skittering like monsters across the blue silk walls and the gilded paintings. Shouting tirades had frothed from unruly mouths as the emperor's shaky hand agreed to the promise of a constitution.

The swarming protestors were overjoyed, pounding each other on the back, yelling, "It's done! It's done! We are free!"

Chancellor Metternich had fled the country in a covered wagon disguised as a washerwoman.

In the darkness of that night, the royal family had crept in disguise from the palace. They'd huddled low in their carriage, the windows curtained in black, and fled to Innsbruck.

As the carriage sped along the bumpy road, throwing them from side to side, Franz had pulled back the black curtain and stared out into the night. The unruly rage he had just witnessed confirmed to him that his mother was right: the power of the army was the only way to keep the Habsburg Empire together. He had been nearly eighteen — he would be a soldier and fight for his empire. After all, he had been a commissioned officer since age thirteen.

Their holdings in Italy were also threatened. The Austrian army, under General Radetzky, had been fighting to preserve the Habsburg territories in Lombardy and in its capital, Milan. It was their richest possession and they could not afford to lose it. Franz's mind was made up.

In May, he'd arrived at the Italian headquarters, determined to fight beside his countrymen. His mother's wrath still burned in his ears: "God selected you to be the emperor. Your head was meant to wear a crown, not to be ripped off by a bayonet."

"Mother," he'd replied, "one day I will be the emperor, and my army must be proud of me."

The Battle of Santa Lucia had been his baptism of war. He'd fought, closing his eyes to the horror of the war, to the fear of the soldiers, to the slaughtered bodies that lay in piles everywhere, the severed limbs, the horrifying screams of pain.

The Austrian army emerged victorious. The Italians retreated. Lombardy had been saved.

When Franz had returned to Innsbruck, Vienna was still under siege but his mother's wrath had turned into pride. He'd stood as a hero before his army.

That summer, his cousins Néné and Sisi had come with their mother from Bavaria for a visit. He'd hardly noticed them. The horror of the war had still remained lodged in his mind.

3

August had been hot and humid. The carriage had rumbled over the rocky road carrying the royal family from Innsbruck back to Vienna for the opening of the newly-formed people's parliament.

Sophie was fuming with anger and humiliation. The new government had commanded their presence. They would be viewed as accepting the new liberal policies and the constitution. But that she never would do. She'd gripped her hands harder. They were helpless as newborn babes in the face of recently granted reforms. Their power had been usurped by the people.

"Temporarily," she had told herself.

She'd looked out the window at the chaos. Barricades were everywhere. Angry faces and shouts were everywhere. Vienna was like a fuse ready to ignite. The horses had jumped and pulled at their bits. And, most disgraceful of all, there'd been no soldiers to protect the royal family.

The mobs were unpredictable. Their passions could have exploded at any moment. The stories Sophie had heard about the murderous rage of the Parisian mobs as Marie Antoinette was dragged through the streets to the guillotine ravaged her mind. Drums had pounded as the queen's head fell. An ecstatic soldier had carried the bleeding head around the guillotine grounds to the roar of a wild, screaming crowd — Marie Antoinette's lips were still moving. True, that had been fifty years ago . . . but revolutions were still sweeping across the continent.

Once safely in the palace behind the massive doors, the royal family had stood together. Sophie was still shaking but Franz had then taken off, up the stone staircase, a spring in his step. She'd wondered what kind of an empire would be left for him to rule. She'd fled to her apartment and slammed the door.

Autumn came. Colourful leaves had covered the ground and flowers taken their last sips of air. The constitution was in force and the royal family lived like prisoners in their palace.

Never had Sophie felt so dejected and helpless. The well-laid plans she had so diligently nurtured for all those years had fled from her control. The whole empire was falling apart. The Poles, the Serbs, the Italians and the Hungarians were screaming for reforms. The new government, with no real experience, were floundering like schoolchildren looking for direction.

The aristocrats and the royals had fared no better. They'd barricaded themselves in their palaces behind huge gates and gulped down wine in dangerous portions, wondering how to save their own skins. Many had panicked and thought of fleeing the country in disguise. "Look what happened in France," they'd whisper among themselves. "The aristocrats were slaughtered by the thousands."

Sophie had picked up Franz's picture from her table. His eighteenth birthday had passed unnoticed by the people, though he had reached the age to rule. Her tears came so fast she could barely distinguish his face in the picture. For the first time, she'd crumbled in defeat.

A pounding on her door sent her flying from her chair.

"Who is it?" she'd called in fear.

Were the people revolting again?

"Please, Your Highness, may I come in?"

It was the trusted voice of her steward. He'd entered and behind him followed a tall male figure wearing a cape and a huge hat that almost covered his face.

"It is all right, Madame," the steward had assured, seeing her terror. "This gentleman is here to help us."

The tall man had removed his hat and bowed to her with a respectful grace she had almost forgotten.

"Prince Felix Schwarzenberg!" she'd exclaimed.

He was from one of the most illustrious families in the empire and had been their most trusted diplomat in many of the Austrian embassies in Europe. He was committed to the Habsburgs and to the empire.

Sophie had barely been able to contain her excitement. The steward bowed his way from the room.

"First let me offer congratulations for Franz on his eighteenth birthday," Prince Schwarzenberg had said, removing his gloves.

"Thank you, thank you," she'd replied, tearfully.

She took his arm and led him to a chair.

Sophie had forgotten how handsome he was, even with those melancholy eyes. The romantic adventurer had flitted through the salons of Europe and England for years. She knew his heart had been broken when, as a diplomat in London, he had fallen madly in love with the enticing Jane Elisabeth Digby, Lady Ellenborough, the wife of Edward Law. Jane had dumped the good lord and married the prince — but not for long, as more bewitching horizons were beckoning. Abandoning their daughter, she'd fled his side, first to Munich and a brief affair with King Ludwig of Bavaria, then to a German baron, then to a Greek count, ending up in the harem of a Bedouin sheik. That's why those melancholy eyes, so the story went.

Sophie had hardly reseated herself when he explained.

"My dear Sophie, the empire is in shambles, but I have a plan." His eyes had brightened. "I respect your integrity and your skills. Between us, we can restore the empire."

Her eyes had almost left their sockets. She knew he was a man of passionate ambition and also that his daring ideas could be reckless. That did nothing to curb her interest.

"I have the ability, my dear lady," he'd charged on, "to restore this empire to an absolute monarchy. But not under Ferdinand. He is tainted with the past, with Metternich's harsh demands, with the wars against our nationalists and, worst of all, his signing of the new constitution. The empire must be re-established with Franz at the helm. He will bring a new beginning and a return to the absolute monarchy."

Sophie had been speechless, motionless.

"I know he is inexperienced, but I will win his confidence and, with the skills you have instilled in him, together we will groom him as the ruler over his people."

His voice was emphatic, his face determined.

She couldn't believe it. She'd wanted to smother him with kisses. She'd tried to calm her racing breath and her thoughts. It sounded like a dream. She'd been well aware that the obstacles were many.

"What about the constitution?" she'd prodded. "An absolute monarch could not rule with that in place."

He'd risen from his chair and warmed his hands by the fire. The flames had flickered on his face. He'd turned to her.

"The constitution, with its first article reading 'All political rights must emanate from the people,' must be revoked." That last word had shot out like venom. "Franz will be sworn in as ruler. He will promise to abide by the constitution. I will declare myself first minister and I, too, will promise to abide by the constitution."

He'd stared into her face. His eyes had narrowed.

"Popular promises and liberal slogans are merely weapons in the art of ruling. It is permissible to deceive the people if it benefits one's country."

She agreed with him wholeheartedly. It was exactly what her father had maintained.

"Will Franz know of your true intentions?"

"No, no," he'd answered quickly. "He must be as innocent as a babe newly-born. He will greet the people with promises of a new order. He has witnessed the brutal power of the masses. He has seen the disaster created. It will not be hard to remind him of the Habsburg belief that he was ordained by God to rule his people and that what he does is for the good of his people."

"Where do we start?"

Sophie's excitement had sent her out of her chair. She'd paced around the room. They had both paced.

"First, we must convince Emperor Ferdinand to abdicate, and your husband to sign away his claim to the throne. And then," his voice had risen triumphantly, "to crown your son Franz as our new emperor."

"I can convince the emperor."

Of that, she'd had no doubt. Ferdinand would be happy to flee and her husband wanted nothing of the throne.

"One last thing," Schwarzenberg had said, still pacing with her. "Joseph should be added to Franz's name, after Joseph I, who was so beloved by the people. They will associate him with his great-grandfather. He must be crowned Franz Joseph."

The candles had flickered. They'd stood in silence, looking at one another, their enthusiasm and their anticipation racing. They both knew their counter-revolutionary plan could put the power of the empire back into their hands.

"But," Schwarzenberg had said, "we must wait for the right moment."

The right moment had arrived with a burst of cannon fire. Hungarian revolutionaries had stormed into Vienna and turned the city upside down. They ripped up railways, smashed windows and sent buildings into flames. Their screams had matched their raging faces.

"Freedom! Freedom! We want freedom for Hungary."

"We want our lands back."

"We want our old constitution."

Drunk with booze and crazy with rage, the rioters had stormed through the streets to the doors of the War Ministry. They'd pounded on them, screaming, "Down with Latour!"

"We must get out of here fast," implored Bach, assistant to Count Baillet de Latour, the Minister of War.

Bach's body had trembled, his heart pounding. The screaming voices were penetrating the room. He had better things to do with his life than challenge a bunch of crazy Hungarians. Not so Count Latour, a disciplined military man dedicated to saving the Habsburg Empire.

"We must stand up and face them," he'd shot back.

But Bach was already out the door. Latour turned and dashed onto the balcony. He saw the orange-red skies lit up by fires. He saw the square below, a mass of screaming, bellowing bodies. He'd thrown up his arms.

"My fellow countrymen . . . " he'd shouted.

His words had been lost in the roaring frenzy. He knew he had made a mistake.

Pounding fists were hammering his door. He fled into a cupboard and hid behind the coats. The outer door crashed down. Yelling voices and thumping boots took over and Latour had quivered with fear. He'd pulled more coats around his body, and buried himself deeper into the cupboard.

He'd remembered his daughter's farewell words: "Don't be too late tonight, Papa, it's my birthday."

The door had been jerked open, the coats torn from their hangers. Angry eyes devoured his face.

Desperately, Latour had pleaded, "My countrymen . . ."

A red-faced man raised a bludgeon high in the air.

"You are not our countryman."

He'd smashed the bludgeon into Latour's head.

Like vicious animals, they fell upon him with knives, broken bottles and the butts of their guns. They dragged him out into the open square. Hysteria peaked. Up on a lamppost they strung him and the people had danced around him like savage animals.

The rain had fallen softly at first, here and there. The winds had stopped. The drops had come quicker, larger, and then in a torrent, washing the fiery faces and drowning their torches.

Within minutes, only the pounding rain and the dead and mutilated body of Count Latour had remained in the square.

During this uprising, the royal family had fled Vienna once more, this time to Olmütz, to the archbishop's palace in Moravia. The miles had accumulated, the city left behind, but the cries of the mobs still echoed in Sophie's ears. Determination had raced in her mind.

We must *put our plan into action,* she'd thought, *before the whole country explodes beyond repair.*

4

On the afternoon of December 1, 1848, Sophie watched the snow piling on the window ledge and coating the mountains and the nearby village. The flakes were large, usually an indication they would stop soon, but the snow had been coming down all day — soft, gentle, soothing to her emotions. It made the roads impassable, but it did guarantee their safety in Olmütz.

Unable to be still, she paced about her salon. Her world could be coming together — the Imperial Army had brought a temporary calmness back to Vienna, the Hungarian sympathizers and the mobs of October had been silenced. The counter-revolution had been successful. The old emperor had a smile as wide as his face when he signed the abdication papers. Everything was settled — except for Franz, who knew nothing of their plan. Yet. She glanced impatiently at the gold clock ticking off the minutes as she waited for him.

A quick knock on the door and then Franz came striding in, his arms swinging with youthful exuberance. A moment of uncertainty touched her. He looked so young with his impish grin, his cheeks rosy from the cold and his eyes sparkling. Sophie caught her breath.

"You've been out a long time in that cold," she said.

"I wouldn't miss a day like this."

He took off his jacket and flung it on the chair.

"I rode right to the edge of the mountains," he continued. "The trails were covered with deep snow. My horse was in ecstasy flying through it all."

"It sounds wonderful."

She glanced out the window. She wavered a moment, uneasy in the pit of her stomach. His world was about to take a dramatic change. She turned back and took a deep breath.

"Please take a chair, Franz. I have something to tell you."

"Was there ever a time you did not have something to tell me, Mama?" he asked, dropping into a chair with a grin.

"I won't mince words, Franz," she asserted, staring him straight in the eye as his grin faded. "The time has come for you to take your rightful place as emperor."

Franz gripped his chair. Snow pelted the windows; the wind crackled the shutters.

"When?" he gasped.

"Tomorrow."

"Oh my God!"

He jumped up and strode to the window. He couldn't see the mountains, the snow was so thick. He was only eighteen. How could he be an emperor? He knew nothing about running a country, and the whole empire was in a mess. He turned back to his mother.

"Prince Felix Schwarzenberg will be your first minister," she'd responded quickly, seeing his panic. "He will advise you and give you help. Your uncle Ferdinand has agreed to step down as emperor. His association with Metternich and events of the past year have made him unpopular."

She paused, giving him a chance to comprehend. He remained frozen in shock.

"Franz, we must start anew," she went on. "It is the only way to regain and preserve the power of the Habsburg Empire. We are countering the rising problems with a new master at the helm and a fresh new start."

He found his voice, but it was a whisper.

"What about all these new promises of freedom, the new reforms, the constitution?"

A soldier at heart, he hardly knew anything about them.

"At your crowning, Schwarzenberg will inform the audience we will abide by the promises given."

She hoped her face didn't reveal the truth.

The room had darkened. The shutters still rattled in the wind. The candles sent flickering shadows across the ceiling. He turned back to the window, perhaps looking for an omen, though he couldn't see much through the swirls of snow.

He was going to be the emperor. He was terrified and yet excited in spite of himself. He would be responsible for almost forty million people: Poles, Ukrainians, Germans, Slovaks, Croats, Hungarians, Romanians and more.

Franz took a deep breath, closed his eyes and prayed silently to have the strength to rule and to bring contentment to his people.

He turned back to his mother. He drew himself into the erect stature of a military general and clicked his heels together.

"I accept, with honour, the throne of the Habsburg Empire. I will do my best. I pray that God will be at my side."

With tears of joy, Sophie had embraced him.

"He will be at your side," she'd assured him. "You are his chosen one. And I, too, will always be at your side."

Her new life was also beginning.

The next morning, December 2, 1848, at nine o'clock, in the banquet hall of the bishop's palace in Olmütz, eighteen-year-old Franz was crowned Franz Joseph, Emperor of Austria.

He took his mother into his arms and buried his face in her shoulder.

"Farewell, my youth!" he cried.

That day, a conspiracy of ravens flew above the little town of Olmütz. Sophie stared in horror. Was it a dark omen of tragedy?

5

On February 18th, 1853, catastrophe again threatened the empire.

Prince Schwarzenberg had died of a stroke and Sophie had achieved her goal. She was now the most powerful person in the empire. The constitution had been revoked, although one reform did remain: the abolition of serfdom. All the ministers and officials were at the archduchess's beck and call, their sole duty obedience to her. The whole court trembled at her nod — to be favoured or disgraced depended upon her and her alone. All decisions were passed through the young emperor to Sophie. Sophie was viewed by all as nothing less than Our Empress.

Vienna had returned to its old splendour. The people had regained their senses, according to Sophie. Nationalistic cries no longer echoed down the avenues. The empire was once again strong and united, an absolute monarchy, so it seemed. But Pilsner beer and wine went down in larger portions and the people danced as never before.

Sophie did accept Franz's appeal to make the army their boot of power. Franz could relate to the army with confidence, better than to his more experienced ministers. And confidence he desperately needed. Dressed in his general's uniform, which had come with his new title, Franz walked with great pride and carried his overwhelming load upon his shoulders.

That day, the afternoon sun sparkled like diamonds on Vienna's spires and the air was cold but invigorating. Arms swinging, Franz Joseph walked briskly along the city ramparts, his aide-de-camp, Captain O'Donnell, struggling to keep up.

"You seem particularly cheerful today," O'Donnell chuckled, almost breathless.

Something was brewing. Franz was beaming with extra vitality, which was unusual for him. O'Donnell tried to catch his breath and struggled to keep up.

Franz was usually reserved, though certainly not with the ladies, who always made his eyes light up. The people, however, often viewed him as cold, almost arrogant. O'Donnell knew he wasn't that. It was an insecure shyness, a shield to hide his youthful inexperience from the forty million people he ruled.

With the ladies, there was no problem. His prestigious rank, along with his charm, polished manners and eloquent glances, ignited their passions. There was always an endless line of beauties, which he never tired of pursuing. His romantic intrigues sent ripples of amusement through the European salons. There were a few disgruntled slurs as well.

O'Donnell envied him. He couldn't imagine what it would be like being the recipient of such a bounty of feminine attention. He himself was tall with muscular shoulders and, he thought, good-looking with a friendly face. But when he was with Franz, the ladies' eyes passed over him as if he wasn't there.

"Yes. I'm very content with life."

Franz was thinking about the ball the night before, about the little countess with the enticing eyes that flashed as fast as her feet danced to the music. He fingered her note in his pocket, a promised liaison that night. His legs moved into double time and O'Donnell was running to keep up.

Suddenly a river of blood came pouring down his uniform. There were screams. There was a man with a crazy face. The screams faded. Then there was only O'Donnell. Then there was nothing. All had disappeared, and Franz had crumpled to the ground.

When his eyes opened, a white ceiling filtered in. He turned his head. He was in his own narrow bed. A blurry face, perhaps that of his doctor, hovered over him.

"What happened?" he moaned.

"Franz . . . Franz . . . Oh, dear Franz. Can you hear me?"

It was Sophie's voice.

"Yes. Yes . . . What happened?"

His vision was clearing.

"Thank God you're back with us."

Sophie was sobbing. He had never seen his mother cry. He struggled to sit up but she pushed him back down.

"You were stabbed, my dear Franz. Stabbed," Sophie said. "You must not move. Not yet. It's a miracle you survived. You turned your head just in time. A woman's scream made you do that. The knife caught your collar's edge. It struck your neck, but the collar prevented a deeper wound that might have killed you."

Franz lay shocked, trying to remember.

"Who did it?" he finally asked. "Who would want to stab his emperor?"

"A nobody. A pathetic young Hungarian nationalist, a tailor's apprentice," Sophie said. "As they held him down, he kept shouting, 'Long live Kossuth.' The miserable wimp will be hung by his filthy neck!"

His mother's spiteful voice resonated with her hatred of Hungarians.

He remembered the name now: Lajos Kossuth. He'd led the Hungarians in their 1849 revolt to secede from Austria. Franz Joseph had just taken the throne. The Hungarians were massacred so terribly he would never forget. His mother had said it was a necessity to save the empire.

"In his eyes, he will die in glory," Franz said sadly.

His mother scoffed.

Franz lay a moment with closed eyes, bathing in the warmth of fatigue. Sophie paced the room, her mind whirling. This terrible incident made it all too clear: they must have an heir. Franz must marry — he must produce an heir or they could lose the power of the throne.

She tried to speak casually, but the words blurted out in her usual commanding manner.

"This terrible incident has made me realize we must have an heir. I must arrange a suitable marriage for you. At once."

"Really . . . ," he laughed.

His mother's face quickly shattered his amusement.

That's when he remembered the beautiful countess and his promised liaison. He had lost touch with time. Was that tonight or last night? He fidgeted around for his pocket. There was no pocket. Where was the note? He threw the blanket off and sat up.

"Lie back. Lie back."

Sophie pushed his shoulders, but he didn't move.

"What day is this, Mama? How long have I been here?"

She was confused. This was hardly the reaction she'd expected.

"It's evening, the same day you were stabbed."

He swung his legs over the edge of the bed.

"What are you doing?" she demanded.

"I must get up, Mama. I have an appointment."

The room turned hazy and his head began to spin.

"You can't get up," she ordering, pushing him down, "or keep any appointments today. Tomorrow perhaps, but not today."

He fell back, troubled. Sophie knew it had to be a woman.

The candles flickered, silence hung in the air. Only the clock ticked. He lay, eyes closed, in helpless remorse. Sophie continued pacing. It wouldn't be easy, but she was determined to settle this.

He opened his eyes.

"Mama, were you seriously talking about marriage for me?"

That was the last thing he wanted. He was only twenty-two and not ready to give up the enchanting little bundles that filled his life.

"I am very serious," she said.

"And I am sure, my dear mother, that you have picked out someone very suitable."

He couldn't imagine who his mother would have in mind. His Hungarian cousin Elisabeth, daughter of Archduke Joseph, Palatine of Hungary, was full of exotic promises. He had even tilted his head in her direction. But his mother had stamped that one out. No Hungarian daughter-in-law for her.

Sophie took a deep breath and sat down on the edge of his bed.

"Yes. In fact, I have. Your cousin, the Princess Helene of Bavaria. If you recall, when you were seventeen, my sister Ludovika and her daughters, Helene and Elisabeth, visited us in Bad Ischl that summer."

He took a moment, then he remembered.

"The younger one, Sisi, was around ten, and she was as wild as a squirrel, flying from tree to tree, and she rode a horse like a gypsy. And the other one, Néné — "

He stopped short. He stared at his mother with desperation.

"That one," he continued, "was tall and skinny and as frigid as winter ice . . . " He faltered as if a thunderous wave had overtaken him. "Is there no one else?"

"This would be a very suitable arrangement."

Sophie stood up abruptly. Her face was stern.

Franz lowered his gaze. When his mother's mind was made up, there was no changing it.

"Bavaria," she went on, "is Austria's most loyal partner in the German confederation and the additional connection between the Wittelsbachs and the Habsburgs would be a great political advantage."

"But, Mama," he said, looking through his fingers at her. "She left me cold. There are so many beautiful women out there. And her."

"My son, that was five years ago when you saw her. I have inquired about her. She is a very beautiful young lady and, I think, very suitable to be an empress."

He fell back. He was trapped.

His mother's voice rambled endlessly. She would arrange a meeting this summer, probably in August, at their summer home in Bad Ischl.

Her words drifted into oblivion. The lovely little countess from the ball the night before drifted into his mind. His body warmed to a pleasant sizzle.

How long, he wondered, *until I have that little one in my arms?*

First Meeting

1

"There is nothing like the valley below in August," Franz called out to Count Grünne, his adjutant, as their carriage rambled along the mountain road.

They were heading to Bad Ischl to meet the Princess Helene of Bavaria. Franz tapped on the carriage window, motioning the driver to pull over and stop.

"Come see," he shouted.

The two men clambered out onto the road. Their eyes feasted on the towering mountains, the surrounding forest and the valley far below. There were tiny villages here and there, peasants tending their flocks in the alpine greenery and a musical tinkle of cowbells.

"And there is Bad Ischl with its red-tiled roofs, on the banks of the River Traun."

Franz took a deep breath, inhaling the pure air. He smiled.

"I'm looking forward to meeting the beautiful princess. Marriage may not be so bad. My friend Prince Albert of Saxony is just back from his honeymoon and he has almost convinced me that a happy marriage can be more satisfactory than transitory affairs."

Grünne laughed. He was surprised at the glow on Franz's face. He had left behind his problems in the empire and threats of a war in the Crimea in his pursuit of love.

"For you, Your Highness, intriguing affairs will be no problem," he said with amusement. "The beautiful countesses and the flirting ladies will always be available to you."

He wished he could say the same about himself. He was short, only to Franz's shoulder even with the high covered heels on his boots. He hardly ever caught a feminine eye — that is, not one of any importance. His impoverished background didn't help. Being the youngest in the family, he hadn't inherited any of the family wealth. At least he was a count, and adjutant to the emperor. Still, he often crumbled with dejected thoughts about his life, especially when watching Franz with the gushing ladies.

"You're right. There will never be a shortage," Franz laughed as he hopped up the steps and into the carriage. "In royal marriages, that is no problem. I will taste their delicious flavours as often as I desire."

That was just what the Archduchess Sophie desired, Grünne knew. They must have an heir. Franz must have a wife, but a docile wife, one who would not influence his heart or his mind. The archduchess was determined to keep control.

Their amusement expanded into smiles, and Grünne hid his bitterness. The carriage continued on the road to Bad Ischl.

2

Ludovika heard her two daughters giggling in the bedroom. She sighed with relief. Sophie's spiteful welcome to Bad Ischl had not deterred them. Their carriage had hardly come to a stop at their inn and there she was.

"You are over an hour late!" Sophie had stormed, pacing like a caged lioness.

"It was our suitcases. They weren't there when we got off the train," Ludovika moaned. "We still don't have them."

She reached out to her sister with a welcoming embrace. Already, her feeling of intimidation was swelling. Sophie always made her feel like a perplexed child and she hated herself for allowing it.

Sophie pushed her aside, eyeing the two girls. It was hardly a pleasant look.

"Your suitcases aren't here, and you are all in black?" Her voice sailed. "It is a welcoming party you are coming to, not a funeral."

"We are in mourning for the Queen of Bavaria's aunt," Ludovika faltered.

"You look ghastly in these clothes and you are due in half an hour at my villa for the reception."

She stared at Helene in distress. Helene's face tensed.

"Franz can't possibly see her looking like this," Sophie said.

Helene's face turned to cement.

Ludovika fidgeted from foot to foot, her headache escalating, and fatigue devouring her. The train trip had been five hours.

"I don't know what to say," she mumbled.

There she was, crumbling like a terrified child.

"Never mind, never mind," Sophie said, taking charge as she always did. "Into your rooms quick and freshen up. I will have my maid come at once and do something with Helene's hair. We can only hope that her youth and freshness will triumph over that terrible black dress."

Sophie had left for her manor, the Villa Eltz, and the maid had come and gone. Now Ludovika's spirits rose with her daughters' happy voices. She tossed the cold cloth from her head and went into their bedroom.

"Girls, girls, we haven't much time."

She tried to look serious, but she couldn't help smiling when she saw Elisabeth clowning around with a book on her head, swishing a fan and tossing coquettish looks.

"Really, Sisi, where do you get the energy?"

"Oh, Mama. I'm just trying to keep Néné's spirits up, reviewing her lessons on how a lady moves about a room."

Again the two girls broke into giggles. Ludovika couldn't hide her titter. At least their sense of humour hadn't been destroyed.

"Néné, your hair is exquisite," Ludovika exclaimed.

Helene looked strikingly elegant beside her younger sister. Her face was slim and her hair, piled high on her head, shimmered with streaks of auburn. Even so, Ludovika sensed a strain beneath her giggles.

"I think Néné knows well enough how to act," she went on. "But Sisi, you've done nothing with your hair and Charles Ludwig will be there."

Elisabeth took a quick look in the mirror and laughed. Her hair was parted in the middle, with long chestnut braids wrapped around her head.

"Oh, I forgot about me."

"Anyway, the black dress does enhance the delicate texture of your skin," Ludovika smiled, trying some humour.

It was certainly too late for Elisabeth's hair.

Elisabeth smiled and whirled around in front of the mirror. Ludovika thought, as she so often did, *How beautiful Sisi will be when she matures.*

"My hair doesn't matter. You know that, Mama," Elisabeth said, her voice bubbling with light sarcastic humour. "But do you think Néné's elaborate hairdo will bring a pleasant look to Aunt Sophie's face?"

Ludovika wanted to add to the sarcasm, but she bit her lip.

"Néné's hair looks magnificent. All she needs is a smile."

She touched Néné's chin tenderly. Helene clung to her mother's hand.

"Oh, Mama. For all our clowning, I'm really very nervous about meeting Franz."

Elisabeth and her mother had sensed this, but it was the first time Helene had voiced her fears. She was always quietly composed, so within herself. Elisabeth often wished she herself was a little more like that. It gave her sister poise, something Elisabeth knew she didn't have.

"He is so powerful and sophisticated, and so handsome," Helene said. "The most beautiful ladies in all Europe are running after him. I am afraid he will find me very provincial."

Her mother took her in her arms and Helene laid her head on her shoulder. Both expressed their sentiments in momentary silence. Then Ludovika held her back and looked into her face.

"You are a most beautiful lady, my dearest Néné. You have great composure and elegant bearing. Even the Munich aristocrats think you will make a perfect empress."

The knock came on the door.

"Your carriage is waiting," a courtier voiced.

Elisabeth steered Helene gently towards the door.

"He would have to be demented not to fall in love with you."

And together they rushed out.

Their carriage rambled along the River Traun and wound through the tree-shaded grounds of the Villa Eltz. It reminded Elisabeth a little of her beloved Possi. Of course, the lawns were more manicured and there were no signs of children and ponies.

Sophie waited at the entrance, impatient and pacing. She scrutinized Helene from the top of her elegant coiffure to the hem of her black dress before greeting her. Ludovika's anxiety began to spin. Elisabeth playfully nudged her sister. Helene stared straight ahead, her face frozen, though she did feel a humorous tickle, wondering whether Sophie had discovered a flaw.

"Don't look so severe," Sophie spouted out to Helene. "This is a party, not a funeral. Put on a smile! Everyone here is dying to meet you, especially Franz Joseph."

That was the last thing Helene wanted to hear. Before she could catch a reassuring breath, Sophie swept up her skirts and spun around.

"Follow me," she ordered.

They marched down the hall and into the formal rooms. At the entrance, they paused before going in. Elisabeth's heart did a flip — in fact, several flips.

The room was pleasant with large windows overlooking a twilight-drenched river. But there were so many people, all strutting around with impatient faces and eager eyes!

The chattering came to a sudden halt. All eyes focused on the entrance, mainly on Helene. Seeing Helene's face, Elisabeth held her hand firmly.

"Relax, my dear Néné. They are all family."

Sophie grabbed the terrified girl by the arm and immediately began the introductions to a quickly forming line of bodies.

Ludovika and Elisabeth followed. They were all relatives, everyone a Habsburg archduke or archduchess. Elisabeth saw Charles Ludwig. He beamed when he saw her, making the most elegant bow. His dark curly hair hung to his shoulders and his dark eyes melted into hers with amusement.

This could be a fun night, Elisabeth thought, producing a smile to match his.

Then there was Franz Joseph. He had the bluest eyes she had ever seen. He was much younger than she expected. He was focusing on Helene, who was now in front of him. Her eyes were downcast, she clutched her evening bag as if she might lose it and her smile had faded.

"You remember your cousin, Helene."

Sophie pushed Helene closer as she presented her to Franz Joseph. He bowed to her, a very eloquent bow.

"Yes, of course," he said, courageously. "It's nice to see you again."

He does have charm, Elisabeth thought, *and what a gorgeous voice, so deep and masculine*. She saw Helene raise her eyes to him with a diminutive smile.

"Your Highness," she whispered.

He took his Aunt Ludovika's hand and bowed elegantly when Sophie presented her. Then his blue eyes were on Elisabeth. His face lit up with such pleasure that a hot blush rose across her cheeks.

"Of course, you remember Elisabeth," Sophie barked. "She was very young when you saw her last."

"I don't believe I ever saw this young lady before."

Franz's tone was playful, his eyes were teasing. Elisabeth was momentarily bewildered. Then he leaned forward, looking deeper into her eyes.

"I think I remember now," he said. "You were the little one who raced across the lawns on the pony, swung on the tree branches and chased through the woods, always picking berries. I never saw you with your face clean. It was always covered in berry juice."

His eyes still teased.

"I guess that was me," Elisabeth giggled.

Sophie quickly latched one arm onto Helene and the other onto Franz and moved them away. She chattered gaily, looking proudly from one to the other. Helene's face remained uneasy while Franz was nonchalant.

Then Charles Ludwig blocked Elisabeth's view. He beamed at her, holding a tray of cakes and ice drinks in his hands. She had forgotten about his big nose, but his humorous face sent her smile to the edge of her cheeks.

"Sisi," Charles Ludwig said, "in the garden is a military band, the best of Austria."

Elisabeth could hear the music. He was swaying with it, as were the iced drinks.

"Will you be my guest? We have so much catching up to do."

Before she knew it, Elisabeth was caught up in an evening of fun and laughter.

Franz's father, her uncle Franz Charles, had a soft, gentle nature. Still, he was quite hilarious, so different from Aunt Sophie. He kept cracking the funniest jokes to make the Bavarian princesses laugh and feel at home. Elisabeth laughed a lot. Helene just produced small stilted smiles. She didn't seem to be having a good time at all — it was probably all the whispers and goggling eyes. Franz didn't seem to be helping her. Elisabeth had fun anyway.

The fiddles sang with Strauss waltzes and the old and the young whistled and sang with them.

Along with cakes and cider, Charles Ludwig kept plying Elisabeth with compliments. She was more than flattered. His kibitzing kept her giggling. Still, he didn't capture all her attention. Her eyes kept straying to Helene and Franz.

Things were not going too well, it seemed. Every time Elisabeth looked at them, Franz's eyes caught hers and he gave her a wink and a smile. It was a friendly gesture, almost teasing. She responded with a big grin, enjoying it. She wondered how the other guests could be so stiff and formal with all the excitement around them. Elisabeth did feel sorry for Néné. She was so sensitive. With everyone eyeing her sister's and Franz's every movement, wondering whether love was pounding in their hearts, it was not easy. And it did not look promising.

When the night ended, Charles Ludwig gallantly bent over Elisabeth's hand and kissed it. In fact, he was so gallant, Elisabeth giggled. Then she bit her lip a little shamefully.

"That's not what an elegant lady would do, is it?" she asked apologetically.

He laughed. Then they both laughed and she knew her true colours showed. Still, he didn't seem perturbed.

"This has been one of the happiest nights of my life," he told her, his face beaming.

"Why, thank you," Elisabeth offered gleefully, "I had fun too. And I hope I will see you again."

His eyes darkened as if there was doubt. Then he bowed gallantly again.

"I truly hope so," he said.

As Charles Ludwig stood beside his mother and watched the Duchess Ludovika lead her daughters to their carriage, he felt a discomforting premonition. He took his mother's arm.

As they headed back to the salon, he said, "Franz likes Sisi much more than Néné. She is the one he will marry."

The archduchess threw her eyes to the sky.

"What utter nonsense," she pronounced. "As if he would look at that little monkey. She is just a child."

The carriage carrying the three women rumbled along the cobblestone road. A large moon shone, the air was warm and pleasant.

"What do you think of him, Néné?" Elisabeth asked, dying to know.

Helene, hands clasped in her lap, looked out at the moon for a moment.

"He's very handsome" she said, trailing off. "Very charming."

"Then you like him?" Elisabeth eagerly inquired.

Helene crawled back into herself. Her eyes stayed on the moon. She was silent.

"Well?"

Elisabeth was almost bouncing off her seat. *How could she not like Franz?* She had to know.

"I think he likes you better than me."

"Likes me better?" Elisabeth sounded puzzled. "That is preposterous. He wouldn't like me better than you."

She turned from her sister to the window. The moon had disappeared behind a cloud. Franz's eyes had been on her, it was true, and he did shower her with amused smiles. She turned back.

"You are imagining it, Néné. He thinks I'm just a child. That was apparent."

"What did you think, Mama?" Helene's voice was full of doubt.

Ludovika's headache clouded down around her eyes. She rubbed her hand across her forehead. She had to be careful. Néné was sensitive and her confidence now so fragile. Still, no one could miss it. Franz had made no attempt to hide his adoring fascination for Sisi. He'd displayed it for all to see. She wrapped her arm around Helene, hugged her and kept a lighthearted tone.

"Of course he delights in Sisi. Why not? She is not yet inhibited by society. She bubbles still in the joyous innocence of childhood. It was a pleasure for all to see. But you, Néné, you are a beautiful, elegant and mature young woman. He will not pick a child to be his empress."

The carriage rumbled over the bumps. All three drew into their thoughts. Ludovika wondered whether she would sleep that night with her headache. Helene wanted go home. Elisabeth wondered whether she really was that childish.

The morning sun glittered on the waters of the River Traun, shimmered through the lovely trees and coated Sophie's apartment in a warm pleasant glow. She stretched out on her chaise, sipping her morning coffee when, without a knock, Franz rushed in. She almost dropped her cup.

"What a pleasant surprise. You're in time to share my morning coffee."

Franz was obviously happy, his arms swinging as he paraded around her room. His eyes had the glow that the young ladies always brought out. Sophie managed to get a coffee cup into his hand before he sang out.

"Mama, wasn't she enchanting? So modest, yet so completely at ease. So gay and charming in her simplicity and her innocence."

He kept pacing with a silly grin. Sophie hoped he wouldn't spill his coffee.

She was completely baffled. She had seen nothing about Helene that would prompt such a dramatic description. She took two sips of her coffee but it didn't help.

"Certainly Helene was graceful, and her social manners were very proper."

But, she thought, *enchanting? Hardly.* In fact, her face was so rigid, she had thought it might crack.

"Oh, Mama. It's not Néné I speak about. It's the enchanting little Sisi. She is as fresh and unspoiled as a green half-opened almond and her eyes are bursting with sunshine."

Sophie's cup almost sailed from her hand. Never had she heard such superlatives from Franz's mouth.

"Even that black dress didn't spoil her adorable figure," he added.

Sophie's emotions were taking off in many directions, and she couldn't put her thoughts together.

"Yes," she said finally. "Elisabeth is certainly quite adorable. But Helene, how elegant and poised she was. And her etiquette is so proper. She would be a perfect empress."

He was nodding but his silly grin told her that her words were totally wasted.

"Of course, that black dress was hideous on Helene," Sophie said, trying again. "It did nothing for her colouring. She really has such lovely porcelain features. Almost like an Egyptian princess, wouldn't you say?"

Her effort was wasted. Franz sat down, cradling his cup slowly, methodically. It was still full. He was lost in thought.

What is coming next? Sophie wondered. She gripped her cup harder and took a big gulp.

He looked at his mother.

"Néné is all you say, dignified and very beautiful, and she does have the makings of a fine empress. But, Mother," his face hardened. Sophie's breath stopped. "She leaves me cold. She is hard-featured. She hardly smiles."

"That's because she was very nervous."

Sophie was out of her chair and marching to him. She wanted to shake some sense into him.

"Perhaps. She lacks warmth, she is so stiff. She has no charm. But Sisi!" His face lit up. "She is different."

His face was so ecstatic, Sophie panicked. Surely he had not fallen in love with a child, barely fifteen with no social graces, no elegance and more like a simple country girl than royalty. Her anxiety flew to a chilling height. She wanted to shake him. But with great effort, she controlled herself and her reason returned. It wasn't unusual for her son to dive into frivolous romantic intrigues, she told herself, but they were short-lived, disappearing like summer clouds. This would no doubt happen. Still, she had to tread carefully. Hopefully, he would return to his senses.

She had a thought. At dinner tonight, she would place Helene in the seat of honour between Franz and his father. Elisabeth she would seat between herself and the shaky old Prince of Hesse, who needed a superb conversationalist to bring him to life. Franz would then judge for himself that she was a child inexperienced in an adult world, with no social skills befitting an empress.

"My son," she ventured, smiling and cushioning her voice, "what are your plans for today?"

"I promised Grünne to show him what it was like to hunt in the mountains around Bad Ischl."

"Then I shall see you tonight at dinner."

Sophie rose, indicating their time was finished.

"The lovely princesses will be there," she offered. "And not in black."

She forced a look of approval. Franz jumped up, made a sweeping bow to his mother.

"Even though I will be doing what I love best, the day won't pass fast enough," he beamed.

Sophie's hands were in knots. She prayed her scheme would work.

3

"Mama, you're not coming to the dinner tonight?" Elisabeth asked, shocked.

Ludovika was stretched out on her bed with a cold cloth on her forehead.

"I can't, my love. This headache is just too much."

"Oh, Mama. We can't go alone."

Elisabeth almost panicked — just her and Néné? She ran into Helene's room.

"Néné, we are going alone tonight, just you and I without . . ."

She halted.

Helene, in her new blue gown, dipped and turned in front of the mirror. She was all smiles, and she looked ravishing.

"What do you think?" she asked, turning to her sister.

"You are beautiful," Elizabeth sang out. "And your dress is gorgeous."

"Thank you." Helene's smile widened. "And you don't look so bad yourself."

Elisabeth twirled once in front of the mirror, trying to copy Helene. She had on her new white and rose gown, but much of its allure disappeared — she was hardly a match for Néné. She turned back to her sister.

"Did you hear what I said about Mama not coming?"

Helene turned her head.

"It doesn't matter. We'll go alone. After all, it's just a small family dinner."

She tilted her face in the mirror again and touched her new hairdo, obviously very satisfied with it. Elisabeth, remembering Charles Ludwig, wondered why she hadn't done something different with *her* hair.

"Let's go, then!" she exclaimed.

It had been at least fifteen minutes since their carriage was announced. As they dashed out, Elisabeth wondered why Néné was not the least bit nervous about the night. Perhaps it was the new dress.

"I will never, never, never marry into royalty," Elisabeth screamed, banging her bedroom door shut later that night.

It had been a night of horror — boring, boring horror. No wonder her father said he wouldn't be caught dead at a royal court dinner.

She ripped off her dress and threw it across the room.

"I even hate my dress!" she moaned.

There she was, the whole night, crushed between Aunt Sophie and an ancient old man who sounded like he had a mouth full of almonds and a voice in rhythm with his shaking hands. She could barely understand a word he said. And Sophie was like an army general, not once giving her a pleasant word or a look of encouragement, just the odd dismissive glance.

"What's the matter with Sisi?" she heard the old man comment to Sophie. "Is she fasting? She has touched nothing but her soup. And she stares at her plate as if she hoped it would run away."

Elisabeth cast surreptitious glances at Franz and Néné. His playful glances back had saved her from total despair. And Néné, she had a great time. She sat in the place of honour between Franz and his father. She chattered animatedly, flashing her eyes and fluttering her fan with such elegance. Never had Elisabeth seen Néné like that. The guests, even Franz, were enchanted, all hanging on her every word. But not Charles Ludwig. His eyes stayed on Elisabeth, sympathetic. He saw her pain and she knew he wanted to come to her.

Now, she buried her face in the pillow and pounded her hands on the bed in anguish. Not even the beautiful rays of the moon shining through her window brought comfort. She just wanted to go home now.

Sophie slammed her apartment door shut so hard, the soldier on the outside jumped to life. The chattering voices were gone and the room was quiet. There was just the ticking clock and her tapping feet. She raged with fury. It had not worked. The little nymph, as Sophie called her, had shown her true colours, but all it had brought was Franz's amused affection.

"Oh please, God, bring him to his senses," she cried out into the darkness.

The sisters were up early the next morning. It was a sunny day, dewdrops shimmered like jewels on the sweeping lawns and birds were singing everywhere.

Tonight was the ball and Elisabeth was as excited as Helene. Her tears had washed away her frustration of the night before. One thing she had chained into her mind: she would never marry an emperor. However, that did not mean that she would miss the ball, even though only the most elite of Viennese society would be present. She had never been to a ball and she loved Strauss waltzes. Besides, she had a beautiful new dress for it, and Aunt Sophie had told them to expect something very special.

"I might be a little klutz on the dance floor tonight," she whined.

Helene was in a great mood, dancing around the room as if she were already at the ball.

"You will be fine," Helene assured. "Charles Ludwig will make sure. He didn't take his eyes off you all last night at dinner."

"Néné," Elisabeth smiled, "what special thing might happen tonight, that Aunt Sophie suggested?"

Helene hesitated. Elisabeth saw a tiny shadow cloud her face.

"We'll see. Let's not worry about it."

Around the room she twirled, this time faster. Elisabeth sensed she knew something more.

They pulled out their dresses for the ball, put them under their chins and paraded in front of the mirror.

"Yours is even more beautiful than I remembered," Elisabeth exclaimed.

"I like yours, too," Helene said.

Elisabeth's dress was not nearly as elegant as Néné's. In fact, it seemed more girlish, maybe childish, Elisabeth thought, looking at it more critically in the mirror as she too whirled around. Why hadn't she decided on something a little more sophisticated?

Ludovika came into the room and playfully tousled Helene's hair.

"Néné, the hairstylist will be here soon. Your hair was lovely last night, but Sophie has suggested a more flattering style, something softer around your face."

Helene's face was grim other than her eyebrows soaring.

Elisabeth attempted a rescue.

"I thought her hair was beautiful last night."

"It was," Ludovika replied curtly. "Sophie just likes the last word."

What about my *hair?* Elisabeth thought, glancing in the mirror. It fell in a cluster of dark, chestnut waves to the middle of her back. She never thought much about her hair, just wrapped it in braids — that was the easiest. *But tonight is special*, she thought, grinning, *a ball with Viennese waltzes and Charles Ludwig. I will surprise him. I will surprise everyone. I'm going to do something special with my hair. The braids are going. I will wind my hair in a cluster of curls high on my head and let it fall down my back. And maybe, just a little softer around my face.*

Suddenly, Elisabeth found it all too much. Hair, clothes and beauty were hardly her interest.

"I need fresh air. I'm going for a walk," she announced to her mother.

"Fine. Don't get lost!" Ludovika replied.

Out in the cool air with singing birds and the gentle sound of the river, her tension mellowed. She sat on the riverbank, pulled her knees to her chin and watched the whirlpools eddying endlessly into intriguing patterns, changing, disappearing, and making room for new designs to form.

So like life, she thought. *Always changing, moments slipping away so fast and forever lost.* She hugged her knees tighter. *My childhood is fleeing as fast as those swirling patterns.*

She thought of Possi. She thought of the forests, the mountain trails, her shepherd friends and her best friend, Allie. She thought of her father. A small breeze lifted her hair. She closed her eyes. She thought of Franz, those blue eyes, his twinkling smiles. Did he really like her better than Néné?

She jumped to her feet. *These are silly thoughts*, she assured herself. *He belongs to Néné.* With amusement, she thought of Maximilian, the king of Saxony. He thought her too flighty to marry his son, Prince George. So why would Franz consider her suitable to be the Empress of Austria, especially after last night? Never would she consider being an empress, anyway. She tore along the path, not looking at the river.

"Sisi . . . Sisi." Helene's head bobbed out the window. "It is time to get ready for the ball."

Elisabeth hesitated, glancing back at the swirling patterns. She took a deep breath, then turned towards the inn. Her childhood might be fleeing, but she would not miss that ball. She ran to the inn, the river eddies forgotten. Ludovika was at the open door.

"Come, girls. The carriage is waiting."

Elisabeth couldn't stop looking at herself in the mirror. Her hair was piled high on her head with a wreath of flowers and she loved it. Her eyes glistened, her smile enlarged.

When she saw Helene, though, she was stunned. She took her hand.

"I have never seen you so beautiful," she proclaimed.

Helene glanced again in the mirror.

"Thank you. Thank you."

The shadow was back on her face. What was it? Elisabeth wondered. She tightened her grip.

"It's going to be all right, Néné."

"Girls. Hurry, hurry," Ludovika called.

Both girls stood momentarily, looking at each other. There were tears in Helene's eyes. Then, they swooped up their gowns with one more quick glance in the mirror before they dashed through the door.

4

In the mountainous region of upper Austria, summer rains can come in torrents. That evening, the clouds opened wide and dashed the hopes of dancing in the gardens of the Villa Eltz. The lanterns were moved inside.

As the rain poured down, the villa glistened inside. There were ladies in glorious gowns with sparkling jewels and there were men in glittering uniforms. There were happy voices sailing through the air, and lively Strauss waltzes flying from the fiddlers' bows.

"It's magical!" Elisabeth exclaimed.

She, Helene and Ludovika stood in the entrance, fidgeting with their evening bags and wondering what to do next. Elisabeth saw Franz. Rather than dancing, he was talking to a young woman whose eyes flashed as fast as her fan. How elegant he was in his uniform with its military decorations and the playful tilt of his head was as he smiled into those coquettish eyes. She smiled too, with amusement.

Still, she had a shiver of panic. All the strangers milling around, their curious eyes flashing, their whispers shaded behind fluttering fans. She didn't dare look at Néné. And where was Charles Ludwig?

Then Aunt Sophie was there.

She examined Helene from top to bottom and her face betrayed that she was ecstatic.

"My dear Helene, you take my breath away. You are lovely. That hairstyle is most becoming. It gives such a warm hue to your face." Then, sharply, "Don't forget that smile."

Helene froze, luckily with a smile.

Sophie's attention to Elisabeth was as quick as her words.

"And you look lovely too, Elisabeth."

She smiled, not with appreciation, but relief. Elisabeth looked like a child beside her elegant sister. Her colours were showing. Franz would never look beyond Helene's beauty to this childlike nymph. That, she was sure of.

Sophie swept up her gown and turned around.

"Now come along. Everyone is dying to see you."

Elisabeth turned so fast, she almost tripped over her gown. She wasn't used to the length.

Into the ballroom they hurried. Although the music played on, the dancers came to a sudden halt. Ladies curtseyed to them, discreetly looking them up and down, while gentlemen bowed.

Sophie secured Ludovika and Helene into comfortable chairs. Then, to everyone's surprise, she propelled Elisabeth through the crowded room to a tall young man with curly dark hair and gentle but curious eyes. Elisabeth was in a panic. What was going on?

"Elisabeth, this is Hugo von Weckbecker, Franz's aide-de-camp."

There was no surprise on his face as he made a courteous bow. Sophie had arranged his evening to keep an eye on Elisabeth and to make sure she did not miss a dance. It was not his right to question why. Still, he was curious.

Sophie was taking no chances. She had forbidden Charles Ludwig's presence at the ball. She did not want him following Elisabeth around with his lovesick eyes. With Franz's unpredictable emotions, anything could happen. It was safer to keep Elisabeth in the arms of Hugo von Weckbecker.

"Hugo would love the next dance with you," she said, ignoring the desperate look on Elisabeth's face.

The music was lively.

"It's a polka," Sophie assured.

Elisabeth's face flamed red. She stared at the young man with stricken eyes.

"Oh sir, I have never danced with anyone but my dance master. And a polka. I've never danced a polka."

She was frantic. Where was Charles Ludwig?

Hugo smiled, but he was a little apprehensive. In spite of their dance masters, Bavarian princesses were known to be no match for the young Viennese ladies he was used to. But with the sharp eyes of the archduchess on him, he quickly reassured her.

"We'll do just fine."

He led her trembling to the dance floor.

At first her feet were lead, then the quick tantalizing beat of the polka doused all her intimidation. Her body took off, whirling to the enticing rhythms. Her face glowed. And her smile appeared.

Dance after dance, waltzes and polkas, they whirled around the room. Hugo was spellbound. Elisabeth showed no signs of exhaustion. Hugo wished the evening would never end. Later, he would remark to his curious friends, "She floated like a dove in my arms."

His curiosity flew almost as fast as the music. As he whirled Elisabeth around, he kept Franz Joseph in the corner of his eyes. Franz stood on the edge of the dance floor, talking and smiling graciously to everyone, especially the young ladies. *Why wasn't he dancing?* Hugo wondered. And where was the Bavarian princess Helene? Was she not here as a promising match for Franz Joseph? She danced with a different partner every time. He was sure everyone saw the ire on the archduchess's face as one young man after another was called over to dance with Helene.

What really sent his mind reeling was Franz Joseph, though, whose gaze rarely left him and Elisabeth. Hugo was a little stunned by the affectionate twinkle in his eyes.

When Hugo guided Elisabeth back to her chair after the evening of dancing, smiling delightedly, he could hardly wait to explain to his friends.

"I suspect I've just been dancing with our new empress."

Elisabeth was in good spirits when she sat down beside Helene and Ludovika. Her feet didn't stay still, though. They kept tapping to the music. She wasn't the least bit tired. She hadn't missed Charles Ludwig one bit.

Helene was fidgeting with her bag, looking perturbed. It suddenly struck Elisabeth that Franz had not danced with Néné all night. In fact, she had not seen him on the dance floor once.

She glanced at her mother, about to ask why, but one look at her expression and she knew. *Another headache*, Elisabeth thought. She glanced at Aunt Sophie, marching back and forth behind them with a most unpleasant face. She wondered what was happening.

Then the orchestra struck up a soft alluring beat, one Elisabeth didn't recognize. The dancers quickly left the floor, gathering on the edge, their eyes expectant.

"It's the cotillion," Ludovika whispered to her daughters.

"What is the cotillion?" Elisabeth asked.

"It's the dinner dance, but a special dance. A young man might present to his young lady a bouquet, showing his love."

Elisabeth felt the excitement in the room. Bodies fidgeted and fans accelerated. This was Aunt Sophie's special surprise, Elisabeth was sure. She turned to Helene.

"This is . . ."

Her voice stopped. Helene's face was white as chalk. What was wrong with Néné? She looked like she might faint. Elisabeth turned back. The music was alluring, her feet kept tapping beneath her gown, but not a soul was on the dance floor. Then she saw Franz crossing the room towards them.

The music soared, but everyone froze except Franz. He was striding towards them, smiling, his arms swinging. The archduchess ceased her prancing. Elisabeth's feet stopped tapping and Helene's eyes filled with terror.

Franz stopped in front of them, still smiling, his eyes on Elisabeth. With sweeping elegance, he bowed to her. The twinkle in his eyes mellowed into affection.

"May I have this dance, Sisi?"

She looked at Helene. She looked at her mother. She heard Sophie gasp. She did not move. She could not move.

"Sisi, may I have this dance with you?" Franz repeated, holding out his hand.

She looked into his eyes, the same dazzling blue eyes. She rose, she took his hand and she allowed him to lead her on to the dance floor.

Eyes popped. Breaths halted. Not a fan flickered. The music played on. Franz Joseph took Elisabeth into his arms. His eyes gathered her in. She smiled as they waltzed around and around and around. Her feet had wings, her body was air. It was magical.

She'd drop her eyes and then look up at him again. Franz beamed and she lost herself in his blue, blue eyes.

Hugo smiled to himself.

The whole room stood transfixed. The archduchess's bitterness momentarily succumbed to the enchantment of the young couple.

Helene sighed in relief.

The music climaxed and then halted. Franz stepped back, then pulled from his jacket a bouquet of flowers. With a sweeping bow and a face full of love, he placed them in Elisabeth's arms.

"My heart is at your feet," he said loudly enough for all to hear.

Stunned silence reigned. Then the roar exploded. The room went wild. Bodies rushed on to the dance floor. Faces were jubilant, voices excited. The fiddlers sent the music to the ceiling.

Elisabeth froze. The flowers fell to the floor. Franz reached out to her. He said something.

She didn't hear. Panic seized her and reason left her. Where was her mother? Bodies crushed around them with gleaming faces. Where was Néné? She cried out. She tried to push through the crowd. Franz reached out to her. She screamed. She pushed him away. Tears poured down her cheeks and smiles turned to shock. Eyes popped and fans halted. She fled to the door.

Ludovika and Helene jumped from their chairs, pushing past the steely-faced archduchess. They tore after her, out and into the carriage.

"But of course you must know what it means!" Helene's voice rose.

Elisabeth, Helene and Ludovika teetered in the tottering carriage heading to their residence. The rain pounded and the horses' hooves sloshed through puddles of water.

"No, Helene, I don't know what it means."

When upset, she addressed her sister by her real name.

"It means he has chosen you."

"Chosen me!" Elisabeth shouted, staring at her sister in shock. "You're wrong, Helene. It cannot be. Mama, tell her that's not so."

Ludovika's head was pounding on all sides. She was distraught, and struggling to constrain herself. She put her arm around her trembling daughter. *My God*, she thought, *Sisi's only a child, not ready for this*. She attempted to keep a calm voice.

"I don't know, Sisi. It could be as Néné said. I will speak to Sophie tomorrow. She will tell us what it's all about."

"Tell us what, Mama?" Elisabeth demanded. "I was not brought here to marry the emperor, Néné was."

"Sisi," Ludovika was massaging her own forehead. "Please. Please let us wait for tomorrow."

The sisters crawled into their own troubled silence.

Helene was truly relieved. She was not attracted to Franz, but her tears fell anyway. She would have to go through this again to find a husband. There would be a difference, she said to herself. Next time, she would settle only for love, like the love she had seen in Franz's eyes.

Elisabeth was numb, staring into the black night. She just wanted to go home. She thought again of Possi, of the forests, of the mountains, then of Count Richard. Her tears ran down. She closed her eyes and thought of the patterns on the river twirling into endless, unpredictable change.

Sophie slammed her apartment door shut and flung her bag across the room. This was her greatest challenge ever and it came from an immature child from the Bavarian hills.

Before reason had time to control Sophie's anger, Franz was in her apartment. He couldn't wait until morning. He was radiant with excitement and bursting with superlatives. Sophie thought he had lost his mind.

"This time, I know you mean Elisabeth," she said.

"Of course I mean Sisi."

Though every cell in her body vibrated with anger, she struggled to preserve her patience. She had to tread carefully.

"She's very charming in her youthfulness." Sophie was surprised how calm, how silky smooth her voice was. "But don't rush into any commitments. Get to know her better. Take time to find out what lies behind that enchanting little face."

"Mama, I don't have to know her better. I want to marry Sisi."

Sophie's patience exploded. She jumped up from her chair.

"She is too immature, too uncultured to be an empress. You will lose all the respect of your people if you choose her."

She marched around the room, gesturing wildly.

"She is a country girl who plays with shepherd children, rides in circuses. She knows nothing of royalty, nothing of court etiquette. She has no elegance, no poise. She is capricious and unpredictable. The Viennese society will never accept her. The whole world will think you mad."

Her face was red with rage.

"I cannot possibly let you make such a fool of yourself."

"Mother, it is what I want." Franz's eyes were steely. "I have always listened to you. Your advice has been meticulous. I could not rule the empire without you, and I have never given you resistance. However, now I do. Now, I must."

His body stiffened to a commanding stature.

"I am the emperor and this is my command. I will marry her."

Sophie collapsed into her chair. Her face went into her hands. It would be a disaster. She rose from her chair and went to the window. She looked out at the dark night. She knew further words would have no effect. He was blinded by love and beyond all reason.

Her challenge was mountainous. She could not lose her power, her control or the security of the empire to the uncertainty of love. She knew Franz's weakness with women and she had to tread carefully. Her only hope would be to postpone the wedding date and hope that reality would reclaim his senses.

She turned back to him.

"I will inform Ludovika of your decision and ask for Elisabeth's hand in marriage."

Franz threw his arms around her.

"Thank you. Thank you, my dearest Mama. Thank you!"

She buried her face on his shoulder. They both sobbed, but for different reasons.

Franz waited in the reception salon of the inn where Elisabeth was staying, his excitement doing loops with his anxiety. The minutes passed like hours since Ludovika and her daughters had been given his proposal. They knew he was waiting, yet no one opened the door.

Panic set in. He could not sit still any longer. He was up and pacing the salon. People started to notice. They bowed at him with curious faces. He tried returning pleasant greetings but he was impatient. *I must have her*, he thought. *I would give up the empire for her.* He looked at his watch again. It had been nearly two hours. What were they doing?

Not a muscle moved in Elisabeth's face when her mother read Sophie's letter to her.

"What about Néné?" Elisabeth's asked immediately.

Tears streamed down Néné's cheeks.

"It doesn't matter about me. You are the one he wants."

Elisabeth stared at her sister. Her tears flowed too.

"Why me? It makes no sense."

"Oh, Sisi. He loves you."

Helene reached quickly out to her sister.

"We all saw it, Sisi. Right from the beginning, it was apparent. I'm not jealous, really I'm not. He is very handsome and very nice. But I do not love him, nor does he love me. I'm not crying because he chose you over me. It's just . . ." She threw up her arms. "It's just all these months, the buildup, the strain. I'm glad it's over, and I just want to go home to Bavaria."

Mixed emotions conflicted Ludovika. She had captured an emperor for Sisi. It was beyond belief. Still, her fears escalated. Sisi was so young — she was not prepared to go straight from childhood into the most prestigious position in Europe. What did she know of love, of marriage, of the unpredictable realities that lay ahead? The Viennese aristocrats were vultures ready to devour anything that alienated their fancy. Ludovika shuddered. What tolerance would they have for Sisi's extreme youth and for the errors she would make?

She looked at Néné, almost nineteen. Was she too old for a suitable match? She looked at the diamond cross lying on the table with Sophie's note of condolence to Helene. She saw Néné's face and her pain returned. She turned back to Sisi.

"Do you think you may learn to love him?" Her voice quivered.

Elisabeth stared into space. *Love? What is love?* She thought of the romantic novels hidden beneath her bed and their glowing descriptions that took her into blissful wonder. She remembered her feelings when she looked at Franz. Was that love?

"Mama, maybe I love him." She burst into tears and moaned. "If only he was not an emperor."

Her mother caught her in her arms and they cried. Helene, too. Elisabeth drew back and wiped her tears. She sat silent a moment.

"Mama," she broke the silence, "I know I'm very young, but I am maturing. I often contemplate life. My books have nourished my thoughts. I do believe our lives are preordained. Our strength is nourished from the seeds of our childhood. That's what Papa always said. And those seeds blossom into our maturity, giving us the strength to adapt to the ever-changing and unpredictable patterns of our life."

She thought of the patterns on the river waters. Her mother's eyes widened at her daughter's wise words. Elisabeth took a deep breath.

"If this is the way of my path, I must not run away. I must accept the change and hope I will be strong. I'm not sure I know what love is, but I will do everything in my power to be a good empress and to make the emperor happy and to be a most loving child to Aunt Sophie."

A frantic Franz greeted Ludovika when she opened the apartment door and invited him in. Her smiling face soothed his anxiety.

When Elisabeth reached out and took his hands, tears flowed down his cheeks. He took her in his arms and held her to him. Their lives were transformed forever.

5

The little town of Bad Ischl was *en fête*. The black and yellow banners of the Habsburgs, mingling with the blue and white colours of Bavaria, flew from balconies and windows. Ten thousand candles sparkled throughout the little town. Fireworks and rockets filled the sky. On the mountainside, Franz Joseph's and Elisabeth's initials were entwined in blazing letters of fire.

The bride-to-be was displayed for all to see as the royal carriage ambled through the little town of Bad Ischl. Sophie forced her smile while Ludovika was *all* smiles. Elisabeth's terror of crowds rose like a sponge, whipping away her seeds of maturity. She raised her hand, only smiling occasionally. She hoped the seeds were well-planted. Franz's whole face beamed. Sophie thought his waving arms might detach from their sockets.

At the town square, full of cheering locals, some hanging from lamppoles and balancing on fountain rails, the carriage slowed to a crawl. Elisabeth's name rose as high as the balconies full of approving, waving townspeople.

Her fear took hold. Maturity fled. A wail escaped her and she buried her face in her hands. Sophie snorted in disgust before her face turned to stone. Franz saw Sisi's panic and took her into his arms.

"It's all right, my little one," he said gently.

He ordered the carriage to return to the inn. Sophie's anger almost sent her from her seat. Her fists pounded in her lap.

"We must complete the circuit — these are her people welcoming her!" she insisted. "Instead of running like a frightened child, she must present herself and accept their homage with the dignity and superiority of an empress."

Her words fell on deaf ears. Sophie bit back her anger and clutched her hands. Her challenges were just beginning.

The next day, the sun showered the town with warmth and the people, dressed in their most colourful clothes, greeted Franz and Elisabeth in the town park. There were musicians and dancing, gay voices and laughter. Elisabeth reached out to the welcoming hands, hugged the children and threw out kisses. In the arms of the locals, she swung to their music with the exuberance of a country girl. It was Possi all over again.

When Franz, caught up in the frenzy, swung village girl after village girl in dance, Sophie went into numb shock. It went against all protocol. She fled to her apartment. It was the final blow.

Max, Elisabeth's father, came for the celebrations. His enthusiasm hardly matched the festivities. Max was sure a terrible decision had been made. He watched his daughter whirl around at the many town dances, he saw her happiness and the love in Franz's eyes and he hoped that he was wrong.

The engagement festivities ended on August 31st, when duties made their claim on Franz. Elisabeth clung to his arm as the carriage bumped along the mountain road carrying them to Salzburg. There they would part, he to the rigour of ruling forty million people and she to the hills of Bavaria to prepare to be an empress. At the fork in the road, Franz escorted Elisabeth to the carriage where her father, mother and Helene waited.

"Our road ahead will have many bumps, but our love will carry us through," Franz said gently, holding her hands, not wanting to let her go.

Elisabeth saw his love — it covered his face, it was in his voice. She was the centre of such devotion. She went into his arms. She closed her eyes and prayed she wouldn't let him down.

Ludovika fidgeted with excitement in the waiting carriage. It was not only the marriage preparations that had her feet tapping, it was the Munich royals. Their disbelief and their excitement would storm through the salons and race across the city of Munich in a chorus of gay voices and delighted faces. What a change in her life it would bring. No more snooty noses. She would be accepted at last in the *crème de la crème* of society.

Max was impatient to get going, having had enough of this celebration.

Helene wondered if Franz would ever tire of kissing Sisi's tear-stained face. Still, she could not dismiss her concerns. What did the future hold for these two young and very different people?

Against the Tide

1

Franz found it difficult to concentrate on his official duties. It was like fitting winter into a summer day and Sophie's impatience was growing.

Often, in the middle of meetings, bogged down with the number of decisions awaiting on the table, his thoughts would drift to Sisi. Sophie's rapping hand and the expressions of his ministers would bring him back. His apology would be a sheepish grin.

When he freed, without consulting Sophie, twenty political prisoners, among them Hungarians from the 1848 uprising, her anger flared like sparks from burning timbers. Franz merely smiled.

"I have such happiness in my heart, I want to share it with my people."

That sent her from her chair. *Not one of those Hungarians deserved to be freed*, Sophie thought.

The ministers drew into themselves with hidden smirks. They thought it quite amusing. Was the charming little princess taking priority over the archduchess?

The Crimean problem was escalating and a decision had to be made. Russia was advancing into Turkey. The French and the

British, to protect their trade routes, were threatening war with Russia. Tsar Nicholas expected Austria's help in return for his having aided Austria during the Hungarian uprising. But Austria did not want war with Turkey.

"Austria must act as mediator to prevent a war or join the British and French," the archduchess explained to Franz, hoping he might have returned to his senses.

When he shot forward in his chair, she was hopeful.

"I do not want war," he said, to her great relief. "I will take this responsibility as mediator at once." Then, with a big smile, he added, "But I must take time to go to Possi."

Sophie snorted with disgust. The ministers tightened their lips to hide their smiles.

In 1854, the Crimean War began and Russia descended upon Turkey. France and England rushed to Turkey's side, Austria with them. And Franz did go to Possi.

Elisabeth sat at her ink-stained desk in her tiny bedroom, staring out at the last rays of the October sun highlighting the fading leaves. The sky was a rosy peach, and a faint mist swept over the lake. Singing birds were sailing through the sky, gathering in flocks to flee to warmer homes.

Her desk was piled high with history books. So many. She couldn't begin to remember all the different nationalities of the empire. There were language books, French and Italian — how could she learn two languages? And there were Franz's titles dating back to the Holy Roman Empire: Emperor of Austria, King of Jerusalem, heir to the Iron Crown of the Lombard Kings, the Apostolic Crown of St. Stephen and so many more. It was like a tangle of threads in her mind.

Sometimes, in desperation, she flung a book across the room, sometimes two or three. Sometimes she felt like throwing them all. One good thing: her professor from the University of Munich had said she had a good mind.

"Sisi. Sisi!"

Her thirteen-year-old sister, Maria, came bouncing in. She did excited hops and loops around the room. That was typical of her. She was always doing somersaults across the lawns, swinging from trees or leaping from rock to rock in the rivers. *She is just like me*, Elisabeth often thought.

"Mama says I can have your room when you get married. I'm so excited."

Elisabeth slammed shut her book and tossed it across her desk. Maria stopped dancing.

"Oh, Sisi. You're crying. Aren't you happy you are going to be an empress?"

Elisabeth looked at her sister a minute.

"I *think* I'm happy," she finally said.

But her tears fell and Maria was bewildered. Elisabeth reached out and put an arm around her.

"How can I explain? It's so wonderful to be in love. And yet, I'm frightened. I'm going to leave you all. I can't bear to hear you discussing things you will be doing when I won't be here to share them. And this little room. I love it, too. I don't want to leave it."

Her tears came faster.

"But you will live in a beautiful palace," Maria said. "Mama says your apartments will drip with gold and embroideries and you'll wear beautiful gowns."

"And soldiers will guard my door and I'll never be able to run through the garden in my bare feet after a warm summer rain."

But how could Maria understand, when even their own mother's impatience was growing?

"Mama says to come to the drawing room. There is news about your trousseau," Maria announced, bouncing from the room with the same lilt that brought her in.

Her trousseau! Elisabeth stamped her feet. What more could there be? Half the summer she'd spent in front of a mirror with dressmakers, even shoe designers. She'd never realized there were so many fabrics to choose from. She even had a special corset for riding. Sophie informed her that an empress must always be laced with a corset for every outdoor exercise.

Elisabeth's head drooped. The medley of the fleeing birds filtered through the window. It was pleasant, soothing. She raised her head and looked out. She watched them sailing through the sky, dipping and singing. Oh, how she envied their freedom. She picked up her quill and her unhappiness poured out:

> If I could but be with thee, flying
> Through blue eternities of sky,
> How I would praise with all my being,
> The god whom men call liberty.
> How soon would I forget all sorrow
> And never fear a sad tomorrow,
> Nor let the tear my cheeks bedew.

She rose from her chair, her face pensive. Then she turned and walked from the room, slamming the door shut behind her.

A fire blazed in the cozy drawing room. Dogs snored on the carpets. Ludovika and Helene chattered over a sheet of paper. As Elizabeth entered the room, Helene waved the paper at her.

"It's a letter from Aunt Sophie with more suggestions."

Her eyebrows sailed with her grin.

"Really," Elisabeth spat out. "What now?"

"Your yellow teeth," Helene giggled. "You must do something about them."

"What yellow teeth?" Elisabeth demanded. "I don't have yellow teeth."

"You aren't different." Helene tried to soothe her. "We all have yellow teeth. Living here in the country, we didn't worry about it. Mama knows just the person to help us."

"But first, the trousseau . . ." Her mother waved another large paper. "It's just to make sure we have judged the requirements correctly."

She handed the list to Elisabeth, who scanned it quickly. Her face reddened by the second: seventeen dresses for formal occasions, fourteen high-necked silk dresses, nineteen thin summer dresses in all colours of the rainbow, fourteen dozen lace-trimmed undergarments, nineteen bedjackets of muslin and silk.

"One hundred and thirteen pairs of shoes!" Elisabeth exclaimed. "What would I do with one hundred and thirteen pairs of shoes?"

"The Empress of Austria is not allowed to wear a pair of shoes for more than one day," her mother said. "And then, my dear Sisi, they are given away."

Elisabeth pounded the table so hard the paper almost flew from her hands.

"And twelve embroidered nightcaps, twenty-four night neckerchiefs, six dozen petticoats of piqué, silk and flannel, twenty-four combing coats."

Elisabeth sent the paper flying across the room.

"I've had enough. I don't want to be an empress."

She fled to the door. This time, maturity was like a dagger in her chest. She sped down the hall, into her room and slammed the door hard, *really* hard. In front of the mirror, she stopped and spread her lips. She did have yellow teeth.

She made a face, reached for her sweater and flew out of the room. She followed the path to the lake's edge, hardly seeing through her tears.

The sun had gone, the sky had darkened. Here and there, the night birds sang and tiny waves lapped the shore.

"What is love anyway?" she asked no one in particular.

Then her father was beside her. He took her hands and drew her into his arms. He didn't try to stop her tears. They turned and followed the trail beside the lake, as they had so many times before. They watched the moon appearing and listened to the stillness. They didn't speak. Their silence was their solace. Elisabeth's mind was calm again.

2

It was October. Franz could no longer endure the separation from Elisabeth. Despite his mother's tirade, he left Vienna with Count Grünne. They travelled day and night. In thirty-one hours, they arrived at Possi. Franz jumped from the carriage into a snarling group of black spaniels.

A slim young groom came running.

"Take care," he shouted. "These are Duke Max's dogs. They always smell strangers. Duke Max insists that dogs have souls and an inner knowledge of humankind. If a visitor is ill-received by the dogs, he need not try to make a second appearance."

Franz laughed. Sporting a green shirt and a Tyrolean hat with a feather cockade, he had not been recognized as the Emperor of Austria.

"Spare your fears, my friend. I know how to conquer the growling blacks. Where is my Sisi?" he demanded.

He calmed the dogs, bounded into the house, embraced his mother-in-law to be, Ludovika, and was introduced to bouncing children and more dogs. There was Charles Theodore, who was two years younger than Elisabeth and known as 'Gackl'. There was Maria, with large sparkling eyes — Ludovika had told him that Maria could challenge Elisabeth on a horse. There was Mathilde, who tittered like a bird and whom they called 'Spatz' (sparrow). There was six-year-old Sophie, named after Ludovika's sister the archduchess Sophie, and four-year-old Max, 'Mapperl'. Both were balancing on the edge of a chair. But none of the bouncing children curbed Franz's anxiousness. He had to find Sisi.

"She didn't expect you so soon," Ludovika said. "She went for a walk. But come, rest. She will be here shortly."

"I can't wait to see her. I'll find her! Which path did she take?"

Ludovika smiled at his excitement.

"Take Spritz and go that way."

She pushed a little white dog into his arms and pointed to a path that disappeared into the forest.

"He will find her," she assured him.

It was a sunny day. Franz sprinted through the pine forest and hurtled through fallen leaves, following the yelping dog. Then he heard her voice calling.

"Spritz, is that you?"

The dog shot forward, Franz on his heels.

"Sisi, it's me."

She stepped from the woods. He stopped. He was speechless. She was dazzling. Her face was flushed, her smile warm, her eyes sparkling.

"Oh, Sisi."

He stepped forward and swept her into his arms. Her face crumbled, her tears came. She pushed him back. He saw her eyes. They were frightened eyes.

"Oh, Franz. I'm so mixed up." It came rushing out; she couldn't keep it in. "I'm afraid to leave my family, I am afraid to go to Vienna. I am afraid I won't be a good empress. I'm afraid the Austrian people won't like me. I'm . . ."

His expression made her stop.

"Oh, Franz," she whimpered. "Do I sound like a child? Do I disappoint you?"

Still holding her in his arms, he radiated love. She pushed him back.

"Franz, do you fear you have made a mistake?"

"No," he said gently, touching her tear-stained cheeks. "I have made no mistake. My heart tells me that. You are very young and very inexperienced. I have asked you to share a great burden." He drew in breath slowly. "But I love you. I cannot lose you. I will do all with my love to protect you, to comfort you, to bring you through whatever lies ahead."

She let him draw her into his arms. She closed her eyes. Had she found love?

She stepped back and took his hands.

"I know I have much to learn. I will not disappoint you. I will make you proud of me." With a touch of humour, she added, "I will read all those history books and remember all your titles."

She hoped she would. Then, seeing the love in his eyes, she knew she would.

Hand in hand, they descended down the rocky path and rounded the corner. Possi glowed in the sunlight but the horizon was not visible.

Nobody but nobody at Possi could keep their eyes off Franz and Elisabeth. Franz's adjutant general, Count Karl Grünne, could hardly believe the change in the stiff young emperor, frolicking like a youngster with the wild, undisciplined children. He challenged them to horse jumps and raced with them through the woods. Elisabeth was always beside him. They were like children themselves. And there were times, Grünne thought, that Elisabeth was better on a horse than Franz. She had a natural touch that made her seem as one with the horse.

As the archduchess's hawk-eye, Grünne had participated in Franz's romantic adventures more times than he could remember. Franz's sexual appetite never ran out and neither did the line of ladies. Grünne passed the juicy tidbits of Franz's liaisons to the archduchess with humorous shrugs. Now he had concerns. Never had he witnessed in Franz such love, affection and delight. Could she be a threat to both the archduchess and to him?

He knew Sophie's fury over Franz's choice of Elisabeth. She feared Elisabeth's influence. Watching them together, so did he. Both he and Sophie wanted someone docile and submissive, she for control and he to preserve his place with the ladies. If Franz's romantic intrigues ended, his own pleasures might also end. There would not be any leftover ladies to quench his passion. And that, he did not want.

Yet, as he watched them together, he often turned away and wandered into the forest. In its solitude, he'd walk the trails and ponder the emptiness of his own life.

Excitement mounted in Munich as the gala Court Ball to honour Elisabeth and Franz neared. Elisabeth could hardly wait.

She loved Strauss waltzes. She had Franz to dance with and she had a new dress — a beautiful dress, very stylish, her shoulders displayed in blue chiffon. She rehearsed Helene's social conversational skills. It was like a game and her amusement bounced. *What a night it will be*, she thought.

The first dance was everything she dreamed of. Franz whirled her around the dance floor — they dipped, they turned, they laughed, they looked into each other's eyes. Then it turned into a disaster — for Elisabeth. Everyone else had a great time.

For the rest of the night, the whole night, Elisabeth and Franz shared a dais with the king and queen of Bavaria. The guests circled around them, smiling graciously. Elisabeth wanted to fly from her seat. Her feet tapped beneath her gown at such a pace, she was sure the queen noticed. She stilled her hands and tried poise and maturity.

"It is the etiquette of the court," Helene whispered to her, sailing by in the arms of a dashing young man.

A ball in our honour, Elisabeth thought, *and everyone is dancing and enjoying themselves but the guests of honour*. Was this a sign of what was to come? She struggled to keep her immaturity in check, though her chit-chat often died on her tongue.

Franz had been gone a week, back to Vienna. The ice formed on the lake, snow flurries filtered through the air. Elisabeth's family moved from Possi to their winter home in Munich.

"Don't take that old thing!" Ludovika ordered when she came into Elisabeth's room in Possi.

In Elisabeth's arms was her old rose blanket she had cuddled with since childhood.

"You won't need that."

It went with her, but her mother never knew.

Elisabeth looked at her narrow bed, already littered with her little sister Maria's possessions. She ran her hand over her empty dresser. The morning sun came through the window. There was no warmth, just tears. She would never live here again. After arriving in Munich, she would be off to Vienna. She didn't think about Franz. She thought of her peasant friends, she thought of Allie, she thought of riding through the forest. She thought of Punch.

She fled her room for the corral.

"Punch!" she shouted.

She jumped over the fence and ran to him. She buried her tears in his mane. The past sailed into infinity and the future went blank in her mind.

As the carriage rumbled along the mountain road, taking the family to Munich, no one except her father understood her unhappiness.

Why would she miss Possi? the others wondered. After all, she was going to be an empress and live in a beautiful palace.

In Munich, the common people welcomed Elisabeth with excitement and joy. They viewed her as one of them. The aristocrats threw lavish banquets and gushed around Elisabeth and Ludovika with glistening eyes, struggling to keep their scornful thoughts behind their stiff smiles, especially when Elisabeth stood with pain in her eyes and lost for words, as she did so often when she just couldn't produce Helene's silky chat. Their whispers accelerated, their fans swished faster and their lips turned into slits.

"*She will never make an empress.*"

Elisabeth hated every bit of it. Their conversations were so boring and their superficial gestures so overwhelming. She struggled as best she could to be gracious. She tried to remember her promises to Franz. But many times she eyed the doors, wanting to flee the salons. Many times she almost did.

"I feel ridiculous with those people," she complained to her mother. "They are a waste of time, so frivolous and insincere. And they never cast an eye on me until I caught an emperor."

She finished with that haughty snort she had picked up from the royals.

"They will improve your social skills," Ludovika assured.

She was getting desperate. Time was moving on and Sisi was hardly changing.

"How will it improve my social skills?" Elisabeth retorted. "When I say anything, they look at me as if it is pure nonsense."

None of them knew anything about Shakespeare or her other favourite writers. They just didn't want to know.

Elisabeth spent more time in her room over her books, and carrying around her favourite parrot, Tusti, as she practised her French and Italian. Ludovika's desperation kept reaching newer heights. Sisi's social skills were not improving and stories flew in from Vienna. People wondered what kind of clouded lenses had covered their emperor's eyes.

"Sisi will never satisfy those Viennese aristocrats," Ludovika moaned to Helene as they pondered the disgruntled voices. "They perceive themselves as the bluest of blood and distinguished from all other humanity. And their latest . . ."

Ludovika stomped across the room, her headache raging, and thrust a sheet of paper into Helene's hand.

"Is it because this is the twenty-second intermarriage between the Habsburgs and the Wittelsbachs, and that hereditary diseases and bouts of madness run rampant because of these intermarriages?" Ludovika raged. "Or is it because she is not of pure blue blood?"

A Wittelsbach, way back, had married a commoner — on her father's side, of course.

"The latest!" she shouted. "They want a beautiful and elegant empress to match the ravishing Empress Eugenie, who is turning Paris into a glamorous and exciting city."

Helene rolled her eyes, picturing Elisabeth's braids. Beauty and elegance weren't her main accomplishments. She smiled.

"Sisi is hardly that."

"They are going to pounce," Ludovika despaired, "and their claws will destroy her."

Still, the goal of a crown for her daughter remained. She raced to her room, snatched up her quill and wrote to Sophie: 'In order to spare Sisi from overwhelming festivities, could the wedding be postponed until June, when the majority of the nobility will have departed from Vienna?'

The archduchess's reply was immediate and unrelenting. 'Such a wish is at odds with prevailing customs in Vienna. The Emperor of Austria does not put off marriage and exclude the public because the future empress is afraid of the aristocrats.'

Farewell

1

April arrived and soon it was the day of her departure. Elisabeth sat on the edge of the bed, her emotions twisting in so many directions that she was transfixed.

A bright sun was in the sky, tree branches hung with white sycamore blossoms, tulips and daffodils were everywhere. Downstairs, a state carriage waited to carry Elisabeth, her mother, her father and Helene through the cheering crowds of Munich to Straubing, where they would board the imperial steamer. Down the Danube they would travel to the village of Nussdorf, and from there on to Vienna and her wedding.

Through her bedroom window, the excited voices of the crowd in the streets below filtered in.

Elisabeth did not want to go.

"Sisi. Hurry, hurry! There is no time to dally," her mother's voice shot up the stairs, impatient and excited.

Elisabeth stood up and put her cloak around her shoulders. She looked at the bare closet, the empty drawers. Nothing lay on her table. Her past was gone.

She closed her door gently and came down the stairs, touching each one with hesitant steps, clearly too slowly for her mother fidgeting below.

She prayed she wouldn't break down and cry in front of the excited faces below. The younger children were doing somersaults in the vestibule and the house staff stood in line proudly, ready for their farewells. To each she gave a little gift. Each hand she grasped in hers, something she would never do again. The latest revelation from Vienna: the Empress of Austria offers her hand only to the most elite. Allie stood last in the line.

"My dearest friend," Elisabeth greeted her. "So many times we have chased each other through the rose gardens and across the lawns on our ponies since childhood, early early childhood."

She threw her arms around her, and their tears flowed like mountain falls.

Her sister Mathilde pushed a bouquet of wildflowers into her hands.

"Don't cry, Sisi. You are a princess going off to marry her prince. You'll live in a big castle. You'll be happy," she exclaimed.

Elisabeth forced a smile.

"I am happy and I love my prince." At least she thought she did. "It's just that I will miss you all so much."

She caught them up in her arms. She didn't add that she hated big palaces, that she just wanted to stay at Possi.

"Look at that gorgeous ship!" Helene shouted.

They had arrived at the dock after filing through crowds of cheering people.

Elisabeth tried to match Néné's enthusiasm, but it was hard. Her thoughts were tangled. Just last year, she, her mother and Néné had set out to Bad Ischl in a small family coach and she had shared the back seat with the maid. Today, the front seat was hers in a state carriage drawn by six of the finest greys and with an entourage of servants, followed by twenty-five cases of her trousseau.

"It is a side-wheeler called *The Franz Joseph*. The most splendid ever to sail the Danube," Elisabeth heard her father say.

The ship pulled out and Elisabeth's eyes took on a sparkle. She had never been on a ship and neither had Néné. They raced like excited children from deck to deck. The upper deck was transformed into a garden with an arbour of climbing roses trailing to the water. Its splendour brought their loudest cries. There, they left the world behind, basking on the garden deck among the roses, as they watched the blossoming orchards of Wachau, the medieval ruins of Dürnstein, the great copper dome of Melk and the towns of Stein, Krems, Tulln and Klosterneuburg pass by. The peasants lined the shores, the women in colourful headdresses shouting her name and the men in tight breeches and short jackets waving their little felt hats.

Elisabeth listened to the waves lapping at the ship. She watched the flying seagulls dipping and singing. Time rolled into soothing infinity. She almost forgot where she was going.

When Nussdorf appeared and her mother's eyes almost exploded with excitement, reality returned to Elisabeth.

Pre-wedding excitement in Vienna had reached a fever pitch. Pictures of the young couple were in every window. There were hundreds of china figurines of them in court dress and their pictures adorned coffee sets and dinner plates. The blue and white colours of Bavaria decorated everything from bonnets in the milliners' windows to the striped awnings on the Graben, and every carriage driver trimmed his horse in blue and white rosettes.

On the afternoon of April 22, 1854, Vienna was almost deserted. Everything on wheels, from the humblest of carts to the grandest of carriages, rumbled down the road to Nussdorf to greet the new empress-to-be.

Franz and Grünne left early, galloping at a fast pace through Vienna. But not fast enough for Franz.

They arrived in Nussdorf ahead of the Archduchess Sophie and the procession of state carriages arranged for Elisabeth and her family. Franz glowed with excitement, throwing smiles, waving to all he passed and calling out salutations.

Love had, one more time, replaced the trials of the war, Grünne thought with a smile. The only thing on Franz's mind was the beautiful young woman who would soon steam into sight.

As the boat neared Nussdorf, Elisabeth let out a desperate wail and Helene took her hands in her own.

The riverbanks were crowded with people, some even stomping into the water, shouting and waving their arms. Carriages were everywhere, and full of cheering people. It was like a massive invasion.

Elisabeth panicked. Even her new bonnet lost its dazzle.

"Take deep breaths," Helene said. "Slow, deep breaths. It will help."

It did not help. Her body trembled like a rickety carriage. She couldn't find a voice or a smile, hardly even a breath.

As the boat neared the dock, the cheers reached a deafening roar. The screams formed her name. *"Elisabeth! Elisabeth!"* She plugged her ears. It was terrifying.

Cannons thundered, church bells rang and bands blared out the national anthem. Ludovika's eyes glowed, every fibre in her body strung out in excitement. She called out to Elisabeth.

"Those cheers are for you, my daughter. You must acknowledge them."

Max turned to stone and Helene again gripped Elisabeth's hands. The boat hit the dock, bounced gently between the pylons, then stopped. Elisabeth froze. This time she couldn't find a breath.

Then, here came Franz down the ramp, arms swinging, smiling broadly. He jumped onto the deck of the boat and raced to her, his blue eyes like sparkling jewels. He made a sweeping bow, then he stood motionless, looking at her.

The crowds also stood motionless, silent. Not a church bell rang, not a drum banged. It was as if the Earth had stopped. Then he reached out and took her hands. His voice rang out for all to hear.

"Welcome to your new home, my dearest Elisabeth!"

The roars tore to the sky. Franz's smile covered his face and Elisabeth's smile emerged. She saw his affection, she saw love. He gave her his arm and guided her up the ramp. Her legs moved without fear, her breath was back. Her face was as delicate as a rose and her smile reached from ear to ear.

Her mother shed tears, her father sighed and Helene's grin was as wide as Elisabeth's.

The magnificent welcome from the people — their joy, their approval, their shining eyes — captured Elisabeth. Her fear of crowds turned to elation. She forgot her yellow teeth; protocol went with the wind as she reached out to all as if they were her close friends.

Archduchess Sophie watched from her carriage with shock and disgust. Her anger festered and her fingers drummed. Even the carriage horseman heard the pelting of her feet. When Elisabeth grasped the hands of a baker, coated with flour, her drumming stopped, her anger turned to horror and her scream reached Elisabeth's ears.

Elisabeth bit back her smile. And Franz turned a blind eye, feasting on his adorable loved one. *Now*, Elisabeth thought, her amusement growing, *my pure hands are forever tainted*.

The royal carriage took Sophie and Elisabeth to Schönbrunn Palace. Franz rode with Elisabeth's family.

Sophie did not shelve her disgust. She was ready to pounce.

Elisabeth saw it coming. She sat rigid but poised on her seat, still enchanted by the people's reception. She glanced out the window at the crowds on the streets shouting her name and took deep breaths. She even waved.

"Perhaps," Sophie said, and no voice could be more bitter, "we cannot expect dignity from a sixteen-year-old country girl whose manners are adopted from the peasants and whose father has the social skills of a barbarian."

Elisabeth almost exploded with anger. Her poise went to shreds. But the gods were with her and the day was saved as the carriage came to a stop at the palace. Franz pulled open the door.

"Welcome to the Schönbrunn, my dearest Sisi," he proclaimed, his eyes full of love.

Elisabeth took her deepest breath ever. She mastered her anger, caught up her skirts, nodded politely to the archduchess, included a smile, and stepped into the arms of her beaming lover. Her maturity had come through.

Sophie dug her nails into her palms. Her mind was made up. If the empire was to be saved, Franz must be controlled. She had to tackle Franz's unpredictable passion for the little nymph. She pounded her fists on her thighs. There was no time to waste. She stepped from the carriage, her chin high, her mind made up.

Reception after reception followed, mostly family. Elisabeth couldn't count the times she ripped off her gloves, exchanging them for fresh ones so the next pair of squishy lips could kiss her gloved hand. She and Franz hardly exchanged a word.

She was so exhausted when she and Helene reached their apartment that the soldier stationed outside her door failed to impress her. She fled into the bedroom, leaving Helene whirling around the salon with eyes agog at the red silk walls edged in gold, at the sweeping floor-to-ceiling mirrors in their rococo frames, at the gilded furniture and oil paintings. Helene caught her breath. Many were of the wedding festivities of Joseph II and Isabella at the Hofburg.

Elisabeth's shout brought Helene racing into the bedroom.

A stiff-looking woman stood inside the room, along with two bowing ladies, whose faces were gleaming.

"Princess Elisabeth, I am the Countess Esterházy."

Elisabeth stared in horror. Finally she remembered her as the new mistress of her household. It was the countess's right to guide her in the etiquette of the Habsburg court, and she had delivered that information as if she was about to take over Elisabeth's life.

"It is very kind of you to be here," Helene quickly responded, "but we will not need you tonight. I will help my sister."

Countess Esterházy's face hardened. The two ladies' sparkles diminished.

"As you wish." Her steely eyes were on Elisabeth. "I must inform you about tomorrow."

She ignored Helene's attempt to interrupt her.

"It has been the custom, for generations, for the emperor's bride to prepare for her entry into Vienna at Favorita Castle. There, the finishing touches to her dress are completed. Your mother will accompany you to Favorita in the morning. From there, with your mother, you will join a procession and make a formal entry into Vienna."

The countess waved a sheaf of papers.

"These are entitled 'Order for the Ceremonial of the Public Entry into Vienna of Her Royal Highness, the Most August Princess Elisabeth'." She thrust them into Elisabeth's hand. "It is a most sacred ceremony. It is imperative that you memorize this for your part in this traditional Habsburg wedding."

With curtseys, they were gone.

Elisabeth and Helene stared at the papers. Then Elisabeth flung them to the floor.

"I'm going to bed, Néné," she announced. "We'll worry about that tomorrow."

Entry into Vienna

1

To Elisabeth, it was a day of horror. To Sophie, it was a glimmer of victory. The bride-to-be made her entry into Vienna, her head buried in her hands and tears pouring down her cheeks.

The royals had extended smirks and the Viennese people were stunned with shock. Who had their emperor chosen? She was more like a scared child than an empress.

Ludovika prayed the wedding would go on.

It began at eight o'clock in the morning. Elisabeth arrived at Favorita Castle with her mother, their eyes still plagued with sleep. There the palace ladies would prepare her for her entry into Vienna.

It was like a circus. It took everything Elisabeth had to keep her sanity embedded in her smile.

There were dresses, there were crinolines, there were shoes. There was jewellery for her hair, her ears, her neck, her arms, her fingers and even her toes. There was hairdressing, there was makeup and there was a continued stream of advice from the archduchess. Elisabeth's deep breaths were getting shorter and shorter as she tried to control herself and keep her immaturity in check.

The palace ladies hovering around her were something else. They chattered non-stop with gossip and stories of other Habsburg brides. At times, Elisabeth ventured a smile.

"Favorita is the castle of tears and broken hearts." Their words were laced with giggles. "Maria Theresa was the only bride to leave here with love in her heart and not tears . . . except for you."

Then their sighs came. "How fortunate for you to love and be loved by the handsomest, most sought-after bachelor in the world."

They eyed her enviously. Elisabeth sat more pinched than ever.

When her tolerance reached its end, she sought refuge in the toilet room. She stayed so long, Ludovika came in without knocking and marched her out.

"Do you not realize that you are the twenty-third Wittelsbach bride to cross this threshold and you must carry yourself as proudly as your ancestors?" she asked.

Elisabeth thought Ludovika sounded just like her sister, the Archduchess Sophie.

She gathered her strength again. It was not easy. It was like digging her nails into bleeding palms.

It was late afternoon when Elisabeth and her mother settled into the glass carriage decorated with Rubens panels and gold-plated wheels. Eight white Lipizzaner horses with red and gold tassels in their manes carried them through the gates of Vienna. They were heading to the Hofburg Palace where Franz waited. Elisabeth shut her mind to what would happen then.

State coaches followed in rank, with forerunners of pages, trumpeters and footmen along the sides. Artillery bodyguards pounded their drums.

The crowds were so ecstatic that the lancers lining the route were powerless at times to restrain them. People even pushed through the barricades and pounded the sides of the carriage.

Elisabeth raised her hand. Her terror was growing. Her smile was frozen, but at least it was there. Her fear of crowds was escalating. Not even Ludovika's obvious delight and waves helped her. Her mother loved it. She hardly noticed Elisabeth.

At the Kohlmarkt, the wild congestion on the narrow road impeded the carriage's progress. The lancers lost control and the people fell over one another banging on the carriage. Faces with gleaming eyes, stained grins and missing teeth plastered themselves against the windows. Elisabeth's face went into her hands. She crouched down so low, the people lost sight of her. She didn't look up again until the carriage stopped at the palace entrance. She knew it was wrong — she was acting like a child. Her mother stopped waving.

Fidgeting Habsburgs lined the palace steps with amused smirks. The news had reached them. Sophie stood in the centre, gloating maliciously with satisfaction. The little nymph's colours were showing and this time the people were aware.

"They are just the Habsburg family," Ludovika said, trying to calm Elisabeth. "And Sophie does have a welcoming smile."

"Do you call that a welcoming smile?" Elisabeth blurted out. "It's nothing but poison."

Ludovika said nothing. But she knew Elisabeth was right. Sophie's smile was poisonous.

Franz hastened down the stone steps and pulled open the carriage door. With her cheeks still wet from tears, Elisabeth reached for his hands and buried her face in his shoulder.

Ludovika prayed the wedding would proceed.

"Thank you, Franz, for giving me this quiet evening alone with just Néné," Elisabeth said.

Franz had escorted her to her apartment door. The day had ended and the mishaps of the day had faded. Franz had soothed her fears. Her only obligations that evening were introductions to the imperial household. The rest of the evening was hers. Néné and she would dine together. And the wedding would proceed.

A stiff soldier with unseeing eyes stood beside her door.

With a flicker of a jest, she said to Franz, "Must soldiers always guard my door?"

"Soldiers will always be outside your door," he replied.

He took her hands and clasped them firmly. She felt his tension. His eyes burned into hers, and she saw a passion she had never seen before. She looked down. Her romantic novels had enlightened her as to the wonders of love, but she feared there was still much she didn't know.

He saw her innocence. He dropped her hands and stepped back.

"Tomorrow is our wedding day and then I will never have to leave you again." He smiled gently, his voice tentative. He bowed. "Until tomorrow."

The coming day moved with uncertainty into her mind.

As Helene and Elisabeth enjoyed dinner in their small but impressive dining room, fears about the wedding day disappeared. Helene's eyes sparkled.

"Imagine a dining room all to ourselves," she said between bites.

Servants kept bringing different dishes, each so good that both girls tasted each one. Elisabeth was thinking of her little room in Possi. Perhaps she wouldn't miss it after all.

The clock ticked on. In exhaustion, they collapsed onto the soft down of the bed. The thought that tomorrow was her wedding day vanished from Elisabeth's mind.

Ludovika, still wide awake, heard the clock strike midnight. Perturbing thoughts were asserting themselves in her mind. She had captured a crown for her daughter, but had she imprisoned her in a society where happiness might never reign?

Until Death Do Us Part

1

It was a fairytale wedding. Greetings poured in from the far eastern borders of Russia to the royal court at Windsor Castle.

At twenty-four, Franz Joseph was Emperor of Austria, King of Hungary and Bohemia, King of Lombardy and Venice — of Dalmatia, of Croatia, of Slavonia, of Galicia, of Jerusalem — and Grand Duke of Tuscany and Kraków. At sixteen, Elisabeth Amalie Eugenie, a princess from Bavaria, was shy, innocently naïve and sublimely beautiful.

Both were very much in love.

The Vienna sky was a postcard blue on that April day. The afternoon sun dropped a coat of gold on the grey exterior of the Hofburg Palace. Beside it, the spires of the Augustinerkirche, the imperial church, sparkled as if embedded with thousands of tiny diamonds.

The city streets bustled with people. The common people's joy had spun to hope, and their hopes were pinned on love. They saw the princess as a revelation, one that could break the stranglehold of the Archduchess Sophie. Hundreds crowded into the church square. With frenzy and jubilation, they pressed into the cordons of police for a better glimpse of the church entrance where the bride and groom would soon appear.

"Love can bring miracles," they smiled. "With her beauty and her youth and the young emperor burning with love, the she-dragon archduchess will lose her power." Their cries escalated as they slapped each other on the back. "Look what love has done! Already the emperor stood up to his mother for the first time by going against her wishes, to take Elisabeth as his bride."

Inside, the church was a glitter in wealth. Fifteen thousand candles flickered on the red velvet that adorned the stone pillars and garnished the pews. They lit up the gold carpet that swept down the aisle. They shone on the embroidered vestments of the prelates, on the magnificent collars of the Knights of the Golden Fleece, on the jewel-encrusted costumes of the Hungarian magnates. They glowed on the elegant ladies, magnifying their extravagant diamonds and pearls a hundredfold.

One thousand guests stared in breathless silence as the young bride walked slowly up the aisle, guided by her mother and the Archduchess Sophie — fathers in that day did not take part in wedding ceremonies.

She was a vision of loveliness in her white satin gown with myrtle and orange blossoms, her face carrying the blush of youth, her deep-set eyes hauntingly beautiful with their mystic glow. Auburn lights showed through the chestnut hair piled high on her head, and diamonds and opals glittered in its folds. Even the most cynical of those who thought her totally unworthy of their emperor stared open-mouthed, their faces flushed with awe. Many tears fell. The vengeance in the hearts of the embittered dowagers, still agonizing over the young emperor's flirtatious eyes igniting their daughter's hopes, mellowed into softness.

Huddled down in her seat was Franz Joseph's beautiful nineteen-year-old Hungarian cousin, also named Elisabeth. She struggled with her anguish.

Two years before, he had laid his heart at her feet, even allowed, for the first time since the revolution, the Hungarian national dance, the Csárdás, to be played at the state ball. He had tried to dance her around to its witty tune, dressed in the uniform of a Hungarian hussar. His loving eyes filled her with dreams unimaginable. When his attention cooled, she blamed his mother, who would not tolerate a Hungarian empress. Or so she had thought, until she heard the rumours. He was passionately in love with a Bavarian princess, more like a shepherd girl than royalty. And against his mother's wishes, he would marry her. When she saw the adoring look he gave his bride as she was led to the altar, she put her handkerchief to her eyes to catch her tears.

Above the altar where Franz and Elisabeth knelt rose a canopy of white velvet embroidered with gold, under which were placed two prie-dieux, also of white velvet. The walls and columns of the church were hung with damask and costly tapestries and the floor was carpeted. From a hundred candelabras, countless tapers glowed. Red velvet tiers hung from the ceiling high above. The cardinal, in gold, was surrounded by seventy bishops and prelates in flaming red velvet with majestic headdresses decorated with gold trim and jewels. The young couple passed shy glances that radiated their love. Elisabeth didn't need her deep breaths.

The cardinal was known for his drone of platitudes. The audience shuffled in their seats and Elisabeth's jewelled crown weighed heavily on her head.

Her faint "I do," when finally required, hardly reached the front row. Franz's "I do" resounded in the ears at the very back rows of the church. Rings were exchanged and Elisabeth, Princess of Bavaria, became Empress of Austria.

Volleys discharged from the cannons on the church roof, their roar seeming to shake the very columns of the church. The ladies clasped their bejewelled ears and Elisabeth buried her face in Franz's shoulder.

Cannons thundered across the city as if an army stormed its walls and every church in Vienna clamoured with bells. The people in the squares went wild. Down the crumbling back alleys where sunshine never penetrated, the thunder of cannons and ringing bells filtered into the dark rooms of the destitute. Their smiles had glimmers of hope.

In the coffee houses, where intellectuals pondered their woes over intriguing aromas, cues were downed and billiard balls came to a halt. The players shook hands, but their joy was restrained, their hopes frayed.

Dr. Fischhof threw his stick down on the billiard table.

"There is doubt on your face," noted Jeb Austoff, an English professor still in his black academic gown.

"Doubt. Yes."

Fischhof swept his bushy black hair back. He was the physician who, five years before, had led the march that sparked the revolution in October 1848. Yet the reforms promised never happened. Franz took the throne, the archduchess took control and all their gains were trashed. He walked to the window and looked out at the rejoicing crowds.

"I'm afraid to have hope," he said sadly, turning to look at Jeb. "Do you really think, my friend, the shrewd archduchess would allow an empress hardly more than a child to take her place?"

The sky had darkened by the time the young couple emerged from the church. Trumpets blared, kettle drums rolled and police fought to control the crowds.

Anxiety grabbed Elisabeth's breath when she saw the crowds. Franz tightened his hold on her hand. The city looked as if a sandstorm had struck. The buildings were ghostly images in the swirling dust swept up by the frolicking masses and the street lamps were barely visible.

Franz waved, the crowds cheered. When Elisabeth waved, they roared. It almost drowned her smile. *Thank God for the carriage*, she thought, jumping into it, not waiting for Franz to help her.

It was a stone's throw to the Hofburg, but the streets were like a ballroom in disarray. People sang and danced, Elisabeth's name on everyone's lips. She saw her name on their banners with the words 'You are our saviour.' She couldn't understand it.

The ride was short and terrifying. Ogling faces pressed against the carriage windows and her smile came to an end. She felt like an animal enclosed in a zoo. Even the eight Lipizzaner horses in their gilded leather pranced nervously, pulling at their reins. The roar was cracking her ears. Franz smiled and waved to the crowds. Again her panic surfaced and she buried her face in her hands.

"Sisi, Sisi. Wave to them," Franz prodded, his impatience showing in his scowling face, his voice chastising. "It is your duty. You are their empress; they are your people."

She took deep breaths and raised her head. She tried a smile. A roar exploded from the crowd. They banged on the window harder, their shouts wilder. She cried out, plugged her ears and let her tears fall.

At the Hofburg Palace, trumpets blared and excited bodies lined the steps to greet them. Elisabeth's father and mother stood in the front, with the Archduchess Sophie. Her mother looked as if she was witnessing a miracle; Sophie looked as if she was viewing a funeral cortege.

When Elisabeth stepped out, her tiara caught the carriage rim and tumbled down. She caught it, but not before horrified gasps turned the greeters into shocked statues. She set it back on her head and calmness returned.

As they quickly mounted the stone steps, Franz leaned in.

"Had your tiara hit the ground, it would have been the worst of all bad omens."

She didn't believe in such superstitions. She closed her lips over her chuckle. It was the only amusement she would have that day.

The archduchess strode down the hall, motioning them to follow. Sentries jumped to attention. Into the Blue Chinese Room they hurried. The small room was papered in blue, white and gold Chinese patterns, representing scenes of Chinese life. Shuffling bodies in glittering uniforms strutted around the blue silk furniture.

"Our first reception," Franz whispered. "These are the generals, the dignitaries and the ambassadors."

Before she could utter a word, they were seated on gold thrones. It was like climbing a mountain to get onto them.

Sophie quickly placed Elisabeth's silk-gloved hand on an embroidered cushion ready for an endless line of pucker-faced ambassadors and generals with chests of shining medals to plant their kisses. Elisabeth tried to smile, but inside she was numb.

They came in droves with shining eyes and a multitude of lips. Some felt like cotton, some were cracked, some nipped her glove. There were wet lips or tongues, she couldn't tell which. Their bows were elegant, their smiles wide, their eyes shaded. Elisabeth thought it superficial and a mockery. There was no affection, just curious eyes.

Her legs were restless. They began to ache and she wanted to stretch them. She didn't dare look for the end of the line — that would make it worse. *Just keep smiling*, she told herself.

"Sisi, did you hear me?"

Franz was standing before her, reaching for her. The procession of uniforms marched away. She snapped back.

"Is it over?"

She was almost afraid to ask.

"This one is. And you were enchanting."

"Was I really?"

Her relief was short-lived. Her feet hardly touched the floor when the royal family, with Sophie at the helm, surrounded them like a swarm of bees.

Their faces were ecstatic — except, of course, Sophie's. It had no affection, more like moulded stone.

Elisabeth's mother, Ludovika, had told her that at one time Sophie stood among the most beautiful women in the world. Her portrait hung in the famous Galeria Schleissheim in Munich. Franz had told her that, at one time, Sophie had been in love. All this seemed unbelievable, with her now-stern features and her icy demeanour. Her mother said her bitterness and the stress of running an empire had taken their toll.

Her mother was in the middle of the group, her face glowing. Her father, Max, was fidgeting like a lion in captivity. Helene was smiling and chattering with a tall young man, a Habsburg from Italy. At least she was having fun.

"We will proceed at once to the Grand Gallery for our next reception," Sophie said, spinning around.

The family jumped aside to let her pass. Then everyone followed her across the room like excited puppies. Down the hall they went. Soldiers clicked their heels and bolted to attention. Bodies jumped from their path.

Helene chattered as fast as she flew. She swished her fan and flashed her eyes at a young man who was trying to keep up. Her mother and father were almost at a run, her father's face twisted with displeasure. Elisabeth and Franz followed in the rear. Elisabeth had no time to ponder their next mission. She struggled to keep from tripping over her gown as she extended her hand for the maid to change her gloves, in order to be ready for the next set of lips.

At the entrance to the Grand Gallery, the archduchess stopped. She stepped aside against the huge mahogany doors. The family halted beside her. The smile left Ludovika's face.

There they were, Ludovika thought: the vultures. The word almost shot from her mouth. To her, no one was more narrow-minded, more pompous and shallow than the Viennese royals. They were a cast-iron, closed society. They knew each other from childhood, shared the same tastes and ideas and had no interest beyond their own closed circle. They lived in palaces, had vast country estates, and competed among themselves in lavish banquets, hunts and gossip.

Their education taught them nothing but aristocratic protocol and where each family stood on the tier of nobility. Gossip with frivolous wit and scandalous intrigues illuminated their conversation. They saw themselves as the *crème de la crème* of Europe and shunned all outside their circle. Except on Saas Sunday.

On Saas Sunday, they displayed their immense wealth to those beneath their almighty tier. Their massive gates were thrown open and, dressed in opulence that would make Paris blink, they paraded through the winding streets of the Prater in gold carriages decorated with colourful frescoes, their horses with high plumes and jewelled harnesses. Their gloved hands fluttered at the hundreds of stunned faces who gaped at a magnificence beyond their wildest dreams. Then they returned to their palatial homes, the massive gates swung shut and the common people trudged down their narrow streets to their tiny rooms, where rats were their most common visitors.

Now the Viennese royals waited with sceptical anticipation to dissect their new empress. Ludovika's jaws tightened with her thoughts. From all reports, she knew their minds were already made up — Elisabeth was a social disgrace. *Dear God*, she pleaded, *give Sisi the strength.*

When Franz and Elisabeth arrived at the door, Elisabeth saw her mother's face. She saw her horror. Then she stared into the room.

It was dazzling. Crystal chandeliers glittering with candles were reflected in the gold mirrors that swept from the floor to a towering ceiling of colourful frescoes embedded in exquisite frames of gold.

Even more glittering were the guests. Uniformed men strutted about in their magnificent regalia. Ladies in gowns of shimmering silk with diamond tiaras flickering in their hair, diamonds shimmering on their bosoms and diamonds dropping from their ears had their fans going in rhythm with their high-pitched chatter.

When Franz and Elisabeth appeared in the doorway, all voices halted, fans folded. Not a sound was heard. It was as if all life had left the Earth. Elisabeth froze.

Not Franz. It was as if adrenalin had pumped into his veins. His face glowed. His body flowing, he almost forgot to bow to his mother as he passed her. With a wide and gracious smile, he tried to pull Elisabeth forward. No motion. Her feet were planted.

He continued nodding, his smile widening, his manner more gracious. His hand on hers, he pulled her harder.

No motion.

"Franz, I can't."

She'd found her voice. It was almost a whisper.

His smile faltered, his eyes still on the guests. He tugged harder — her hand hurt. His nodding went up a notch. His eyes stayed on the guests.

"Franz, I can't," she repeated, terror in her voice. "I won't go in there. I can't. I can't."

No one moved. No one spoke, not even a whisper. Not even a fan fluttered, not even a gasp.

Franz's smile froze. His nodding stopped. His eyes stayed on the audience. He gripped Elisabeth's hands like pliers. Her knuckles scrunched in pain. He tried to pull her forward.

She wrenched her hand free. His startled eyes were on her. She saw his horror.

"I'm sorry."

Her panic had taken over. All maturity had left.

She caught up her skirts and turned abruptly around. She fled past the frozen-faced archduchess, past the gaping royal family. Hearing her mother gasp, she paused, staring at her with desperate eyes.

"I'm sorry, Mama."

Then she crashed through a maze of bodies, past shocked faces, and raced down a hallway. Where she was going, she didn't know. Her tears were like a river. She pushed open a door, escaped into an empty room and crashed face down on the embroidered cushions of a couch. She sobbed as if the world had come to an end.

Sophie acted immediately.

"Stay here!" she ordered the flustered Ludovika, who was attempting to follow her. "I will handle this."

She pulled the leather-faced Countess Esterházy down the hall with her. When they entered, Elisabeth buried her face deeper into the cushion. She had disliked the countess from the moment she met her. She was the archduchess's spy. She had a thin unsmiling face and eyes that turned into slits when her rasping voice spat out the orders of the archduchess. Already she had informed Elisabeth that her vocabulary was inadequate, that her voice sounded more like a whisper because her mouth was like a buttoned pouch and that her yellow teeth could do with more improvement.

"Elisabeth, you have shown great disrespect to our guests." Sophie's breath sizzled on the back of Elisabeth's neck. "Not only have you disgraced the House of the Habsburg, you have also disgraced the emperor."

Elisabeth shook so hard she thought she might come apart.

"I couldn't help it. I couldn't help it." Tears poured with her words. "Those people . . . so many. I just panicked."

Although she knew she was acting like a frightened child, she couldn't help herself. She wanted to cry out, "Help me. Help me!" But the archduchess heaving over her like a surging steam engine sent her deeper into the cushion. For a moment, only the ticking clock kept pace with Sophie's heaves.

"The emperor," Sophie's voice shot out, "is the highest in this land. He was chosen by God to rule this great empire. You are now the empress, the highest woman in the land." Her tirade increased in bitterness. "You are now the chosen one. I have told you. I have warned you, though it seems it has not penetrated your childish ears, you must stand above your subjects at all times. To display human fragility in front of your people is abominable." Her voice was thunder. "It degrades you, puts you at their level. You are now the superior one. You must separate yourself from your people to reinforce their humbleness, their subservience." She sucked in her breath. "This, Elisabeth, is how we retained our power over our subjects. You must *always* be the superior one."

Sophie was hanging over Elisabeth again, like a raging animal. Her voice dropped to a low, cunning growl.

"But you, terrified of your own people, are running like a snivelling shepherd child."

Elisabeth half-expected her to pound her shoulders.

"What kind of respect will that bring?" Sophie demanded.

Elisabeth felt like she was flattened at the bottom of an abyss so deep, there was no way up. She was wrong to run. She knew that. But how could she explain? She herself hardly understood her panic. She had acted like a terrified child. She buried her face deeper in the cushion and moaned to herself. There was nothing superior about her.

"I should never be an empress," she wailed.

All she wanted was to go back to being just Sisi.

"That we all know."

Sophie's contempt was like a razor-edged knife. She was pacing.

"I warned Franz," she said. "I warned him the first time he set eyes on you. I pleaded with him. 'She's nothing but a wild, little country girl,' I told him. 'No one has made any attempt to discipline her. She has no social graces, no idea of proper conversation. She is just like her father, a social disgrace. Not a royal house in Bavaria will have him at their table.'"

Elisabeth gasped. How dare she speak of her father like that!

Sophie continued to pace. Then her words turned to total disgust.

"And what did he teach her? To entertain the peasants by dancing at county fairs? 'What kind of an empress will that produce?' I asked Franz. But he didn't hear. He was in love. Yes, in love." A haughty laugh shot out. "With a pretty wax doll-faced child who blinded all his reasoning. But mark my words," she shook her fist at Elisabeth, now up and balancing on the edge of the couch, "he will pay dearly for going against my wishes."

Elisabeth jumped from the couch so fast the archduchess stumbled on her long skirt, trying to avoid a collision. What right did this woman have to chastise her father? Elisabeth saw the cunning smirk on the older woman's lips and knew her thoughts. Sophie saw herself as the winner. Elisabeth's weakness was glaring like the sun in a cloudless sky and Franz would pay dearly for his error. Her father's words flooded into her mind: "The nourishment of our strength comes from the seeds of our childhood." She knew that. The strength he instilled in her was still there.

Elisabeth straightened her tiara. With a sweep of her hands, not even drying her tears, she gathered up her skirts and sped past the gaping women.

Down the hall she ran. Then she slowed to a majestic pace, her head high, her face calm. She ignored the inquisitive looks, the gasps, the bowing bodies jumping aside to let her pass. She saw her mother holding her head. Another headache — and no wonder. Her father was pacing, looking disturbed.

"Mama, I'm fine!"

She offered her hands to her mother. Ludovika's face was full of concern.

"Oh, Sisi. I knew you would be all right."

Elisabeth pulled her hands back and stepped in front of her father. His eyes shimmered in tears. Her heart filled with love. She threw her arms around him.

"And Papa . . . oh, Papa, I love you. You were a wonderful father. You taught me so much. Thank you. Thank you for everything."

They clung together tightly, remembering. More tears came.

"I will be fine."

She backed away, and gave them both a reassuring look.

Then she saw Franz. He stood at the door where she had left him. Her sympathy swelled. He was struggling with gracious courtesies to those milling around him. Yet, how distressed he looked, his smile like parchment. No doubt, she thought with a touch of amusement, his mother's predictions were filling his thoughts.

She went to his side and slipped her hand onto his arm.

"We will go in now."

Her voice was soft, her eyes shining. She was still resolute, but she hadn't yet looked into the salon. Franz's face turned to instant relief. He saw the tears dried on her cheeks. He saw no fear.

"You are ready?" he asked, his voice strained.

She smiled decisively.

"Yes, Franz, I am ready."

"I love you," he murmured.

He quickly assumed his polished presence. He led her through the massive doorway into the room of restless bodies, goggling eyes and fans swishing faster than ever.

Heels clicked, voices stopped, fans halted. The young emperor, his head high, nodded proudly and graciously to the guests as they curtseyed, bowed and quickly made way for the couple to pass.

The crowd's eyes were like saucers — her tear-stained face did not go unnoticed. The fans began to flutter and the whispers, mixed with knowing looks, didn't escape Elisabeth's eyes. She took deep breaths. Deep, deep breaths. She carried her head high and walked like an empress.

On the gold throne she settled, placing her hand on the embroidered cushion and awaiting the mocking lips.

Feet scuffled on the shining floor as the line assembled, and voices sailed again to an excited pitch. Elisabeth did not dare ponder the length of the line.

She breathed deeply. She tried to focus on the beauty of the Grand Salon and let her body sway to the echoing minuet.

The procession proceeded according to rank. The archduchess, of course, headed the line. Elisabeth looked her straight in the eye, without a flicker.

"Remember," Sophie whispered harshly, almost making Elisabeth clench her fists, "you must ask each guest a question. No one is allowed to address you until you address them with a question."

That almost sent her gloved hand flying from the embroidered cushion.

She looked down the line of shuffling bodies. There were beautiful young women, their eyes bulging with indignant curiosity. There were haughty young matrons, their disdainful noses high. There were dowagers, their large bosoms decked in jewels, bitterly resenting their daughters' loss. There were the gentlemen in uniforms with elegant manners and knowing smiles, their medals flickering.

Elisabeth's panic sparked. What kind of questions could she ask? The music escaped her ears and she couldn't even find breath to catch. The line moved fast — people curtseyed, kissed her hand and then moved on with pinched brows and indignant looks. She could hardly find a word to say, let alone a question, and many times not even a smile. Sophie had been right. She was just a country nymph. She had no social graces. Artificial conversation was as foreign to her as another language.

Then her two cousins from Bavaria were standing before her, smiling and trying to catch her attention. All protocol went to the wind.

"Alice! Jane!" she called out.

She was out of her chair, tripped on her gown and almost lost her tiara. She caught them in her arms and hugged them tearfully. The room went stony silent. Even the music stumbled. Franz's gracious nods to the ladies smiling and curtseying at him with their adoring eyes stopped. Her sanity returned. She had committed a crime.

The archduchess took her roughly by the arm and pushed her back on to the throne. The cousins fled. The line moved on, the music flared and Franz cast anxious glances at her.

When the last billowing gown and military legs trailed from Elisabeth's sight, Sophie was there, rasping a command.

"A banquet is next. In the Gold Salon. Follow me."

As they sped across the floor, Elisabeth had no time for terror. Again she was ripping off her stained gloves and replacing them with new ones.

Into the Grand Banquet Hall they flew. Windows swept high to a ceiling of gold-trimmed frescoes created by Guglielmi. Gold chandeliers hung on long golden chains. At a table that wound around the length of the room, guests fidgeted, their faces disgruntled and their hopes dashed.

Though they did rise, their glances at Elisabeth were hardly admiring. She certainly was not the Empress Eugenie they wanted and they wallowed in humiliation. All Europe would be wrapped in sneers. "How could our emperor be so blind?" they whispered as they gulped down their wine greedily and their food lay hardly touched.

Still, Franz's eyes shone and his face beamed as he sat beside his bride.

Servants in red jackets that matched the chairs ran around with steaming dishes. There were five courses, each with a different wine sparkling in a fresh glass.

The first course was an assortment of game: roasted hare, quarter of stag marinated overnight in salt, stuffed chicken, loin of veal covered in German sauce with sugar plums and pomegranate seeds, and pies with a mixture of deer, gosling, capon, chicken, pigeon and rabbit, covered with saffron and flavoured with cloves.

The second course was sturgeon cooled in parsley and vinegar, covered with powdered ginger.

The third was vegetables in a cream sauce, sprinkled with fennel seeds preserved in sugar, roe deer, and pig and stuffed capon covered in yolks of eggs and sprinkled with a spice powder.

The fourth was cheese slices with strawberries and plums stewed in rose water.

The fifth was a selection of prepared wines in vogue, served with fruits and a wide assortment of pastries.

Of course, no one was allowed to eat until the emperor took his first bite.

It's like a medieval banquet, Ludovika thought. As each serving ended, her anxiety escalated another notch. Every time she glanced at Elisabeth, her guilt dug deeper. It was the wedding night. She had not prepared Sisi for the bedroom encounter. She was afraid that Sisi would not understand and, as a consequence, the marriage might not go on.

Royal marriages were the unifying bond of dynastic families and love was not always in their destiny. That's why she forbade romantic novels. They might spark delusions. Ludovika knew Elisabeth devoured the romantic novels she hid under her bed and her perspective of the sexual relationship between a man and a woman would be hazy. Royal princesses were so naïve when it came to sex. The word itself was forbidden. The peasants knew more about love and sex than they. And, like in a romantic novel, Sisi had fallen in love with love — she would hardly comprehend the reality of her wedding night.

Ludovika glanced at Sisi, bent over her dinner and producing the odd smile but hardly tasting a morsel. What were her thoughts? She glanced at Franz, devouring his food like a starved animal. She reached quickly for a glass of wine and gulped it down.

She did have one consolation. Sisi would not suffer the Habsburg ritual that brides and grooms had been exposed to for generations. The custom was that married princesses and chatelaines would escort the bride to her room, assist her with her preparations and put her into bed. Then the groom would be escorted in by married princes, cardinals and prelates. In their presence, he'd climb into the marriage bed. The cardinals would remain, though they would turn their backs, until the marriage was consummated. Ludovika had stood up to Sophie on that issue.

She took another gulp of wine, then two gulps, and hoped the young emperor would prove a seasoned gentleman who would treat his innocent bride.

Franz took his last bite. His fork went down, his eyes on Elisabeth. All forks went down. There were many unfinished meals and disgruntled faces but the dinner ended when the emperor finished.

Franz's eyes gleamed like diamond studs. No one but no one missed his passion. The gentlemen had knowing smirks; the ladies turned their heads away in envy.

The archduchess motioned to Ludovika. It was time for their procession to the bridal apartments.

Servants scurried to pull back their chairs. The chatter ceased and the guests rose. The servants bowed themselves backward to the walls and stood like sentries, except for the gleam in their eyes.

Elisabeth rose. She glanced at Franz, fidgeting like the impatient lover he was. His eyes wrapped her in their passion. Her eyes widened, her breath caught — but not with love. With fear.

She took her mother's outstretched arm. They walked from the dining salon, preceded by twelve pages carrying bright candelabras. The guests stared after them with a mixture of emotions. Elisabeth stared into space.

2

A page opened the apartment door and stepped aside to let Elisabeth and Ludovika enter. The magnificence they saw toppled their fears and boggled their eyes. Elisabeth dropped her mother's arm and ran into the room.

"And this will be my home," she declared.

They moved swiftly through the salon, running their hands over the shining lacquered tables beneath golden candelabras, glancing at the mirrors sweeping up the walls and porcelain vases filled with flowers. She let out another squeal of delight when she saw the gold toiletry set. She ran her hands over it with a dreamy look of disbelief.

"And look at these Rubens paintings!" Ludovika exclaimed.

Elisabeth was speechless.

They went into the bedroom. They stopped and gazed spellbound.

"It is beautiful," Elisabeth whispered.

The room was all in blue, from the silk-lined walls to the massive bed. Cushions piled high against a mahogany headboard carved in gold and blue designs.

"This was Maria Theresa's bed."

Countess Esterházy's voice shook them back to reality. There she stood with four palace ladies, their excitement bursting.

"What are you doing here?" Elisabeth asked.

The countess made a sweeping bow.

"We are here to assist Your Majesty with your preparation for bed."

The ladies made sweeping bows.

Elisabeth stifled a scream. Her mother dismissed them with calm politeness. And somehow, just somehow, Elisabeth managed a polite farewell.

"Goodnight. Thank you."

They marched out with pinched faces, especially Countess Esterházy.

The room was peacefully quiet. A large gold clock ticked the movement of time. Ludovika settled Elisabeth into bed, puffed up the huge cushions around her back and tenderly draped her long auburn hair over her shoulders.

Sisi looked more like an adorable child than a bride, Ludovika thought, and she didn't seem at all nervous. Still, Ludovika struggled with her anxiety. But she told her nothing and Elisabeth didn't ask — at least, not about her own wedding night to come. Her mother's wedding night had often aroused Elisabeth's curiosity. She didn't know if the hearsay was true.

"Did you lock Papa in the closet on your wedding night?"

Elisabet's quesion broke into Ludovika's thoughts. A surprised Ludovika laughed. How did she know about that?

"Do you believe all the gossip?" she asked.

"No. I usually close my ears to gossip. But I have often wondered about that. I would never ask you, except it is my wedding night . . ."

Her voice trailed off. Ludovika sat down on the edge of the ruffled bed.

"It was a different situation," she said finally. "Your young husband loves you dearly. On my wedding night, your father spitefully told me that he did not love me. He loved another and had married me only because he was afraid of my father, who was then the King of Bavaria."

She paused. Elisabeth saw a misty expression catch her face.

"I, too," she continued, "loved another, whom I wanted to marry. My father had thought him unsuitable. Though I kept it to myself, my heart was broken. Your father's cruel confession was all I needed. So yes, I did push him into the cupboard and locked the door. And I slept in the large bed all by myself and I loved it."

"I would have done the same thing," Elisabeth laughed. "And who was the young man you loved, Mama?"

She couldn't visualize her mother young and in love.

A knock came on the door.

"They're here," proclaimed Ludovika, jumping up. "That is a story for another time."

Archduchess Sophie swept into the room, the young emperor on her arm. Not a particle of warmth was on her face. Franz was beaming, straining like a racehorse ready to break the gates. Ludovika's anxiety returned in a flash.

"I bring my son to his bride," Sophie announced.

There was no smile, no warmth, just the tone of a death sentence.

Ludovika forced a smile. Franz almost pulled free from his mother's arm. Elisabeth's fear turned to shock at the bitterness in Sophie's eyes.

She hates me, she thought, and she buried her face in the pillow.

Days later, when sunshine drenched the spring flowers in the palace grounds and white and pink magnolia blossoms waved like tiny hankies in a soft breeze, Elisabeth huddled over her ornate desk in her apartment. Her quill raced across her diary, her tears flowing with it.

> Oh, but had I never left the path
> That would have led to freedom.
> Oh, that on the broad avenue
> Of vanity I had never strayed.
> I have awakened in a dungeon
> With chains on my hands
> And my longing ever stronger.
> And freedom, you have turned from me.

A Dream Buried in Dust

1

"It's humiliating," Elisabeth said. "Franz and I are to attend breakfast at eight o'clock at the request of the archduchess, in her apartment."

It was the morning after her wedding. Franz had fled to his office before dawn, planting a quick kiss on her cheek and consoling her shock with "Duty calls. World politics will not wait for our honeymoon." His appointments began at five-thirty every morning he told her as he sped out the door.

Elisabeth and Helene had escaped to the garden room that looked over the palace grounds. There, they were free from probing eyes. Still, the warm sunshine pouring through the windows and the birdsong echoing among the trees were hardly soothing to Elisabeth.

"And when I begged Franz to please let us have our breakfast alone in our apartment, as I was so tired of all the receptions, he said it would be an insult to his mother."

It was a festive breakfast, with the beaming and inquisitive eyes of excited guests. And so many: her mother, her father, Néné, Franz's two brothers, the Habsburg archduchesses and archdukes, and, of course, Sophie at the head of the table.

Franz was all smiles as he led her in. She had a hard time finding one.

"And furthermore," she moaned to Helene, "everyone seemed to be waiting for some revelation. You saw their eyes. Especially those young archdukes with their smirks and whispers, not missing a movement we made. I was afraid to even blink. And Sophie looked almost angry. What's it all about, Néné?"

Helene was her sole support. She wondered desperately how she would manage when her family returned to Possi in two days. Helene couldn't hide her amusement.

"You are so naïve, Sisi," she said with affection. "I hate to embarrass you, but all Vienna is on pins and needles waiting to hear if the marriage has been consummated."

Elisabeth's hands flew to her cheeks.

"Oh, Néné. Is that what it's all about?"

Even in front of her sister, her face flamed red.

"That's why Sophie probed you so vigorously," Helene said. "She probably hadn't slept a wink all night wondering if an heir had been conceived."

"And those staring eyes . . . they were looking for a sign?" Elisabeth gasped.

Helene nodded, smiling.

"And mark my words, bets are flying around the palace and all Vienna."

Elisabeth's face went into her hands. She was mortified. Even the privacy of her wedding night was the talk of the town.

Her face strained, she closed her eyes. Her wedding night was hardly one of love, that is, not like she expected. Not like the love in her romance novels.

Her mother and the archduchess had barely closed the door when Franz ripped his clothes from his body. He'd stood there bare. Before the shock had completely terrorized her, he was in the bed with a face like she had never seen before. She'd cried out and pulled the blanket over her head. He'd snatched it from her. Their eyes had locked. He'd seen her terror, her innocence and his face had softened. He'd reached out with gentleness and touched her frozen face. His fingers had gone through her hair, lifting it slowly, with tenderness. She hadn't moved. She hadn't spoke.

"There is no rush, my little one."

His voice had been soft and tender. He'd breathed in deeply, calmed his shaking body, dropped his hand. He'd turned away and blew out the candle.

Elisabeth raised her head now and looked at her sister.

"Oh Néné. I want to go home. I want to be just Sisi again. I want to race through the forests laughing out loud and singing at the top of my lungs. I want to go home." She closed her eyes, her voice shaking. "I don't want to be an empress. I don't even want to be married."

Helene took her hands.

"Sisi, laugh about it. That is the only way. Imagine, your wedding night is the talk of Vienna and think of all the jealous ladies out there."

Elisabeth stared at her — it wasn't funny, it was hideous. Then her smile came, a distorted smile.

"It is ridiculously funny. All Vienna, the court and the servants hanging on pins and needles wondering if the princess has given her love to her prince." Then her face crumbled with tears. "It's also pathetic."

Their moments of escape were short-lived. Countess Esterházy was soon on top of them with a bundle of papers in her hand.

"This is your schedule for today."

And it was only the first day of her marriage.

Helene looked at Elisabeth, Elisabeth looked at Helene and their smiles turned into dejection.

Reception after reception filled the day. Elisabeth, parked between the archduchess and Franz, struggled with smiles for departing guests from Lower and Upper Austria and from places she had never heard of. Each official event required a change of clothing. She stepped into gown after gown. At least there was no time for despair.

When their apartment door finally closed behind them that night and exhaustion drained from her like water from a squeezed mop. Franz reached out to take her in his arms — this time more gently. For a moment she gave in, feeling her love. His arms tightened, his breathing impatient. She panicked.

She pushed him back. Her fear took over. She knew she was acting like a child, but still, she couldn't help it.

"I'm sorry, Franz," she wailed.

She fled into her boudoir. She slammed the door, telling the maid to go. She collapsed into tears. She was so weary, she was almost sick. Her anxiety was wrapped in distorted pictures. What would happen tonight? She could hardly move from her chair to prepare for bed.

"Come to bed, my little one," Franz called.

He called again. His voice turned edgy. Fatigue and fear were crushing her. She couldn't sit here all night.

Finally, she ventured out, having no choice — her hair hung long, her face was gaunt, she wrapped her chemise around her, high to her neck. She was numb, more numb than afraid.

A candle flickered on the bedside table. He lay on the bed. He shot up. She saw his naked shoulders. He didn't move. He watched her cross the floor and smiled. She wrapped her chemise tighter around her body. He swung to the edge of the bed. She fled to the far side. He quickly pulled the blanket down. She climbed onto the bed. She avoided his eyes. She kept her chemise wrapped protectively around her. She curled into a ball on the far side of the bed, her back to him, and buried her face in the pillow.

He brushed her shoulder. His hand lingered, tightened. She felt his breath. He murmured her name, gently, softly — still, she lay motionless.

"Goodnight, my love," he sighed.

And he blew the candle out.

The next day at breakfast, the climax came. Franz and Elisabeth were hardly in their chairs. All eyes were on them like starving hounds. The smirks were a dimension wider, the whispers faster and the servants, dashing around with steaming dishes, had bated breath and eyes bulging from their sockets. Sophie was sizzling in her chair.

"It seems that love has flown the coop," she rasped.

Max's fork went flying to the floor. A servant moved hastily to retrieve it.

Everyone sensed Franz's trauma. Though he tried to hide it, no one could miss it. Sophie saw the leers of the young archdukes and their amused eyes. They knew his appetite for sex and his skill with ladies.

The whole country knows, Sophie thought, digging her fingers into her hands. *And now he wavers. In the eyes of his people, he will be judged a weakling.* She dug her nails in further. And it was all because of a whimpering country nymph.

"I can assure you, my dear Mama, that love has not flown the coop. I am the happiest man on earth," Franz said.

Then he cast such a look of love upon his bride, all eyes reflected hearts of envy. All, that is, except those of the archduchess. She sniffed dismissively. Still, the strain was there for all to see. Franz did not gulp down his food and the napkin in Elisabeth's hand twisted into a knot. She knew the choice would not be hers. The marriage would be consummated that night.

Distant bells echoed across the cobblestone courtyard of the Habsburg Palace, declaring nine p.m. Heavy rain pounded on the closed shutters when Franz arrived at their apartment. An urgent meeting with his mother had followed dinner that night.

Elisabeth sat in her boudoir waiting. Every part of her body quivered. The maid had just fled with a distinct glow on her plump face, forgetting to dim the candles. Elisabeth wondered if she, too, had a bet.

Her hair fell in luscious waves over her pink robe to the middle of her back. Her face had a rosy blush, but it came from fear. "Make yourself attractive and seductive," Helene had told her. *What is seductive?* she wondered. She looked at herself in the mirror — she still looked like a child, a frightened child. *Why does he love me?* she whimpered to herself.

The boudoir door burst open. He appeared in her mirror, straight and tall, his face flushed, his blue eyes gleaming. His fists were clenched. He caught her eyes.

He saw her trembling chin, her quivering body. His face softened, his affection warming. Then without a word, he crossed the room and put his arms around her. But it wasn't gentle, it was fierce.

She felt his breath hot on her neck, his trembling body powerful and unrelenting, his groans and his passion engulfing, smothering her. He ignored her panic, her frightened whimpers, her feeble attempt to escape. He ripped the robe from her body, picked her up, crossed the room and threw her on the bed. Her eyes closed, her mind closed. She succumbed to his violent passion.

The clock struck seven-thirty. Sunshine rippled across the room. She heard him come through the door. He touched her shoulder.

"We must go to breakfast."

He leaned over her, dressed in his general's uniform, having already given public audiences. He had risen at five a.m., leaving her huddled in bed wide awake, though he did not know that. She had not slept all night, pondering the terrible experience called love and her ignorance, her romantic notions, her future.

"Please, Franz," she cried, reaching up to him. "If you love me, let us eat alone, just this one time, in our own apartment."

She couldn't face the archduchess and all those eyes. They would know, and she could imagine their thoughts.

"My dearest Sisi," his voice was impatient, "you know we must not offend my mother."

He motioned the maid waiting in the background to help her dress.

"I don't need her!" Elisabeth screamed.

She threw off the blanket, jumped from the bed, flew into her boudoir and slammed the door.

When she reappeared, dressed, apprehensive and reluctant, Franz caught her in his arms. He looked into her face. Love overwhelmed him. He felt a passion so different than any he had known before.

From his earliest youth, women had thrown themselves into his arms. They flattered him, they cajoled him with promises, they wooed him with their flashing eyes and willing bodies. There were times he felt almost contempt, not gratitude, as he tasted their flavours. But Sisi, so pure, so innocent — no one had fired his passion or his love as she had and no one had lain so innocently in his arms.

"My dearest Sisi," he murmured, cradling her face gently in his hands. "I love you. Having you is the greatest gift a man could ever have."

"Oh, Franz. I was afraid. I didn't know what was expected. I just didn't know."

The horror of the night vanished. She buried her face in his chest.

"I understand. And your innocence gives me my greatest pleasure. I want you just as you are."

She closed her eyes and melted into the gentle arms that only hours before had crushed her into sheer terror.

The sun shone through the tall windows of the archduchess's breakfast salon that morning and vases of spring flowers were everywhere. The excited voices escalating in the hall changed into smiles when Franz and Elisabeth arrived. They all knew. Elisabeth saw that.

Franz's smile covered his face. Elisabeth wanted to flee the room. She almost missed the chair the grinning servant pulled out for her.

The archduchess's salutation came with smug satisfaction. Her mother looked as if she had stepped into paradise and Helene gave her a wink. Elisabeth didn't smile. She just wanted to disappear.

Platters of food came and went. She couldn't swallow a thing. Voices raced excitedly, all eyes latched onto her burning face. *What are they imagining?* she wondered. *And who won the bet?*

"My dear Elisabeth," the archduchess's voice sailed, with a mixture of contempt and humour. "why sit so pinched? We are well aware your marriage was consummated last night. By dinnertime, all Vienna will be celebrating. So sit up and take pride."

Laughter rippled like river waters in spring. Franz continued to devour his breakfast and Elisabeth twisted her napkin nervously.

"My dear Elisabeth," the archduchess continued, "privacy is unknown in the marriage bed of the Habsburg emperors. An heir is the prime concern. Because of your delicate nature, your mother begged me to forgo our tradition of cardinals witnessing the consummation of a Habsburg marriage. So look pleased, and be happy at your great accomplishment."

That's when her father's fork went flying to the floor. A servant rushed to retrieve it and Max tipped over his chair trying to avoid a collision.

"Really, Max, one would think you had never handled such utensils." The archduchess tried to sound humorous, but the sarcasm prevailed. "Perhaps in the Bavarian hills they are not used."

Elisabeth's eyes shot up from her plate. They narrowed on the archduchess. Her tolerance was at an end and her fear toppled. She jumped from her seat. A second servant stepped forward quickly to pull back her chair. Her face was white.

If ever in her life she wanted to scratch the eyes from another person, it was then. If ever she wanted to release the venom that boiled inside her, it was then. But she did neither — she retained her composure, her eyes on the archduchess. She clenched her fists so hard, she felt the pain. No one moved. Not an eyelash blinked. The servants stood like robots. Even Franz stopped eating and looked up at her. Her heart thumped, her body shook, her hands knotted. But her words flowed out like silk.

"My lady," she said to the archduchess, "the breakfast has been delightful. Would you please excuse me?"

With her head high, a nodding smile to the guests, she turned and walked from the room with the elegance of an empress. Her steps went faster and faster as she fled down the halls. Heels clicked and soldiers jumped to attention. When she reached her apartment, she was running, her tears running just as fast. They poured into her pillow.

They were not tears of frustration — they were tears of satisfaction, of accomplishment, a discovery of strength. She had stood up to the archduchess. And she hadn't ripped out her eyes as she wanted to, she had done it with elegant dignity.

A day that had begun immersed in despair ended like a burst of spring, Elisabeth thought as she watched the evening sun disappearing.

The maid was preparing Elisabeth's bath for one more reception. She was excited about this reception — it was the Hungarians. She remembered, back in Possi, her tutor's description of them. "Viennese royals view them as wild and unmannerly," he had said, "but they are charming, chivalrous and romantic. And they have a mad passion for horses and colourful costumes." Then a sudden sadness crossed his face. He never explained why.

Franz had hurried after her from the breakfast table that morning. She smiled to herself remembering his concern. "I am fine," she had told him.

"Mama can be difficult. Her life is devoted to the empire," he'd said tenderly, taking her face into his hands. "But try to remember, her intentions are for the good." Then, with a smile and amusement lighting up his eyes, he'd added, "I have a surprise. Our honeymoon starts tomorrow."

"You mean we will go away?"

"Tomorrow, my beloved, I myself will drive us to Laxenburg and — "

"What is Laxenburg?" she'd demanded, jumping up and taking his hands.

"It is a palace, where you can ride your horses over its rolling countryside and walk in its beautiful grounds to your heart's content."

She'd clapped her hands.

"And your mother — ?"

She'd held her breath.

"She disapproves of our going. But I told her you were ready and, for a short time, we must go."

"But, I mean — " She'd stopped, not wanting to sound rude. "I mean, will she come with us to Laxenburg?"

He'd thrown back his head and laughed.

"No mother. Just you and me."

"Oh, Franz," she'd cooed, her pleasure evident. "I can't believe it. I can't believe it."

"And . . ." He'd touched her nose playfully. "Can you take another surprise?"

"What? What?"

"Did someone tell me that you like Herr Renz and his circus?"

"Herr Renz!"

Herr Renz was king of the sawdust ring, the greatest circus rider of all times, the master of Haute École, a man her father worshipped and talked of as a god.

"Oh, Franz. Are you teasing me?"

"He is performing this afternoon in the Prater. We will picnic there and watch him. That is, if you could stand changing your clothes one more time."

She'd danced about, still clapping her hands.

"I don't believe it, I don't believe it!"

In the end, the day had also brought sadness and more tears as she bid her family goodbye. How she would manage without them, she didn't know. Helene's tender hugs didn't hide her concern. Her mother, fending off another headache, tried encouragement with loving advice. Still, her headaches gaining in frequency, she was clearly delighted to be on her way home.

Elisabeth told her father she was going to see Herr Renz that afternoon. Max's eyes lit up momentarily and then they darkened. He bent and whispered to her.

"If you ever want to see me, you will have to come to Possi. I will never set foot in this palace again."

That afternoon, Herr Renz's performance in the Prater had made up for it all. She and Franz watched it as they picnicked in the park under a marquee. Elisabeth was so engrossed in the performance that the crowds milling around them with goggling eyes did not bother her. She knew Sophie was outraged. It went against all protocol. Her eyes had narrowed when she and Franz swept past her on their way out.

On their return to the palace, Sophie had turned her back and marched away.

2

"Madame, your bath is ready," Astera, her maid, called out.

Elisabeth returned to the present. The sky had turned into twilight. One more function, then tomorrow they would leave for Laxenburg. Horses, horses, horses and no Madame Mère, as the archduchess was called. She gave her hands another clap.

On the bed lay the dress she was to wear.

"How charming it is," she remarked to Astera.

She examined it as intensely as her maid. It had a mauve velvet bodice and an embroidered mauve skirt with many other colours. It was very simple, hardly like the gowns she wore to the other receptions.

"It is the dress of a Hungarian noblewoman," Astera said.

Astera was Hungarian and excited about their evening function. Her idol, Julius Andrássy, would be at the reception. She kept his picture in her dresser, as many young Hungarian women did. She hoped she'd get a glimpse of him.

"How could I forget the Hungarians?" Elisabeth chastised herself.

Franz had said it was a most important function. A delegation of Hungarian noblemen would present their wedding gifts and their best wishes. He'd told her Hungary was the largest part of the empire.

"We cannot afford to lose their favour," he'd explained.

She remembered his voice, tense and serious.

"They want more independence, a separate government, which we will not grant, but it is best not to raise their ire. I will wear the uniform of a Hungarian Hussar, not an emperor, and you, the dress of a Hungarian noblewoman. This will keep them mellow."

Astera wound Elisabeth's hair high upon her head, wanting something intriguing. She placed her tiara among the waves.

"You look lovely," Astera said, as Elisabeth took a few swoops in front of the mirror. "And you will love those Hungarians. I hope you meet Julius Andrássy."

"And who is he?"

"The hero of our country and, oh, so good-looking."

Elisabeth was all smiles.

"It will be a fun reception. I might try out a few words of Magyar that my tutor taught me."

3

Julius Andrássy came to an abrupt halt when he saw Elisabeth. The Grand Hall of the Hofburg Palace, lively and gay, faded from his view. An emotion completely foreign to him filled his heart and mind.

Beautiful women clustered among the marble pillars, their fans racing, their jewels glittering and their eyes flashing as never before. There were the pompous Viennese men, their eyes on the décolletage of the ladies' gowns. There were the Hungarian noblemen, the centre of all this fun, in their fancy dress costumes with leopard skins flung over their shoulders and gold-trimmed boots with jingling spurs. Their boisterous voices bubbled with laughter. There were the servants scurrying around with smiles as broad as their faces.

And there was Elisabeth.

Andrássy pushed his way through the crowd to see her better. She stood between the emperor and the archduchess, welcoming the Hungarians jostling to get into the line. Her face glowed with excitement.

Andrássy had heard of her beauty, but actually seeing her left him speechless. Her spontaneous delight was most enchanting as she reached out to welcome her guests. Yet how elegant she was in her Hungarian dress, her slim neck and her tiny waist charmingly displayed. He found himself imagining that auburn hair falling upon those delicate shoulders.

"Oh my God," he muttered to himself.

She was the most enchanting creature he had ever laid eyes upon.

"Come on, Julius."

His friend Count René took his elbow, propelling him forward.

"We'll miss meeting our new queen if we don't get into line."

They jostled through the crowd and took their places in the line. Andrássy's eyes hardly left her. He could hear her voice. It had the gaiety of a child frolicking in a park. Her playfulness intrigued him. Yet she stood with stature, magnificent and with poise. And she was so young. *She likes us*, he thought, watching her reach out to the Hungarians. His excitement grew — that dainty hand would soon be in his.

He saw the archduchess frothing with displeasure. In fact, her face was so red, it appeared she could explode. He saw the humour of the situation. Everyone in that room knew of Sophie's dislike for the Hungarians, whether aristocrats or not. She never hid it. She viewed them as traitors, wild and unmannerly. She was not at all pleased to see Elisabeth bubbling with such welcoming gestures, often reaching for them with outstretched hands and tossing out the odd kiss.

Franz Joseph gazed on his bride with affection. He was glad to see her so happy.

Hungary needed Franz Joseph, Andrássy thought. And Elisabeth might be a valuable asset. Julius carried a dream, a great dream, to one day free Hungary from its total domination under Austria. The archduchess would never grant such change. Franz Joseph was their only hope. Seeing Elisabeth's reactions, he thought perhaps she might be the guiding light.

"Wipe that silly look from your face, my friend," Count René said.

He was aware of Andrássy's eye for beautiful women. In Hungary, he was a hero with a romantic appeal to both men and women. Men shook his hand in adoration and reverence for his bravery and daring achievements in the 1848–49 revolution against Austria. His chivalrous charm and his dashing good looks brought women from throughout Europe to his feet.

He hardly looked the nobleman he was, René thought, eyeing Andrássy's mop of black curly hair and his theatrical attire, an elaborate lion's skin across his shoulder. Still, that didn't stop the flirtatious eyes of the Austrian court ladies. They were buzzing with excitement, just as the archduchess was fuming with disgust. Still, René had to admit, not only was he a hero with wit and charm, he was an intelligent diplomat welcomed in the most prestigious homes in England and in Europe. The future of Hungary might well lie with him.

"You might turn the hearts of half the women in Europe," Count René whispered to Julius, sensing his excitement as they neared Elisabeth, "but she is your empress. She can never be anything more if you wish to achieve your ambitions."

Then Julius was before Elisabeth, looking into her eyes. She was smiling, her voice as soft as a whisper. She slipped her hand into his. It was so delicate and so soft, he froze. He couldn't utter a word. He just held her tiny hand in his. René pushed him on, reaching out to take her hand in his.

Julius heard René's elegant exchange as he bowed. Still, he stood speechless. He heard her few words in halting Magyar, uttered with such sincerity and warmth. His eyes moistened.

"I have never seen you speechless in front of anyone, let alone a woman," René later remarked.

René was laughing as he pushed Julius into the festive crowd of Viennese aristocrats and Hungarian noblemen.

Julius lifted a glass of champagne from the gold tray and stared, unseeing, at the smiling, flirtatious ladies, jewellery hanging like ropes around their necks. Still, he could say nothing.

"Never mind, my friend," René informed him, "every Hungarian in this room is impressed with the lovely Elisabeth. And look at Franz Joseph. He is elated by our affection for his lovely bride, and he has promised to bring her to Budapest."

For the rest of the evening, Andrássy hardly spoke. This was also unusual for him, René thought. He was known as an exceptional communicator at such occasions. He performed this skill with elegant expertise, gaining for Hungary prestige from the rest of the world. Usually, he never missed a chance to extend a hand to the ladies, but that night only Elisabeth was in his sight.

Julius took in her every movement, her tall, graceful body, the delicate bosom beneath the Hungarian blouse, the childish glee that radiated from her eyes. A strange premonition stole his thoughts. This woman would somehow, somewhere, be a part of his life.

4

The city was bathed in sunlight, birds sang as they whipped through the air and Elisabeth's excitement raced with the gusting breeze as the carriage sped through the Hofburg Palace gates and onto the cobbled streets of Vienna. It raced along the Prater, past waving and smiling crowds. Elisabeth and Franz were on their way to Laxenburg, with its woods and lakes, medieval ruins, gothic bridges, horses to ride and even a model dairy. And she was permitted to bring Tusti, her parrot, with her.

She cuddled close to Franz with his green cocked hat and Tyrolean jacket, skillfully manoeuvring the excited horses. Her eyes sparkled, her smile covered her face and her hand waved wildly to the people along the roads.

Into the rolling hills they drove, past green valleys tucked here and there. She breathed in the cool sweet air. It was like Possi. Her new life was just beginning.

They tore across an ancient bridge and along a sun-drenched lake lined with pines and flowering aspen. Even the horses quivered with renewed energy, pulling at their bits. When she caught sight of the Laxenburg Palace, she squealed in delight. It was a magnificent jewel enclosed in a forest of greenery.

"It has a thousand acres of parkland, with riding trails to satisfy your every whim," Franz told her as he manoeuvred the carriage into a courtyard and stopped at the entrance.

Elisabeth was like a child at Christmas time, bouncing to get out.

There it ended.

The mahogany doors flew open. Smiling servants hurried down the stone steps to greet them. Archduchess Sophie appeared in the entrance, standing like an imposing general. Elisabeth could hardly believe her eyes. Franz had no explanation.

The promises were never kept. They had merely changed palaces.

Sophie took up residence at the Schönbrunn, a few miles away, and spent much time at Laxenburg. Countess Esterházy moved into Laxenburg, forever perfecting Elisabeth's imperfections. And Franz's schedule remained the same.

It was hardly a honeymoon. What could have been paradise with the beautiful parkland, the sparkling lake, the forest of nightingales and golden orioles, and the stables full of horses, became a prison. The riding trails had only the squirrels racing on them.

It was a routine of rigid etiquette training. There was etiquette, etiquette and more etiquette. Sophie, out to crush any resistance, was determined to make Elisabeth docile and submissive.

"We will mould the little country nymph into a suitable Habsburg empress," she informed her ladies, making sure it reached Elisabeth's ears.

The ladies jumped in glee — such fun they would never miss. And Franz ignored the whole thing.

Every day, every single day, there was instruction on how to rise from a chair, how to dress, how to eat, how to pay visits, how to receive visitors, how to walk, how to talk and even how to dance. You would think she had come from the depths of the jungle.

Dinner was a catastrophe. She and Franz never shared it alone. There was always Sophie and a multitude of guests — boring, boring guests who looked down their long noses with disdain. Sophie informed her that it would improve her social skills.

Elisabeth summoned all the strength she had to hide her despair. And her anger. She tried to keep her head high and a smile on her face. The last thing she wanted to act like was a whimpering child. And she did need a little polish.

It was not easy. There were times she pulled the blanket around her ears when the insistent knocking of the ladies began her morning. Not until irritation strained their voices did she rise from bed. She often pleaded a headache, but that brought the archduchess thumping at her door.

She tried walking in the palace gardens to escape the ladies and soothe her frustration. That created a riot.

"It is inappropriate for an empress to walk unaccompanied by her ladies," the archduchess pronounced, marching across the lawn to accost her, the ladies at her side.

The ladies did not hide their amusement.

Elisabeth realized she had to hide her anger.

"How about shopping in the village? With the ladies, of course," she ventured.

The nearby village was so like the one near Possi, she thought.

The archduchess's face tightened with contempt.

"Do you not realize the stores would have to be closed to the public and a squad of policemen brought in before you could appear on their premises?"

And Franz? She hardly saw him alone. He'd collapse in his own apartment on a small iron bed except when he invaded her body. And his eyes still lingered on the young ladies. Elisabeth resolved to throw away every one of her romantic novels.

It was the palace ladies that drove her to escapades which aroused her amusement and relieved her despair. It helped save her sanity. Sophie would go into a furor, and that was amusing as well.

These ladies were something else — young, single, the *crème de la crème* of Austrian royalty. They came as a troop, daily from Vienna, with Sophie's approval.

"They will enhance your manners and improve your ability to converse with the court royals," she'd told Elisabeth.

They had haughty faces, noses that pointed to the ceiling, distant smiles and eyes that glittered with constant curiosity. They were always searching for something to gossip about. Elisabeth knew she was their prime target.

They never read a book — outside of romantic novels, that is. Their only interests were the latest available aristocratic gentleman, who had nabbed an inheritance, the Burgtheater where the gentlemen flocked to see young girls and who was cheating on whom. To Elisabeth, it was all frivolous, shallow and boring.

Furthermore, one would think they were much too pious to step into the wicked world of romantic intrigue that coloured their continual revelations. Yet Elisabeth knew that was hardly the case. Their eyes glowed when talk of amorous affairs slithered from their lips. Elisabeth turned away to hide her mirth. They were nothing but frivolous balls of envy.

Though the ladies tried to hide their vengeful jealousy of her exalted position, Elisabeth didn't miss it. She knew their bitterness. How had a little country nymph — not even of pure blue blood — snatched, from beneath their noses, their illustrious emperor? When Elisabeth thought her reason might evaporate, she tried her first touch of humour by adding to that insult and upsetting them even more.

She elaborated on her stories of playing with the peasants' children, sharing meals in their cottages, dancing at country fairs and holding out her apron for rewards. Their eyes almost popped out! They could hardly wait to circulate the stories. And it almost made Sophie hysterical — all the rumours were true. It was the only bit of humour Elisabeth had until the jewellery express.

Her jewellery became her best weapon. She knew that although these palace ladies were of the bluest of blood and from the noblest families, most were impoverished and many had no jewellery. It was the eldest male in an aristocratic family who inherited the family's wealth and jewels. When an eligible gentleman with an inheritance came on the market, their mothers went on a rampage.

To Elisabeth, jewellery meant little. An earring had never hung from her ear before she'd met Franz. In this dismal atmosphere though, she discovered its usefulness.

Day after day, when the palace ladies required her time, she paraded out in her finest jewellery, from diamond tiaras embedded in her hair to strings of glittering jewels circling her neck and shoulders. This abundance, this ever-changing variety left them speechless. Their faces reddened, their lips tightened, their eyes hung on her like hungry dogs. And often, solemn-faced and thin-lipped, they turned away. Elisabeth just smiled sweetly.

Then one day, Countess Darlaine — young like Elisabeth, her face plain, sadness often on its pinched contours — lifted the thin diamond necklace she wore.

"My brother inherited our family wealth," she said. "He gave me this necklace. It is my only piece of family jewellery. His wife drips in jewellery. The gods are not fair." She sounded more bleak than ever. "My mother says I must marry for wealth and jewellery. But I do not have your beauty. Only an old man waits at my door. His beard is white, his face is carved. He offers me jewels, but there is no love."

She looked at Elisabeth, her dark eyes in despair.

"It is a marriage of necessity for us both."

The ladies dropped their eyes, all except Countess Sara. She sat back in her chair with a smile — a tight smile — on a hardened face. She was the only one decked out in jewellery.

The tiny Countess Lola did not have one attractive feature and never expected to find a husband, though her mother said never to give up.

"You, Sara," she ventured, "are the lucky one to have captured a rich husband."

Sara's smile disappeared. Her eyes turned down. She covered her face with her hands. The ladies looked away.

"She loves another," Lola murmured to Elisabeth. "They danced at the balls. They held hands on summer evenings and watched the moonlight on the Danube River. But he was a younger brother who would not inherit the family wealth. He was not suitable. She married another, but he does not love her — he loves another also."

Elisabeth looked away. For the first time, she felt empathy for the ladies. They were human. Imperfection in life does not have preference. But for them, she thought, it was not the fault of the gods. It was the ignorance of their society.

The jewellery express came to a halt and her boredom began to fester.

Horses, she thought, *might be my escape.*

5

It was early morning, the sun had just dropped its warmth on the Laxenburg Palace grounds and dew still glistened on wildflowers snuggled here and there on the rolling plains. Franz had fled to his duties and the ladies had not yet knocked on her door when Elisabeth threw on her riding habit and rushed to the stables. She had not consulted the archduchess or Franz. She knew their answers.

She demanded Senta — her favourite horse, the one she had plied with treats — and a groom from the stiff-faced staff. To their shocked gasps, she threw herself up on the horse with no help. She motioned the groom to follow and out on the trails they galloped.

With the racing horse beneath her, the vast empty plains in the morning sun and the air so pure and fresh, her jubilance overflowed. She felt like a prisoner newly freed from a dungeon. She jumped over streams and sailed over fences. She lost her groom many, many times — he couldn't keep up. Often, she'd pull her horse to a stop and gaze at the plains around her. She felt almost alone on Earth. It was ecstasy, but an ecstasy short-lived. Back at the stable gates, it ended.

The archduchess was there, with her troop of ladies, stone-faced but sizzling.

Elisabeth jumped from the horse, smiling. The terrified groom seized the reins.

"The Empress of Austria does not ride anywhere unless she is properly attended," Sophie shouted, stomping over to her.

Elisabeth had never seen such anger.

"I had a groom with me," she returned as sweetly as she could.

The groom was shaking at her side, his eyes on the ground. You would think he was in front of a firing squad.

"He is not sufficient. Only the emperor must accompany you."

"He is never here," Elisabeth said, her sweetness disarming.

The groom quickly led the horse into the stable.

"No, my dear," Sophie replied contemptuously. "There are matters more urgent demanding his time than galloping across the plains."

She spun around and marched towards the palace, her troop following with flying steps, hiding their amusement. Then she spun around again, pushed the ladies aside and glared at Elisabeth.

"Do you not get enough food at the table?"

The ladies could not stifle their giggles. Elisabeth wondered what all this was about.

"I have reports that you sneak from the kitchen with food in your hands."

"It is to feed the horses . . . ," Elisabeth protested.

"To feed the horses?" Sophie was incredulous. "Really, Elisabeth. How undignified it is for the empress to run to the stable with carrots and sugar lumps to feed the horses. Will we ever make you into royalty?"

Her eyes narrowed and Elisabeth knew more was coming.

"And one more thing. Perhaps your time could be better spent practising your own enunciation instead of teaching your parrot to talk."

That was when Elisabeth sent her riding crop sailing into the air and charged past the archduchess and the gaping ladies. She went immediately to her apartment and didn't unlock the door until Franz arrived that evening.

Franz's eyes had a twinkle when he dashed in.

"Mama says you were misbehaving?"

He reached out to her. She pulled away and stomped across the room.

"You have no idea how they treat me," she blurted out.

She had lost control and did not care if she sounded like an immature child.

"I'm like a caged animal being trained how to dress, how to eat, how to talk. Even how to breathe. I can hardly be myself. I must be impeccably dressed at all times. And I must never be seen without gloves."

She picked up her long white gloves from the table and flung them across the room.

"And we are never alone. All the riding you promised, what happened to that?"

She was shaking, her anger rising.

"We don't even share our evening meals alone. There are always eyes watching, waiting for me to make a mistake. And I hate that boring old imperial general your mother insists I sit next to at every meal, just so I can learn to converse. And what am I supposed to say to a grumpy old man who can hardly hear anyway?"

She wanted to scream that she would never be royalty, and she missed her best friend Allie, and more than anything in the world, she wanted to go home to Possi. Her tears poured down in buckets.

She let him take her in his arms. His strength and warmth momentarily calmed her. It was the first time she had let out her frustration. She had struggled to hide it from Franz, hoping her maturity would prevail. But now she realized it wasn't all just her immaturity — it was another woman determined to crush her into submission. To deprive her of herself.

She stepped back and looked up at his face.

"And what's wrong with talking to Tusti? She even chastised me for that."

He laughed with amusement which only rekindled her anger.

"It's not funny."

She pulled away and started to stomp across the room. He took her hands and pulled her around to face him. He was no longer amused.

"My dear Sisi, I think it's delightful that you want to feed your horses and speak to your parrot. You may. We will ignore her wishes on those issues. But for the riding, you must ride with me. It is a rule of the court. I solemnly promise you, on the weekends we will ride together. There won't be a trail we'll miss. But please . . ." He considered his words. ". . . listen to my mother. She only wants to help you."

"She's not helping me. She's destroying me!" Elisabeth screamed, pulling her hands from his and charging back across the room, faster than before. "Furthermore, she is trying to make me shameful in your eyes. To make you see your error, that you should have listened to her and never married me."

"What she does is for you. She is accustomed to demanding obedience and she has earned that respect. Believe me, she wants to help you."

He looked deeply into her eyes.

"She wants to groom you into a perfect Habsburg empress. Her ways are harsh. I know, I am her son. But believe me, Sisi, her intentions are good."

His face turned stern.

"During the revolution, it was she who saved this empire. With her skill and her tenacity, she brought the Habsburgs from a dangerous precipice to the power we are today. We are the greatest empire in all Europe because of her."

He reached out and took her hands again.

"The Habsburgs were called upon by God to rule, and we live our lives in His service. Our sole purpose is to care for our people, to bring them contentment and happiness. We must sacrifice our own comforts and our lives for this purpose. Our own imperfections and desires must not stand in the way." He cleared his throat, then continued in a gentler tone, "Please try to understand why I say this. It is not to hurt you, it is to help you. You are now a Habsburg. A great responsibility lies upon your shoulders. You must stand beside me and give to our people as I do. You are very young, very inexperienced. But you must learn." Then, firmly, he finished, "You do not want to be a flaw in this great empire."

Her eyes widened. She stepped back and pulled her hands from his. She stared at him a moment. Then she fled to the window.

The night was dark, as black as her tangled thoughts. *A flaw.* His words did not incense her, they frightened her. She was only sixteen, but fate had brought her into a world she could never have envisioned and would never have chosen. Like the everchanging patterns in that flowing river, she could never go back. She was afraid. Her heart beat harder. Her destiny was chosen and she could not run away. She must move forward and adapt. Somehow. She closed her eyes and held her hands tightly together.

Could she do it?

She turned back to Franz. She looked at his face, saw his concern, his love.

She picked up her white gloves and pushed her fingers into them. She attempted a mature voice.

"I promise I will not be a flaw in our great empire."

Her journey into adulthood was brief. On the first step, she toppled.

That night at dinner, she filled the old general's ears with chatter — 'palace lady' chatter, that is. She wasn't sure what fell from her lips. She remembered Néné saying that no one hears what you say anyway, unless it's gossip. "Just keep your words coming, and charm with a smile." She even threw in coquettish looks.

At times, the old general looked surprised, at times perplexed. He never smiled. It didn't matter. It was practice. Even the archduchess stared at her, lost for words, and Franz gave her a couple of winks.

Spurred on by her new goal, she ventured that evening into the drawing room where Franz and his mother were in a heated discussion. She was a little uncertain, but she persisted and in she went.

Franz paced the floor, his brow pinched. The Crimean War had brought horror beyond belief. There was no money to finance his military, his people were suffering from famine and his soldiers, along with French and British soldiers, were dying by the thousands in roadside ditches, from cholera and famine.

Of course, Elisabeth was never informed about this. Her place was not in politics, Sophie had told her. When she saw the terrible tension on Franz's face as he paced the floor, she clasped her hands in terror.

Sophie jumped from her chair, reaching for Franz. Elisabeth had never seen her so distraught. Then they spotted her.

"Sisi!" Franz rushed to her side. "Please wait outside until we are through." His voice was frantic. "We have a great emergency. It is the Crimean War and — "

Seeing the expression on her face quickly triggered a different reaction. He kissed her hands.

"My dearest," he said, "I'm sorry. Stay if you wish, but, please, take a seat by the fire. I will be with you shortly."

"It's best she leave, Franz," the archduchess barked. "This is of no concern to her."

"Oh, but it is," Elisabeth blurted out. "I want to know. After all, I am the empress. If there are problems, I want to share them with my husband."

"These are not problems for a child's mind," Sophie shot back.

Elisabeth saw Franz's face. He looked concerned. But he made no attempt to counter his mother.

Elisabeth quickly picked up her skirts and found a chair by the hearth. She was hurt. Still, she listened to their voices. The only thing she knew about the Crimean War was Florence Nightingale, the 'angel of mercy' who at seventeen had heard the voice of God, calling her to serve. She'd sacrificed all, even the man she loved, to nurse the injured soldiers. She'd sailed to the Crimea with thirty-five nurses she had organized. She'd revived the filthy dilapidated hospitals and had nursed and given comfort to the soldiers, who worshipped her like an angel.

The disappointing evening did not deter Elisabeth's aspirations. In fact, they motivated her. The next day she bravely took a carriage to Vienna. In the antechamber of Franz's reception room, she demanded to see him.

"Your Majesty," the attendant said with a courteous bow. "Everyone in the room is waiting to see the emperor."

The room was filled, from well-dressed men with meticulously curved moustaches to peasants in traditional apparel.

"But I am the empress, and I demand to see the emperor at once."

Again he made a gracious bow, his voice emphatic.

"The emperor has a strict protocol," he said. "Every day, he gives audience to hear his people. Whether it is the highest dignitary in the land or a peasant, each one must take his place in line."

When she complained to Franz, after a two-hour shuffle in the anteroom where curious eyes hung on her like chains, he replied that it was the degree of respect that he granted his people from the most elite to the poorest.

And the empress, the emperor's wife has no prestigious advantage? she wondered. But she didn't voice it.

She told him her mission — she wished to be by his side and share with him his problems. In time, she would learn and might be of help. She smiled most charmingly.

"How else can I learn?" she asked, seeing the amused expression on his face.

His smile enlarged. That was when he closed his books and gave her an endearing hug.

"Today will be a short working day. I have a surprise for you."

He escorted her back to Laxenburg, driving the excited horses himself. He took her riding far out into the plains and his smiles were full of love.

Her journey into adulthood brought her to a disturbing realization. She was the empress, but her only duties were to stand beside her husband at receptions, to grace the royal drawing room with stilted conversation, and to provide an heir. Her shining horizon diminished into the clouds, and her path ahead was mired in shadows.

When they returned to Vienna, to the dull and distressing atmosphere of the Hofburg, Sophie emerged stronger than ever and the royal court had self-satisfied sneers. They focused on Elisabeth with coldness and disdain. She was merely the daughter of a non-royal duke, not worthy of the honour placed upon her.

Elisabeth fought to keep her smile. She did not want to appear as the troublesome child Sophie so frequently told her she was.

She still loved Franz, loved him dearly. She felt a thrill of delight when she heard his footsteps and the sound of his voice. But, little by little, her love was shifting into anguish. More and more, Franz drifted from her side, attending to affairs of state, the hunt and the smiling eyes of the ladies.

A small room beside her bedroom became her retreat, her salvation. She decorated it like a tiny altar with a hanging crucifix of onyx and silver and golden candelabras that raised perfumed candles from a wreath of snowy blossoms. Here she would flee when her anguish overtook her. With her arms on the altar rails and her face buried in her hands, her frustrations became sobs that shook her whole body. Her only consolation was to cuddle the two Great Dane puppies Franz had given her and let her tears fall.

Then, with lingering anguish, she'd stand up and walk out of her rooms with a smile on her face.

6

In June 1854, Elisabeth's doctor informed her of her pregnancy. The country went wild, Sophie's smiles became permanent and Elisabeth went into shock.

"I am too young," she told herself.

Desperation took over. Her sixteen-year-old body was not yet fully developed and a new life was blending with its growth.

"Motherhood belongs to my mother."

Still, the delight in Franz's eyes brought her a soothing resignation and another step into maturity.

Sophie informed Franz that for the next nine months she was in control. Elisabeth did her best to perform the duties expected of her, but her horror grew when Sophie informed her that she owed it to her husband and the monarchy to show herself for all the world to see. On the palace balconies, in the carriages, in the parks, in the salons and at the foreign receptions, where everyone was suddenly less interested in her beauty than in the emerging life growing beneath her gowns.

The archduchess stood always at her side. Elisabeth fell into docile contentment. She did not raise an eye when Sophie wrote to Franz: 'I do not think Sisi should spend so much time with her parrot, for if a woman is always looking at animals during the earlier months, the child may grow to resemble them. She'd fare better either looking in her looking glass, or at you.'

Tusti was removed.

Her deformity grew into a nightmare. She had her mirror removed. She couldn't bear to have Franz view her nude. She turned him from her bed. The first crack appeared.

Franz seemed undaunted by her decision. In fact, she thought, he seemed quite happy. He planted a goodnight kiss on her forehead, then he was off to the Burgtheater, known as the theatre of the young ladies. And the gossip exploded with renewed fervour. His sexual passions would never be put aside for pregnancy.

All Vienna was caught up in the excitement. The fans whirled faster and the royal eyes gleamed brighter than the diamonds hanging from the ladies' necks. Down the palace halls, through the royal salons, the whispers flew incessantly. The gossip pushed aside even the Crimean War.

The archduchess had a smile like a thousand twinkling lights. This was just what she wanted. Franz could again taste the alluring wares offered him. She hoped it would clear his mind and cool his overwhelming passion for Elisabeth.

The palace ladies had so much fun countering their jealousy by dropping every story they heard within Elisabeth's range. Elisabeth plugged her ears, but that did not rid her of fear.

There was a change in Franz.

He visited Elisabeth every evening, but his impatience was evident. His goodnight kisses were quicker and quicker. His eyes had a glow, but not for her. They hardly touched her, whipping over her as fast as his kisses. She was perturbed and also angry. She desperately wanted to scream at him about the rumours, but she didn't.

She tried to hide her fears, hanging on to her innocent ideas of love. She often poked fun at her ladies gossiping.

"What would you ladies do if you didn't have something to gossip about?"

Countess Levy, the only one of her ladies she trusted somewhat, gave her quite a serious look.

"Perhaps, my empress, you should pay heed to what the ladies say."

The other ladies looked uneasy, trying to hide their excitement. Still, their eyes sparkled maliciously. Elisabeth looked at them and then away. She didn't want to hear. They were out to poison her like everyone else.

However, her curiosity was piqued. She turned back to Countess Levy and her ladies. Their eyes enlarged into saucers. She took a deep breath. She even smiled, though admittedly a tight smile.

"And what do they say?"

They came to life, swarming like bees pouncing on a new source of honey. They all talked at once, each one trying to outdo the other.

"They say the empress is naïve and very immature," said one.

They all fell silent a moment, biting their lips, then seeing Elisabeth waiting for more without anger, they continued.

"They say she has the passions of a child, and she could never satisfy the desires of her experienced husband known for his sexual appetite," offered another.

Then they looked down, as one. Elisabeth could almost hear their hearts racing.

"And they say," adding another, her fan fluttering, "it is only a matter of time until he takes a favourite."

Up came their eyes to see her reaction.

Elisabeth gasped. They believed it. She saw it in their faces.

She struggled to her feet — her body weighed a ton and her baby was kicking. She turned and stomped out of the room without saying goodnight. She slammed her bedroom door with such a bang, the maid came flying out. It was the first time she had let her emotions show in a long time.

She collapsed in her chair in tears. She ran her hands over her protruding stomach, feeling the movement inside. It was warming and soothing. She closed her eyes. Much of what they said was true — she'd been naïve when she married. Even now, she understood so little about sex and the overwhelming passion in Franz. She gave herself to him, but it was a labour of necessity, not her vision of love. She covered her face with her hands. In fact, she hated sex. She hated seeing him charge into her room with those fiery eyes.

She rose from the chair and walked to the window. She gazed into the darkness. She believed marriage was a bond of trust. If Franz engaged in a romantic intrigue, her faith and her love for him would be destroyed forever.

7

Countess Levy couldn't wait to pass the latest news to Elisabeth. It was the night of the Court Ball. The countess felt a little guilty, but she loved intrigues, especially romantic intrigues, and her discretion often flew with the wind.

"You should have seen her," Countess Levy beamed, as she puffed up the pillows on Elisabeth's bed. "She is the most gorgeous thing I have ever seen. And her gown was sensational, from the salons of Paris."

She had come from the ball to assist Elisabeth with her preparation for bed. The countess was excited, yet careful of her gown, as she had full intentions of racing back to the ball as soon as possible. Too much was happening there.

"Who are you talking about?" asked Elisabeth.

"The countess, the Italian countess! The emperor hasn't left her side all evening. He's completely enraptured by her. And who wouldn't be?"

Elisabeth bolted upright in her bed. Franz had begged her to come to the ball, but she'd refused, of course. To display herself would have been detestable to her.

"Did he dance with her?"

That was strictly against protocol. When the emperor hosts a court ball, most of his evening is spent on the dais smiling charmingly to his guests.

"Almost every dance, and everyone is talking about it. And the archduchess . . . You wouldn't believe her smile."

Countess Levy caught her own smile. She shouldn't have said that. Elisabeth was speechless.

"The whole ballroom is in an uproar," the countess said. "I've never seen such excitement. Everyone is whispering and wondering where she came from and why she was invited to this ball. No one has an answer. Some say . . ."

She glanced quickly at Elisabeth and bit her lip, but she couldn't hold it in.

". . . she's Madame Mère's protégé."

Elisabeth was out of the bed, pacing the floor. Her steps were short and heavy. Her stomach felt like an iron lump.

"Is she attractive?"

"I said she was gorgeous. Very chic, very sophisticated. And so well-mannered. She tilts her head so fashionably. Her voice is exquisite. And such a nice accent."

"And why, do you suppose, they said she might be Madame Mère's protegé?"

She stared the countess straight in the eye. The young woman drew back when she saw Elisabeth's face. She lowered her eyes. Perhaps she had blurted out too much.

"Well," she searched for the right words. "They say . . . they say . . ."

"What do they say?" Elisabeth screamed.

Her baby kicked as if it was raging too. She marched across the room and stood in front of the countess, her hands on her hips.

"Well . . . they say . . ."

"What? What?" Elisabeth shouted.

"They say . . . the archduchess has a plot . . ."

"A plot? What kind of a plot?"

"They say she wishes the emperor to return to the habits of his bachelor days."

"His bachelor days," Elisabeth screamed louder. "Why? Why?"

"My lady, you know what they say. You've heard the stories that you cannot satisfy the emperor." Her eyes fell to the floor. "They are saying he is ripe to take a favourite."

Neither heard the Countess René bounce into the room. Elisabeth bit back her scream when she saw her. She had the silkiest, yet meanest mouth ever. Gossip and ridicule fell from her lips like poison candy. She was stunning and vibrant with her dark eyes flashing. She had no fears of catching an heir. Elisabeth knew what brought her: why let Countess Levy have all the fun? Her smile broadened at the two women. Her eyes sparkled.

"You missed a great ball tonight, my empress."

Her silky voice sent Elisabeth's irritation flying, her composure in tatters. Countess René swirled around the room, showing off her beautiful dress and her slim figure. Then she stopped with a bigger smile.

"I have great news," the countess continued, her voice excited but still silky.

Both women stared at her.

"Her Imperial Highness the Archduchess Sophie has a new maid of honour, a perfect jewel."

"And who is this perfect jewel?" Elisabeth demanded.

"The ravishing Italian countess. She has created such a sensation at the ball tonight."

Elisabeth clung to the bedpost. Her face turned so white, both ladies rushed to her.

"No, no," she whimpered, frozen, the bedpost in her hand. Through lips barely moving, she moaned, "This cannot be."

And she fainted to the ground.

Elisabeth's baby girl arrived the next morning, on March 5th, 1855, and her loud screams echoed through the halls as if she were six weeks old. Franz and Elisabeth clung together tightly and cried. Elisabeth reached out to draw the archduchess into the circle.

"Sophie will be the child's name," the archduchess declared, pulling back. "I will, naturally, be her godmother."

That announcement did not mar Elisabeth's pleasure in her baby. She fondled her tiny feet, her little hands, the fingers so perfectly formed, and a love beyond her wildest dreams crept through her with the softness of warm honey. All her anxieties disappeared.

She wrote her mother: 'Now my existence cannot be said to be utterly useless. And there is hope that everything will be all right. Children form an unbreakable tie, even between husbands and wives who are otherwise absolutely indifferent to each other.'

One week later, as Elisabeth lay peacefully in bed, watching the archduchess cuddle the tiny Sophie in her arms, her happiness was slashed into shreds.

"My dear Elisabeth," Sophie said, looking up, "I will supervise the raising of this child. I have personally selected the staff for the nursery."

Elisabeth bolted up.

"You didn't consult me."

"There was no need. You are very young and inexperienced. You may visit the baby, but only with my consent or when I am present."

Elisabeth's face was stricken.

"You must understand," she added, "it is best for the child."

And the nursery? It would be beside the archduchess's apartment for her convenience, of course. Elisabeth fell back, speechless.

Sophie laid the baby back in its cradle. She was unmoved by Elisabeth's expression.

"This is for you to read."

She flung a paper on the bed and marched to the door.

"And don't forget," she added, turning back, "your responsibility has not ended. It is a male heir we desire."

The door slammed behind her.

The baby wriggled in the crib. Elisabeth lay numb, staring at the ceiling. Then she picked up the faded, handwritten document. Its heading was 'The Habsburg Creed.'

'It is ordained the Empress shall have no birth rights as other women. She is her husband's bondwoman and must offer to her lord offspring made in her own image before she receives the thanks bestowed on mothers for the suffering of childbirth.'

Elisabeth buried her tears in her pillow.
Franz, silent through it all, did not offer any help.

8

Spring disappeared into summer. Tusti was back, perching on Elisabeth's shoulder, his elocution as good as hers. Life at the royal court in Vienna was reception after reception and endless lines of diplomats with a variety of lips sponging on her gloved hand. Elisabeth's only recreation remained in the royal salons, where the bluest of blue bloods mingled and gossip created the only hint of humour on their stiff faces. When Elisabeth tried conversation other than gossip, both men and women sent cigar smoke into her face, eyeing her as if she didn't know what she was talking about.

Had she been allowed to attend the salons of the aristocrats, a level below the royals, she would have fared much better. They were fun, sumptuous banquets and festive balls, and the music of Mozart, Haydn and Strauss flowed down their halls. Their measure of blood was below the pure blue of the royals, however, and Franz informed her that their impurity of blood was a barrier that could not be broken.

Franz came to her side occasionally. He said his time was spent mostly in his mother's office solving the problems of the empire — of course, Elisabeth was never informed of the problems — or chasing with his hounds to clear his mind. She closed her ears to the gossip and to the palace ladies' giggles. The only good thing: the Italian countess was gone.

Her times with her baby were short, much too short. Nursemaids and the archduchess had replaced her. Often when she held her little one and love poured through every vein of her body, she buried her face in the tiny bundle and her tears came. When Sophie saw this, she snatched the baby from her viciously.

"Do not show your affection in front of your staff. It displays your emotions and lowers your prestige."

She did complain to Franz, when she could find him. His reply was always the same.

"It's the way of court life. You must adapt."

In the bedroom, only his sexual passion reigned. There was no love — at least, none that she could see. In his heart? She didn't know. In her own heart? She was beginning to wonder.

Loneliness came. It came like a black winter cloud. She missed her family. She had no friends, no real ones like her shepherd friends. The palace ladies still gathered around, but gossip had reached a new low and their passion for it was gone.

Despair began its descent. Her smiles were now rare, her face cast in gloom. The diplomats, who once flocked to see the beautiful empress, were rare as well. She was meek and submissive, and the archduchess's smile reflected her satisfaction. The little nymph was under her control.

But then Elisabeth's sanity was saved. It came on the wings of love. Franz discovered a poem she had written.

Summer is here once more,
The flowers bloom more tenderly.
But what is the charm of this to me
In this land of exile?

Under the azure sky, I languish in my prison.
The hands are bound that once were free.
The cold bars of my windows
Make a mockery of my yearnings.

He saw her desperation.

He rose from his desk. He went to the window. The breeze blew softly over his face. The helplessness within him surfaced. It was a helplessness he buried in the overwhelming demands of running an empire and in his mother's despotism. He loved Sisi, yet he didn't know how to reach out, to give her the comfort and the love she needed. She needed her family. She had to go home to Possi for a visit.

His mother had to be convinced. It was like breaking through the walls of a fortress. Sophie's bellows echoed down the halls. Her fists shook in fury.

"You must not give in to her childish whims!"

Elisabeth went to Possi and the bars of her prison window began to lift.

9

Elisabeth bloomed with the radiance of the flowers that shimmered on the Bavarian hills. There were joyous activities and non-stop chatter with her mother and sisters. A suitable husband had not yet been found for Helene. When she saw Franz's earlier affection for Elisabeth, she had vowed to marry only for love. Now, hearing of Elisabeth's trials, she hoped she would recognize real love. Everyone was talking about a royal match for their fifteen-year-old sister, Maria, already a beauty. Her mother had her sights on another crown.

Elisabeth tossed her shoes aside and chased the children, barefoot, across the lawns. She was Sisi again. Vienna disappeared from her world. She galloped bareback through the valleys, the riding gear required in Austria cast aside.

"It's the only way you feel the soul of the horse," Elisabeth called out to the shocked palace ladies who accompanied her to Possi, whose presence the archduchess had insisted upon to keep her posted.

She performed for the locals in her father's circus. The ladies gasped in horror and hid their faces in their hands. If the Viennese saw that, the shock waves could produce a riot.

The local Bavarian aristocrats buried their heads in shame.

Freedom was her greatest delight, losing herself in the quiet beauty of the valleys and hiking the mountain trails with her father. They watched the sunsets on the lake and the stars in the sky and they listened to the evening cries of the birds. He never asked how things were in Vienna. He didn't have to.

She shopped with Helene and Maria in Munich, the ladies they left behind in Possi — and the stores didn't close to preserve her identity.

They stopped at a zingara's stall and put forth their palms for the gypsy woman to view their futures. Helene would marry a wealthy man whom she would dearly love. The zingara hovered over Maria's palm.

"You will become a queen," she said, "but amid blood, war and disasters, you will lose your crown."

The gypsy took Elisabeth's hand, and her face hardened. She looked up at Elisabeth, solemn and hesitant.

"Your hand," she said in a whisper, "is written with tragedy. When you least expect it, the tragic end will come."

"Of course, I don't believe in gypsy predictions," sniffed Maria as the young ladies returned to their shopping.

Helene turned her eyes away in doubt. Elisabeth knew it was true. She sensed a dark omen on her horizon.

One afternoon, after chasing through the garden and playing hide-and-seek with the children, Elisabeth struggled into the salon and collapsed on the couch in pleasant but overwhelming fatigue. Two snoring dogs were reluctant to share it, but the choice was not theirs. Down on the floor she sent them and she stretched her legs to the armrest at one end. Contentment and happiness soothed her.

From a nearby chair, Ludovika smiled at her radiant face.

"Sisi," she exclaimed, "you have become a ravishing beauty."

"Me, a ravishing beauty?" Elisabeth sat up, beaming.

She was certain motherhood had robbed her of all beauty. She couldn't remember the last time Franz paid her a compliment.

"It must be this wonderful countryside and my freedom," she grinned, her smile teetering on a giggle.

She hadn't given Vienna a thought — except for her baby. That always brought an ache.

"Your face is slim with soft elegant contours," her mother said. "And the mystical hue in your dark eyes is very bewitching."

"Oh, Mama. Keep going," Elisabeth giggled. "I haven't heard anything positive about me in a long time. Aunt Sophie tells me I'm nothing but a country nymph. She says I don't even know how to walk properly."

Ludovika scoffed. How typical of Sophie, with her callous superiority, chastising Sisi with degrading comments. *It's just as she has treated me*, she thought. She knew Sophie was still fearful of Sisi. She had become the subservient daughter-in-law she wanted, but her maturing beauty could be a greater threat.

"You walk beautifully and you are not a country nymph," Ludovika said firmly. "You are a lovely young woman, tall and so well-rounded. And your hair . . ." Her smile widened. ". . . would be gorgeous if you got rid of the braids."

Elisabeth bit her lip in amusement. Never had she heard such superlatives falling from her mother's lips. Ludovika was pensive, but still her eyes kept their sparkle. Her voice intensified.

"As you mature, your beauty will grow. Your road ahead is not easy. Use that beauty, Sisi, to conquer, as men use their power to conquer."

Elisabeth stared at her mother.

"My beauty could be my power?"

She didn't know whether to laugh or be serious.

Ludovika hurried over to the couch and took her hands.

"Sisi, you know what your father said: 'Your inner strength is nourished from the seeds of your childhood.' He gave you strength. Dig it up."

Although her voice was lighthearted, Elisabeth could tell her intent was serious.

"With your beauty and your strength, you might even surpass the archduchess. You might become the powerful one."

They looked into each other's eyes, sharing this new thought.

The ladies did not miss Elisabeth's new radiance and their whispers mingled with their awe and their jealousy. They did not report it to the archduchess. Such reflections would only fuel her anxious fears.

They did report that Possi was absolutely appalling. Unruly children were everywhere. No discipline. The gardens were a mess, dogs and ponies everywhere, along with the odd cow that wandered in. And dinner, you wouldn't believe — the duchess always had her two spitzes on her lap! She fed them continually and amused herself by picking off their fleas and depositing them on her plate. They did add that "the plates were instantly changed." Needless to say, the entourage was delighted when they returned to Vienna and handed the empress over to the emperor.

Franz's welcome at the station festered in their pious faces, envy challenging their smiles. They had never seen him so ecstatic — not with Elisabeth, that is. His face beamed as he caught her hands.

"You are beautiful," he said, "a vision from the past."

He swept her into his arms and covered her face with kisses. Elisabeth was overwhelmed, so overwhelmed she was almost speechless. Such affection she had not seen in a long time. She remembered her mother's words. The ladies returned to their homes with solemn faces and downcast eyes, wondering why such love had passed them by.

10

The bliss of Possi disappeared like a summer sky beneath the rage of a thundering storm. Life at the Hofburg Palace returned to reality, and boredom became Elisabeth's permanent companion. Her radiance disappeared, her eyes lost their glimmer. Archduchess Sophie was back in command and the doldrums of court life in full force. As for Franz, she couldn't be sure where he was: at the Burgtheater or chasing a chamois, a hare, a boar or, perhaps, an Italian countess. Most times she found him amid a cluster of young ladies. The ladies who accompanied her to Possi wore satisfied smirks — their lives weren't so bad after all.

On an autumn day, when rain pounded the shutters and Elisabeth's spirits were darker than the day itself, she pulled out her mirror. She stared at her face. She undid the braids and her dark brown hair tumbled down far past the middle of her back, slivers of auburn shining through it. She tilted her face in the mirror, fluffing her hair in different styles. She whirled around once, twice, many times, eyeing her figure and her long hair. She liked her figure, tall and well-proportioned, and she liked her poise when she held her head high and displayed her long, slim neck.

She had never thought of herself as beautiful. In fact, beauty was as foreign to her as the palaces of Vienna. Not even Count Richard had complimented her so effusively. She remembered the pleasure in Franz's eyes when he welcomed her back. Was it her beauty?

Excitement ran through her like a sparkle of champagne, the rain on the windows disappeared. She laughed good-humouredly to herself. Perhaps she really could challenge the Empress Eugenie of France, the most beautiful woman the world.

She whirled around again and then stopped. Another thought, this time intense. Power. Could she achieve the power to take control of her life? Could she challenge the hold of the archduchess and the royals? She could see the humour of it. Wouldn't she just love to trample them with her superiority!

She heard the rain again. The candles flickered. Her heart raced, her body was taut, her eyes gleaming. Her mother's words were recalled with fervour. Power could, perhaps, be hers.

The braids went first. Egg and cognac became her favourite shampoo, and her hairstylist arranged her hair into lavish styles that brought the royal eyes from their sockets. Her childish look went with the braids. She became a woman.

She bathed her face each night in masks of strawberry and egg. She watched everything she ate. It was challenging and amusing and she forgot to be bored. Though there were times when, spending so much time on her beauty, she wondered if she was losing her sanity.

The eyes of the palace ladies were always on her and Sophie's face had an added pinch.

Though the foreign envoys and dignitaries again flooded the court to meet the lovely empress, her greatest satisfaction came from Franz's glowing eyes and his whispers of affection. The chamois, the hare and the wild boars had a break and the young ladies at the Burgtheater were wondering what had happened to their favourite visitor.

Elisabeth's self-confidence bloomed like dry plains in spring rains. Even the birth of another daughter, Gisela, who was also placed in the nursery beside the archduchess's rooms, did not put a crinkle in it. In fact, the arrival of another girl retained her importance. It was a male heir they wanted. She was still in demand.

Her yellow teeth remained her flaw. She tried to hide them, never parting her lips more than necessary, but her words were muffled, so she discovered.

"The empress is a wonder of beauty," an American envoy was heard to say, "tall, well-formed, with a profusion of dark auburn hair, a low Greek forehead and a sweet, gentle smile. But she whispers and one cannot understand a word she says."

Elisabeth fled to her apartment. She emerged three weeks later with a perfectly articulated voice. It was low, silky and enticing. And she kept her yellow teeth hidden.

The envoy returned home with glowing superlatives.

"Not only is she beautiful, she has a voice with an enchanting musical lilt."

The royals, who had desired a beautiful empress, were not happy at all. Jealousy and fear laced their condescending voices. How had this little country nymph risen to such heights?

Elisabeth, recognizing her new power, begged Franz to let her children return to her side. He took her hands and smiled.

"They will be yours."

He wrote to Sophie: 'Could you be gracious enough to understand Sisi's feeling of pain seeing our children enclosed in your apartment? I think the time has come for change, so she, too, can show off her babies. Sisi will never deprive you of the children and she asks me to tell you that they will always be entirely at your disposal.'

For the royals, the sun almost departed the Earth.

"Sophie is losing her power and the little nymph is taking over," they screamed in terror. Of course, they kept it under their breaths.

Sophie refuelled her fervour. Her anger boiled. She ripped the declaration to shreds and tossed it away. She drew on her strength. She had to tread with care. Franz was too unpredictable when it came to Elisabeth. Her eyes were venomous.

Elisabeth won back the control of her children. Their rooms were moved next to her apartment. Her beauty she placed on hold. Her children became her life. Little Sophie was shy and docile. She would look at Elisabeth with her large blue eyes, then run and jump into her arms and hug her. When Elisabeth took her on walks in the palace grounds, she always raced to the same tree with a long branch to swing on and never wanted to leave it. She swung with such exuberance, the nurse and the attending ladies stared in horror, but no one reported it to the archduchess. They saw the child's enjoyment. And Elisabeth thought of herself long ago.

Triumph and Disaster

1

Trouble was brewing in the Habsburg territory of Lombardy-Venetia. The revolutionary cries of the Italians calling for an end to Austrian rule and for the unification of Italy had reached a boiling point. No longer did the sidewalk cafés beneath the sycamore trees ring with the boisterous songs of Italian baritones. It was now dangerous to be caught singing these songs. In protest, few Italians would touch a cigarette or gamble, as the revenues from these activities filled the Habsburg coffers.

Alexander Bach, Austria's minister of the interior, appealed to Franz.

"The archduchess's repression of the Italian people is a failure. Our General Radetzky rules there with an iron hand, torturing, flogging and sending to the gallows or the firing squad suspicious young Italian patriots who might conspire against Austrian authority."

He didn't mention the latest. Two young women, Italian singers accused of singing subversive songs, had been savagely beaten. Dressed only in chemises, they'd been roped to a flogging bench. Like a madman, the provost marshal had beaten them with a rod, pausing between each stroke to add to their torture. Their screams had penetrated the castle walls. For days, they'd lain in the castle until an ambulance took them home.

"And furthermore," Bach told Franz, "England and France are siding with the Italians. And Cavour, the Piedmont-Sardinian Prime Minister, has threatened to drive Austria from Italy at any cost. We must have a more peaceful solution. And fast. Before the country explodes."

Franz knew he was right, but how would they convince the Archduchess Sophie? She was against any appeasement. To her, power was the only way to control an insurgent population. "There is no negotiating with those crazy Italians," she'd exclaimed many times. "They must be controlled by force."

Franz challenged his mother on a sunny afternoon in the garden room of the Hofburg Palace. He handed her coffee and settled himself across from Bach. He warmed his cup slowly in his hand. He'd almost rather lead an army into battle than stand up to his mother.

Elisabeth sat beside him, fighting her excitement. She was going to Italy, so she hoped, if Madame Mère could be convinced.

That Sophie was suspicious was obvious on her face. Her impatient glances at Elisabeth were almost menacing. *What has the little imp concocted this time?* Sophie wondered.

"My lady."

Bach stood up and bowed graciously to the tense Sophie. He fought his own nervousness. He was terrified of the archduchess.

"I feel that the continued use of force in Italy will not solve our escalating problems there. Europe and England are siding with Italy. Franz and I believe that only the presence of the emperor . . ." He took a deep breath. ". . . with the lovely empress at his side, might pacify the citizens and regain their respect."

"Elisabeth!" Sophie shouted.

Elisabeth almost dropped her cup.

"My lady," Bach continued, "the Viennese people adore her beauty. It is almost a cult to them. The Italians are notoriously susceptible to feminine beauty. She will sweep into their hearts, especially with little Sophie at her side."

"Sophie!"

This time she was out of her chair.

Elisabeth took her first step into politics. She and little Sophie went to Italy with Franz. The archduchess reached for her Bible and prayed to God to give her the strength to save the empire.

Their reception in Italy was hardly friendly. It was a country beautiful beyond anything Elisabeth could have imagined, yet with a populace drenched in despair. The streets were full of solemn faces and the sidewalk cafés stood silent.

"What a charming spectacle we made," Elisabeth said to Franz on the evening of their first day in Venice, "but what a disappointment."

They were spectacular as their carriage wound through streets lined with spectators — Franz said the army had forced their presence. Franz was so handsome in his field marshal's uniform. She was in her mauve dress with matching hat and Sophie bounced from window to window waving her tiny hands. But not a hand rose in welcome. There wasn't a smile. It was like a city in mourning. Her enchantment with Italy was short-lived. The city was like a hostile camp.

When Elisabeth and little Sophie visited a park for play, it was quickly deserted by the people.

Not one aristocrat attended the performance of Mozart's *Magic Flute*. Instead, their boxes were filled with their servants, wearing black and purple gloves.

"A sign of mourning," Franz told Elisabeth. "It is their way of showing their resentment."

At La Scala in Milan, Marshal Radetzky demanded the attendance of the Italian aristocrats. Soldiers with loaded weapons were posted at stage entrances and anyone who refused to rise for the Imperial Anthem could be shot.

The gala ball was cancelled. The aristocrats refused to attend, soldiers or no soldiers. The archduchess was right — it was a hostile country, ready to ignite. What had happened to this once carefree populace?

In the quiet of their Italian quarters, free from Madame Mère, Elisabeth found a new comradeship with Franz. He began to share the world of politics with her. He often broke down while expressing his concerns for Italy. She took his hands, gave him her sympathy, gave him her love. He talked and talked and she listened.

She learned of the devastation of the conquered land. The Italians viewed the Habsburgs as robbers and oppressors. All freedoms were denied them. Young Italian patriots who conspired against the Austrian authority went to the gallows or to the firing squads in city squares. Not only were the Italian aristocrats harnessed with fines and sequestrations, many had lost their lands and hundreds were imprisoned when the Habsburgs took control. Elisabeth understood their desperation and their hatred. They were a country oppressed, robbed of their identity.

One evening, Count Grünne, the archduchess's watchdog, usually chained to Franz's side, stomped into their apartment with decisive advice from the archduchess. His boney face beamed with smug authority.

"Your presence here as mediators is not working," he said to Franz. "The people have shown no respect for their emperor."

He didn't mention their empress.

"They must accept your authority as a divine right. The army must stamp their resistance to the ground if Italy is to be saved."

Elisabeth grasped her hands. Visions of the sorrowful faces, the anger and bitterness she had witnessed flashed through her mind. Grünne's sharp, high voice set her nerves on edge. His ideas were disastrous, and she wanted to spring from her chair and voice her opposition. Armed repression was not the answer, she wanted to scream out. The people must be listened to and understood. Their feelings and their rights must be respected. Still, she knew he would never accept such advice from her.

Franz's face was buried in his hands. She held her breath. She prayed to the gods, *Don't let him make an error.* He looked up.

"Let me think it over," he said.

Her breath was back. Now, she had to reach him before it was too late. She breathed a silent prayer.

The next night, after a disastrous gala reception which the military had forced the Italian aristocrats to attend, her time came.

There was not one pleasant remark at the affair, not even a smile all night. One lady openly suggested that Elisabeth change her French tutor for an Italian one. She had conversed in French because she was unsure of her Italian.

That night, in the silence in their apartment, where their helplessness mingled with despair, Franz's eyes rested on the crackling fire. His face was dejected, his eyes unseeing. Elisabeth sat at his feet. She reached up and took his hands. She felt warmth in her heart. She felt love.

"You cannot gain respect of the people by crushing them like ants," she said softly. "You say you are the father of the people. But children grow up, and a father must change his ways to retain their respect."

She was surprised how easily her words came. His eyes were on her, still unseeing for a moment, then alight. He tightened his hands on hers.

"Give freedoms and a voice to the people? It is the last thing my mother believes in," he said. "But it is the only way. We cannot grind them into submission. We must respect them and we must gain their respect."

As the night moved into morning, they talked of the repressions, of Radetzky's military rule, they talked of the people and their hopes. Gradually, the clouds parted.

"I am the anointed ruler, chosen by God to protect his people. Whatever I do, it must be for the good of my people. I must prove this to the Italians."

He lifted her hand to his lips.

"My darling, why have I failed to see the depth of your understanding in your eyes?"

The next day, Franz began to grant clemency. Count Grünne was not consulted, only informed. Elisabeth stood beside Franz proudly as he dictated his decision. She did not once glance at Count Grünne.

Within a week, Italy was once again joyful. The people cheered in the streets as the imperial family passed by. Little Sophie's smiles were bigger than ever. They were invited to Italian aristocrats' salons and there were no complaints about Elisabeth's French. At their final gala at the renowned Fenice Theatre, every box was occupied and not a soldier was present.

Elisabeth felt her greatest happiness when a little peasant girl in a colourful dress and a bonnet upon her head presented her with a basket of wildflowers, and a card that said 'We love you' in Austrian German.

2

Waving arms and wide smiles did not welcome them back to Vienna. The royals were snarling like a pack of angry wolves over the concessions given to the whining Italians. Count Grünne's distorted stories of Elisabeth weeping on her knees, pleading with Franz to bring about what would be ruinous changes, did not help.

"Giving in to the Italian whims is degrading to the prestige of the empire," the royals growled. "And," they had to add, "it's all because of that little Bavarian country nymph."

The archduchess prowled like a caged animal, fighting her anger. She knew she had to step carefully. She saw Franz's eyes when they settled on Elisabeth, full of love and admiration. She clenched her fists. But in her apartment her fury would explode. She pounded the table with both hands. Hard. Hard. Hard. Her patience had run out. The little nymph had to be stopped.

Elisabeth walked among the tiger-like eyes and the slandering whispers holding her head high, smiling pleasantly. She clung to her pride in her achievement in Italy. No matter what the royals thought, she had calmed the cries of revolution. Her hair was gorgeous and her dresses the latest French fashions from Paris, made popular by the Empress Eugenie. She added a lilt to her voice. The eyes of the dignitaries were shining again.

But Franz had changed. Elisabeth feared Sophie's dagger had made its descent.

Elisabeth found an anonymous note beneath her apartment door: 'A good wife would do her duty to her country by producing a large flourishing family instead of getting mixed up in subversive politics.' She ripped it up and threw it in the trash, but not before an amused smile crossed her lips.

Count Grünne strutted, his demeanour superior, watching her every move. She knew something was up. He hardly left the archduchess's side. His irritation inflamed every time she was granted a friendly smile — there were a few from the lower-ranked aristocrats.

When another message came, Elisabeth wasn't happy. This time, it was on her bedside table. It was yellow with age and dated 1784 — an ancient pamphlet directed to Marie Antoinette. A portion was heavily marked.

'The destiny of a queen is to give an heir to the throne. . . . And the king said to his wife, "Madame, we look to you to give us sons and not advice." This puts the ambitious creature in her place, has taught a lesson to all. If the queen is so fortunate as to provide the state with a crown prince, this is the end of her ambition.'

Elisabeth gave a disgusted snort, then she read on.

'She should by no means meddle in the government of the Empire. If she is a foreigner she may be sent back from whence she came.'

This time Elisabeth folded the pamphlet and put it in her drawer. She didn't tell Franz about it, though she fumed with irritation. It was Sophie, she was sure.

Her anxiety crept back and Franz was a part of it. He hardly sought her out. He was almost inaccessible. The whole court saw it. Their fears were gone, their smiling faces brighter than ever and in their eyes, that silent mockery. It seemed he had taken up residency in his mother's office — that is, when he wasn't at the Burgtheater entertaining the court ladies or hunting. And there was no love. It seemed her sole duty was to provide a Habsburg heir. Franz never lay, after his brutal passion of sex, and held her in his arms. He never soothed her with affectionate words. It was as if their glorious relationship in Italy had never been.

The juice masks returned and the egg shampoos came back. Elisabeth wound her hair, hanging now to the floor, into magnificent styles that sent the royal ladies rushing to their mirrors. She even outdid the French styles. And she charmed with added skill. Over and over, she fed on her father's words, 'Our strength is nourished by the seeds of our childhood.' She was determined not to give in to Sophie, but she had a hard time finding the strength.

The visiting dignitaries smiled again and visitors sought her presence. Still, Franz sought the latest beauty and again the whispers began. This time, it was a Polish countess, more beautiful than the Italian one. Elisabeth's fortitude began to crumble and her smile was getting harder to find.

Charles Ludwig came to court for a visit. He was good fun and good-looking and kept the European courts rattling with his love affairs and scandals that appeared to be without number. He had married three times and still had a reputation as being the reveller of the Habsburgs. But love had evaded him.

When he came to court, his eyes never left Elisabeth. His affection for her still lingered and would perhaps do so forever.

They'd laugh and joke like they had so many years ago. Sometimes, he had to turn away to hide his emotions. He watched her put her hand out to bowing visitors and often wondered whether her eyes would be so sorrowful if *they* had been allowed to marry.

When Franz announced at a family dinner a state visit to Hungary, Elisabeth felt a tremor of excitement.

"The Hungarians are calling for more concessions than we granted to Italy," Franz said. "Their passions must be curbed."

He smiled, his eyes on Elisabeth. Eyebrows went up. Something was coming. Not even Sophie knew what it was. But her hands tightened.

"My dear Elisabeth," he said with a twinkle he usually reserved for flirting ladies, "your presence is necessary. The Hungarians are mad about you. You were a treasure in Italy. Perhaps with you at my side, I can gain their respect."

Elisabeth heard the archduchess gasp and took a deep, deep breath to keep from showing her emotions.

"I would be delighted to be at your side in Hungary," she smiled most charmingly. "And this time . . ."

She came forward in her chair, retaining her sweet smile, without a glance at the archduchess.

"I will take both my children."

"That is impossible," declared the archduchess.

The forks almost flew from the guests' hands. Sophie was out of her chair, marching over to Elisabeth.

"Little Sophie is ill. She cannot go," she proclaimed, her face raging red.

"The doctor has said her cough is not serious," Elisabeth's voice sailed out, wrapped in silk. She added with a musical lilt, "If the children don't go, I don't go."

Both children went to Hungary.

From the first day of her arrival, Elisabeth took Hungary to her heart.

On May 4th, 1857, they made their state entry into Budapest. Franz, in his field marshal uniform, rode a white horse. Elisabeth, dressed in the national costume with a colourful bodice and lace sleeves, rode in a glass coach with her two little girls giggling and waving.

She loved the Turkish architecture and she loved the people, their gaiety and their vitality. They dashed around in costumes so colourful that both her girls wanted a Hungarian dress. She was enchanted by the music of the gypsies and the Csárdás. She had never heard anything like it. At a ball, she could not resist flying to the floor to dance the Csárdás, especially with Julius Andrássy, the tall Hungarian whose bushy hair and elegant charm was almost as enticing as the dance. Franz couldn't dance the Csárdás. At times, Julius held her as spellbound as the music. Then the whirling strains took over and their feet flew and their laughter sailed as they looked affectionately into each other's eyes.

Then, on a day when the sun drenched the blossoms of Budapest's sycamore trees, on a day when it was least expected,

God took little Sophie. She died in her mother's arms. She returned to Vienna in a casket and Elisabeth's guilt never left her.

✦ 3

In her Hofburg Palace apartment, Elisabeth lay on her bed staring at the candles flickering in the chandelier. It was late afternoon and the room had darkened. December snow fell gently against the window and a fire crackled in the ceramic stove.

The archduchess had just left the room with the most renowned specialist from Berlin.

"She is in no condition to give birth, not in this mental state," he had muttered.

The words did not surprise Elisabeth. Her pregnancy was hardly a reality to her, nor was her life. The past few months she could hardly remember — they had disappeared in her overwhelming grief. The whole court feared for her sanity.

She remembered hovering over Sophie's casket. She couldn't bear to say goodbye. After twenty-four hours, she collapsed in fatigue.

Not a day had passed without her descent into the blackness of the crypt. Over the tomb she hovered with tears and prayers for forgiveness. She could not forgive herself for taking Sophie to Hungary, no matter what the doctor had said.

The snow flickered on the window. She moved her hand across her stomach and thought of the specialist's words. A new life moved inside her. She felt the movement. Warmth went through her body. Was this God's way of forgiving? She closed her eyes. Perhaps it was.

Elisabeth moved from her tear-drenched apartment in the Hofburg to the beauty of Schönbrunn Palace. Sophie welcomed her move and parts of the gardens were allowed for her private use, free from her palace ladies. She sat beside the ornate fountains with their statues of brook and spring nymphs, listening to the waters bubbling over the edges and down a narrow gorge. She walked through the Zoological Gardens, talking to the lions and the tigers and often reaching out to pet the lonely giraffe. Many times, she sat and read her books beneath a large sycamore tree with umbrella boughs that touched the ground, under which Maria Theresa had often sat with a box of state papers. Elisabeth became docile and submissive, giving in to her mother-in-law and the hovering doctors' every whim. She read everything, absolutely everything, and carried gypsy charms to ensure the birth of a boy.

In June, Ludovika and two of Elisabeth's sisters, Helene and Maria, came to visit. Their visits were always a highlight in Elisabeth's life. Their tongues were never still and smiles returned to her face.

Helene was engaged to the very handsome Prince of Thurn and Taxis and both were madly in love. Elisabeth thought her mother's eyes might pop with excitement.

"And Maria," her mother's voice rose excitedly, "is betrothed to Francis, the Duke of Calabria and the heir to the Kingdom of Naples and the Two Sicilies. She will be married by proxy."

Ludovika was so elated. She had captured another crown for a daughter.

Elisabeth shot forward, stunned.

"By proxy!" she cried, looking at Maria's sparkling face.

She would marry by proxy a man she had never seen. And from the rumours, Elisabeth heard he was delicate, almost feminine and perhaps feeble-minded. She was horrified.

"But she's only sixteen and she doesn't speak his language!"

Her mother stiffened.

"Not everyone has the luck to fall in love and capture a fairytale prince who is the most powerful ruler in all Europe. Or, instead of thanking God for her good fortune, to do nothing but feel sorry for herself."

Elisabeth fell back in her chair, speechless.

"But Mama," Elisabeth said, finding her voice again, "how can you say such a thing? My life is a nightmare. I'm a prisoner in a society to which I can never belong. I have no freedom. I am bound by etiquette and protocol. My days are nothing but schedules. And furthermore . . ."

Tears filled her eyes.

"I'm so lonely. I have no love. I have no friends, no real friends."

She thought of Allie, now a trapeze artist.

"I have just the gossiping palace ladies. And Franz?" She threw her hands to the air. "I don't know what love is. I hardly see my husband. Every brigadier general has a prior claim, as well as the Burgtheater and the hounds."

She didn't mention the Italian countess or the Polish countess or the cluster of young ladies.

Her mother stood up. She had her sister Sophie's tight, unforgiving face.

"I consider that you have reached the height of human happiness in becoming an empress. Just think of it, a Bavarian princess raised with peasants and with no dowry or cultured manners. It is a splendid dream. You are surrounded by every possible luxury. I cannot understand how you cannot bow to the necessities of your position."

Helene and Maria were on the edge of their seats, their faces stunned.

"People must learn to grow accustomed to their surroundings," Ludovika went on. "It gives me much pain to see you trying to pose, without any reason, as a saint and a martyr. Reflect upon it and I hope you will see that the fault must lie, in part, on your side. You know that in life we must make compromises. So do not condemn the marriage of your sister."

The sisters were astounded.

Ludovika rose and turned to her younger daughters.

"Come, my dear Néné. Maria. It has been a late night."

When the door closed on them, Elisabeth collapsed into a chair. Was her mother right? Was her despair a fault of her own? Should she be able to adapt to her situation with humble acceptance? Yes, she lived in a prestigious world. Yet it was shallow, empty, devoid of human warmth. She covered her face.

"It's like swinging on a star when a world of happiness and of love is lost in the mist," she said aloud, as if reciting a poem.

Elisabeth's baby arrived at midnight, August 21st, 1858. It was a long and difficult labour. The baby's cries echoed down the halls. Ears were saturated and soldiers standing in the halls jumped to life.

"It's a boy! It's a boy! My dearest Sisi! It's a boy!" Franz proclaimed.

"A boy . . ."

Elisabeth opened her eyes. *A boy!* She saw Franz's tears, she saw Sophie's satisfied smile, almost a smirk.

"He will be named Rudolf, after Count Rudolf, who began our great empire in 1273," Sophie announced.

Elisabeth said nothing. She could not argue. She fell back on her pillow, exhausted. The exploding guns and the chiming church bells filtered in. She heard excited voices in the halls. An heir. She closed her eyes and let the screams of the crown prince take over. She smiled softly as a warm feeling filled her heart.

Congratulations poured in from all parts of the world. Schoolchildren crafted sonnets and parents named their newborns Rudolf.

"Heaven has given us an heir," Franz, full of pride, declared to his people, "and he will find a new, greater and more elegant Vienna. The old city walls will be replaced by a broad splendid avenue that will encircle the inner city!"

The Ringstrasse was born, and Vienna began its march into the splendour of a new world.

But perfection did not reign for long before Sophie pounced again.

"As you are too young and too inexperienced to raise the heir to our great empire," the archduchess informed Elisabeth when her baby boy was two days old, "I will take full control of his education and development. Your time with him will be scheduled."

Elisabeth sprang up in her bed.

"But Madame, he is my son."

Her full breasts were in such pain she was close to screaming. She had begged to nurse her baby, but a buxom Tyrolean girl with rosy red cheeks, handpicked by the archduchess, was awarded that privilege.

"You deny me the sacred right of motherhood, one that the lowliest woman in this empire is allowed, to guide the first steps of her child."

Her anger began to spiral.

"He is not just your son," Sophie said. "He is the heir to the throne. To expose him to your liberal ideas and your unorthodox upbringing would be fatal."

Elisabeth fell back on her pillow. She was in shock. She had never felt so helpless.

"Please . . . please," she whimpered, "don't take my baby. Let him give meaning to my melancholy life."

"Do not grow morbid and sentimental," Sophie said. "You are the most privileged woman in the world. You have the finest jewels and you live in the grandest residence. And you call your life melancholy?"

She shook her finger. "You have played the role of victim far too long. One gets weary of watching such a performance from the luckiest of all human beings."

With that, she picked up her skirts and marched out.

Franz did not oppose his mother. The nursery was again beside the apartment of the archduchess. Elisabeth's daughter Gisela was moved there too.

"The children should not be parted," Sophie informed her.

No one sympathized with Elisabeth.

The royals were ecstatic. "She is unfit to bring up her children." They walked about with satisfied sneers.

Elisabeth's visits to the nursery were strictly scheduled. They became her greatest bliss. She saw his first smile, his first steps, and he called her 'Mama'. When the nurse would take him, saying "Your time is up, Your Majesty," Elisabeth could hardly let him go. Often, he would cry, clinging to her, and Elisabeth would bury her face in his body to hide her sobs.

The distress this caused her, was really taking its toll.

Autumn came. She was back in her apartment, loneliness again her constant companion. She tried to fight despair, but anything good in her life was hard to find.

Franz had again taken up residence in his office, attended the Burgtheater or was out hunting. She hardly saw him. When she complained to him of her boredom and her loneliness, his aide brought his written reply: 'My poor darling Sisi, how happy I would be just to spend one hour in your company. But here I am, tied to my desk, literally snowed under with paper.'

She knew the situation in France and Italy was again accelerating; there was a threat of war. Yet he never shared anything with her. The gossip was also accelerating — it was not of the war.

The palace ladies were whispering and giggling with renewed excitement. Franz was eyeing a dancer from the theatre, so they heard. When Elisabeth tried playfully to question him, he laughed.

"Gossip is the court's entertainment. It adds a bubble to their champagne."

But her anxiety did not go away, nor her heartbreak. She broke down to the Countess Levy one day.

"If my husband is unfaithful, my love would go, for marriage is to me a bond for life."

Countess Levy sat with her hands in her lap, contemplating her reply. No one in Vienna sympathized with Elisabeth. There was nothing wrong with Franz's romantic endeavours. Romantic adventures in royal marriages were normal. Everyone knew that. Even the archduchess had told Elisabeth, "Take on a lover of your own."

However, if she did that, Elisabeth knew her fate would be sealed. Never again would she be a threat.

Sophie did make attempts to put young dashing men in her path. Elisabeth was never persuaded.

"Everyone knows Franz's heart belongs to you," Countess Levy said gently. "But love affairs in royal marriages are common for men, and wives accept their husbands' affairs without complaint. They are repaid by the exalted position they occupy by the virtue of their marriage."

"I did not marry for an exalted position," Elisabeth countered. "I married for love. If Franz destroys our bond of marriage, my respect and my love will be destroyed."

Countess Levy's eyes went to the ceiling. How naïve could Elisabeth be? Half the women in Vienna had slept in his arms. Yet, she felt sorry for her and knew that no one else in Vienna did.

4

Elisabeth's sister Maria arrived in January, a stopover on her journey to Naples. She had been married by proxy to Francis, the Crown Prince of the Two Sicilies. She was now the Duchess of Calabria.

Maria dazzled everyone, from the frozen-faced sentries who lined the halls of the Hofburg Palace to the Archduchess Sophie, who raved about her beauty. She was eighteen, jubilant, with the innocence of youth quenching her fears. Franz followed her with enchanted eyes. He often remarked that she was Elisabeth all over again.

Around her neck, Maria wore a ribbon with the picture of the groom encased in diamonds. Elisabeth was hard put to find a favourable comment.

The sisters chattered and rode horses though the royal grounds. Elisabeth couldn't bury her concerns. She tried tactfully to prepare Maria for the disillusionment that might await her, but her warnings fell on the deaf ears of innocent youth. All she could do was pray.

Elisabeth accompanied Maria to Trieste, where the Neapolitan royal yacht waited to take Maria to Naples. The ceremony was like a medieval play. A ribbon stretched across the reception hall of the government's palace to symbolize the border between Bavaria and Naples. A large table had two legs in the Bavarian section and two legs in the Naples section. Maria was seated on the Bavarian side. Trumpets blared and bowing dignitaries escorted her to the Naples chair. There, the Naples dignitaries were presented to her. More trumpets blared, hands clapped as she was escorted to the royal yacht.

Elisabeth clung to the railing of the dock, watching her sister sail away. Maria was now the Crown Princess of Naples. She sailed on the royal yacht amid strangers, whose language she hardly understood. The only living creature to console her was her canary, Hansi. Elisabeth looked up at the azure sky.

What a tangled-up world this is. Love has lost all meaning.

Italy did not remain peaceful. War again threatened. The Austrians were enforcing more regulations. Elisabeth was concerned, yet Franz would not discuss it with her. Sophie saw to that.

Piedmont's President Cavour, sympathizing with the Italian desire for unification, vowed his assistance.

"I will help you drive every Austrian out of Lombardy. It will be the beginning of a new Italy."

In April 1859, Austrian troops marched into Piedmont. The archduchess insisted Cavour was dangerous and must be crushed. The war in Italy began, and it became an infamous disaster for the Habsburg Empire.

Austria was not prepared for such a war. Supplies to the troops were poorly organized, medical aid was hardly available, communication was vague and Austrian bodies filled the ditches. Franz insisted on going to the front lines. Sophie stormed in protest. Elisabeth shuddered in fear.

"We must save Italy!" Franz proclaimed. "And I must be at the side of my troops."

On the morning of June 14, Franz led his troops into battle in Solferino.

"Follow me, my brave men!" he ordered. "I, too, have a wife and children."

It was his final hope of retaining Lombardy.

The morning was sunny, hot and humid. The armies — one hundred and twenty thousand men, forty thousand horses and seven hundred guns — lined a fifteen-mile front.

That afternoon, the war ended. By two o'clock, what remained of the Austrian troops had fled in defeat to the Solferino hills. The dead and wounded lay in the fields among the sprouting corn.

The Austrians saw fourteen thousand men killed or wounded and more than eight thousand missing or taken prisoner; the Franco-Piedmontese saw fifteen thousand killed or wounded and more than two thousand missing or taken prisoner.

As if it was God's revenge against man's horrific passion for war, a violent storm swept in. A tornado swept up billowing clouds of dust. There was thunder, there was lightning. Then sheets of rain came with hail, blotting out the field of the dead and the wounded.

When the storm swept away, a brilliant sun replaced it, and the sky was again azure. Twenty-nine thousand men lay dead or wounded. They lay in the fields for days without help. Thousands died of hunger, of disease, of exhaustion. The peasants returned to their ravished farmlands. They buried the dead and burned the horses. It took eight days.

Lombardy, Austria's most important territory in Italy, was lost.

That evening, Franz wrote: 'It was the most tragic day of my life. I have learned what it feels like to be a defeated general.'

He returned to Vienna a dejected man. He found himself cringing with humiliation before his mother, before his wife, before his people, before all of Europe. But more so before his troops.

A young heartbroken man named Henri Dunant also looked for solace. He walked helplessly among the dead and wounded. Those heartbreaking moments nourished his vision and brought into existence the Red Cross.

The Austrian populace was unforgiving. Their cries filled the air. They blamed Franz Joseph for the horrific deaths of their sons, their brothers, their husbands and their fathers, who had given their lives for a country they considered foreign. They screamed, "It is all for greed. The emperor puts the interests of the dynasty before the interests of his people." They called for his abdication. Many refused to remove their hats when Franz passed by.

The world viewed the Austrians as aggressors. A European newspaper wrote: 'The courageous Austrians were beaten, not by the French and Italians but by the overbearing imbecility of their own emperor.'

Franz crawled deeper into dejection, fleeing Vienna for the solitude of Laxenburg Palace. Sophie barred herself inside her apartment. Elisabeth begged to be at Franz's side in this time of need.

"We can ride together. We can talk."

In spite of her good intentions, he turned away.

"I must have the solitude and the escape," he told her.

In the quiet of the shaded trails, he searched for answers and for the strength to walk proudly again as leader of his people.

Elisabeth remained in the Hofburg, disappointed and hurt, but not crushed. The horror of the war had opened her eyes and she looked beyond her own personal struggle. The empire had to be saved. Her son stood on the threshold. She devoured the foreign newspapers, still illegal in the empire, and visions of the outside world began to mould her thoughts.

She walked through the cobblestone streets of Vienna and sat in the parks, her identity hidden. She talked to the people, she listened to them. She heard their fears, she saw their dejection and she sensed their helplessness. For the first time, she understood the messages on the pamphlets that had flown about on her wedding day: 'We hope you will be our salvation.'

Her sympathy grew and her views deepened. She thought of Italy. Could she help bring the change they needed in the empire? She watched the tiny clouds flying across the sky. She thought of Archduchess Sophie, who would always be a barrier to her son. He must have an empire to rule. But answers didn't come. She felt strongly that the only way to save the empire was to let the people stand up and be heard.

Franz returned to Vienna. His faith was restored, his mind made up. He put his errors aside. He was at the helm, the father of the people, chosen by God. They must respect him as a child respects his father. This was the Habsburg creed that had kept the empire under Habsburg control for generations. His mother was right — power was the only way to preserve the empire.

Sophie came quickly to his side. They locked themselves in his office for hours. Elisabeth was never included. This did not stop her.

One morning, she intercepted Franz as he hurried to his office door.

"Franz," she pleaded, "I can help you with the people. I have talked to them and I have listened to them. Please listen to me."

He stopped. He looked into her eyes. He let her hands linger in his for a moment. Then, without a word, he dropped them, pushed past her and walked swiftly into his office. She heard him greet his mother as the door closed behind him.

The bulging eyes of the staff hung on her like starving dogs. She kept her poise and walked out. She was angry and bit her lip so hard it brought tears.

Her anger grew. Elisabeth became more determined than ever. She'd try again — another day.

The next time, she marched into Franz's office, ignoring the footman's frantic orders that the emperor was not to be disturbed. The archduchess had just left and no one else waited to see him.

Franz hardly raised his eyes from his papers. His welcome barely slipped through tight lips. She took a chair; he didn't offer it to her. She didn't hold anything back. Her feelings for the people and her suggestions flowed out. She spoke of their frustration and their unhappiness. She spoke of their needs. She spoke of change. She didn't give him a chance to stop her, neither did he look up, nor did a word come from his lips.

When she'd spoken her piece, Elisabeth waited for his response. She waited and she waited until her patience gave out and she exploded. She was out of her chair and around to his side. She wanted to gather all his papers and hurl them to the ceiling. His fingers were tapping, his mouth tight. Still, his eyes remained on his papers.

"You listen to your mother as if she were God. But she is destroying the empire. All of Europe, even your own people know Cavour tricked your mother into starting that terrible war. It made you appear the aggressor. And still you believe her decisions are infallible. You close your eyes to all other reason. All you have to do is listen to your people, hear their desperation and realize there must be change or the rest of the world will leave us behind."

She was shaking. Still he said nothing. He did not look at her. She turned, fled to the door and yanked it open. Then she stopped and turned back.

"And furthermore, do you still think she knows best how to raise Rudolf? She is old. She is old-fashioned. Don't you see that?"

She collapsed in angry tears. Franz's eyes remained on his papers. Elisabeth crumbled into her agony. She wanted her children back desperately.

"Please, Franz," she begged.

She let the door go. She moved back to his desk, still in tears.

"Please give my children back to me. Please let me be a larger part of their lives."

Franz looked up. He rose from his chair. His voice was as cemented as his face.

"You are not ready, my dear Sisi, to have Rudolf returned to your care."

He walked around his desk and, taking her arm, propelled her out the door.

"Goodnight," he bowed, adding, "And please, Sisi, stay out of politics."

5

When November snows draped Vienna in a blanket of white, carnival time brought a world of make-believe.

It was a time of celebration. The young and the old tossed aside their woes, their unpaid bills, their prejudices, their inhibitions, their unhappy love affairs. They drowned their woes in champagne and Pilsner beer and flung themselves into the exhilarating world of make-believe. Even the disasters of the war sailed from their minds. Fiddlers sawed out music on the streets. One thousand orchestras warmed up their instruments and Strauss waltzes and minuets floated through the salons and the ballrooms, down the streets and through the alleys.

It was also a time when gossip rose to ecstatic levels, mingling with the liveliest of the musical strains. Who was dancing with whom and whose face was hidden beneath the masks at the many masquerade balls?

These balls were the most exciting and intriguing. The gentlemen had no idea who they whirled around the dance floor. Was she a peasant girl or a royal lady? Ladies found partners that excited their dull lives. It could be a country girl who practised her elocution as she cleaned the royal stables, but on carnival nights, she could whirl across the dancefloors in the arms of an elegant gentleman plying her ears with enticing fantasies. There were ladies who covered their ugly faces and used a silky voice to capture a glimmer on a young man's face.

That year, the gossip had an extra-syrupy spin. A mysterious lady was in town. Fran Roll made her first appearance at the Royal Imperial Theater, the most elite theatre in town. Nothing was known about her except that she came from the provinces. She had no claim to fame, but her charm and her ravishing beauty held everyone spellbound.

She attended the Royal Ball at the Hofburg. Not a drop of royal blood flowed through her veins and the royals cemented in shock but not for long. Their curiosity feathered into excitement. Who was she? Everyone was in a frenzy to dissect the mystery. The rollicking dancers spinning in the hundreds of balls rumbling throughout Vienna were tripping over each other to catch the latest flying whispers. Even the rats were scampering with an extra lilt into their hovels.

Of course, it didn't take long. Everyone knew. It was just more fun prolonging the suspense.

And it was no surprise.

She was another of Madame Mère's protégés. Poor distressed Franz needed more gaiety and more congenial company — and what better than a beautiful lady?

Back to the ballroom floors he came, dancing Fran Roll around and around. His eyes flashed and his grin was wide. Politics and war were smothered by his joy.

Elisabeth searched for new facial wraps and enticing hairstyles, tried her most alluring smiles. No one noticed. They watched her fidgeting distress, her expressions, her desperate eyes. And dancing bodies continued to tumble and trip as their whispers and smirks flew like gusting winds. The archduchess has done it this time, they said. Franz was totally captured.

On top of all this, Elisabeth received news from Naples. A year had passed since Maria's marriage. The old King Ferdinand had died, Francis had taken the throne and Maria was now the Queen of Naples. Sadly, love had not found its way into her life.

Her timid husband knew what was expected, but found it impossible to do and spent most nights on his knees in prayer.

Now disaster threatened. The Sardinian Garibaldi, dedicated to the full freedom of Italy, threatened to invade Sicily. Maria was terrified. Everyone they could depend upon had fled and their Swiss guards had mutinied. Maria begged her sister for Austria's help.

Elisabeth dropped the letter. Terror took over. Her beloved sister could die at the hands of ruffians.

Her mother's desperate letter lay beside it, her final words being: 'Entrance Franz with all your charms. We need Austria's help to save your sister.' Elisabeth jumped from her chair.

"What charms do I have?" she asked herself.

Her feet were almost tripping over themselves as she paced the room.

"Not only am I barred from politics, every beautiful woman in court brings a brighter gleam to Franz's eyes than I."

She picked up Maria's letter. Helplessness invaded her, desperate helplessness.

"How can I help Maria?" she cried.

Her tears did not solve her desperation.

Two nights later, Franz raced into her room. His smile covered his face, but she knew he hadn't come for love — Fran Roll was still in town. He took her hands.

"I have a surprise," he said, "come to Bad Ischl with me. It will bring a shine back to your life. We will take little Gisela as well."

Affection showed on his face and his manners seemed genuine. Still, suspicion swelled.

She went to Bad Ischl and her biggest hope went with her. Perhaps this could be her opportunity to gain Franz's help for Maria. Gisela bounced from window to window as the carriage rolled along the road to Bad Ischl. Franz was jovial, with big smiles, laughing at Gisela's exuberance and watching excitedly out the window as well.

Franz dropped smiles on Elisabeth but there was no real affection. He never reached out and took her hand. He stared out the window as if he was searching for something. Her uncertainty was present. She did not mention Maria.

The carriage bounced over the bridge and into Bad Ischl. Flowers and streamers were everywhere. *Is it for us?* Elisabeth wondered. Then she saw the portraits. They hung from the balconies and they filled the store windows.

"That's Fran Roll," she said in a bare whisper, looking at Franz.

He didn't hide his excitement.

His eyes beamed like glittering candles.

"The season is closed, and she is here for her holidays."

"Papa," Gisela asked, "whose pictures are those?"

"A famous actress and she is here in Bad Ischl," Franz said.

"Oh, Mama," Gisela smiled, "she is beautiful, like you."

Elisabeth walked the garden paths with Gisela. They sat on the riverbank and watched the swirling patterns on the waters. They searched for tiny fish. They shopped in the stores, which Gisela loved. And she raved about the pictures. Elisabeth didn't utter a word.

Franz they saw mainly at dinner. Elisabeth never asked him what he did with his time. She never questioned where he went after dinner. She knew. She wanted to claw out his eyes and shout out the venom that roared within her, but Maria was in her mind and she put aside her bitterness. She needed his help for Maria.

Over coffee one evening, she made an attempt. She gathered her charm, wrapped her best smiles in it and kept her voice calm, even as he checked his watch with a jockey's passion and downed his coffee in quick gulps.

"I need your help for Maria," Elisabeth said.

The last drop of coffee went down in a gulp. He rolled the coffee cup in his hand, slowly, pensively. He was clearly uncomfortable with what he had to say. He looked up at her.

"Sisi, I do not have money to send them, and I cannot send troops. And furthermore," he took a deep breath, "all Europe shuns us for our invasion of Lombardy. I cannot risk another Italian adventure. I cannot send help to Maria."

He rose from his seat and grabbed his jacket. She stood up and looked him in the eye. Her smile was gone, her charm was gone. Her words were a command.

"Then I give you a choice. Either Fran Roll leaves Bad Ischl in twenty-four hours or I go . . . forever."

Fran Roll left the next day, though not very far. For the first time, Elisabeth's thoughts of leaving her husband came closer to reality.

6

On their return to Vienna from Bad Ischl, more bad news awaited Elisabeth. Garibaldi had marched into Naples — he would unite all Italy, the Kingdom of Naples would be no more. Elisabeth's hands trembled as she read the report from the Austrian minister in Naples: 'Maria and Francis were forced to seek refuge in the Fortress of Gaeta. There is virtually no one left on whom they can depend but, still, the eighteen-year-old queen is determined to defend her crown. And, my lady, all Europe marvels at her bravery. Garibaldi cried out, in spite of his victory, "She is a woman on whom praise must stand."'

Elisabeth flung the letter across the table. *My sister Maria,* she thought, *struggles with a small army to defend the Fortress of Gaeta. The whole world praises her courage and her bravery, yet no one comes to her aid.*

Franz fled to Mürzzuschlag with a group of boisterous gentlemen to hunt pheasants and ducks. The only comfort he'd given Elisabeth was "I will be with you tonight."

She'd nodded, but with little confidence.

Franz did not return that night, nor did he return the second night when the shooting party returned. Excuses were vague — he would remain another day at Mürzzuschlag. At least, Elisabeth thought, Fran Roll was not at the lodge.

She hid her frustrations, as she always did, in her impending duties. The afternoon tea in her apartment for the court ladies was, on that first day, tedious and boring. Gossip was at a low ebb. Even Fran Roll's allure was wearing off.

That Franz hadn't returned with the other hunters on the second night roused curiosity. The ladies' fans fluttered faster, every eye watching Elisabeth to see her reaction. Elisabeth hid her stress, something she was good at now. She smiled and chattered as if in the best of spirits. Inside, her anger boiled like an unleashed geyser. When Countess Katra raced into the tea party, eyes popping and face flushed, Elisabeth knew there was trouble.

Newly married, it hadn't taken Katra long to pry from her husband, who had just returned from the hunting lodge, a choice piece of scandal. Of course, she'd promised him she would not breathe a word, but it was just too exciting to keep it a secret.

It was not weariness nor illness that delayed the young emperor. It was the pursuit of a buxom peasant girl who danced to the zithers, straining every muscle in her beautiful body.

Eyes goggled, fans flew and every word, including the stifled squeals, reached Elisabeth's ears. The ladies made sure of that.

Elisabeth's face paled, but still she retained her composure. Neither her chatter nor her fan betrayed her true feelings. But her anger had reached its limit. She had to get rid of the ladies before she exploded and treated them to the show for which they were frothing.

With grace and dignity, amazed at her own composure, Elisabeth caught the ladies attention.

"Please excuse me, ladies, but I must cut my reception short this evening as I am very tired."

She extended her hand for farewell kisses. It didn't tremble, nor did her smile. The ladies reluctantly left, pouting indignantly.

When the door closed on the last pair of goggling eyes, Elisabeth collapsed in a chair. This was the end.

"Matti, come!" she screamed to her old nurse, whom she had brought from Possi.

Matti came flying in.

"Fill a travelling bag with the necessities. We are leaving."

"Are we going for long?" asked the nurse, shocked.

"Perhaps forever."

"Oh, Miss Lisabeth . . . ," she said, tears in her eyes.

"Go! Do as I tell you!" Elisabeth screamed, stamping her foot. Matti was out the door.

Elisabeth fell back in her chair, covering her face. She knew how the tongues would wag in the court. It would be just what they expected. The little country nymph was running away. It would be the most satisfying piece of gossip they would have had in a long time.

She sat up straight. She dropped her hands to her lap, clutching them tightly. Yes, she was running away before she was totally destroyed, before they sucked out every bit of strength she had. She knew she had to find answers. But where? She had no idea.

Within an hour, they were out of the Hofburg Palace in a carriage heading for the Südbahnhof, the southern railway station, where they boarded the first train leaving for Trieste on the Adriatic coast. No one recognized them.

The next morning, the archduchess received the news. The empress had not spent the night in her apartment. Countess Katra's scandalous stories were exposed. Sophie threw up her hands.

"The little Bavarian goose, will she never learn?"

Of course, Franz was not to blame.

It did not take Sophie long to discover Elisabeth's plan. The royal yacht was moored in Trieste. Sophie sent a telegram to Trieste to stop Elisabeth's departure. The yacht must not be put to sea. She dispatched to Trieste a special train carrying an envoy.

Elisabeth and Matti boarded the yacht the next day. Elisabeth was momentarily suspicious when the captain did not seem surprised to see her. He led them graciously to a sumptuous stateroom.

"Your Majesty," he said, "there is a slight breakdown in the engine room. We cannot sail until tomorrow."

Elisabeth was too exhausted to care and sleep came with no effort.

She awoke the next morning with the captain knocking on her door.

"My lady, an official from Vienna has arrived. He wishes a word with you."

Elisabeth rolled over on her back and stared at the ceiling. It hadn't taken the archduchess long to track her down.

The envoy was a pleasant man with gentle eyes, short and hunched over. In a soothing voice, he pointed out the wicked scandal that would fall upon her if she fled with no explanation.

"They will blame you. You must consider your children. How will they view you in years to come? Come back," he told her, "and defend your actions. It is the only way for you to gain respect."

Elisabeth stared out the window. The morning sun shone on the gentle water. She saw seagulls flying and swooping, chasing each other, calling to each other. She knew he was right. She cared not what the Viennese thought, nor the archduchess. It was her children that mattered. They were too young to understand. She must assure them of her love.

In her Hofburg apartment, Elisabeth sat with her hands tight in her lap. She listened to Franz's pleas.

He knelt before her, on his knees, begging with tears, his voice shaking, asking for her forgiveness. He confessed his love for her. He promised like a guilty child never to be unfaithful again. He even declared that he would brave his mother's anger and reproach her for the harshness and the injustice she had inflicted upon her.

But Elisabeth's heart remained cold and unmoved. She saw his weakness, his cowardice, his shallowness. She saw a man with no imagination, no depth. She saw a man whose values were justified only by his heritage and who knew not what love was. But she knew with certainty that her love for him was gone forever.

She refused to see the archduchess.

She took her children into her arms and assured them of her love. Their tears mingled, their hearts entwined.

Excuses were provided to the people. The empress was ill. She must find rest in a warmer climate. A yacht was arranged through Queen Victoria of England.

On November 17th, 1860, Elisabeth boarded the royal sailing yacht in Antwerp for the 2,700-kilometre voyage to Madeira. She took her old nanny, two ladies, a doctor, numerous domestic staff and her two dogs, Derry and Sita, who shared her life more than did her husband.

As the yacht pulled out, she sat alone on the deck, watching the land disappear and listening to the waves splashing against the sides of the ship. She watched the seagulls swooping with goodnight calls. There was a full moon. She thought of her children. She dropped her head and let her tears flow.

From her purse, she pulled a letter from her mother. She read the words again: 'My dear child, there are two types of women, those who achieve what they want and those who never do. You, I am afraid, belong to the second category. You are very intelligent, you are contemplative and you don't lack character, but you are too uncompromising. You don't know how to live or make allowances for the ways of modern life. You belong to another age, the time of saints and martyrs. Don't give yourself the airs of a saint or break your heart in agonizing to be a martyr.'

Elisabeth dropped the letter onto her lap and stared out at the sea. A light spray touched her face. Her mother had given her life for her children. She'd had moments of regret that she had never worn a crown and that love had deserted her. Although she succumbed to her grievances, her mother had found solace within herself.

Should we succumb to our grievances, accept them as patterns of our life, Elisabeth wondered, *or can we rise above them, be our own person and search for a better way?*

She looked out at the sea. She saw the horizon. It was shrouded in mist. There was nothing beyond.

Part 2
Love and Tragedy
1860–1898

The Search

1

It was a twelve-day crossing to the island of Madeira, in one of the worst Atlantic storms in years. Rain hammered down and wild winds hurled the yacht about. The *Victoria and Albert I*, provided by Queen Victoria, rolled and pitched as if demons manned its helm.

Elisabeth's ladies huddled in their beds with blankets over their heads, clinging to their rosaries, regretting the day they set foot on the ship. Her doctor couldn't stand up, her cook was too sick to prepare her meals and her dogs howled endlessly in their kennels. Elisabeth, however, was in ecstasy being wrapped in nature.

She stood beside the captain on the bridge, clinging to the steel rails and struggling to keep her tottering feet on the floor. Her eyes blazed with excitement.

"It's beautiful!" she kept repeating.

The captain, struggling to keep the ship afloat, wished she would stop nattering and disappear into her cabin like her ladies before she toppled and hit her head, making him responsible for a royal injury. But her excitement only grew.

"I must go outside on the deck!" she announced.

The captain almost dropped his hands from the wheel as the ship rolled into a crashing wave.

"Your Majesty, that is impossible!" he shouted.

Their feet almost went out from beneath them.

"I insist," she said. "And I am the empress. Tie me to a seat on the outside deck. Please. Please. I beg you!"

He had no choice, and visions of the end of his career flared in his mind. His first lieutenant took the wheel. The ship rocked and the twosome could barely make it to the door. The roaring sea almost ruptured their eardrums when they managed to push the door open. The winds almost took the hair from their scalps.

"My lady, this is too dangerous!" he tried again.

Her only reaction was a beaming face.

The captain managed to get Elisabeth into a chair, almost crashing across the deck in the process. When he had tied the last knot that secured her and tucked the blanket around her shoulders, he stepped back and balanced himself by holding on to the deck rail. He gasped. She rested her head against the back of the chair, her eyes closed; her face showed contentedness. The sea spray touched it and she sighed in ecstasy.

The sun sparkled in a cloudless sky when the royal yacht anchored in the tiny harbour of Funchal on the island of Madeira. The seas were calm, tropical flowers bloomed everywhere and colourful birds with unfamiliar songs circled in the air.

"It's like stepping from a winter night into summer!" Elisabeth exclaimed, racing down the ramp.

Her ladies struggled to follow, after twelve days at sea their legs having forgotten how to walk. The Madeirenses were there to greet her with smiles and flowers.

When Elisabeth saw her charming villa, she cried out happily. It was perched on the edge of black volcanic cliffs. She jumped from the carriage as excited as a child at Christmas. She ran through the gardens and onto the terraces that hung on rocky ledges high above the sea.

"Look at the sea birds nesting in the crevasse!" she pointed out, turning to her ladies. "It's paradise!"

They weren't convinced. Already they missed Vienna. And what kind of gossip would they find here?

Elisabeth's days were hours of discovery. She walked on the cliffs, breathing in the sea air. She sat on her balcony listening to the songbirds and to the waves lapping at the rocks. She devoured her books as never before: Dante, Shakespeare, Byron, Keats and Heinrich Heine, her father's favourite and also hers. She shared their thoughts on the incurable misery of human fate with its tragic enigma of suffering and death and agreed more and more with their views about the problems of society and social class. Their awareness of the sacred rights of the individual resonated with her deeply. When she thought of the people trapped in her own empire, she closed her books and looked out at the sea. The world she came from was the epitome of all she read.

Still, the future remained unclear. There were no answers and she could not see where her path might lead. She missed her children desperately — when she thought of them, her tears flowed. She wanted to hug them and hug them some more.

A telegram with news of her sister Maria brought mixed emotions: 'Maria gallantly fought Garibaldi's invading forces, but no help came from other countries. On February 13th, 1861, the Bourbon flag flew no longer. Francis and Maria boarded a French frigate and fled to Rome where they would take up residence in the Palazzo Farnese.'

Elisabeth set the telegram down and sighed with relief. At least Maria was safe. But tragically, at only nineteen, she was a queen without a country, married to an impotent husband and doomed to spend the rest of her life in homeless exile. What an imperfect world.

Elisabeth watched the sun slip below the horizon and the sky turn a misty orange. She listened to the waters lapping the shore.

She picked up her mother's latest letter: 'The greater one's social position, the less one has the right to give way to one's grievances and neglect one's boring obligations.'

Again, Elisabeth thought of Maria. She had fought to the end with strength and determination. She had not run away. A soft breeze touched Elisabeth's face. Hands held tightly together, she gazed out at the sea.

In April 1861, she boarded the British royal yacht to begin the return journey to Vienna. Confused and fearful, her path uncertain, she prayed to have Maria's strength.

Spring was the only warmth to greet her in Vienna. The sun burst in the sky, the tulips bloomed and clusters of blossoms hung on the sycamore trees.

Franz was happy to have her back, or so he said. Yet the flirtatious eyes of the young ladies still caught his attention. His passion for her awoke only at her apartment door when he attempted to take her into his arms. But she wasn't ready, and she doubted that she would ever be.

Nothing in the Viennese court had changed. The stiff-faced royals milled around the salons with unwelcoming eyes shadowed with disguised contempt. The palace ladies didn't waste a moment drawing her attention to the latest beauty in court. Count Grünne, who usually ignored her, was quick to point out a ravishing young lady with a Hungarian accent who was capturing Franz's attention.

"It's Elisabeth, his cousin from Hungary," he said with a twisted smile that was as irritating as his sharp, high-pitched voice. "Perhaps you did not know that at one time their love was the talk of the court. She had hopes of being an empress."

Elisabeth's eyebrows went up in surprise. No. She did not know about her namesake.

Franz's cousin Elisabeth was tall with an elegant figure. She was dressed in the very latest French fashion and had dark curls that fell magnificently down her back. She was hardly docile — she laughed with the boisterous lilt of the Hungarians and her eyes sparkled as flirtatiously as her smiles. When the fiddlers started up the Csárdás, she took Franz's hand and pulled him to the floor and he tried it once more.

Not a royal moved to the floor. They thought the dance vulgar. Not Sisi — her feet were tapping, her body swaying. She thought of pulling Grünne to the floor until he leaned in slyly,

"The archduchess would not tolerate a Hungarian empress. But the whole court knew Franz was in love with his cousin."

And probably still is, Elisabeth thought, watching Franz devour his cousin with his eyes and smiles and hold her very close when the music slowed, burrowing his face in her hair.

Elisabeth gave Grünne a nonchalant sniff. She turned and walked away, not allowing him the satisfaction of seeing her reaction. She moved through the crowds, smiling and chattering as best she could. As the dance music ascended, the dancers whirled and laughed, but it faded from her ears. She moved about, smiling but feeling as if she were standing alone on the sands of the desert.

That night in her bed, sleep lost its way. Despondency was again creeping in. She realized her children were her only salvation. She had to gain back their control and wrap her life within them. They were shy with her and resisted her embraces. She understood. She had deserted them. She had to regain their trust to regain their love. As for Franz, she had to convince him to stand up to his mother, even if it meant opening her bedroom door.

The next afternoon in Franz's office, her heart beat hopefully. She could not have looked more beautiful. Her hair hung loose around her face, giving her a gentle look. Her silky mauve gown showed her slim neck and the roundness of her body — it was a new style from Italy. She had prayed his mother would not be there, but she was. Elisabeth hoped her determination would hold.

Franz rose from his chair and greeted her with a surprised smile, complimenting her on how lovely she looked. She saw a familiar glint in his eyes and she flashed her sweetest smile. The archduchess clenched her jaw. She suspected something. Franz took Elisabeth's arm and guided her to a chair. Then both of them eyed her impatiently, especially Sophie, whose fingers tapped her chair, as they often did whenever Elisabeth was present.

Elisabeth smiled.

"I am sorry," she said, "to impose upon your time. I know your problems are urgent."

Sophie's fingers tapped faster.

"I have a wish," Elisabeth continued, "that is very close to my heart."

Sophie's eyes went to the ceiling.

"Don't we all?"

Elisabeth took a deeper breath, more determined than ever, and clenched her fists tightly. She hoped Sophie could not see that she was shaking.

"In Madeira, I had time to contemplate my problems. I have matured. I have put my life into perspective and I am ready for responsibility. In fact, I need responsibility."

Elisabeth's voice shook. Sophie saw her fear and her satisfaction swelled. Her fingers stopped tapping. Franz's eyes went back to his papers.

"As you have requested, I do not participate in politics. But my children . . ."

She waited until Franz looked up.

"I wish to have the care and education of my children in my hands. I have spoken to Count Joseph Latour, in whom I have great faith. He would be my guide."

Latour had long been a friend to the royal family.

The archduchess was out of her chair in a flash. She marched over to Elisabeth like an animal ready to pounce on its prey.

"You have no idea what you are asking. Your head is obviously as empty as ever. Why, you abandoned your children for months."

She was trembling with anger.

"Rudolf and Gisela are my children," she continued. "I will never surrender my mission of nurturing and educating them. Providence has entrusted that to me."

Elisabeth was stunned.

"That is a terrible insult," she raged, flying from her seat, almost knocking down the older woman. "They are *my children* and I will have them."

She turned to Franz. He was up, moving towards them.

"She hates me," Elisabeth screamed to Franz. "She wants to destroy our marriage. If you love me, Franz, I beg you to listen to me. Give me back my children."

Franz's face was drawn, his fists clenched. Weighed down by years of his mother's authoritarianism and advice, he could not succumb to the emotional cries of his wife, no matter how much he loved her. And he *did* love her. He wanted to hold her and soothe her and kiss away the tears.

"Sisi," he said instead, "my mother is right. The children must remain under her authority. Please try to understand."

He reached out to her. She pushed him back.

"Understand what?" she screamed. "That I am not capable of raising my children? Is that what you think?"

"Please, Sisi."

But the answer was in his eyes.

With a scream, Elisabeth turned and fled to the door. She pulled it open, almost toppling the footman who had his ear pressed against it. She turned back and looked at Franz.

She wanted to scream again. In fact, she wanted to claw out his eyes, and Sophie's as well. Instead, she took a deep breath and, somehow, her voice came out controlled.

"The court refers to your mother as the empress. Not only has she robbed me of my position, she has robbed me of your affection and that of my children. And you . . . you say you love me and yet you never stand up for what I want. You never attempt to put an end to the gossip that flies through this court."

Her face tightened, her eyes narrowed.

"There can be only one empress in this court. I cannot remain as long as your mother insists on taking my place. I am leaving. My return will depend upon you."

In 1861, shortly after Elisabeth return from Madeira, the court doctor announced that a galloping consumption was plaguing the Empress and that she must recover on the island of Corfu.

2

The beauty of Corfu and its soothing waters wrapped her in a world of unreality. Her palace was surrounded by gardens that sloped down cliffs into the sea. Elisabeth sat on her balcony overlooking the Ionian Sea, reading her books and gazing out at the sea, her dogs snoring at her feet.

She immersed herself in Corfu's ancient past, exploring the ruins of the once-fabulous kingdom of the magnanimous Alcinous and the maiden Nausicaa, of whom Homer wrote, 'She is akin to the immortals by her grace and her beauty.'

Homer's *Iliad* and *The Odyssey* were her favourite stories as she tried to lose her sorrow and find understanding through the mythical gods and goddesses. Many stories, such as the one of Adonis, conceived by the union of Cinyras, King of Cyprus, and his daughter, brought a smile to her lips. He was so handsome, his name was used as a metaphor for youthful male beauty. Aphrodite, the goddess of love, fell in love with him, as did Persephone, queen of the underworld. Zeus decreed that Adonis spend part of the year with each of them. The seasons of spring and fall were born from his imagination. *If only life were that simple*, she thought.

When Elisabeth closed her books, the silence was so loud that she seemed alone on Earth. She missed her children, missed them desperately. She missed their bouncing bodies, their hugs and their kisses. Tears slipped down her cheeks when Gisela's sobbing words came back to her: "Mommy, don't go!"

Letters came from Franz begging her to return. Letters came from her mother, urging her to find her common sense before her world was lost. Her latest letter drowned Elisabeth in despair: 'You are an intrinsic part of a great nation's honour. You are faithless to the trust and to the tradition of your ancestry when you thus act on the power of personal injury and passion.'

She gazed out at the sea. How little she had known of life when Franz swept her off her feet. Love was a romantic illusion. She had been a child of fifteen, stolen from paradise and imprisoned in a world to which she could never belong. Yet her mother was right and Franz was right. In this imperfect world, one must learn how to adapt. She closed her eyes. But how?

Franz said he loved her, he would guide her through their problems. But he never took her hand in sympathy, made no attempt to understand her turmoil. Perhaps he didn't know how. He lived a life of strict routine — love could never stand in the way of that.

His passion for sex never satisfied, his intrigues and affairs — though he said they meant nothing — had broken all her trust and destroyed her innocent perception of love and marriage. Yet in the eyes of all, she was the weak one, the one at fault. They never saw the other side of the coin. She rose, went to the edge of the balcony and looked out.

"I cannot keep running away," she whispered into the darkness. "I must take control of the realities of my life and adapt to them."

She thought of her father. Max hated the frivolousness and the insincerity of their aristocratic society, but he did not run away. He lived among them in a manner that gave him pride and satisfaction.

The moon sank into the sea, the breeze still warm. She was her father's daughter. Again she asked herself: Did she have his strength?

The last rays of the moon sifted into darkness and the ripples on the water settled into sleep. Still, her thoughts were hardly soothed. Accomplishment and pride do not come from running away. This time, she said the words out loud.

"They come from strength and determination."

Again, she thought of her father. She could do it too.

As sure as the sun would come up every day, there would be no love awaiting her. Franz would always succumb to other feminine charms. There would always be flirtatious women who turned his head with their attractiveness — and no doubt his head would always turn.

The archduchess had replaced her in the lives of her children.

My destiny has been chosen, Elisabeth thought. *Still, I must be true to myself. Only then can I walk with pride.*

"Vienna, here I come!" she promised. "Like my father, I will live by my own terms and in my own way."

She closed her eyes and uttered a silent prayer: *May I have the courage of my father and the determination of my sister.*

The waves lapped gently against the rocks, soothing her.

But fears still lingered.

Return — 1862

1

Vases of flowers and a warm fire in the ivory stove eased the tension in Elisabeth as she greeted Franz in her Hofburg Palace apartments.

Franz stood motionless at the door, staring at her. Then tears flooded his eyes. He crossed the floor, dropped on his knees, bent his head over her hand and kissed it gently. His lips were trembling, as was the slim hand he held.

"May God keep you with me," he murmured.

She sat motionless for a moment. Then, with the tenderness of a mother, she laid her other hand on his head.

"We both have much to forgive."

There was no hint of warmth in the welcome of the Viennese royals. They turned their noses sky high and scoffed, "She is nothing but a childish empress racing about the world on every whim."

The citizens of Vienna, however, welcomed her back joyously, with open arms. They formed a twilight procession, marching into the courtyard, chanting, "Elisabeth. Elisabeth. Our beautiful empress! Welcome. Welcome back!" She waved to them from the palace balcony and, beside her, Franz beamed with pride.

Her eyes glowed on seeing their radiant faces, on hearing their exhilarating cries. "Our beautiful, beautiful empress!"

That night in the quietness of her room, with her excitement still high, her mother's words came flying back: "Use your beauty as your power."

Elisabeth paced around the room. What better way to fortify herself? Her eyes shone and her smile widened into a playful grin. This time, she would really challenge the Empress Eugenie.

Her beauty became like a cult and her mirror became the focal point of her life.

The diets returned, juice and lean meat, and her five-foot-seven-inch figure developed into a solid 110 pounds. Her tiny waist sent her palace ladies into paroxysms of envy. They starved on diets, bought new corsets and tightened them until their faces turned white. But not one waist shrunk to Elisabeth's 19½ inches.

"Just stop eating," she smiled at them.

Her maid, Astera, rubbed her face with nightly masks of raw veal with warm olive oil to maintain the softness of her skin and to prevent new lines. During the appropriate season, she added a dash of strawberries. Her soft skin radiated the gentleness of her face. Damp towels covered her hips and legs to maintain their slenderness as she slept the night away. Her hair became her crowning glory. Now it fell to her heels, a dark chestnut with auburn streaks. From the Burgtheater, she snatched the most famous hairdresser in Vienna, Fanny Angerer. Hours and hours it took, shampooing and brushing, then skillfully winding her mass of hair into artful styles that turned the court's eyes into saucers and Franz into a dazzle of smiles. Cognac was added to the dressing for a sweet smell.

When she replaced the ornate furniture in her apartment with gymnastic equipment, swings and bars so she could work out daily, the royals were aghast. No one but no one had ever heard of a woman on exercise bars, let alone an empress in a gym outfit with no gloves.

The servants cast aside their reservations and fear of Madame Mère's reprisals, and rushed to please Elisabeth, smiling and bowing respectfully. Sophie paraded around with a face so grim that Elisabeth's playful smiles were mixed with a little concern. She knew Sophie would not give up and she steeled herself, clinging to her sister's willpower and her father's strength.

Her niece, Countess Marie Larisch, who loved scandal and gossip even more than her palace ladies did, said to her with laughter, "Your beauty is an all-consuming passionate love. You worship your beauty like a heathen worships his idols."

She didn't explain to Countess Larisch that her beauty was the power that fortified her way of life. She would only turn away and smile.

In fact, her beauty was an all-consuming burden. Every moment of every day, from the time she left her bedroom until she returned to bed at night, she was on view. And the reactions were mixed. The ladies of the court, still bitterly determined to trample and humiliate, dissected her figure, her skin, her attire, her jewellery, her hair, looking for flaws. Elisabeth didn't miss the resentment triggering their false smiles. She found them amusing. Their whispers stayed behind their fans. They wondered, spitefully, how a Bavarian country nymph had become a world-famous beauty.

Elisabeth forged ahead on her new path. Her confidence was growing. Even Franz looked at her with appreciative eyes. She tossed aside the rule of nobility that said an empress must be at all times accompanied by an appropriate attendant. She walked unattended through the palace grounds and into the woods. There she lost herself in the solitude.

Sophie slammed her shutters whenever she saw her.

Elisabeth chose which court receptions to attend. The royal whispers became fearful. Was the archduchess losing her power? "Could Elisabeth become the strongest in court?" they wondered, their fans sailing into higher speed. "If Franz gives in to her whims, it will be a disaster for our empire."

The Spanish Riding School in Vienna became her favourite place. Her riding skills became the talk of Vienna. The horsemen watched her with admiration. It was as if she had a natural instinct. Horses responded to her as if she were a part of them. She thought herself a better rider than Franz and so did many others.

When she rode in the Prater, often without a groom, the people flocked to the curbs calling her name and throwing flowers. Her smiles and her waves captured their affection. The royal court wondered how many more rules she would break before Franz stepped in.

And what had happened to Archduchess Sophie?

When Elisabeth began socializing only with the Hungarian nobility, the Viennese royals gulped more wine and waved their fans in contempt. She had truly lost her wits. The Hungarians were far below even the rank of the Viennese aristocrats — not a drop of blue blood ran through their veins.

For Elisabeth, the Hungarians were an intoxicating escape. She loved their boisterous laughter, their charming affection and their fun-loving nature. She loved their lavish buffets and the music and dancing that raced through their palace salons. Furthermore, they were magnificent horsemen. Elisabeth was challenged by their riding feats and she delighted in the approval she saw on their faces when she performed.

Elisabeth ignited eye-popping shock when she appeared at a royal court opera wearing a magnificent gold-embroidered headpiece worn by the wives of the Hungarian Magyars.

The archduchess's angry disgust sent her from her seat, striding out the door. The doormen were almost trampled by the entourage of indignant royals and aristocrats who followed her. The opera house was left nearly empty.

Elisabeth sat back and enjoyed the music with an amused smile that almost turned into a chuckle.

With her father's courage intact, she took her biggest step. She dismissed Countess Esterházy. The countess's condescending rebukes had tormented Elisabeth from the day she arrived in court. The countess's face went beet red with rage, but Elisabeth stared into her eyes with charm and dignity. She replaced her as her chatelaine with a Hungarian, the Countess Königsegg.

She didn't consult Franz, she informed him. It did bring his eyes up from his papers. She didn't consult Madame Mère at all.

For the first time, the Vienna court went into silent shock. Even their fans dropped to their laps and wine stayed in the bottles.

When they regained their voices, their anger exploded like a volley. "This is a threat to our position, and it is a threat to the established principles of the empire." Fans vibrated so fast, it was like a cyclone racing through the salons. "Not only is this countess a Hungarian, but in her new rank as chatelaine, she is the privileged head of the empress's household. And," their anger still rising, "she is not entitled to that position, for she does not have one drop of royal blood. She is merely a countess by marriage. And now she has precedence over all the ladies of the land, including the highest royal nobility."

Now they were sure the archduchess was losing her power. What was going to happen to their empire?

Elisabeth's beauty became the talk of Europe. Dignitaries, ambassadors and foreign visitors came in droves. Their bows were gracious, their smiles wide, their eyes bright, sometimes with tears, when she extended her hand to them.

A dignitary wrote: 'The empress is . . . beautifully formed with . . . gentle eyes, very red lips, a sweet smile, a low musical voice, and a manner partly timid, partly gracious.'

Another wrote: 'The beauty of the empress draws many people to court who would otherwise stay away.'

Franz beamed at her side. The ladies with the swishing fans and the coquettish eyes searched for a new prey and the deer and the hare had a break longer than they'd ever had before. And Madame Mère? It was as if she had left the planet.

When the Shah of Persia arrived in Vienna with his colourful entourage of soothsayers, astrologers, forty gelded rams, six dogs, four gazelles, horses with pink manes and his harem of 190 women, he begged for an audience with the empress. He had a snooty air of condescending superiority towards women, though he never left his harem behind. He could not believe a woman's beauty could create such effect throughout Europe. Of course, he thought, European men were too easily distracted by the feminine charm. What they needed was a harem.

The shah, with his turned-up nose and a superior air, marched in to meet the empress. He took out his golden eyeglasses and eyed her from the top of her stylish hairdo to the tips of the shoes that showed from beneath her gown. His face turned red. His hand began to tremble.

"She is beautiful."

It was a hoarse whisper. He stood paralyzed. Then he dropped to his knees. When Elisabeth smiled and put her hand out for his kiss, he almost toppled to the floor.

During his allotted one-hour audience, he could hardly put a sentence together. He remained as red-faced and bashful as a lovesick schoolboy. Elisabeth smiled sweetly, struggling to keep her amusement in check.

He told her, as he bowed his way out, their visit was the highlight of his European tour. She hid her chuckle and told him sweetly that he too was charming.

But love is not mine, she thought that evening, alone in her room. *Though men are lavish with their devotion and Franz lies beside me exhausted from the passion of sex, I am empty.* She opened her bedroom door to Franz only when his passion could no longer be contained. *I lie beside him like a frozen corpse, for my love for him is gone. I feel only contempt.* These thoughts came many nights as she watched the flickering shadows of the fire dance across the ceiling. She allowed her sadness to slide deeper. *A royal marriage is an absurd institution. As a child of fifteen, I was sold. I was then made to take vows which I did not understand and from which I have never been able to free myself. I am walking my path, but I am so lonely.*

2

Elisabeth engaged Ida Ferenczy, a country girl from the lowlands of Hungary, not nobility, for the prestigious position of reader to the empress. She gave her the title 'Frau von Ferenczy.' The Viennese court was shocked and suspicious.

"She is a spy," they whispered, "for Hungary. And for that villain Julius Andrássy." They were sure of that. Andrássy had escaped the hangman's rope in the 1848 Hungarian rebellion, after actively pressing for Hungary's independence from Austria.

Ida hardly looked like a spy. She was tiny and docile with a warm gentleness that, at times, mellowed the royal venom. She walked with a limp, one leg shorter than the other. This embarrassed her. It always showed whenever she walked into a reception. Elisabeth told her it was her sweet smile and her blue eyes that captured people's affection.

To Elisabeth, Ida became a lovable and trusted companion, something she had craved from the first day of her marriage. Her Hungarian became almost as good as her German and her fascination for Hungary grew from Ida's love for her country and her fascinating stories.

For Ida, it was a step into a society whose doors would normally have been closed to her. She had never been inside a palace, let alone lived in one. She couldn't believe the gilded ceilings, the paintings, the mirrors, the winding staircases and her adorable bedroom. In her small country home, she had shared a bedroom half the size with her four sisters. A young man she left behind vowed to wait forever for her return. He knew she had a mission. The horrors of the Hungarian uprising had never left her mind.

She had been forced to stand in Budapest Square and watch the thirteen Hungarian generals condemned to hang following the revolution. As each man stood up to have the noose slipped around his neck, he shook the hand of the man behind him in line. The last man had no live hand to shake, so he shook the hand of the last dead man. The last man had been her uncle.

It was several years since the revolution had ended, but the Hungarian people were still beneath the boot of the Austrian Empire. Julius Andrássy had become Ida's hope. He had a plan, a wonderful plan, for more freedom for Hungary from Austria. Not by war, but by peaceful means. Such a tragedy as the revolution they could never risk again. They needed Elisabeth.

With Andrássy's encouragement, Ida hoped to capture Elisabeth's sympathies by making her aware of Hungary's plight. They hoped Elisabeth could influence Franz to act, in spite of the opposition of the archduchess, who hated the Hungarians and rejected any idea of autonomy for them.

Elisabeth knew little of the 1848 Hungarian uprising, and Ida fed her curiosity. She began to understand the sadness in her long-ago tutor's eyes when he had spoken of Hungary.

Franz always changed the subject of Hungary's oppression whenever she brought it up.

Ida told her of the desecration of the Hungarian lands and villages by the Austrian and Russian invaders. She told of men who had their eyes dug out, their noses and ears cut off and were then burned to death.

"The invaders stripped the women and young girls," she told Elisabeth, "and raped them in the village squares and in the streets of Budapest. Then they cut off their breasts and beat the women to death."

Elisabeth covered her face. Such cruelty she could not imagine. Her sympathy for the Hungarian people grew.

"The Hungarian people have never condemned Franz Joseph," Ida said. "He is not responsible. He was only eighteen and just put on the throne, with no experience."

Ida didn't tell her that Franz Joseph was now their hope. That had to wait.

Elisabeth never asked who they blamed. She did not have to. She knew.

When Ida told stories of Julius Andrássy, Elisabeth couldn't help smiling. Ida's eyes glowed. He was certainly her cherished hero.

"And what is Julius Andrássy like?" Elisabeth asked.

She had met him only briefly during her wedding ceremonies, but she had danced with him during her visit to Hungary. She knew a little about him. And she liked what she knew.

"He has a mop of dark curly hair and a rugged face with a beard, trim and adorable. And oh, he is charming."

Ida's smile danced across her face.

"You should see the ladies' excitement when he is in the room," she cooed. "They can't keep their eyes off him. When he escaped the Austrian gallows and fled to Europe, the Parisian ladies nicknamed him *le beau pendu*, 'the handsome hanged man,' in exile."

They both laughed.

"In Hungary," Ida added affectionately, "we call him 'the saviour of our country.' He, and only he, can restore Hungary's historic rights."

"Look at your face," Elisabeth grinned.

Ida was blushing.

"You worship him. He sounds like a romantic hero who has stepped from a gothic novel."

"He is that. And more," Ida said softly.

Elisabeth's smile broadened. She could hardly wait to see Julius Andrássy again.

In November 1862, Elisabeth received an urgent letter from her sister Maria to come at once to the Ursuline Convent at Augsburg. There was no explanation. It had been a year since Maria had fled to Rome, a queen without a country. Now what? Elisabeth was concerned.

"Oh, I have caused such a scandal for our family," Maria wailed, embracing Elisabeth when she arrived.

Maria quickly pulled her into a sparsely furnished room with stone walls. A fire burned in a hearth.

"Papa has fled to Africa," Maria continued. "And poor Mama is wondering how she will ever find a suitable husband for dear sixteen-year-old Sophie, with her elder sisters' antics spinning out of control."

"What have you done?" Elisabeth implored.

"I am about to give birth to an illegitimate child."

Elisabeth gasped. She looked at her sister's body for a moment, then she held her silently.

"I fell in love with a handsome Belgian count," Maria sobbed on Elisabeth's shoulder.

She pushed Elisabeth back, smiling through her tears.

"It was wonderful. I had never been so happy. Our love bloomed like the Roman spring. We rode our horses across the great Italian plains, we walked through the woods, we listened to rippling streams and we found love. And all the while, my sanctimonious husband knelt in his private chapel, surrounded by cardinals, confessing his anguish and his imaginary sins."

She smiled cynically. She walked about the room. She stopped and looked at Elisabeth. Her tears were gone, her courage back. Her voice held no despair, just determination.

"My lover will take our baby. He will raise it. I will never see it. In our world, there can be no other way. Our family cannot be destroyed by scandal."

The pain showed on her face. Elisabeth turned away, thinking she might burst into tears. How does one give up a baby?

Maria collapsed into her chair, her face calm in spite of her tears. She ran her hand gently around her protruding stomach.

"He gave me love. He brought me happiness beyond my wildest dreams. This life inside me swells with our love and with memories that I will have forever. I have no regrets, even though I must give up the child."

Church bells chimed outside.

Two days later, the baby arrived. Maria turned quickly to the wall.

"Please take it, Sisi. Take it right away. I cannot look at it or I could never give it up."

Elisabeth carried the tiny red-faced bundle, wrapped in a white blanket, into the next room. She put it into the arms of a tall young man who waited. They stared at each other, their pain reflected in their eyes. Tears fell down their cheeks. Then, clasping the baby tightly to his chest, the young man turned and fled from the convent.

Elisabeth returned home. When her apartment door closed that night, there was only the ticking clock and the flickering fire. She thought of Maria. She envied her. She knew her pain would never leave her, but she had found love. Though it might pass from her life, it would never leave her heart.

That night, like so many other nights, she soaked her pillow with tears.

It was a time of stress in the royal court. All Europe was in the turmoil of change. Family dynasties were falling into the hands of more powerful countries and the powerful Otto von Bismarck would become the new chancellor of a united Germany. With Lombardy free from Austrian control, he was determined to restore all the German lands the Habsburgs had acquired through generations. His threats echoed throughout Europe: "At the earliest opportunity, I intend to make war on Austria."

The Austrians prepared for the worst. Franz searched desperately for solutions and Elisabeth prayed the empire would be saved for Rudolf.

In the midst of this chaos, Franz's youngest brother, Maximilian, and his wife, Charlotte, arrived in court with dreams of glory. It was the last thing Franz needed.

Max was a gentle man, tall with dark wavy hair. He had the charm of an ancient chivalrous knight. He sympathized with the oppressed, he wanted more freedoms for the people and his liberal ideas had drawn Elisabeth to his side in full agreement.

Franz knew that Max was his mother's favourite. His other brother, Charles Ludwig, had fled the family, although he had never forgotten Elisabeth. Though Sophie often disagreed with Max, she could not resist his charm and Franz struggled with a jealousy that was never far from the surface.

Max had found a mission: he was going to Mexico. His excitement made the royal family, gathered in Red Room of the Hofburg Palace, both curious and fearful.

"Emperor Napoleon is determined to restore French influence and uphold the Catholic religion in Mexico," Max exclaimed.

Elisabeth had never seen him so excited. Charlotte was almost jumping from her chair.

"He sent French troops to overthrow the powerful Benito Juárez and establish a Mexican Empire," Max beamed. "Mexico will be ruled by Catholics. He has offered me the imperial crown." He took a deep breath, smiling proudly. "Charlotte and I will rule as Emperor and Empress of Mexico."

He was ecstatic.

"Oh my God," Sophie shrieked. "You must be crazy. This is a pipe dream. You cannot trust the French. And furthermore, do the Mexican people want a foreigner as their emperor?"

Elisabeth could not hide her concern.

"How can you give up your fairytale Miramare Castle to rule over a country of savages?" she demanded.

Charlotte sprang from her chair. She marched over to Elisabeth, her hands on her hips.

"I will then be an empress like you," she announced.

She had long concealed her resentment, but now it exploded. Elisabeth, a poor Bavarian princess, was an empress while she, the daughter of the King of Belgium, was a mere archduchess.

"I will have a crown on my head. Already, I have made up the lists of my palace ladies and established the order of the court ceremonies. I have waited a long time for this."

Sophie fled to her apartment and slammed her door. Franz wished Max luck. He was glad to see him go. He knew the Austrian people sympathised with his liberal views and so he might have been a threat to his rule.

In April 1864, in the town of Trieste, they said goodbye. Max and Charlotte boarded the Austrian freighter that would take them to Vera Cruz. Archduchess Sophie sobbed uncontrollably. Elisabeth actually felt sympathy for her.

Max waved from the ship's ramp, but his face was grave. Charlotte waved so excitedly that even the sailors smiled.

Sophie broke from the crowd. She rushed up the gangplank and threw her arms around her son. She knew she would never see him again.

Back in Vienna, all thoughts were on Bismarck. Franz embedded himself in his office with his mother. Elisabeth turned to her horses and prayed Bismarck would disappear. The people downed their Pilsner beer in larger proportions. In the coffee houses, the billiard balls clicked rapidly and the future was pondered with grave anxiety.

Bismarck did not occupy Elisabeth's mind for long.

Baroness von Welden, her children's nanny, burst into her apartment one day with desperate cries.

"They are separating Rudolf from Gisela and moving him into his own apartment."

It was the day after Rudolf's sixth birthday.

"We cannot permit this," the baroness said. "They need each other. They are not exposed to other children."

Her words pierced Elisabeth's heart. She turned away and nodded sadly.

"It is the Habsburg custom. When the heir reaches six, he must have an all-male household with a tutor who ensures strict military training."

"But his tutor, Count Leopold Gondrecourt, is too strict and too brutal in his tactics."

Elisabeth knew this also. Stress covered the nanny's face.

"I went to the emperor," the baroness continued. "I begged him not to allow that man to be in charge of the young prince. 'Rudolf is too delicate,' I told him. 'He is not a soldier. He is an intellectual. Books are his passion.'"

Elisabeth nodded. She knew this, too. Gisela, with her cluster of curls, sparkling eyes and tiny red mouth that was always chatting was of average intelligence. She loved dancing and parading around in pretty dresses. Elisabeth plied her with smiles, often saying, "I think you will be a ballerina." Rudolf, on the other hand, was remarkably brilliant yet very sensitive. He needed love and affection. The brutal training of a soldier was not for him — at least, not this early in his life.

"And what did Franz say?" she asked, struggling to keep her voice steady.

"That his intellectual achievements were a cause for worry," the baroness replied. "That he was further developed mentally than the average child his age. His mental development must be subdued so his body can keep pace."

Again the nanny broke down. She could hardly find her voice, it shook so.

"He said," she finally continued, "he had ordered Gondrecourt to drill him hard and make a good soldier out of him. And Madame, he is only six years old."

Elisabeth stared out the window. The freezing rain poured down. She couldn't hold back her anxiety. Franz wanted a physically strong son who would love soldiering, but Rudolf was not that. He was gentle and sensitive, far more like a Wittelsbach than a Habsburg. Franz was determined to change that.

"You must help, my lady, for Rudolf's sake. He is much too timid and afraid to complain to his father. The children cannot be separated. They need each other. And little Rudolf needs affection, not soldiering."

Elisabeth's face showed her concern. The power of her beauty had brought Franz to her side and enhanced her position in court, so she lived her life more contentedly. Still, the control of her children remained beyond her reach. They were lost to her beneath the thumb of the archduchess. Rudolf was the heir to rule the empire and she, his mother, had no say in his life. She was helpless.

She took the distraught nanny's hands.

"I will do what I can."

Her voice broke. Her tears came. The women clung to each other. It looked hopeless.

Elisabeth tried. Franz turned a deaf ear. Sophie passed her by with her chin in the air. She could do nothing.

Gondrecourt carried out the emperor's instructions in his own way. Rudolf was drilled to a point of exhaustion with military exercises and physical and psychological toughening.

Baroness von Welden recounted, to Elisabeth's terror, how Rudolf's tutor instructed him in heroism. He was locked in his bedroom while Gondrecourt fired bullets through the windows. He was shut in the game preserve, unprotected, with a wild boar coming, and left to defend himself. He was only six years old.

Elisabeth's anxiety accelerated every time she saw him. He became almost a permanent invalid with fevers, nervous anxiety and stomachaches. Count Joseph Latour, Gondrecourt's subordinate, came to Elisabeth with concern. He had not dared to approach the emperor, for he knew Gondrecourt was carrying out his orders. After his visit, Elisabeth hardly left her apartment. Not even the visiting diplomats brought her out, just her horses. She raced them across the plains like a woman gone mad.

On a winter morning, before dawn had cleared the skies, shouts and screams brought Elisabeth quickly from her bed. She ripped open the shutters. Snow and ice pellets pounded the window.

She gasped in horror.

A blizzard raged, the cobblestones were white, but there was little Rudolf, shivering and terrified, cringing under the bellowing of Gondrecourt, drilling the seven-year-old boy in the blinding snow.

Her room was still dark. She hurried to her desk. Her hand shook when she lit the candles. Picking up her pen in stony-faced anger, she wrote the ultimatum. Not a tear dropped. Her helplessness was gone. Determination was its heir.

She sped down the dark halls. The sentry's eyes blinked from sleepy lids. She did not stop for the attendant's announcement, she charged into Franz's office. It was only six o'clock, but she knew he would be there with his head in his papers.

He jumped to his feet.

"Good morning . . ."

His smile was quickly replaced by a perplexed expression. She plunked her ultimatum on his desk.

"Either Gondrecourt goes or I go."

She didn't wait to hear his reaction. She whirled around and stormed from the room.

Franz picked up the ultimatum.

'I wish to have reserved to me absolute authority in all matters concerning the children, of the people around them, the place of their residence, the complete supervision of their education, in a word, everything is left entirely to me to decide, until the moment of their majority. I further wish that as to my personal affairs, such as the choice of people around me, the place of my residence, all arrangements in the houses etc., be reserved to me alone to decide. Elisabeth — 1865.'

Elisabeth's wish was granted.

The archduchess slammed her door so hard the sentry dropped his gun.

Elisabeth took charge of Rudolf's education. Count Latour became his new tutor while Gondrecourt returned to the military. Within weeks, Rudolf regained his health.

The royals were aghast and threw up their hands. Their worst fears had become a reality — Elisabeth was now the stronger one. . . .

Her beauty had fortified her strength. Her strength and resolution would be the tools that saved the great Habsburg Empire from collapse . . . and love would come into her life.

Julius Andrássy

1

Elisabeth fell in love with the gallant, courageous hero. Tales of his amorous adventures and heroic deeds not only entranced all Hungary, they flooded the salons of Europe and England. It was January 1866. Elisabeth was twenty-eight and at the height of her beauty. Julius Andrássy was forty-two.

He was a man with a vision, dedicated to bringing his beloved Hungary out from beneath the Habsburg heel, to regaining its independence and restoring its unwritten thousand-year-old constitution. To Elisabeth's life he brought new meaning and purpose and a love that would never leave her.

As a general in the 1848–49 Hungarian revolution, Julius had led the dedicated Hungarians into a hopeless and bloody conflict with Austria and Russia. Elisabeth knew from her companion, Ida Ferenczy, that he had been captured and condemned to death for high treason but had escaped the gallows and fled to Europe. The executioner had nailed his name to the gallows.

His charisma and his dashing good looks, especially his dark flashing eyes, kept the hearts of royal court ladies throughout Europe and England in a constant flutter.

He spoke several languages, including Hungarian, French, German and English, and he used his diplomatic skills to attract powerful European men to his cause. He was invited into the most prestigious homes, where he filled their ears with the plight of the Hungarian people to gain their sympathy, respect and help.

When he was finally pardoned, Julius Andrássy returned to Budapest. He found a submissive and disillusioned populace and his dedication was cemented.

"A nation oppressed is not a nation destroyed!" he had shouted to the people. "Spirit and hope can be buried, but they never die."

He'd then promised that Hungary's goals would be achieved peacefully with Austria, not by revolution. The people had raised their heads in hope — he became their saviour.

He and Ferencz Deák, a liberal lawyer who shared his passion, formulated a plan that would benefit both countries. Hungary needed Austria for economic reasons. They created a plan for an Austrian-Hungarian dual monarchy where both nations would be united for a common good while preserving each one's independence. To convince the archduchess, who saw power as the only way to keep control, would be impossible. They had to reach and convince Franz Joseph.

With Bismarck emerging as a threatening force determined to free the German lands from the Habsburg Empire, Andrássy hoped their time had come. Hungary was Austria's largest and most profitable possession. He knew Austria could not afford to lose it.

"We must stand up now and make our voices heard," he exclaimed to Deák. "The empire is roiling in fear. With Bismarck pounding at their gates, the last thing the Austrians want is revolt in Hungary. And we do not want war with Austria. We must put forth our ideas. Negotiation is the only way."

Deák stared across his desk at the determined face. He agreed, negotiation was the only way. However, with the stranglehold of the archduchess, it would be like banging their heads against a stone wall.

"It is a pipe dream," Deák said, looking down. "If the emperor ever considered a dual monarchy, the archduchess would rip him apart limb by limb."

"There is a way to reach the emperor," Julius smiled.

Deák stared at him.

"Oh, really? And what is that?"

"A fair angel. Our victory might come on the wings of an angel, the beautiful empress."

Julius's fascination for her had never left him. He knew everything about her.

"You must be joking!" Deák shouted, "Why, the archduchess has that childlike empress under her thumb and the emperor jumps like a scared rabbit to his mother's orders."

"Ah, you are behind the times," Julius laughed. "Our little friend Ida has succeeded very well in providing me with information about the Viennese court, and especially about the empress." He smiled. "I'm also well-informed about the marital relations of the royal couple."

Deák's eyebrows shot up.

"What does the royal bedroom have to do with this?" he asked.

Julius laughed.

"It seems you have not heard, Ferencz. Your childlike empress has lately emerged powerful in her own right. Her beauty dazzles the world and her growing influence in court has sent the Austrian royals into fits. They are afraid their gold-plated privileges are threatened." Julius chuckled. "And rumours fly that Elisabeth is the strongest in the court. The emperor gives in to all her wishes."

Deák rolled his eyes. It sounded improbable. He looked dubious.

"Elisabeth," Julius continued, "is fascinated with Ida's Hungarian stories and she sympathizes fully with our situation. And," he smiled broadly, "she has an ardent — and I mean ardent — dislike of our anti-Hungarian archduchess. You see, my friend, our success might lie with her. I truly think she will rise to our challenge, overstep the archduchess and convince the emperor."

Deák threw his hands into the air.

"This sounds even more like a pipe dream."

"Never underestimate the charms of a beautiful woman," Julius laughed.

Deák snorted under his breath.

"Julius is certainly one gentleman who would know that," he told himself.

It was a cold, snowy day in January 1866, but that didn't prevent the excitement racing through the halls of the Hofburg. The Hungarians had arrived! They created a gypsy-like ambiance with their tribal costumes and their boisterous laughter. The sentries at the door felt the excitement, servants scurried around smiling and even the royals, especially the ladies, couldn't hide their amusement. Though their noses were tilted skyward, you could almost hear their hearts beating.

The Hungarians came to give belated birthday wishes to Elisabeth, to gain her affection and to beg her to visit Hungary. Their hearts beat with hope — but not Ferencz Deák's. He still thought it was a pipe dream.

Filled with Ida's stories, Elisabeth could hardly wait to see Andrássy again. The Hungarians had begged for a private audience with her. Ida hadn't told her, but from her glowing face, Elisabeth was sure Julius Andrássy would be there.

Elisabeth swirled in front of her mirror in the Hungarian national costume, a white silk dress with a black bodice, trimmed in diamonds and pearls and set off by an apron shimmering in rainbow colours. Over her small diamond crown she carefully placed a Hungarian bonnet.

"Do you like it?" she asked Ida.

"I love it."

Ida gave her a hug and Elisabeth was gone. Ida stood with mournful eyes. Oh, how she wanted to go with her, just to see Julius Andrássy.

Sitting gracefully on a throne in the Red Salon, Elisabeth waited with her Hungarian ladies. She couldn't sit still — her feet were tapping, her heart was beating fast. The huge doors swung open and the show began.

In their native Magyar costumes of gold and red, the Hungarians made a theatrical entrance with sweeping bows, wide smiles and glowing salutations. Elisabeth's amusement almost turned into giggles. She wanted to jump from her chair and join hands with them.

A tall man stepped forward. He was broad-shouldered with a head of bushy dark hair, a trim beard cradling his face. He was so dashingly amusing in the gold-embroidered ceremonial dress of a Magyar nobleman, golden spurs on his boots and a lion's skin flung over his shoulder, Elisabeth almost laughed out loud. Then she recognized him. She caught her breath and she smiled, her broad smile matching his.

He bowed. His eyes, mischievous in amusement, drew her into their depth.

"I am Count Julius Andrássy, vice president of the Hungarian Chamber of Deputies."

She put her hand into his. It was warm, firm, but gentle. Her heart burned with love from that moment on.

It was an afternoon of greetings, smiles and chatter. And no eyes lingered longer together than Elisabeth's and Julius's.

Dress after dress flew from Elisabeth's closet. What to wear that night at the gala dinner?

"This is the perfect one," Ida announced, holding a white gown with a low neck. "The flattering lines will show off your tiny waist."

"Of course it is the right one."

Elisabeth held the dress and whirled around with it.

"Oh, Ida. What would I do without you?"

Not even with her sisters did she share such intimacy and trust.

Ida smiled.

"And tonight," she said enviously, "you dine with our gallant hero."

"Julius Andrássy," Elisabeth nodded.

She stopped her whirling. She knew Ida's admiration for Andrássy and wished she was coming with her.

"Oh, Ida. He is charming and his voice, so deep and melodic. No wonder all the ladies are crazy about him, even though he looks more like a gypsy than an aristocrat." Seeing Ida's face, she added, "I think you are a little in love with him yourself."

"And who isn't in love with him?" Ida laughed. More seriously, she added, "He's not only charming and witty, attractive with his gypsy-like aura, he is also as clever as a cage full of monkeys. He has made Europe aware of our sufferings in Hungary." She smiled. "Yes, he is as vain as a prima donna, he loves his Casanova image, and I know that in Austria many regard him as a villain who should have died on the gallows. But in Hungary he is our hero."

Elisabeth took her hands.

"My dear Ida, you have brought to me a world hidden from my eyes. You have nurtured my love and my hopes for your country."

That evening, Elisabeth sat beside Franz, poised and elegant. Her hair hung long in a tangle of pearls to the middle of her back. Her face glowed. She basked in smiles and admiring eyes. Julius Andrássy's eyes seemed never to leave her. She had to struggle to pull hers away.

Hungarian voices and booming laughter rang through the dining salon. Servants with shining smiles raced, and good humour even softened the stern faces of the Viennese elite. Most feminine eyes glistened. Franz was smiling more than usual, but still a little hesitant. The archduchess was not present.

Julius Andrássy rose and proposed a toast to Elisabeth. His eyes gathered her in. With a low, virile voice, he spoke of the Hungarians' unbounded love for her and their loyalty. He hoped, as all Hungarians hoped, that he would one day welcome her return to their capital of Budapest.

She lowered her eyes, gathering her breath. At first she couldn't move. Then she rose.

Not a glass moved. Not an eyelash flickered. She looked into Andrássy's eyes. Then she turned to all and spoke in a soft voice, in perfect Magyar.

"There is no wish dearer to me than to return to your country," she said.

The room sat momentarily spellbound. Then, like a bursting volley, their voices exploded.

"Elien Erzsebet! Elien Erzsebet!" *Long live Elisabeth!*

After dinner, the royal couple moved about, conversing with everyone, Elisabeth in hesitant Magyar, Franz Joseph only in German. He could not master the Magyar language and, by the Hungarian reaction, he knew they were not at all pleased that their emperor could not even speak their language.

Elisabeth moved to Julius Andrássy. She reached out her hand to him. He accepted it tightly, his composure momentarily distracted by its delicate slimness.

"I walk in the shadows of your dreams," she said.

She let her hand lie in his, enjoying its masculine strength.

"I hope," she smiled, "one day to hear them from your lips."

"I have a plan . . ."

Franz was quickly at her side, his face pensive. He grasped her arm to move her on. Elisabeth felt his tension, but she held back and whispered something to Julius. Then she moved forward with her husband. Her smile was contained, but her heart sang. The dark corridors of her life had caught rays of sunlight. A new meaning had moved into her life.

Ferencz Deák came to his side.

"I see you have exhibited your usual charm, Julius. The empress is enchanted by you. What did she whisper in your ear?"

Andrássy smiled.

"She said, 'When the emperor's affairs go wrong in Italy, it pains me. When they go wrong in Hungary, it is death to me.'"

2

Bismarck continued to stomp like a wild boar vying for female favours. The German states were in a state of high anxiety — not all wanted to break from Austria. The Austrians were wondering if Bismarck really would go to war against them, as he threatened. Still, Elisabeth and Franz went to Hungary.

Elisabeth insisted.

The archduchess's anxiety was refuelling. But it wasn't due to Bismarck. It was Elisabeth she didn't trust. Elisabeth and Julius Andrássy both, especially with the disturbing whispers. No one could miss the attraction between Elisabeth and Andrássy. With Franz teetering under Elisabeth's thumb, he could be per-suaded to grant concessions to Hungary which Sophie did not want. She paced about her room praying that Franz would keep his head.

"We are not giving in to those wild Hungarians!" she declared.

Elisabeth fell in love with Hungary. There were receptions and balls with a gaiety unseen in Vienna. She felt free as a bird tossing aside all protocol, shaking hands with everyone and dancing the wild Csárdás with none other than Julius Andrássy.

In Vienna, the Hofburg walls began to rattle with shocking stories and Sophie's nails went deeper into her clenched fists. Was Franz still in control?

Elisabeth did share Julius's hopes with Franz. She did let Franz know her hopes for the Hungarians. He had listened, but she was not sure if she had succeeded in convincing him of the changes needed.

On their final night, Franz addressed the Hungarian National Diet. His mind was made up: his mother was right. The total control of power must remain in Austria or Hungary could go the way of Italy. The Hungarians waited, excited and hopeful, but anxious.

Before he rose, Franz leaned in to whisper to Elisabeth.

"Continue to charm the people, my beloved Sisi. That is your contribution. But you must leave the politics to me and accept my decisions."

He addressed the assembly in German. He warned the people they must be content with Austria's authority. He would grant some concessions, but Austria must continue to rule.

Elisabeth held tightly to her shaking hands to hide her distress. Her anger flared. The archduchess had done it again. She saw Julius's face and she fought her tears.

When Franz sat down, the assembly sat in stunned silence.

Then she rose. She ignored her husband's startled eyes, his tightening jaw. In flawless Magyar, she spoke of her love for their country and for the people.

"May the Almighty attend you with His richest blessings," she finished.

As she folded her hands, tears rolled down her cheeks.

The assembly, so moved, could not utter a word. Tears streamed down the faces of the young and the old, on all except Franz Joseph. Julius buried his face. His tears were there also.

When boarding the train to Vienna, Elisabeth turned to Andrássy.

"I have failed you," she said.

He took her hands in his. There was no bitterness in his eyes. There was love. She turned and stepped past Franz into the train.

3

On June 15th, 1866, Bismarck declared war on Austria. It was the beginning of a new Europe. Family dynasties would disappear and new boundaries would change the map of Europe forever. In one week of war, all Habsburg lands in northwest Germany were overrun by Prussian troops. They occupied Hesse-Kassel, Baden, Saxony, Bavaria, Franconia, Hanover and parts of Bohemia. Prussia annexed Schleswig-Holstein, Frankfurt, Nassau and parts of Hesse-Darmstadt.

Elisabeth's children, Gisela and Rudolf, were sent to Bad Ischl, but Elisabeth stayed at her husband's side. She worked caring for injured soldiers in the hospitals that overflowed with the wounded. The soldiers called her their angel. One young soldier refused his operation until Elisabeth was at his side.

On the evening of July 3rd, Elisabeth sat with Franz in his office, lost in the beauty of the sunset. The horrors of the war momentarily faded into its natural tranquillity.

The door burst open. Archduke Albrecht, the commander-in-chief, raced in.

"We have lost the Battle of Königgrätz."

It was one of the bloodiest and the most horrific battles in history. Two hundred and fifty thousand Austrians fought against an even larger Prussian army. At the end, twenty thousand Austrians lay dead or wounded in the fields. They had fought bravely on the final day of the battle. Exhausted and shattered, the Austrians had marched forward with flags flying and drums beating. Their chances were slim, their hopes high. In twenty minutes, Austria lost two hundred and seventy-nine officers and ten thousand men. The war turned Prussia into a great European power.

In Vienna, Johann Strauss wrote "The Blue Danube" waltz as a tribute to the Austrians who had fought in the battle.

The road to Vienna was now open. The Prussians were on the outskirts of the city. Panic tore through Vienna. The winding cobbled streets once filled with Strauss waltzes were now filled with rattling carriages of frantic people fleeing in terror, taking their trunks and their furniture. The treasures of the Hofburg Palace and the important files of the Foreign Ministry were shipped to Budapest. Valuable paintings were removed and hidden. The royal family, with exiled Habsburgs who had fled Bismarck's occupation of their Italian and German lands, now huddled in the Hofburg wondering if their great empire was crashing down to its final end.

Ludovika, Elisabeth's frantic mother, sent her a telegram asking if she and Franz would flee Vienna.

Elisabeth replied: 'We do not know what is going to happen. We still feel we are in a dream . . . One blow after another. And we are told we must trust in God.'

Perhaps it was their trust in God. The Prussians did not move into Vienna. France intervened and a ceasefire was negotiated, resulting in concessions that would have consequences for the

Habsburg Empire. They would lose all their German and Italian holdings, including Franz's jewel, Venice.

Franz wavered, desperation devoured him. He could not accept the terms, yet what could he do? His money was gone, his army destroyed, the lights of Prussian campfires glowed on the outskirts of Vienna and the people hovered in fear.

To make it worse, the Hungarians were demanding more freedoms. Franz knew they could not lose Hungary as well. If Hungary went, the smaller counties such as Croatia and Serbia would go with them, and that could mean the end of the Habsburg Empire. Somehow, Hungary had to be brought under control.

4

After sleepless nights and struggling days, Franz made a decision. It was a decision that tormented him to the depths of his soul. Still, he knew there was only one way to keep Hungary. *My country must come before the whims of my heart*, he thought, staring out into the starless night. *Only one person can reach the hearts of the Hungarian people. My dearest Sisi.*

His decision was made. He didn't consult his mother.

The following day, in the Hofburg salon, the Habsburg family huddled anxiously. Franz paced before them, his face tense.

All eyes were upon him; they knew the news was not good. Uncertain about Bismarck's terms for peace and fearful of the situation in Hungary, the family was desperate for a solution.

Franz stopped and stared at them. Elisabeth had never seen him so distraught. An ache touched her heart.

"Hungary wants change and more freedom. Bismarck is on their side. We cannot afford to lose Hungary."

He was pacing again.

"If we lose Hungary, the empire could collapse."

Elisabeth saw tears in his eyes, bringing tears to her own. She wanted to embrace him, her sympathy almost love.

"What chance do we have?" The archduchess threw up her arms. "Bismarck has promised Hungary freedom."

"That is right. And we cannot afford another battle," Franz said. "There is another way."

He turned and stared into the hearth. He fought his anguish. He was throwing his beloved Sisi into the arms of another man. He knew the attraction between them. He loved her more than anything in the world. The flirtatious little countesses meant nothing to him. But he never knew how to convince Sisi, how to show her his love or how to give her the affection she craved. His regimented life had not prepared him for human compassion. And now he had no choice. Julius Andrássy was Austria's only hope of conciliation.

He held his breath. His country came first. He closed his eyes. *Please God,* he prayed silently, *don't let me lose Sisi.*

He turned back to the group. He walked over to Elisabeth, took her hand and raised her to her feet.

"In 1746, when Hungary launched its greatest threat to break from Austria, our empress, Maria Theresa, rode into the midst of the roaring populace begging for their loyalty. She held in her arms the little successor to the throne. Her beauty, her bravery saved our empire."

Elisabeth held her breath. Nobody in the room moved except Sophie. Her mouth almost dropped to the floor.

"My dearest Sisi, our empire needs you to win the hearts and the minds of the Hungarian people. You are much loved in Hungary. You speak their language. You have the respect of Andrássy and Deák. You can follow in the footsteps of Maria Theresa. War cannot save us. We must convince the people, in a diplomatic way, to remain within our empire. Andrássy is the man who can help us."

He paused to gather himself.

"You must go, with the children at your side, to convince him that Hungary must stay with Austria."

He took her into his arms. Tears ran down their cheeks. For him, they were tears of despair. For Elisabeth, they were tears of exhilaration. She was needed.

On July 10th, Elisabeth arrived in Budapest with her companion Ida Ferenczy and with Gisela and Rudolf.

When she stepped from the train, Julius Andrássy met her. Ferencz Deák was at his side. Julius's eyes shone as he took her hands.

"The sun shines again on our beloved Hungary," he said.

Cheering and waving greeted them as the carriage wound through the streets of Budapest heading for the royal chateau.

The children bounced like excited puppies and Ida's glowing eyes hardly left Andrássy. Elisabeth smiled and waved — she was as excited as the children.

Andrássy sat across from Elisabeth, his eyes on her as if no one else existed. She turned and smiled at him.

Deák turned away. They were a magical couple, but heartbreaking. *How,* he wondered to himself as he stared out the window, hardly seeing the crowds, *will this turn out when there is no place in their world for such a love?*

Andrássy's voice brought him back.

"My dear Elisabeth," he said, hesitant yet firm, "do not be overly optimistic about their thunderous welcome. Their hearts still burn for change. If peaceful relations with Hungary are to be, Austria must make concessions and make them quickly. The moderates have made their demands. We do not want to break away from Austria, but we insist on our historical rights. The constitution must be restored."

"Mama. Look!"

Rudolf's excited call caught their attention. He was half-hanging out the window.

"There is a plaque with my name on it."

Elisabeth looked out and saw the plaque. She smiled. She turned back to Andrássy.

"Help me and I will do everything in my power to convince the emperor."

She turned back to the window with a silent prayer. *Please God, let there be an empire for Rudolf to rule.*

5

"From what I hear, your riding skills are the talk of Hungary, so I am here to challenge you."

Julius greeted her the first morning. He was struggling to manoeuvre two impatient horses that were pawing the ground and pulling on their bits.

"I'll give you ten minutes to get ready," he added.

She was on the porch of a small country home, basking in the sun and listening to the birds. Julius's beaming face brought out a note of pure pleasure.

"It won't take me ten minutes. And beware, I might put a dent in your pride."

It was the beginning. Two people united in their passion for riding, their passion for a common goal and their passionate love for one another. Yet they both knew, as they ventured through the forest trails, it was a love that could never be realized.

For days, they rode through the woods, basking in the solitude of nature, leaving the world behind. Elisabeth struggled to keep up. She hated to admit that he was a better rider than she. He had magnificent grace and his powerful legs manoeuvred the horse with a skill and ease she had never seen.

"You ride as if you were born on a horse," she exclaimed.

He reined in his horse and they trotted together at a slower pace.

"From time immemorial the Magyars were the greatest of horsemen." His eyes had an amused glint. "They rode into history on horseback in 895 A.D. They crossed the great mountain ranges, settling in this valley, the Carpathian Basin. And are you ready for this one?"

She tossed him a smile.

"Our first parliament was held on horseback."

"On horseback?" she laughed.

"Yes. They were determined to establish authority in this wild land. For thirty-four days, they held sessions with horses as their chairs."

"Then you will be a hard one to challenge," she giggled.

She whirled her horse around and took off down the trail. Their laughter sailed into the breeze, his rising higher as he swept by her.

Hours turned into days. They galloped across the plains and through forests, hurtling over fallen branches. They sauntered along the bubbling streams and the roaring rivers.

"You are pretty good on a horse," he said.

In fact, he was astounded how good she was.

"You would think you had a drop of Hungarian in you."

The twinkle in his eyes made her laugh.

"Not only Hungarians have riding skills," she tossed back in fun. Then she added seriously, "And I have the skills to help you bring together your hopes for Hungary."

They would dismount and walk along a small river, watching the tiny fish playing in the water. Stories of Hungary fell from his lips. Sometimes his eyes held tears. She gained a deeper awareness of his people, their generations of struggle, their hopes, their pride, their spirit. She grew more and more in love with Hungary and more and more in love with Julius.

Often, he would take her hands when his stories brought her tears, holding them gently, caressing them and then dropping them quickly. He would turn away and they would stare into the rushing stream and at the hills beyond. Their sadness mingled in their silence. Both knew she was an unattainable jewel, the emperor's wife. If they crossed that threshold, their hopes for Hungary would never be.

One day, they reined in their horses on the edge of a rocky ledge. Below lay a barren plain stretching unending to the horizon.

"When the Turks invaded in the sixteenth century, they devastated this great plain."

He stretched out his arms to the desolate land below.

"There were forests with animals and birds and flourishing villages. The Turks marched across, ravishing and burning all that was there. Hungary was on their road to Vienna. From Vienna, they would march into Rome. The Turkish general, Köprülü, swore he would stable his horse under the dome of St. Peter's and drive Christianity from the world."

A smile lit his face.

"The Turkish general had a passion for women. He had an army of three hundred thousand when he arrived at the gates of Vienna and he had a hundred carriages for his own harem."

Elisabeth smiled and offered what she knew.

"The Duke Kent of Lorraine defeated the Turks in Vienna and saved Christianity in the western world."

She remembered that part of her history. The King of France had called it a miracle.

"You are right."

His bushy brows furrowed, his face hard.

"But when the Habsburgs drove the Turks from our land, they had no sympathy for the displaced people. When the Hungarians returned to claim their lands, they found them confiscated by Austria and given to new settlers from the German regions. The Habsburgs had replaced the Turks. From that day on, they have viewed the Hungarians as rebellious for wanting their rights restored."

At sundown, they rode slowly home.

"The spirit of the Hungarian people will never be broken," Julius said. "But we are willing to compromise, to put aside our differences and reach an agreement with Austria."

"I understand," Elisabeth said.

It came from her heart.

That evening, when the children were in bed, they sat in the salon of her country home. A fire glowed in the huge fireplace that reached to the ceiling. Ferencz Deák was with them.

Deák knew they all agreed wholeheartedly that an Austrian-Hungarian dual monarchy would bring Hungary peacefully to Austria's side and could save the Habsburg Empire from collapse. Still, he was uneasy. The horseback rides had not as yet produced the hoped-for solution. Their time together seemed more important to Elisabeth and Julius than reaching a decision.

Deák leaned forward, eyeing them both.

"Time is running out. The people are restless. Unless the emperor accepts our concessions soon, our people will turn back to Kossuth. Austria has banished him from our country. Still, the British and French sympathize with him."

Julius understood his impatience. The past days with Elisabeth had almost replaced the outside world. He stared into the fire transfixed with emotion. He saw that Deák was impatient.

Julius looked up and turned to Elisabeth. He took her hands.

"You are our angel," he said softly, "our providence, our saviour. We must depend upon you to be the mediator between the Court of Vienna and the Hungarian people."

That night, July 13th, she wrote to Franz:

'Andrássy has expressed his views clearly and precisely. I am convinced that if you trust him, we will be saved, not only Hungary but the monarchy too. But in any case, you must talk to him yourself and quickly. Any day, matters could take a turn. You are not dealing with a man desirous of a position at any price. On the contrary, he is risking his present position. Please, I beg you for Rudolf's sake, do not ignore this last chance. Please telegraph me the minute you receive this letter, stating whether Andrássy should leave for Vienna on the night train. If you are not willing to listen, then in the future, you will be relieved from any further interference on my part. And nothing will remain to me but the consciousness that whatever may happen, I shall one day be able to say to Rudolf that

I did everything in my power, that his misfortune is not
on my conscience, but on his father's.'

Elisabeth returned to Vienna with hopes that her concept
of the Hungarian situation might be convincing. But the
atmosphere in Vienna was like a powder keg and the last thing
Franz needed was pressure from Hungary.

The war with Prussia had been a disaster. Farmlands and
villages had been turned into battlefields and the people
still huddled in tents in the forests, fearful for their lives and
scavenging for food. Roads and ditches were still littered with
Austrian troops dying of cholera and typhoid fever. The hospitals
were filled with the wounded. And still, Franz could not bring
himself to accept Bismarck's demands for an armistice.

Worse, bad news had come from Mexico. Franz's mother,
in despair, locked herself in her room. France had withdrawn
all their troops from Mexico and Max, as the new emperor, was
likely to be deposed. It was quite possible that his life was at risk.
Franz could offer no aid as there was no money in the Austrian
treasury and certainly there were no available troops. Max's
wife, Empress Charlotte, had fled to Rome to beg the Pope to
aid the Catholic Mexican Empire. The Pope had refused. She'd
collapsed and her Mexican residency was exchanged for a mental
institution in Trieste, near Miramare Castle.

On top of all this came Elisabeth's call for immediate
concessions for the Hungarians. Franz, his head bent with the
weight of it all, knew something had to be done. But it would
have to wait.

Elisabeth did convince Franz to see Andrássy and Deák. The
Viennese at court were disgusted. The whole empire was
struggling and Elisabeth was asking for concessions for Hungary.
There was no doubt in the court's mind that Elisabeth was tainted
by the seductive charms of that ruffian Julius Andrássy and that
he was out to divide the empire. What fanned their fear into

hysterical heights was the freshness of Elisabeth's beauty. Might that influence Franz?

Andrássy and Deák arrived at court. They presented their demands for a reinstated constitution and their hopes for a dual monarchy.

Elisabeth was excited, but also nervous. She took the children for a walk in the garden, but their chatter and bouncing somersaults did not distract her. She waited impatiently.

When she saw the faces of Andrássy and Deák as they hurried down the path towards her, she knew the answer.

"It took all of ten minutes," Julius said. "He made no concessions."

They returned to Hungary disappointed and dejected. Elisabeth locked herself in her room.

6

"Do you not realize the urgency of the Hungarian situation?" Elisabeth implored Franz.

She had charged into his office unannounced. This time, the footman jumped aside when he saw her coming. Andrássy and Deák had been gone two days but she was not giving up. Archduchess Sophie was with him.

Sophie's face turned red with rage and Prime Minister Count Belcredi sprang up as if a pistol had exploded.

Franz raised his head, his expression tense. Elisabeth saw his stress. He eyed her almost vaguely.

"Do you not," he asked in a voice both low and cutting, "comprehend the disastrous consequences of the war with Prussia? The armistice is not yet signed, but we stand to lose most of our German territories as well as our possessions in Italy and the Danish Duchy of Schleswig-Holstein. Furthermore . . ." His face went stony. ". . . our people are desperate for clothing, food and shelter. And I don't have the money to remove and bury the six thousand dead soldiers and six thousand horses still in the battlefields of Königgrätz."

He pounded his desk.

"My obligations are overwhelming. Yet you, my dear Sisi, cry for Hungary. Hungary!"

Again, he pounded his desk.

"Hungary has hardly suffered in this war. I am not sorry for the Hungarians at this time."

Elisabeth understood his anguish, yet not his logic. She stood motionless. She understood the humiliation he suffered by giving into Bismarck's demands and from the angry populace blaming him for the disasters. Granting more independence to Hungary at this time would further demonize him in their eyes. Yet the Hungarian situation was urgent.

"Hungary is a crisis too," she said, trying to keep her voice controlled.

The archduchess fumed. Elisabeth knew she was about to explode, but still she went on.

"Hungary is on the verge of revolt. I saw it. The people are fired by Kossuth's cries for total independence. But they do not want another revolution. They want peaceful negotiations."

She leaned towards Franz.

"Think of Rudolf," she implored. "Do you realize that if we lose Hungary, it could be the end of the Habsburg Empire? Andrássy's solution of working together for a dual monarchy is the only way to preserve the dynasty."

Count Belcredi jumped from his chair. He believed passionately in the power of an absolute monarchy.

"You are deluded! If Hungary is allowed to break from us and if the emperor is not the supreme figure, all our possessions would rise up and that would be the beginning of the end. Two independent parliaments functioning without a central control would be a colossus with feet of clay."

"And one other thing." Franz's voice was low and decisive. "Andrássy is an honourable man, but I fear he is neither strong enough nor does he have the resources in his country to carry out his goals."

Elisabeth flew from her chair.

"He is the only one who can do it," she declared. "You sent me there to win the hearts of the people. I saw into their souls. I understand their desires. And you do not listen to me!"

She was boiling. She turned to the hostile eyes of the archduchess.

"You are all too closed-minded to understand. You are blinded by your desire for power and control. But the world is changing. People are changing. Now is the time for change in the empire or you will be left behind. You are destroying yourselves with your own greed."

She picked up her skirts, whirled around and strode from the room. The next day, she fled Vienna for Budapest.

"I have failed you," Elisabeth said.

She and Julius rode their horses slowly through the woods. Chirping birds did not soothe her.

"I have failed the Hungarian people. I have failed the Austrian people. But more frightening, I have failed my son. He may never have an empire to rule."

"We cannot think failure," Julius said gently. "Change does not come overnight. We must have patience."

She reined in her horse and looked at him.

"But your people, will they have patience?"

"They burn with determination, but they do not want war. We must strive to keep their faith and their trust."

His face brightened.

"And today," he grinned, "we will cast aside our disappointment and have some fun."

He spurred his horse. It reared and shot ahead.

"Follow me," he shouted over his shoulder.

They galloped fast through the woods, emerging on a high ledge. Julius reined in his horse. Elisabeth reined in beside him.

The sun had dipped from the sky. Below them lay a grassy plain with woods of pine. Tiny fires lit up the boughs of huge trees and shimmered on canvas tents.

"The gypsies!" she declared.

"You're right. And we are going to a Tzigane wedding."

"Oh no!" she exclaimed, her voice pure delight.

Elisabeth's eyes shone as their horses picked their way down the winding trail of rocks and roots. The sky was darkening. The nightingales sang. The breeze was gentle. It was almost a mystical splendour.

They bent low to dodge the hanging branches.

"The bridegroom is sixteen," he said, "the bride twelve. Age is not important, only the physical and mental development."

They stopped and dismounted in a clearing where they could see the young couple. They stood hand-in-hand in front of a huge fire of pine logs. With his back to the fire, the vajda, in a long crimson mantle, stood performing the ceremony.

"They worship fire as their ancestors did when they lived on the slopes of the Himalayas," Julius said quietly. "The Earth has existed eternally and is the origin of all that is good, as a raging fire burns in its bowels. They do not believe in afterlife and they have no word for Heaven or paradise."

The fire lit up the shining faces and the colourful costumes of the people encircling it. The groom had a crimson dolman thrown over his shoulder, high-tasselled boots and a small velvet cap with a heron's plume. He towered over his tiny, extremely pretty bride in her scarlet skirt and bodice, her dusky braids hanging long and a gold necklace gracing her neck.

When the vajda finished his address, an earthen vase was smashed against the ground.

"It symbolizes the ending of their past and the beginning of a new life," Julius whispered.

The couple were sprinkled with a mixture of salt and brandy. Julius leaned closer to Elisabeth.

"That puts into flight any evil spirits that might be lurking around them."

Elisabeth smiled in amusement.

Then the festivities began, with passionate musicians playing madly on their violins and crashing the cymbals. Their music was so lively and intoxicating, Elisabeth's body swayed and her feet tapped.

"The gypsies know not a note of music," he explained, his feet tapping too.

"It comes from tradition, from the souls of the past. It is the harmonies of nature, of the nightingales, the babbling streams, the windstorms tearing through the pines. They reveal the passion of love, of pain, of life and of rapture."

The men, with embroidered capes on their left shoulders and long spurs jangling on their boots, whirled around. Elisabeth wondered how they kept from tripping over themselves. The women wore colourful skirts held high above their knees.

"Their dancing is as wild as the Hungarian Csárdás," Elisabeth laughed.

"It is a mixture of that and the minuet," Julius explained.

Their horses picked their way home through the dark woods on a moonlit trail. They rode in silence, still mesmerized by the beautiful simplicity of the life they had witnessed and the enchantment of youth and love.

At her chateau, Julius helped Elisabeth from her horse. He held her hands.

"Do our duties and our ambitions blind us to the deeper meaning of life?"

She closed her eyes. She wanted to lay her head on his shoulder. She didn't. She let her hands lie in his. Then she pulled them away. He made no attempt to prevent her. She turned and rushed into her chateau to hide her tears.

Two evenings later, when winding through the darkening forest paths, they heard faint sounds of wailing voices. Quickly they spurred their horses through the pine trees, ducking the branches and wading through tangles of bushes. They came upon gypsy fires, glowing through the darkening trees. The moon lit up a small area where the trees had been cut and removed. They reined in their horses. There, a woman was bound to a stake. Her body was clothed in nothing but her long raven tresses. Her large black eyes revealed her agony. Blood dripped from incisions on her body.

She was surrounded by the Tzigane gypsies: men, women and children chanting sinisterly.

"Another Tzigane ceremony," Julius said.

"What kind is this?" Elisabeth asked, horrified.

"You will see."

The vajda, this time in a mauve mantle, was beating the woman mercilessly with a leather thong. He flogged her back, her breasts and down her legs. The woman whimpered and cried. The people chanted louder.

Elisabeth was out of her saddle. She ignored Julius calling to her. She raced to the vajda before he could stop her.

"What has this woman done that you should treat her this way?" she demanded.

The vajda almost lost his balance in shock when he saw her. He straightened, catching his breath and his dignity.

"There has been love, and of the love, sin, and of the sin, a curse would come upon my tribe if it were not punished," he said. "This woman has betrayed the man to whom she was honour-bound, and I must avenge the disgrace upon one of my people. She must be punished."

"Please, please, I beg you — forgive her for her crime. She has suffered enough!"

Tears were in Elisabeth's eyes.

Julius caught her quivering hands.

"It is their way and we must respect it." he said, "To them, it preserves the sanctity of their wedding vows."

"Nothing," the vajda continued defiantly, "can help the culprit. For twenty-four hours, she must remain tied to the stake. Then she will become a wanderer on the face of the Earth. No tribe will ever allow her to rest in their midst."

He took a deep breath.

"We are just. We warn our women of what awaits them should they sin. It is for them to keep themselves pure."

Only the woman is blamed. What about the man?

Elisabeth turned and strode back to her horse, her fury escalating. Why hadn't Julius stepped in? She threw herself up into the saddle and hurried down the trail. She didn't wait for Julius.

Julius caught up. He took hold of her horse, pulling it to a stop and looking her in the eyes.

"I will help her," he said.

"You promise?"

"I do."

She reached out and took his hand.

"Thank you. Thank you, Julius."

The woman was given a home on a Hungarian estate, where she stayed the rest of her life.

In the cozy salon of Elisabeth's Hungarian country home, Julius sank into a big chair, enjoying the crackling fire and reminiscing about his day with Elisabeth. It had been two days since they had seen the gypsies. That day, he had showed her Gödöllő Palace, on the outskirts of Budapest. He hoped one day it would be hers as a gift from the Hungarian people for her dedication to their freedoms. He thought of her face when she brought her horse to an abrupt stop and gazed at it. It was love at first sight.

Elisabeth came into the room. He jumped up with a smile as she offered him her hands. She was enchantingly beautiful in her gown of soft mauve and her hair falling loose and long. He wanted to wrap her in his arms and never let her go.

Her sober face cut his smile. She pushed a letter into his hand.

"Please read this," she said.

He glanced at it and then he looked up in surprise.

"It's a letter to you from Franz Joseph."

"Yes," she said. "Please read it."

She was disturbed, pacing around the room.

He read it: 'I would like to ask you for something very important to me. If you would pay me a visit, it would make me endlessly happy. I simply cannot get away from here at the present, though I would like to come to you. I long for you so. Perhaps you would come to see me again at this difficult time.'

Julius dropped the letter. It slid to the floor. He stared into the fire. Franz wanted her back. He loved her. Jealousy, anger and desperation stabbed. This week of paradise was over. These delicious moments of joy and temptation had come to an end. The fire blazed, the flames rose. Reality returned.

He was out of his chair, pacing the room. His panic was rising. He did not look at Elisabeth. She knew his thoughts, as he knew hers. At the window, he pulled the drapes open and stared into the night. A tiny crescent moon hung alone in the sky, the gardens hidden in darkness. His thoughts raced. They began to race into dark thoughts. Then, logic returned.

Franz would do anything to have her back. Perhaps, just perhaps, he would grant her wishes for Hungary if she gave him another son as he so desperately wanted. Would Hungary gain the freedom they desired? This could be their opportunity. Their hopes could become reality.

Yet the knot in his heart did not unravel, it tightened. He could not put her into the arms of another man. He loved her; she was his. He couldn't let her go.

He felt Elisabeth's hand on his shoulder. He turned. They stared into each other's eyes like desperate children. If he touched her, he would never let her go.

He stepped back. Anguish gripped him like iron chains. His face steeled itself. His words came out decisively. It was as if they came from somewhere else.

"You are our beautiful providence. Hungary needs you. Go to your husband. Give him the son he wants. He will grant you what you wish." His voice lowered. "And Hungary will always be indebted to you as our saviour."

Tears fell down their faces.

"My child will be my gift to Hungary," she said.

With her children, Elisabeth returned to Vienna. But their love was never put to rest.

7

Suspicion raced through the Viennese royal salons. The tongues shifted again into high gear and the wine glasses clinked with renewed fervour. Something was up. The maids and servants, eyes popping, almost stumbled over their feet whenever the empress and the emperor appeared. Their curiosity raced also. Was their empress really back to stay? And was that love in their eyes?

Elisabeth assumed her full responsibility as empress, following the etiquette of the court with gracious smiles and overwhelming charm. She never missed a function. Her beauty was more alluring than ever and lines of diplomats circled the halls. The Hungarian aristocrats had lost their favourite guest. But there was fear in the royals' eyes.

Franz hovered around Elisabeth passionately and coquettish young ladies sought refuge in other admirers. The Burgtheater lost its favourite attendee.

Archduchess Sophie desperately pondered her next strategy, especially since the Hungarian Magyars seemed to have taken over Franz's office and that traitor Julius Andrássy had become a fixture there. Furthermore, Andrássy charmed the ladies of the court, even though they struggled to conceal their excitement when he was present.

Count Belcredi's anger flared every time he saw Andrássy and Deák leaving Franz's office, smiling and slapping each other on the back as they sailed down the hall. He was never consulted on any of this.

He knew it was about Hungary when Sophie stormed from Franz's office and raced past him.

"I hope he regains his common sense before he destroys our empire," she shouted.

For Elisabeth, it was like playing a part in a play, almost surreal. She presented herself with dignity and charm and, for all to see, affection for her husband. They all knew her apartment door was open. The pain of her love for Julius never left. Their eyes met, their thoughts entwined, but not their voices. They knew that curious eyes never left them.

Julius saw his dream moving closer. Still, when he looked across the room and caught Elisabeth's eyes, memories tore him with pain.

"I have many masters," he remarked to Ida one day, in a trembling voice, "the emperor, the Hungarian people, the lower house, the upper house of Hungary. But I have only one mistress. Only one woman commands my heart."

On February 17th, 1867, Hungarian hopes were realized. A dual monarchy was established. The Empire of Austria became the Austro-Hungarian Dual Monarchy with two capitals, Vienna and Budapest, and two parliaments. Only the ministers of war, finance and foreign affairs served both countries. The five-hundred-year-old Hungarian constitution was re-established. Franz Joseph remained Emperor of Austria but would also be crowned King of Hungary.

Julius Andrássy had the broadest smile in a long time. He became prime minister of Hungary, but his expectations continued to grow. He must become the minister of foreign affairs for both countries, for then he could influence the affairs of Austria and, with that, have more power in his own country.

In the Austrian assembly, Deák gave special thanks to Elisabeth.

"You are the beautiful Providence bestowed upon Hungary by the grace of God." he said. "You and Julius Andrássy have brought Hungary to its rightful place of recognition."

Franz rose and bowed to Elisabeth in humble respect.

"With your foresight, not only have you saved Hungary, but also the Habsburg Empire."

He took her hands and looked into her eyes.

"Thank you for bringing the light to my eyes."

Her face glowed as she thought with relief that Rudolf would rule an empire.

To the Hungarians, it was as if the heavens had opened. To the Viennese court, it was as if demons had destroyed the world as they knew it. They accused Elisabeth of 'magyarizing' the empire and diminishing their God-appointed status. "The Hungarians are a horde of wild gypsies," they cried into their wine. "Now they share the governing of our great empire." It was almost too much for them to bear. They crawled into their despair with one last pitiful moan. "Julius Andrássy is responsible for this humiliation. He is her lover. He deserves the gallows now, far more than he did in 1848."

Sophie fled to Bad Ischl. She could not stay in the same city as Elisabeth.

The Austro-Hungarian Dual Monarchy became the foundation of the flowering economy that shaped the near future.

Elisabeth escaped the discord by fleeing to Munich for the engagement of her younger sister, Sophie, to King Ludwig of Bavaria. Ludovika was ecstatic. She had secured another crown for another daughter.

Though he was young and intriguingly attractive with the classic profile of a Greek god, dark curly hair and a smile that could charm the devil, there was a peculiar side to Ludwig. It was the talk of all the royal courts in Europe.

Elisabeth was concerned. She knew that generations of mixed family marriages were rampant in the royal houses of Bavaria, and that insanity and many other medical defects tainted the blood. Ludwig's brother, Otto, tragically insane, was locked in a mental institution.

"Ludwig worships Richard Wagner and his music as if he was God," bride-to-be Sophie told her. "He appeared at a court banquet dressed as the Swan Prince, twirled around and then quickly disappeared."

Elisabeth may have been amused but now she was more concerned for her sister.

"He ignored me for days," Sophie went on. "Then suddenly, he appeared in the middle of the night with a bouquet of flowers and left them at my door. And one night, he fled from the ballroom, leaving me alone in the middle of the floor, with no explanation."

Sophie had mixed emotions. Elisabeth saw that. She also saw her mother turn away, trying to close her ears.

"What do you think, Mama?" Elisabeth asked her.

Ludovika was not about to throw away a crown. They were too hard to find these days, especially for a family with a reputation such as theirs. She calmly looked up from her book and smiled at her daughters.

"No one was more eccentric than your father. I did not run away and he did not wear a crown," she said.

The pre-nuptial celebrations continued, but Elisabeth returned home, still worried. *Royal princesses are like horses*, she thought. *Put on a block for the highest bidder. Love plays no part. When will they find their pride and rise to their feet?*

She thought of her sister Néné — she envied her. Néné had escaped the trap and had married for love.

On June 8th, 1867, in the St. Matthew Church in Budapest, Franz Joseph and Elisabeth were crowned King and Queen of Hungary. It was a medieval ceremony. Franz Liszt's *Coronation Mass*, composed for the occasion, echoed through the cathedral.

Elisabeth stole the show in her Hungarian national dress of white and silver brocade with a black velvet bodice laced in pearls, her long auburn hair entwined with white camellias, hanging loose to her waist. She was, in Franz Liszt's words, "a celestial vision."

Julius Andrássy presented to her the key to Gödöllő. She clasped it to her heart tearfully. Both remembered their first glimpse of Gödöllő. Neither could say a word and their eyes met and lingered, until Deák coughed.

At the station, surrounded by excited crowds, Elisabeth clasped Julius's hand.

"Until we meet again," she said in soft Magyar.

Then she turned and stepped onto the train. Both knew their remembered moments of the past were all they would ever have.

Upon the Habsburgs' arrival back in Vienna, a telegram awaited from Mexico: 'On the morning of June 19th, 1867, under the blazing sun in Santiago de Querétaro on Cerro de las Campanas, Ferdinand Maximilian was shot down like a criminal on the order of the Mexican Benito Juárez. He died like a hero. Not once did he show fear.'

Franz was the one who broke the news of his brother's death to his mother. Sophie was never the same again. Charlotte, Max's wife, remained in the mental institution in Trieste for the rest of her life.

There was more bad news. Helene's young husband, the Prince of Thurn and Taxis, was flung from his horse and died in a ditch. *Poor Néné*, Elisabeth thought. She'd been the only one of her sisters to marry for love, and she was still destroyed by fate.

A glimmer of relief came in a letter from Ludovika. Sophie's engagement to King Ludwig was broken. Elisabeth's father, Max, had informed the king that unless a wedding date was set, Sophie would be released from their engagement. Ludwig's reply to Sophie had been short: "Your parents desire to break our engagement, and I accept their proposal." Life moves in interesting patterns. Ludovika's letter went on: 'Sophie has met a dashing prince, Ferdinand, Duke of Orléans, and they fell in love instantly. I have never seen her so happy.'

Perhaps the gods reached out in sympathy and shielded her with their protection. Soon, Ludwig's dementia escalated to such proportions that a squad of police and doctors were called to his royal palace. Shackled, he was taken to the country palace of Berg and placed under the care of a psychiatrist, Dr. Gudden.

The next evening, Ludwig and the doctor went for a walk around the lake. He appeared quite stable and the doctor had no concerns. They did not return that night. The next day, they were found — the doctor's body floating in the lake and Ludwig's body in the waters near the other side.

A post-mortem was held. It was felt a terrible struggle had occurred — the doctor's body was scarred and his lungs were full of water. He had been forcefully drowned. Had the waters taken Ludwig as he attempted to escape, or was it suicide that led to the peace of the world beyond?

8

Vienna began to return to its old ways. The wars were over, the loved ones were back home and the battlefields were again filled with crops. Fairs and circuses flourished in the Prater, people chattered in the sidewalk cafés and artisans and musicians flocked to the city. Once again, tunes flew from the bows of fiddlers on the streets and echoed down the dark alleys. The rats had an extra lilt in their tiny steps.

In September 1867, Elisabeth announced her pregnancy. The country went into a wild ecstasy that ended in a crash. She announced her baby would be born in Budapest. If it was a boy, he would be christened Stephen, after Hungary's patron saint.

The empire almost toppled. "Julius Andrássy is the father," people proclaimed. Cries for a miscarriage were rampant. Elisabeth kept her smile and prayed for the miracle of a boy. Her duty was almost done.

On April 22nd, 1868, in the Buda palace, one year after the signing of the Austro-Hungarian Dual Monarchy into law, Elisabeth gave birth to a baby girl, Marie-Valerie. Franz's hopes for a boy were crushed, but Elisabeth found a rewarding joy. Valerie became the pinnacle of love in Elisabeth's life. Elisabeth took charge of every part of her life. She referred to Valerie as 'the little divinity' or 'the one and only'.

When she installed a complete Hungarian nursery, the Viennese royals let out one last helpless gulp. "It is an affront to our society, Hungarians raising a Habsburg princess."

Gödöllő Palace became her escape.

"My dream has become reality," Elisabeth exclaimed to Rudolf and Gisela.

They gazed at the small palace nestled in gardens, with blossoming chestnut trees and orange trees with hanging fruit. Beyond were the plains with riding trails out into the infinite silence of nature.

Every day, she rode into that silence. She'd stop in the woods and close her eyes. And many memories came.

Her way of life changed and the Vienna salons vibrated with the stories of her 'disgusting' lifestyle. It did not deter Elisabeth. The gay, fun-loving Hungarians were always present at her salon parties. Her social functions included not only the highest on the social tier (the Hungarian tier, that is), but the lowest as well. Once, she invited the whole village of Gödöllő. The strains of the Csárdás echoed though the salons, down the halls and out into the gardens. When the circus came to town, she invited the gypsies. Their musical instruments almost shook the trees outside. Gisela and Rudolf joined in their dancing. Gisela loved it so.

"I could easily be a gypsy!" Gisela told Elisabeth.

Julius came to her parties, but he didn't come often.

When they danced, he said, "You are as wild as the Hungarians."

Their smiles and their eyes lingered, but not for long. There were always eyes ready to fuel the minds of the rumour-mongers in the Viennese court. Julius, as the prime minister of Hungary, had to protect his image if he wished to retain Franz's trust. He still carried his grander hopes for Hungary.

Elisabeth returned to Vienna only for functions she considered important. She felt no guilt deserting Franz, as she could not masquerade her affection. Her duty was done. She had hoped for another son, but God had other plans.

Franz knew it wasn't love that brought her back. He knew he had destroyed her love many years before. He also knew he could not change. Still, he loved her and often wished, especially when the ladies gushed around him with their adoring affection, that he could grab her in his arms and bury his face in her hair and never let her go. Sometimes when he chased the chamois he would rein in his horse and call out to the silent woods, "Sisi, I love you."

When he'd tried again to win her back — he had tried many times — she had brushed aside his pleas.

She wrote him: 'You know me and my habits, and if you don't like me as I am, well, I must be pensioned off.'

He turned back to the coquettish eyes, the Burgtheater and chasing the boar. Still, he missed her. Sometimes he would drop his papers, bury his head in his hands and sob.

Fox hunting, the English model, was newly introduced in Hungary. Elisabeth took to it with a passion. It was a way of blocking Julius from her mind. She picked her riding friends not for their rank, but for their horsemanship. The finest of Hungarian horsemen, young aristocrats, free from the obligations of earning a livelihood, rode at her side.

Her beauty and her daring escapades charmed them, and they all raced together with laughing voices. She wore high laced boots with tiny spurs and three pairs of white gloves to protect her hands — that always brought extra smiles. She displayed her tiny waist with an extra flare and she always had the latest riding hat. She basked in their worshipping eyes.

But she still missed Julius.

He did ride at her side — occasionally. When he did, they became one. They reined in their horses and let the others go on. They would ride in silence, neither one daring to touch the other.

However, more and more, Franz claimed Julius's time. More and more, the young horsemen were losing their appeal. And more and more, she watched the stars flickering in the night sky, and pondered the patterns of her life.

One afternoon, without warning, Julius arrived at Gödöllő. He had two horses pulling at their bits and a smile. It was a strained smile. Elisabeth dropped Shakespeare on the table and, in minutes, she was in her riding clothes.

He took her hand and helped her into her saddle. He kept her hand in his momentarily, then dropped it. He grabbed his horse's bridle and threw himself into the saddle. He whirled the horse around.

"Let's go," he shouted.

Into the woods they tore. They jumped over fallen boughs and small streams. They raced across a grassy plain. He rode like a madman. She struggled to keep up. She dug her spurs into her horse. Still, Julius bounded ahead of her, the turf flying from his horse's hooves. She even called out desperately, but it had no effect.

Then, back into the woods they galloped. He slowed down, his expression tight. They arrived at their favourite lake. They reined in their horses. She tumbled from the horse with exhaustion. Her legs could hardly hold her up.

"I thought you were trying to lose me," she whimpered.

He didn't smile.

"I didn't think speed was a problem to you."

She saw his tension. He turned and looked at her.

"I might lose you in the woods," he said solemnly, "but never from my heart."

He tied the horses, then turned quickly and charged down to the lake. She followed, knowing something was up — and that it would not be pleasant.

The sun was descending and shadows forming. Birds still sang. Elisabeth and Julius found their favourite log. Ripples lapped the rocks, denting the silence. As Elisabeth sat on the log, Julius stood staring out at the lake. She waited.

The dying sun's rays touched their faces. He turned to her.

"I must move this empire on to achieve my goals and to bring better times to the people. The empire is antiquated. We need to grow with the world."

She knew what he meant.

He sat down beside her.

"I believe we must work with Bismarck and establish a dual alliance with Prussia. That is the growing power. It would preserve our empire. But the emperor still wallows in humiliation. He cannot accept the Prussian catastrophes and the loss of his German and Italian holdings."

He turned to her.

"I have a solution. As prime minister, I do not have the authority to convince the emperor that my plan is the only way to go. Only the minister of foreign affairs can do that. I must gain that appointment from Franz Joseph, so that I have more influence."

Elisabeth turned away. The sun had dropped into the lake. The sky was a rosy gold. She knew what lay beneath his words. He had chosen Hungary over her. Franz had replaced her.

Rumours that they were lovers still enhanced the gossip. When they were in the same room, every eye was on them. If there was the slightest suggestion of an affair, Franz would never appoint him. All contact between them must end. No connecting eyes, no smiles, no rides in the woods. It was over. It must be as if they existed on separate planets.

She looked up at the sky. This was goodbye. There was no other way.

From the distance came the evening cries of the nightingales. The sky was darkening. She rose from the log, her feet sinking into the sand. She looked at him. His eyes were tormented, as were hers.

"I understand," she said. "You go back ahead of me. I'm not quite ready to return."

Tears edged his eyelids. He breathed in slowly and let them fall. His arms reached out to grab her. She snatched her breath, and stepped back. If they went into each other's arms, they would never say goodbye.

"Go," she pleaded. "In this world, there is no place for us together. We have always known that. This society does not recognize genuine love. It is merely a tool for power and to manipulate gossip."

He whirled around and raced back up the path. He threw himself on his horse and galloped away.

Elisabeth turned back to the lake. She listened to the lapping water, the breeze caressing her face. The stillness wrapped her in its comfort. She didn't cry. She looked up at the darkening sky. Life would go on. She was the delicious fruit that would taunt and intrigue, but she would always be unattainable to taste.

She turned and walked up the trail slowly. She untied her horse and climbed into the saddle. The trail had darkened. She found her way home, her thoughts darkening like the shadows on the trail.

Julius fled to Vienna. She remained in Gödöllő.

Her children and her horses were her salvation. Jovial young Hungarian horsemen rushed to her side. Often, with her bevy of young horsemen, she would ride four or five different horses a day.

She basked in the young men's shining eyes and their admiring whoops when she took high jumps. Rudolf often came, sharing her passion for horses. Not Gisela — her love was shopping in the small town.

Count Nikolaus Esterházy, or Niki, the undisputed master of the hunt, rode at her side. He was out to replace Julius Andrássy in her affections and no one could miss his. Rudolf often teased her about it. The count was a Hungarian aristocrat, dashingly good-looking and so wealthy and independent he was completely undeterred by her being the wife of the emperor. He was out to challenge everyone, even the emperor, for her love.

She was amused by his attention and she displayed the coquettish smiles of the court ladies. Rudolf said she was better than them. She built a riding school on the palace grounds where she practised with Niki and many other of the best and the handsomest horsemen in the country. If the count stepped onto forbidden grounds, her smiles turned the other way — she didn't have her husband's morals. It only brought his smile and more grace to his charm, more determination to his desires. He would have her. Nothing would stand in his way.

The stories sailed into Vienna, and Franz wrote her. 'I hear a dashing young Hungarian has caught your eye.'

She wrote back: 'My eye, but not my soul.'

Europe was again spiralling into disaster. Bismarck was again on the march. In 1870, Bismarck went to war against France. The French Empire collapsed and was proclaimed a Republic. Napoleon III was a prisoner in German hands and the beautiful Eugenie fled, with her son, from the wrath of Paris mobs. Prussia became the most powerful nation in Europe.

Franz now had no alternative. He had to sign the final peace alliance with Prussia. He finally lost his German and Italian holdings, including Venice. In 1871, the German Empire was created. Archduchess Sophie broke down in despair. The empire that she and Schwarzenberg had restored now lay on the brink of collapse. Even more humiliating, that Hungarian traitor Julius Andrássy was appointed foreign minister. Franz had lost all touch with reality.

Disillusioned and helpless, her indomitable spirit crushed, Sophie fled Vienna for Bad Ischl, where she died in May, 1872.

In this troubled time, Elisabeth packed up her children, left her Hungarian household and returned to Vienna to be at Franz's side. Rudolf's protests echoed across the palace grounds — he wanted to stay in Gödöllő. Horse-riding was his passion and he was determined to outride his mother. Gisela, on the other hand, bounced in excitement. She wanted to go to Vienna.

"I am fifteen now, and there might be a young man for me in Vienna," she said.

Elisabeth was shocked.

"Fifteen."

She had been fifteen when Franz came into her life. She grabbed the pudgy little girl into her arms.

"Is it really time for me to find you a husband?"

Where had the time gone?

Elisabeth found Franz overwhelmed by stress and quickly offered her sympathies. The success of the Austro-Hungarian Dual Monarchy still feathered her confidence. Perhaps she could be of further help.

Franz was not receptive to her the day she sat in his office as he and Julius discussed the Prussian situation. She agreed with Julius that to fan the economy of Austria, they must have closer ties with Bismarck. To Franz, it was still an offence to his dignity.

Elisabeth ventured her opinion.

"You must set aside your hatred. We must go forward. I believe closer ties with Bismarck will build a stronger empire."

That was as far as she got. Franz rose.

"I appreciate your opinions, but they are not needed now."

He took her arm and, very gallantly, led her to his office door. He bowed with a forced smile.

"There are many duties you have long neglected here in court. It would please me to see you take that responsibility."

She looked at Julius. His eyes were on her but he did not say a word. She removed her arm from Franz's grasp. She didn't jerk it away, though she wanted to. She walked through the door. She didn't slam it, but she desperately wanted to. It took all her determination to walk past the attendants and down the hall with the poise of an empress. She never again ventured into politics.

A husband for Gisela became Elisabeth's pursuit. Her sympathies for the poor and the helpless brought meaning into her life, which she desperately needed.

She worked in the hospitals and in the orphanages, where children's faces took her heart. On Mundy Tuesday, a traditional ceremony during Lent, she washed the feet of twelve men and women from the almshouses. They brought a solemn empathy. They looked at her. Small smiles dented their cracked, thin faces and she smiled back with affection and a separate ache.

She never felt fear when she and Ida Ferenczy ventured into the dark squalid quarters of the poor. They hopped over the open gutters gushing past the front doors, where the people dumped their slop, and up the damp mouldy staircases. In one or two rooms, which as many as five families might share, beds were lined up in the halls, in the toilet rooms and in the kitchens. Elisabeth and Ida brought food, clothing and help for the sick. Elisabeth laughed with them, cried with them and held hands that were pained with illness. She reached into their souls, and they called her their 'Queen of Mercy'.

There were incidents that challenged her kindness. One day, when riding through a dark alley, a piercing scream shot from a crumbling hovel beside them. Elisabeth and Ida jumped from their horses and flew inside. In a room of filth and odours, a large man with shaggy hair and venom spewing from his lips was flogging a woman. He held her to the floor and punched her vigorously. Elisabeth dashed her hunting crop across his face. The man dropped his victim and stared at them in amazement. Like a shot, the ill-fated damsel was on her feet, her hands on her hips, her anger flying.

"Why do you hussies interfere with my husband?"

She didn't know it was the empress.

Elisabeth let out a laughing whoop. She pulled from her pocket ten gulden pieces and placed them in the man's hand.

"Beat her, my friend," she said. "Beat her all she wants. She deserves it for being so loyal to you."

With the help of four hundred ladies and noblemen, Elisabeth brought the first Volksküchen (public soup kitchens) to Vienna. It catered to the poor, to the beggars and to the homeless. In one day, over ten thousand people would dine there from early morning to evening supper.

Tears of pity for her own sorrows melted into the past.

I am just like my mother, Elisabeth thought one day with a smile. *I am eyeing all Europe for a suitable crown for my daughter.*

Gisela was hard to please.

"He must be tall, handsome and ride a horse like you, Mama," she demanded.

Elisabeth thought she might know just the one. Prince Leopold was the most skillful rider in Bavaria and handsome as well. There was a problem. He was not entirely free. Negotiations for a dowry of fifty thousand guldens were on between his family and the family of Princess Amalie of Saxe-Coburg.

Elisabeth pondered a solution. But not for long. Mapperl, her youngest brother, arrived at her apartment with a revelation.

He had galloped non-stop from Bavaria. He was a captain in the Bavarian Army, tall and slim, with unruly red hair and a jovial face and gentle eyes that most ladies could not resist. But that day, his gentleness was rugged with fear.

"I'm in love with Princess Amalie and she is in love with me," he declared in Elisabeth's apartment, after making sure his words could not be heard. "We have loved each other since the Possi days, when we raced our horses through the woods. I have never loved another. Now, what chance do I have competing with Prince Leopold and the dowry of fifty thousand guldens? Amalie is desperate over such a marriage."

Tears brimmed in his eyes. Elisabeth grabbed his hands, her eyes sparkled, her amusement took off.

"Let me see what I can do."

On a weekend hunt in Gödöllő, she invited Prince Leopold to compete. He was a skillful hunter. Gisela was there and their attraction was instant. Gisela thought him very attractive and charming. Leopold was enthralled with Gisela's sparkling eyes.

"They have the charm of innocence and mirth," he said with an affectionate smile.

It was love at first sight.

Elisabeth threw her eyes to the heavens. Her smile could not have been bigger. *Thank you, thank you*, she intoned in silence.

A dowry of fifty thousand guldens was quickly accepted. The marriage of Gisela and Leopold took place in the summer of 1873.

That autumn, under the boughs of Possi's sweeping pine trees, Mapperl and Princess Amalie exchanged their vows.

Elisabeth smiled to herself. She felt quite proud of her accomplishment. She was again the 'providence saviour'.

In 1873, the World Exhibition came to Vienna and brought with it the royalty of Europe. Elisabeth picked the receptions she would attend and they were few and far between. The royals saw it as an insult to the visiting aristocrats. When the Shah of Persia again arrived with his entourage of soothsayers and astrologers, his harem and his favoured horses with their manes dyed pink, he informed them all that it was the empress he wished to see. Elisabeth's amusement brought her out. This she would not miss.

The shah was just as arrogant as on his previous visit. He stomped around viewing himself as above all European royalty — in fact, above all royalty. Elisabeth's smile grew wider. He participated in exactly what he pleased and he refused to have a woman presented to him unless she was young and pretty. Franz didn't know whether to laugh or be angry.

At the state dinner, the shah spotted Elisabeth.

Elisabeth had dressed with care that night, in her favourite white and silver gown with a purple sash. She had put on a crown of amethysts and diamonds and let her hair fall down her back in curls. She had thought it might be a fun night.

The shah, stout and short, stomped into the dining salon late. With him was his grand vizier, who always stood behind him at state dinners to taste every dish to make certain it was not poisoned. The other guests were already seated.

He stumped through the room looking impatiently for his seat. He ignored the disgruntled faces of those he disrupted as he lumbered into his chair. His telescopic eyeglass came out at once. He surveyed the room with wide eyes pushing from their sockets. When he saw Elisabeth, everyone at his table heard his gasp. He examined her from every angle, as if she were parked on a ramp in an eastern slave market. His joy bounded. Then he sat back with the genuine naïveté of a child. Elisabeth smiled at him. He didn't touch a morsel of his food. His grand vizier ate it all. And it was not poisoned.

For Elisabeth, it was a highlight of the exhibition, though not many words passed between her and the pudgy shah.

9

In January 1874, Elisabeth became a grandmother. She threw her arms in the air.

"I'm only thirty-seven and I am a grandmother!" she cried.

The horror of aging raced through her and her voice became a whisper.

"Is there anything more terrible than to feel the hand of time on one's self?" she asked Ida.

She stared into her mirror, running her hand across her face. She moaned with agony.

"And to watch the skin wrinkle and to wake up one morning and realize that one is no longer desirable?"

Ida shrugged sympathetically, but she felt no sorrow. Everyone gets old, if they are lucky enough to live that long.

"Life without beauty would be worthless to me. It is my power and my salvation."

This time, Ida understood.

"Don't forget your grandchildren. They can be your new world."

Elisabeth remembered the little bundle she had just held in her arms. She nodded but was not quite convinced.

When Franz referred to them as "a settled middle-aged couple," out came the masks of egg yolks with raw veal and crushed strawberries. Her figure she scrutinized as if with a magnifying glass. If an extra half-ounce appeared, so did the diet of oranges and raw meat juice. The treadmill, a luxury available to few others, went into overtime. She enhanced her smiles and her charm. The diplomats lined up to admire her with shining faces, gracious bows, a touch of flirtation, lingering lips and hopeful eyes. Many times, Niki Esterházy stood in the line.

Carnival time came and Vienna exploded with renewed jubilation. It had been a desperate year. The Vienna exhibition was the greatest venture of its time. Millions of people indulged in its glittering world. It ended in financial disaster.

The stock markets crashed and private banks collapsed. Most disastrous was the orgy of gambling. It infected people, rich and poor. Fortunes were lost and lives destroyed. The rich shot themselves in their palaces and others drowned themselves in the Danube. Bodies floated, some in costumes, some naked with colourful ribbons tied around their necks, some with masks.

During carnival season, the populace threw aside their financial worries, their broken romances and their frustrations and fled into the glorious world of music and dancing. The smell of frying doughnuts and roasting chestnuts filled the chilled air and the lilt of happy voices was everywhere.

The music of Strauss and Liszt and many more frolicking tunes echoed along the icy streets, down the dark alleys and into the cellars of the poor. Even the rats perked up their ears. The excitement drifted through Elisabeth's open window. She could see the streams of coloured paper draping the snow-laden trees. She saw the confetti dust flying through the streets, and the smell of frying doughnuts filtered in. Her fears of aging flared.

"Only the empress is not allowed to enjoy this excitement," she moaned. "I am shut up in this palace, spending my evenings at our court balls, sitting on a dais, and even the stiff-faced royals dancing around me are dying to escape to the outside, where all Vienna dances at the carnival balls."

Her distress turned into anger.

"All this time I am growing old and I have never been to one carnival ball."

She slammed the shutters closed and turned to Ida.

"If I remain imprisoned in this palace, I will be an old woman in a year. We are going to a ball. To the ball of the Musikverein."

It was the gayest and most splendid ball of all. The ladies wore elaborate costumes with tantalizing masks. With her identity hidden, even the most virtuous lady could indulge in flirtatious adventures with any man who took her fancy. The men milled around with glowing smiles and passionate glances.

"I will dance every dance and no one will know who I am. I am going to dress like a peasant girl."

Franz was out of town inspecting the troops in Prague. The gods were with her. They whipped through the closets.

"You will have to be a well-dressed peasant girl," Ida laughed. "We are limited on peasant clothing."

They settled on a daring mixture. Elisabeth displayed her elegant figure — her neckline plunged and her arms were bare. Giggling, they raced to the market for masks to hide their identities. Elisabeth chose a colourful one with no jewels. It covered her face, just her chin showed. *No one will know me*, she vowed. Ida dressed as a peasant girl too, though she let her lower face show.

"Do I look like a grandmother?" Elisabeth demanded.

She whirled like a teenager in front of the mirror.

"You look absolutely ravishing, though more like a bourgeois than a peasant girl," Ida laughed.

Even she was tingling with excitement.

There was one young bachelor, charming and elegant, out to reap the excitement of the carnival. He ended the evening with an empress in his arms. Fritz Pacher von Theinburg was his name. Elisabeth thought him a young bourgeois. She told him her name was Gabriela. They waltzed around the dance floor, their eyes radiant, their smiles entwining.

Never had Elisabeth enjoyed herself so freely.

"I love this!" she squealed as her body dipped and spun.

At times, Fritz picked her up and swung her around and around. His arms were so powerful that she had no fear. She did not feel like a grandmother. And no one was smiling more happily than Fritz. He was a flamboyant lawyer who hadn't, as yet, found a woman to love. He knew she was a lady, a special lady. He was curious.

"No one has captured me like you!" he told her as they whirled around and around.

Elisabeth smiled even wider, with eyes more enticing. She responded to his curiosity flirtatiously. He could barely resist pulling her mask from her face.

When night turned into dawn and the dance music drew to an end, he escorted her to her carriage. He didn't want to say goodbye. Neither did she. He offered his name and pleaded for hers. He had to see her again. Daring to try to remove her mask, he caught a glimpse of her chin. She gasped and snatched it down. He saw the terror in her eyes, making him even more curious. Ida saw it as well. Taking Elisabeth's hand, she pushed him away and firmly pulled Elisabeth into the hired carriage.

"I will write," Elisabeth promised him as the carriage parted.

As they rattled over the cobbled streets towards the palace, his face stayed in Elisabeth's mind.

She did send letters, many, but not from Vienna — she couldn't risk that. They were posted in Munich, in London and from many other parts of northern Europe. That protected her identity. They never met again.

For Fritz, it was an unfulfilled love he carried in his heart. He never told the wife he later married. Elisabeth never told Franz.

Years later, the letters would be found in Fritz's home, buried in a drawer, yellow with age. Gabriela would be identified. But by then, both would have left this world.

Carnival time drifted away into winter. The revellers crawled back into their lives and the Hofburg Palace became Elisabeth's unbearable prison.

Rudolf's companionship lifted her a little from the doldrums. He was emerging into manhood with a witty charm that enraptured everyone. *He certainly inherited his father's traits*, Elisabeth often thought with amusement. The young ladies from every level of society clustered around him adoringly and he basked in their adoration. She did wonder how true the stories were of his romantic adventures — there were many for one so young. Franz just turned an unconcerned eye.

Rudolf was alert and shrewd in his studies. Elisabeth loved their walks in the gardens, discussing his liberal ideas, so similar to hers. Franz would hear nothing of them. They were not appropriate ideas for a future emperor.

When Rudolf voiced to his father his belief in the sacred rights of the individual, Franz came to life.

"It is the emperor who has the sacred rights, not the people," he thundered at Rudolf. "Never forget, or the empire will be lost."

Elisabeth took Rudolf's hands, but she had no power to ease his disappointment. She also had concerns. Emotionally, Rudolf was tender-hearted and sensitive, almost docile, with thoughtfulness and affection. Yet when something thwarted him, his temper flared beyond control. His rage was terrifying. He was like a monster. Many times Elisabeth ran from the room when he pounded the walls. Many times she was terrified.

He kept in his room a human skull and often she watched him caress it with an almost sinister pleasure. Sometimes a shiver went through her as she watched him. He also kept a collection of small pistols. They held a fascination also. He was always ready to shoot from his window at anything with wings and bring it down, whether it was an eagle or a tiny finch. It was almost a passion.

Franz said it was normal. She didn't agree, and she couldn't push it from her mind.

The winter days darkened. Her children didn't need her neither did her granddaughter. Franz was buried in work, or in the Burgtheater, or chasing the chamois — she didn't really know which. The dignitaries had lost their charm and the fear of old age consumed her. Depression tightened its grip. Sometimes she even thought of death. That's when she collected herself and made plans to travel.

"Franz, please come with me on a holiday. Maybe to England, or even the Mediterranean," she begged him, trying to hide her desperation behind her smile. Then in a softer voice, she added, "We could be together, just you and I."

She hoped that might make a difference.

He did look up from his desk. He saw her great need but it did not garner his sympathy. The rigidity of his life had left him almost without compassion. Her whims, her need to escape he still did not understand. Nor did he understand her complaints of loneliness. The salons were always active, there were always receptions. Her need for attention and love he couldn't help. He didn't know how.

He rose and took her hands in his. They were stiff, but warm. A warm feeling went through him. He loved her. He found his voice and tried to show empathy.

"My dearest Sisi, my days are planned for months ahead and, as you know, my duties to my country come before my pleasures."

When her face crumpled, he persisted.

"The future of the Habsburg Empire is far more important than my personal happiness."

She turned and walked from the room. She felt no anger, just despair. Deep, deep despair.

A letter from her sister Maria saved her. 'Come to England,' she wrote. 'Come see my new hunting lodge. The weather is great, and there is nothing like the hunting in England.' With little left in her life, Maria had turned to horses. She was a brilliant shot in the hunt.

England would become Elisabeth's new world. And Bay Middleton would come into her life.

Bay Middleton and the Queen of the Chase

1

"What is an empress to me?" scoffed Captain George Middleton — known as Bay — to Lord Spencer, who had asked Bay's assistance to pilot for the Empress of Austria during the hunting season.

It was the beginning of March and the English hills were covered in green.

"How would I find the patience for her?" Bay said. "I am not a cautious pilot suitable for a woman. I ride only with the most daring of male riders."

Elisabeth had rented Easton Neston, one of the finest country homes in England. She arrived with her daughter Valerie, her full staff, her best horses and her Hungarian riding friends. Niki Esterházy was among them. But not for long.

She hardly noticed the elegant manor, but gazing at the vast lands stretching to the horizon, her excitement sent her feet hopping.

Her sister Maria resided not far from her. Now, she repeated Bay Middleton's remark to Elisabeth. With a grin, Maria went on.

"He is a Scotsman. He is neither rich nor does he come from a well-known family, but he has an irresistible charm and he is always present at the aristocrats' country homes. And," her smile broadened, "he is renowned as one of the finest riders to the hounds in the country."

She rolled her eyes, with a touch of humour.

"They say he is difficult to follow and takes challenging risks. Lord Spencer says it's just a matter of time until he breaks his back. However, he has agreed to take you on. Whether this is good or bad, only time will tell." Coyly, she added, "They say he can be rude."

"He sounds interesting."

Elisabeth's words were playful. "What is an empress to me?" he'd said. Well, she would show him.

"He will never find me boring. I will always be a challenge," she promised Maria.

"Tread with care, my dear sister."

Maria knew Elisabeth's habit of alluring her horseman friends into almost slavish devotion and dedication.

"You see, he is engaged to be married and his fiancée is not the least bit happy that he will be in constant attendance to an empress reported to be the most beautiful woman in the world."

Her words fell on deaf ears. Elisabeth could not wait to meet her new prey.

The morning of their first hunt, the sun was bright and she was mounted on her favourite horse, Jumbo, who reacted skillfully to every movement of her hands. She was dressed in a blue riding habit with yellow buttons and a tall hat, the latest English style. She felt stylish.

Bay Middleton had never seen such tiny spurs. And a black umbrella?

"What's that? You pull out an umbrella when it rains?"

What a sarcastic voice, Elisabeth thought. But she did not let him enjoy his rudeness.

"It shades me from the admiring crowds that I often attract when I ride," she said, smiling sweetly.

He was not a tall man, but muscular. Elisabeth didn't think him particularly good-looking. He had a slightly arrogant face and red hair that stood up short and straight. Elisabeth thought him totally moulded in his own superiority. She felt a little distaste. Could he really have the charm her sister had described?

She rode skillfully at his side, and they left their fellow riders behind. Not once did she show a hint of fear or hesitation on jumps that twisted his face.

When they dismounted and the grooms took the horses, she put her hand out to his.

"Thank you for your superb guidance."

He took her hand, and he held it. He was dumbfounded. Never had he seen a woman so exquisitely lovely — with such dainty hands, enclosed in not one but three pairs of gloves — have such complete mastery of a horse.

"With your tiny hands, with the slightest touch, you control every movement of your horse. You have what I have never seen before. You seem to reach the soul of the horse. What a joy it will be for me to ride at your side."

He dropped her hand and bowed. Elisabeth knew he had been conquered.

From that time on, for six years, Bay Middleton rode at her side at hunts. They were two people entrenched in the love of the hunt. He picked her horses. He helped her from the saddle. He pulled her out of the ditches when she tumbled into one. He spurred her on, hardly ever attempting to discourage her daring exploits. He praised her, yet at times he was rude, chastising her for disobeying him. She knew his rudeness came from fear and affection. She became a part of his life and a part of his heart.

Elisabeth accepted criticism as a willing and docile pupil from this young Scotsman, nine years her junior. She accepted, with almost girlish delight, his affection. The Hungarian horsemen left her side, returning to Hungary with downcast faces. Niki Esterházy was devastated.

The hunts were exhausting. Elisabeth never complained. Large horses were ridden at great speeds, flying over ditches and jumping fences. On a day Bay turned head over heels, she managed to remain in the saddle hurdling the same ditch. He didn't apologize, just swallowed his pride with a smile. The ditches were always full of people. There were bruised skulls and broken limbs and also horses tripping and falling, some so painfully injured they had to be shot. It was dangerous but challenging and Elisabeth didn't miss a day. She tossed aside her gloves to control the reins more skillfully. Out of a field of a hundred riders, only a dozen would finish. She always did and, most of the time, she was the only woman to finish. She loved the admiring eyes.

Valerie was always the first to greet her when she returned. The young one was never allowed on a hunting horse.

"Every day I pray, dear Mama, that you will come back safe and sound," she announced one day, throwing her arms around her mother.

Her admiration showed in her eyes.

The British hunters were mostly aristocrats. They were good company and fun, a far cry from the dull Viennese royals. Their country manors were rustically charming and their dinner parties elegant, yet full of carefree chattering voices. Horses were their common bond and the conversation was devoted mostly to hunting and racing. Elisabeth enjoyed this the most. Of course, she always had a smile when they remarked about her riding skill. "There isn't a woman in England better than you are on a horse," they said often.

Like autumn ending and winter dropping its icy pellets, scathing gossip began to filter into the hunting seasons. Elisabeth knew there were jealousies, mostly among the women. She captured too much male attention. She tried to close her ears, hoping it would go away. She was her most charming entertaining at lavish dinners, trying to keep their hearts. Still, the tongues wagged and the champagne glasses clinked.

"Bay Middleton is always at her side. Look how he looks at her." "Look how she looks at him. She treats him more like a royal prince than a guide. The finest horses in the stable are at his disposal." "He escorts her to every meet and she never misses a competition he is in. She travels miles across the country to see him perform." "Look how solicitously he worries about her safety. It is obvious he is in love with her." "What does the emperor think?" "He's never here." And "When does Bay ever see his fiancée?"

The gossip did nothing to hinder her love of hunting. She tried to put it all aside. When the day was over and she closed her bedroom door, drank her bedtime tea and gazed into the fire, her heart was content, the gossip forgotten. Only the expectations of the next day's hunt filled her thoughts.

When her son Rudolf, now nineteen, arrived in England for a state visit, the stormcloud broke.

He charmed everyone, including Queen Victoria, who paid him the honour of inviting him to Osborne, her country home. The Prince of Wales took him to explore the nightlife in London and he voiced his amusement.

"The young man is really a man of the world. What flair he has with the ladies."

"And do you chase the hounds as well as your mother does?" the prince asked Rudolf jokingly.

Talk of his mother's hunting escapades raced through London, as well as her supposed amorous intrigues.

Rudolf had tried desperately to master the skill, but he could not outdo his mother. His mother had jokingly said to him, "Perhaps in England, you should not hunt." In his eyes, he felt a failure. He looked at the prince.

"I am not one to chase with the hounds," he said. "I see it as cruelty to animals."

The prince shaded his eyes. He recognized it as a cover to hide Rudolf's inferiority.

"It's all over London," Rudolf howled to Elisabeth, ripping off his gloves and throwing them on a chair.

He had just arrived in Summerhill, his mother's latest hunting retreat. The gossiping British had sent her fleeing to the quiet rural plains of Ireland. Here she had found heartwarming contentment. The Irish country people clamoured around her with warm cheers of welcome and they did not gossip.

Rudolf stomped around the room, wringing his hands. Elisabeth was still dressed in her riding habit and glowing from the exhilarating day. She reached out to him, but he pulled back quickly.

"Did you not hear me?" he said. "It's the talk of London. And everyone made sure it reached my ears. Even the queen."

"Of course, Rudi, you are talking about Bay Middleton."

"Of course I am."

The very name of the man fuelled his anger.

She sank into a chair, took off her gloves and laid them on the table. At the misery on Rudolf's face, she sighed a pained sigh.

"They say he never leaves your side, that he is your lover, that you sneak into London, incognito, with him. Is that true, Mama?"

His face was red.

"He is not my lover."

She jumped from her chair and strode over to him.

"I am your mother. Such words from you insult the very essence of our trust."

She fled to the window. The light in the sky still shimmered through the trees. After deep breaths to calm herself, she turned.

"He is my dearest friend," she said, "filling in for a husband who has no time for me. Though your father indulges his hunting friends, chasing the pheasants or whatever crosses his path."

And ladies as well, she thought to herself.

"Did I sneak into London with Bay?" Elisabeth said to her son. "Yes. I dressed as an ordinary lady and I had the time of my life. We dined in a quaint inn bustling with the common people and sipped our wine in the candlelight. And no vengeful eyes spied upon us."

She remembered how they had laughed and chattered about silly things. The world they had left behind. They'd glowed with mutual affection, with the joy of each other's company. The horses had been forgotten. But not that she was the empress. When he'd reached out and taken her hand, she had let it lie momentarily in his. She'd felt his hand tighten. When she had slowly pulled away, he had let go. His jaw had tightened in anguish. That night, she had cried herself to sleep.

She looked hard at Rudolf.

"Furthermore, Rudolf, do I question your love affairs? They are the talk of Europe. Even your father has suggested we must find a wife for you."

Women from every rung of the social ladder vied for Rudolf's attention and he had no resistance. Just like his father, she had thought so often, pitying the woman he would marry.

"But Mama, you are different," he countered. "You have more responsibility."

"Yes, I do. And I respect it." Looking him squarely in the face, she said, "I do not overstep the boundaries of my marriage."

He looked back at her hard, momentarily. Guilt slithered across his face.

"I know that, Mama," he said quietly. "I really know that. You are skilled in politics. Julius Andrássy told me that. You have a deep understanding of the change the empire needs. Yet you never try to persuade Papa. You flee to this frivolous life of chasing the hounds or travelling from country to country. You show no interest in the political crisis at home. This is the empire that I must someday rule, and I am desperately worried. We must have change."

She took a deep breath.

"I know all that goes on there. Julius Andrássy keeps me posted. Julius influenced the dual alliance with Prussia. I am very happy about that. I pleaded with your father to recognize the changes in the world. If we do not keep up, we will be left behind and we will lose the empire. Do you know what he said to me?"

She looked straight into her son's eyes.

"He said, 'Stay out of politics. This time, I truly mean it.'"

She picked up her riding gloves, twisting them.

"And how does he view Bay Middleton and all the gossip?"

She didn't wait for his answer.

"Bay Middleton and horses keep me amused, freeing him from that responsibility and keeping me out of politics. My horses are my escape from a society which views me almost as a foreign impediment."

She smiled.

"What I might have accomplished in politics I have accomplished in the skill of riding."

She reached out to him when they said goodbye. This time he did not pull away. She looked into his eyes.

"Maybe someday you will understand and judge me differently."

He wrapped her in his arms and tears ran down their cheeks.

When Rudolf had left, Elisabeth opened and read the letter he had brought her from Franz: 'The relationship has worsened between England and Ireland and Queen Victoria fears your presence in Ireland might be exploited for political reasons. Please leave Ireland at once and stop in London to call on the queen, as she views your stay in Ireland as a deliberate insult to the English monarchy. We do not need conflict between England and Austria.'

Elisabeth threw the letter across the floor. She could not believe it. She loved Ireland. It was Hungary all over again. She loved the affection of the people, showering her with flowers and travelling miles to get a glimpse of her on horseback. She loved her Georgian manor, Summerhill. But most of all, she loved the high banks she and Bay galloped over, the miles and miles of green hills and the valleys with soft springy turf that clung to her horse's hooves.

The next year, Ireland came to an end. Elisabeth's heart was broken. She knew there was no other way. Her last day of the hunt brought sadness but it also brought glory. She rode three different horses and twice she and Bay were thrown into mossy embankments — luckily, they had no broken limbs. Then came her final feat. She ignored Bay's glaring protest and she took the highest jump in all Ireland. The horse pulled so hard at the reins as his powerful body soared into the air, her bare hands were wet with blood. But she did it. It was like sealing a farewell note to a lover and dropping it into a postbox.

When she was back at the stables, nerves still tense with excitement and painful hands immersed in water, Lord Spencer came up to her and made a sweeping bow. He was an arrogant man, but known to be the best rider to the hounds in the country.

"I have only one opinion," he said. "You are incomparable both as a rider and as a woman. I have suffered a thousand deaths just watching you."

That night, draped in melancholy, she walked slowly down the hall to her farewell banquet. She heard the jolly voices and the whooping laughter. Her tears came. This was farewell. She would never again hear those Irish voices.

When she appeared in the doorway, everyone was on their feet, her name on every lip. She found a smile, forced back her tears, and into the room she went. Before she could sit down, they joined hands with her and swung her around and around. Their voices rang out:

> To the Queen of the Chase
> The Queen, yes, the Empress.
> Look how she flies,
> With a hand that never fails,
> And a pluck that never dies.
> Hark horn and hark hallo.
> Come for a place.
> The Queen of the Chase

She let her body swing with them. Then her tears came. Everyone stood motionless and silent.

"I thank you for the wonderful days I have spent with you in Ireland," she said in a choked whisper, "they will be among the most treasured memories of my life."

The room went wild. Bay's eyes flashed as he joined hands with her and the fun began. It was a farewell, but it was a rollicking one, with passion and affection. There was no more time for tears.

It was a farewell to Ireland and it was also a farewell to her closeness with Bay Middleton. Though, at that time, Elisabeth did not know that.

A telegram from Franz awaited Elisabeth back in her room: 'The engagement of Rudolf to Princess Stephanie of Belgium has been negotiated. Would you kindly stop in Brussels on your way home to welcome the young lady into the family?'

Her face turned deadly white.

Ida ran frantically to her side.

"My lady," she asked, "is it tragic news?"

Elisabeth let the telegram drop to the floor. Her voice quivered.

"Let us pray it does not turn out to be that."

Rudolf

1

"I am not ready to be a husband, and I don't propose to be one for as long as I can help it."

Rudolf grinned at his companion, General Joseph Latour, as the train steamed through the green valley that edged the Belgian mountains.

"Well, your father has determined that you marry soon," Latour retorted.

It was early March of 1879. Rudolf was twenty-one, and they were on their way to Brussels to meet Princess Stephanie, the youngest daughter of King Leopold of Belgium. As the wealthiest man in Europe, he would certainly produce a suitable dowry.

To Rudolf, the most sought-after bachelor in all Europe, bachelorhood was like lying in the arms of the gods. He had no intention of letting that life come to an end.

He was tall, with auburn brown hair like his mother's that framed his slender cheeks and an elegantly-trimmed beard. The ladies raved about his blue eyes with their fascinating depth. "They hold you in a spell," they chanted, to Rudolf's amusement.

Latour had to admit that Rudolf did have charm and charisma. The young schoolgirls called him their 'fairytale prince' and carried his picture in their schoolbags like a keepsake to treasure. However, his father was desperate to get him married. Scandalous gossip raced nonstop across the country.

It was a time when Vienna was booming. The financial crisis was over, the bourgeoisie had flourishing businesses and the middle class had jobs. Only the poor still huddled in their dark alleys, with rats remaining their constant companions.

Sexuality also flourished as fast as the economy. Crinolines were tossed aside, replaced by bustles, plunging necklines and exposed arms displaying the charms of the feminine body as never before. It was not unusual for the ladies to toss aside their virtues, as others saw it, and march in equality with men. The demimondes' romantic intrigues darted through society like lightning streaks across the skies. This brought some of the most reserved gentlemen soaring into sexual orbit. They prowled, and ladies were always waiting. Vienna became the sexiest city in the world and Rudolf was out to taste every flavour offered. Elisabeth joked, but with concern, that he probably outmatched his father.

Rudolf's romantic intrigues brought jealous husbands and outraged fathers seeking reprisals, especially from the royals. The Russo-Turkish war had not given Franz Joseph nearly the headaches that Rudolf did. He had to find him a wife — and quickly.

Catholic princesses were hard to find and Rudolf harder to please. Or to be convinced that marriage was for him, Latour thought as he looked out the train window at the darkening sky. The niece of the Saxon King Albert was quite attractive, though her figure extended the seams of her gowns. Latour had actually thought her charming. Rudolf, however, had taken one look at the stout Matilda and they'd fled Dresden the following day.

They did not fare much better in Madrid, where the skinny infanta was displayed for his inspection. Rudolf spent more time petting the royal dog than speaking to the lady. Still, Latour had to drag him from Madrid — not because of the infanta, rather the vibrant guitars and the Spanish señoritas in the beer gardens.

When the royal ladies were found unsuitable, Rudolf's spirits sailed to new heights. He headed back to Vienna, where he lost no time renewing his sexual prowls. Franz Joseph's desperation escalated. So did Elisabeth's amused taunts, but they did not curtail Franz.

"Only a marriage bed will bring him to his senses," the emperor exclaimed.

Elisabeth's eyes went to the ceiling. That had hardly trimmed Franz's desires.

Franz's only hope was the Belgian princess, though Rudolf had dismissed her picture with a snort.

Franz's sharp rebuttal hammered the walls.

"Go see her anyway," he yelled, pounding his desk.

Latour smiled to himself as the train halted in the Brussels terminal. Rudolf had covered his bets. On the same train was an enchanting Viennese actress with whom he intended to find solace, no matter what happened.

Princess Stephanie would never forget the afternoon of March 5th. She was fifteen, her schooling just finished. Her father summoned her to the reception hall of the palace. He wasted no time.

"The crown prince of Austria is here to consider your hand in marriage." His tone was decisive. "Your mother and I are very much in favour of this union. You could one day become the Empress of Austria and Queen of Hungary."

Stephanie froze, speechless. Her mother offered no sympathy. Her father took her arm and they crossed the floor to the two men standing by the window.

"Stephanie, may I present General Latour and Crown Prince Rudolf."

Rudolf made a sweeping bow with a charming smile. A twinkle lit his eyes. Latour held his breath. Rudolf saw a rose-blushed face. He saw her shyness, her childish coyness. He saw her innocence, her youthful freshness. He was captured. For a short time, that is.

Stephanie saw her fairytale prince. The frost went from her face. She fell in love in that moment.

Rudolf wrote his father: 'Stephanie is nice-looking, good and very sensible. In her, I have found a real angel, a sweet and faithful being who loves me, a charming and tactful companion who will help me and stand by me in my difficult life ahead.'

The Viennese actress was not forgotten. She filled his spare time in Brussels.

When Elisabeth arrived in Brussels after her Irish holiday, the Belgian royal family greeted her on the railroad platform. She looked radiant in her blue velvet travelling suit. Stephanie curtseyed, her eyes apprehensive.

One look at the awkward girl in a bonnet so big her face seemed lost and Elisabeth struggled with her aversion. She forced her smile. Her fears were confirmed. This child would never satisfy the appetite of the young man standing beside her. She looked into Rudolf's eyes and she saw his fear.

She cut short her visit and fled to Vienna before her frustration exploded.

Into Franz's office she marched with her travelling cape still on. The footman made no attempt to hold her back. In fact, he pushed the door open as soon as he saw her coming. Franz dismissed his visitor.

"She is not for Rudolf," Elisabeth declared. "Their lives would be a disaster if they marry."

Used to her outcries, Franz looked down. He took a deep breath, then raised his head calmly,

"She is the only one who has captured his interest," he said decisively. "We must complete this arrangement at once."

Elisabeth collapsed into a chair. Her pleas didn't budge him at all. She threw herself on her knees reaching for his hands.

"Do one thing for me. Please. Please wait one year."

Rudolf might then realize his error.

Franz had the same thought, but for him it was fear. He pulled his hands from hers and pounded his desk.

"The wedding will proceed as soon as possible."

She flung out one last plea.

"She hasn't even started her menstruation periods yet."

The wedding was postponed for a year.

Rudolf returned to his bachelor ways with the exuberance of a condemned man escaping the gallows. In desperation, Franz appointed him colonel of the Thirty-Fifth Infantry Regiment, garrisoned in Prague. Such responsibility, he hoped, might counter the feminine charms.

With a newfound diligence, Rudolf took on his duties. It gave him a pride he had long sought. Not only was he flattered by the respect of his fellow officers, he gained his father's recognition. He had often felt a condescending disrespect from his father. Now he was a part of his administration. The ladies were tossed aside and new visions and hopes took over his mind.

In the coffee houses, where the professionals, doctors, lawyers and university students voiced their liberal ideas, he found a common bond. They reawakened thoughts he had buried long ago in helpless distress. His excitement took off like a horse freed from the reins.

He understood their view of the empire as a frail, outdated structure. Twenty million heterogeneous people with no national unity huddled submissively beneath the dominating hand of the emperor, who used power with no respect for the people's wishes. His new views were aired on a visit to this mother.

"The empire is not moving with the changes of the world. It is lost in its past," he told Elisabeth, echoing her thoughts. "The people want change. Their frustrations are mounting. No longer is the word of the emperor sacred. Franz Joseph, as the father of the people, as the undisputed hand of God, is losing his halo. Unless there is change, there will be no empire for me to rule. Can't you understand? I must convince Papa."

With these visions fuelling his mind, he rushed to his father's office and took his place in line. Elisabeth kept walking the woodland paths. She had no hope.

Change was the last thing Franz wanted to hear. He dismissed his son condescendingly.

"You are talking nonsense."

Rudolf walked out into the afternoon sun like a helpless and bewildered child. Elisabeth could only wrap him in her arms to console him. Their helplessness they buried in tears.

The soothing charms of the opposite sex were quick to whip reality from Rudolf's mind. The champagne, which enhanced his sexual skills, went down in greater proportions and his amorous adventures rocked the country with new fervour.

Franz prayed the year would pass without a serious calamity, and Elisabeth fled to Gödöllő Palace with a morbid premonition that tragedy lay on the horizon.

It was the first winter Bay Middleton had not come to Gödöllő. Elisabeth harboured fearful thoughts. She missed him. He always brought colour to the dark winters. Her Hungarian horsemen were thrilled, though, especially Niki Esterházy, who had not given up.

When word came, it brought her a scary consolation. Bay was flat on his back from a riding accident. However, he assured her he would ride with her in England in the spring. She closed her eyes and thanked God.

In February 1881, Elisabeth went to Cheshire, in northwest England, with her entourage and her patient daughter Valerie, now a flowering teenager. Valerie enjoyed the freedom from the royal court and she adored her mother. She hoped she would have her mother's strength to stand up for what she believed in. She did fear her mother's violent riding feats and she was always relieved when Elisabeth arrived home safely. She was never allowed on a hunting horse, just a pony, but she went to the stable and fed them treats.

Elisabeth's residence, Combermere Abbey, was on a large lake surrounded by miles of wooded parkland. She was offered the room William of Orange used in 1682, with a bed so high she would have to climb up to it on a chair. With an apologetic smile, she chose instead a small cozy room that reminded her of her tiny Possi bedroom. She would gaze out at the lake, so much like Starnberger See, and muse about that nature girl of so long ago and the tangled roads of life.

Bay Middleton was well again and she met him at the Whitworth station. His smile sent the distress of the winter flying. She took his hands and held them tightly.

"This is Major Richard Burkley."

The young man at Bay's side bowed graciously.

"He knows this countryside like the back of his hand. He can even put me to the test in the hunts."

"Look at you!" Elisabeth said to Bay, after a quick nod to Burkley.

How she wanted to hug him. She was so happy to see him.

"You are totally recovered," she smiled.

He grinned, his red hair standing as straight as ever.

"I am ready to challenge this Cheshire terrain that even the mountain goats find terrifying. And we won't miss Ireland."

Elisabeth had some doubts about that. Already she missed Ireland.

For the next three weeks, often six days a week, they galloped through the hilly terrain, jumping fences and flying over ditches. Elisabeth did forget Ireland.

But there was something different. She saw it in Bay's face when they stopped on a ridge and viewed the surrounding beauty. She felt it when their horses slowly meandered back to the abbey. She saw it at social functions, when she caught his eyes on her, solemn and almost sad, and then when he would quickly turn away. Many nights, when she lay in her bed and watched the moon moving across the sky, she feared a change was coming.

It came on a night when they ventured incognito into a small country inn hidden in the trees on the edge of the village. The dining room was dark and cozy with wood panelling. Candles flickered on the table, lighting up their faces, and music and laughing voices echoed through the room. As they sipped their after-dinner wine, she eyed him.

"What are your thoughts?" she asked.

Bay looked into the wine shimmering in his glass. For a moment, he was silent. Then he looked up at her.

"For weeks this winter," he said slowly, "I lay flat on my back from my injury, staring at the ceiling. I had time to think. I pondered my life and my responsibilities."

She clasped her hands tightly, an outlet for the pain she knew was coming.

"Much of my time I have spent with you."

He looked into her eyes.

"For six years, I have stayed at your side and they have been the happiest, yet the most frustrating, years of my life."

She stared down at her hands.

"I have loved you as passionately as any man can love a woman. Sometimes I thought I would go crazy with the passion that boiled in me."

He reached out to her.

"But I can never have you. We can never belong to each other. You are forever unattainable. To preserve my sanity, I must step away."

He dropped her hands. They stared at each other and their tears formed. She closed her eyes — first Julius and now Bay.

The candles flickered. He put his glass of wine to his lips and gulped.

"My fiancée, Charlotte Baird, has waited all these years, suffering with her jealousy as I rode like a lovesick child beside the most desirable woman in the world. She knew my passion but she was patient, and still she wants me. She is attainable."

He looked away.

"I have given her a promise of marriage. It will be in two months. We cannot ride again. That is why I have brought along Major Burkley. He will be your new guide."

There were no answers.

That night, Elisabeth did not shed distraught tears into her pillow as she so often had. She sat quietly in her room and stared at the fire crackling in the ceramic stove. She would always be the delicious fruit that could never be tasted. That fruit would dry with time and fall from the branch, then her world would vanish and her dreams never be realized. For love would never be hers.

The next day, she rode across the fields, over ditches and stone barriers, through valleys and down hills so steep the ground seemed moored against the horse's body. There was no Bay. Burkley was by her side. He ended the day with a smile.

"You look like an angel, but you ride like the devil."

Her smile was faint.

The next day she packed her entourage and returned to Gödöllő. She never rode in a hunt again.

2

As Rudolf's wedding date approached, Elisabeth watched her son's tension spiral. Sometimes he was so distraught she just wanted to comfort him in her arms. The champagne went down in greater proportions. Elisabeth was desperate. Franz couldn't wait for the wedding.

The day before the wedding, the whole court went into shock. Rudolf had ordered a cage with five wildcats delivered to the zoo grounds of Schönbrunn Palace. The cage door was opened and drummers pounded their drums. The terrified animals fled out. With a grin of passion almost surreal, Rudolf shot each one, slowly, deliberately. Even Franz was shocked. Elisabeth locked herself in her room.

The May sun bloomed in full glory, but the wedding in Vienna's Augustinian church was a cold and loveless affair. Elisabeth looked stunning in her blue gown with diamonds and flowers twined through her hair. But her face was stone.

Stephanie, the bride, was red-faced and awkward in an elaborate gown. She looked more like an overdressed child than a bride. Rudolf had no smile. In fact, he looked ill. No one was smiling. The archbishop's voice boomed out dazzling promises of eternal happiness, but not one soul in the room believed it, not even the bride.

The wedding carriage bumped over a rocky road taking the young couple to the Laxenburg Palace. Rudolf stared out at the rain hammering the window. Stephanie huddled down, frightened and frozen to the marrow. Not even their hands touched.

It's a nightmare, Stephanie thought. She had left her home for another country, married a man she hardly knew who had nothing to say and who did not love her. The desolate countryside sped by, the clouds hung lower and the rain hammered harder on the windows. She was close to tears.

The Laxenburg Palace was as cold and damp as the outside air. No plants or flowers welcomed them, just a few sleepy-eyed servants and a waddling old chambermaid with an accent Stephanie could hardly understand. She led Stephanie to a cold, damp room with no carpet, no toilet, no bath and the fire in the stove miserable. Rudolf did not come. She spent her wedding night alone.

She huddled down in her bed shivering with the cold, but relieved that he hadn't come. Like Elisabeth before her, she hardly knew what was expected of her. Her romance novels only went so far. The rain pounded on the window and sleet was an added touch.

The next night, Rudolf came. There was no love. His attack was brutal.

She wrote in her diary the next morning: 'What a terrible night. What agony. What loathing. I was not prepared. My illusions, the dreams of my youth were destroyed. I felt that I must die of disappointment.'

Rudolf knew his mother had been right. He had made a terrible mistake.

After a brief time in Prague, the impressive-looking, though spartan, Hofburg Palace became their home. Stephanie's agony never ended. Her apartment had no bathroom and no water closets. Two large buckets of water on a shelf were her shower and a red rubber bowl was the toilet. The maid would carry the slops down the halls at all hours of the day. The oil lamps would go out after a few hours and there would only be a candle to light, if the maid remembered to leave one.

And her husband? You wouldn't know she had one. Rudolf retained his own bachelor apartments, where she was never invited.

Stephanie sat among the court ladies, smiling desperately and wondering how true the stories were. Did young ladies come in droves to Rudolf's apartment, as everyone said? Did his valet escort them from a secluded entrance through hidden halls to the apartment of the beaming prince? The court ladies never had such fun. They watched everything that went on and the servants looked for evidence in the garbage containers. It was like a comic opera.

The whole of Vienna raced with excitement as rumours rattled down the palace halls and through the salons. Even the dark alleys vibrated. The royals were at it again. Bright-eyed, vibrating with curiosity, the court ladies dissected every movement Stephanie made. Their whispers accelerated with giggling excitement.

"Is this what a royal marriage is in Vienna?" Stephanie cried to Elisabeth.

Elisabeth dropped her eyes. People said that she was not very sympathetic, even though memories of her own early marriage came back to her. But what could she say? It had been obvious from the start.

In 1883, Stephanie and Rudolf's daughter, Elisabeth, was born. Rudolf's feet landed back on the ground. He was a father and he had responsibilities. There was an empire to inherit.

He travelled to London, Rome and Madrid. He saw a different world, a liberated world. In Paris, he marvelled at the remarkable changes brought about by the French Revolution. The French Empire had become a republic. He saw a contented populace.

He saw his father as an antiquated martinet. Again, he echoed his thoughts to his mother.

"He has no understanding, nor does he respect the people's feelings. He rules only to preserve the power of the Habsburgs, and his tactics just won't work."

Elisabeth took his hand.

"Fight for what you believe in. Save this empire for your children," she advised.

To his liberal friends in the coffee houses, Rudolf promised, "I will never rule this empire as an emperor. I will rule as the president of a republic."

Rudolf's liberal ideas brought cheering from his coffee-house friends. But could he convince his father?

It was another week before Rudolf finally met with Franz in his office. Still, his determination was fired. He sat in front of his impatient, stone-faced father.

Franz knew of Rudolf's liberal leanings and he had no time for such nonsense. Control, not change, was frozen in him since the days when Prince Felix Schwarzenberg and Archduchess Sophie ruled with iron fists.

"Please get out quickly what you wish to say," he said to Rudolf.

Rudolf gripped his hands and gripped harder to keep his courage. After only two sentences, Franz cut him short.

"You are talking nonsense again. I have no time for this."

He leaned forward, arms on his desk.

"I give you freedom in your private life, but not in state business until your common sense returns. Until then, you are dismissed from all political discussions with my ministry and with my ministers."

Franz rose, ignoring Rudolf's attempt to respond. He took Rudolf's arm and led him to the door.

"Like all other subjects, you are not permitted to question or speak to me about matters that concern this empire and government business."

He closed the door on Rudolf's red face with one final comment.

"Furthermore, like the populace, you are not permitted to question the emperor."

Rudolf sobbed like a child in his mother's arms.

"The emperor stands isolated on a pinnacle. He is losing the love and respect of the people. Mama, there will never be an empire for me to rule, nor for my children."

Elisabeth went to the window and stared out. Fall had cast an early chill. Coloured leaves swept along the paths and across the lawns. For a moment she stood silent, then her anger exploded.

"Fate holds in store for Austria nothing but dire calamities. There is nothing for us but to resign ourselves to the worst. The House of Habsburg is in the grip of an implacable fate."

Rudolf clasped his mother in his arms. He knew she was right.

Rudolf turned to hunting with a vengeance. It soothed his raging helplessness. His father's chastising disrespect went like a knife into his soul. He chased deer, hare, partridges, squirrels, pheasants, wolves, wild boars, goats, foxes, lynx and bears. He chased them with a frenzy that shocked his fellow hunters. The Habsburgs were passionate hunters, keeping meticulous lists of their kills. During Rudolf's hunting life, around thirty thousand animals were shot.

His faithful valet, Loschek, escorted a larger procession of young ladies through the tunnels of the Hofburg Palace. Gossip spread with new vigour. Stories sailed of exotic carriage parties under the trees of the Prater and in the hunting lodges, where peasant girls with their rosy cheeks and buxom figures outshone the Viennese ladies. The champagne flowed freely and it was said that morphine became an added spark.

Once again, Stephanie, who had hoped that a daughter would make a difference to her unhappy life, wallowed in despair while Elisabeth helplessly turned her back.

In the autumn of 1888, Vienna again became the city of dreams, the gayest in all Europe. The new Imperial Theatre and Opera House brimmed with shining new stars and the beautiful Ringstrasse boulevard with its magnificent tree-lined streets was full of gilded carriages. The music of outdoor musicians once again echoed through the streets. Wine glasses were raised with jovial voices in the sidewalk cafés.

It was true that the emperor's fist still held the people in a firm grip, but a strong middle class was emerging and industry was expanding. Smoke from the piano factories rose in the air, and fortunes were being made. To the hopeful tycoon, a good marriage was not an affair of the heart, it was the pursuit of power.

Although the homes of the new bourgeoisie rivalled some of the aristocrats', even their newfound wealth could not break through the social barriers of the Viennese court. The royal salons did not welcome them, for not an ounce of blue blood flowed through their veins.

Nothing had changed for the poverty-stricken, sheltered in the dark alleys and fleeing the cold in the windproof sewers.

Vienna, 'the city of dreams, the gayest in all Europe', had more suicides than any other city in the world. There were the unidentified who jumped into the Danube and whose bodies washed ashore, colourful ribbons tied around their necks. There was the elegant young lady who boarded the Budapest express with a small suitcase, then emerged from her room in a bridal gown with a veil, opened the car-end door and stepped onto the railbed below the flying train.

There was the young couple who gaily picnicked on capon and champagne inside the gates of a cemetery. When finished, the sunshine still sweeping through the rustling trees, the young man placed a pistol into the girl's mouth and exploded her skull. Then he blasted his own. Why? They were attractive, wealthy and given permission to marry. What more perfection could lie beyond? Was it a dazzling world of joy with no responsibilities?

There was the tightrope walker who jumped from his window with a rope around his neck. He left a note: 'The rope was my life and the rope was my death.'

The most spectacular death of another tightrope walker left an audience with cries of horror. It was performed with spotlights and a blaring orchestra in Vienna's best variety theatre. He had argued with his wife minutes before his act. At the show's climax, poised high up on the rope to beating drums, he dramatically threw away his balancing staff and dove headfirst down to the marble floor.

When Rudolf expounded on the advantages of voluntary death and praised the courageous ones who "threw away their souls in defiance of God," Elisabeth was terrified. When he painted a theatrical picture of escaping this world of turmoil in the arms of a beautiful woman, she fled to Franz.

"Your fears are a figment of your imagination," he said, attempting to dismiss her fears. "Rudolf is well, just a little tired. He parties too much."

Elisabeth fled to Gödöllő, morbidly terrified. In her diary she wrote: 'I fear Rudolf is condemned to a tragic fate, to a slow agony more hideous than death.'

3

In June of 1888, Mary Vetsera came into Rudolf's life. She was the beam of light at the end of his dark tunnel. But it was a light in the tunnel of death, shining with illusions.

Mary Vetsera met Rudolf at the racetrack in Freudenau. She was seventeen. He was cheering the horses with Edward, the Prince of Wales.

When the prince introduced them, Rudolf's eyes lit up with the sparkle a new woman in his life often produced. They greeted each other and then he walked on. But their mutual attraction was sealed. In her diary she wrote: 'On that afternoon, a passion was born.'

Baroness Marie Alexandria von Vetsera was born in Vienna in 1871. Her father was a baron of the lower nobility; her exceptionally beautiful mother came from the wealthy banking family, the Baltazzi. Mary, as she was called, was considered a 'good imperial mixture'.

She was brought up denied nothing — money and prestige were ingrained in her as were visions of a royal alliance. She attended the Institute for the Daughters of the Nobility. It was a preparation for life among the ranks of the royal court, a dream that had bypassed her mother.

At seventeen, Mary was also exceptionally beautiful. Her tutor remarked, "It makes me happy just to look at her. She is mature for her age. She has a perfect figure, a magnificent wealth of dark hair, a snub nose and large blue eyes." Intellectual pursuits she tossed aside. Fashionable clothes, jewellery, ice skating, the racetrack and flirting took all her talents. Romantic intrigues were not new to her. In Cairo, where she spent her winters, her extraordinary beauty and her flirtatious manner kept the buzz running and her mother's hair greying.

Mary had a dream that turned into reality. Since childhood, she had collected photographs of Rudolf. She knew of his life. She knew of his unhappy marriage. The day she met him she confided in her maid.

"I know I have no right to say this and he may not remember I exist, but he is mine. I feel it in my heart. I swear I shall never love another."

With the frivolous determination of a teenager, she set out on her mission. She begged her friend, Countess Larisch, whose marriage allowed her access to court, to take a letter to Rudolf suggesting they meet again.

"I must try," she told the countess. "I belong in his life."

The countess's eyes lit up. She was also eighteen, and she had a passion for romantic intrigues. She rushed with the letter to Rudolf, excitement charging through her veins like gushing spring waters.

"The enchanting little one has barely left my mind," Rudolf said, fingering the letter.

He smiled, but with an expression the countess found really hard to read.

"It was amusing, yet thoughtful," she told Mary later, "as if he saw something in the future."

She didn't tell Mary that he picked up a real human skull that lay on his desk and rubbed it almost affectionately, with a strange expression. She didn't tell her that a revolver lay on his table beside the latest press releases of suicides — an elegantly dressed young woman had stepped from her balcony and fallen six storeys into the next world; a young man had shot his girlfriend and then himself because his father thought him incompetent.

The countess did add, with an amusing smile, his final words: "I have a lively desire to meet and talk to her." The girls hugged each other in excitement.

On an October afternoon, Mary and Countess Larisch jumped from their carriage in the alley behind Vienna's Grand Hotel and dashed into a waiting carriage. The wind almost took their hats. Bratfisch, Rudolf's coachman, quickly closed the door and off they went.

The horses galloped at full speed onto the Ringstrasse and down winding streets to the hidden entrance of the Hofburg Palace. They kept their faces concealed in their collars. Then up the stairs and along dark halls they rushed. Mary's eyes sparkled, her excitement ready to burst. Countess Larisch was so thrilled she had a hard time catching her breath.

At the apartment door stood a beaming Rudolf. His elegant bow was so enchanting that their smiles burst into giggles.

"Please, ladies, come in."

His smile was almost a giggle too.

It was the beginning — an afternoon of chatter, of laughter and eyes aglow with excitement. Rudolf himself guided them back through the dark halls and down the steps to their carriage. His eyes were on Mary but he spoke to the Countess Larisch.

"Please bring her back to me . . . soon."

Mary snuggled down in the carriage, hiding her face.

"He is just as adorable as I imagined," she murmured.

Days became weeks and their secret rendezvous continued in a rambling carriage driven by Bratfisch through the deep silence of the Vienna woods. There was only the odd chirping bird and Bratfisch's melodic whistle. It was a passionate and intoxicating connection, more spiritual than romantic. They held hands and looked into each other's eyes, but it was free of physical fulfillment.

Her youth, her beauty and her devotion intrigued Rudolf. For him, it was not love. It was like the beginning of a spiritual journey, perhaps a glorious escape from the despair that shadowed his life. He let his imagination run free. The world beyond was beckoning him with fascination in the arms of a beautiful woman.

For Mary, it was ecstasy. She felt like the heroines in her romantic novels come to life: the hero of her dreams, a future emperor, and passionate love roiling through her. She floated in a world of stars.

They formed a pact. They clasped their hands together. They looked into each other's eyes and they made a promise.

"If ever our love is discovered, after a few happy hours at a place nobody knows, we will enter the world beyond together."

On a stormy January night, Mary fled from her carriage straight into her bedroom and collapsed on her bed with her fur coat still on. Her maid had to pull it off.

"You can't sleep in it," she implored.

She couldn't miss Mary's dreamy expression, so radiant. Mary couldn't keep it to herself.

"I have been with him," she cried, springing up and catching the older woman's hands. "We both lost our heads. Now we belong to each other in body and in soul."

She looked away.

"I no longer belong to myself, only to him. From now on, I must do everything he asks of me."

In Vienna, intrigues never stay buried, especially royal intrigues. 'Rudolf and Mary Vetsera' — soon it filled every ear.

Mary's mother screamed that this was not the way to gain prestige in the royal court. She threatened to put her daughter in a cloister. Rudolf's wife, Stephanie, wondered what next could happen in her marriage. Elisabeth hung her head — she had the darkest of premonitions.

Franz furiously ordered Rudolf into his office and pounded his desk.

"This time, you are a fool," he shouted. "You have overstepped your boundaries. And you did it without discretion."

He marched him to the door. The valet heard his last words.

"You do not deserve to be my successor. If you do not break off this relationship at once, I will disinherit you."

Rudolf pulled his arm from his father's grasp. He looked him in the eye steadily. The fear of his father was gone; the fear of his future on the Earth was gone. His chin went up. He smiled.

"I will see her only one more time," he promised, firmly.

Deep in the Prater, in a carriage beside the ice-covered lake, with the falling snow protecting them from ruthless eyes, Rudolf and Mary planned how to complete their suicide pact.

They would go to the hunting lodge, Mayerling, the next day. From there, they would depart into a glorious world of freedom and joy where they would never part.

Mary was not frightened. She clung to Rudolf. She was dazzled with love. Rudolf saw this as closure to his defeat. In his father's eyes, he was a failure. His life was doomed. He would escape this unjust world into the glory of the unknown in the arms of a beautiful woman.

January 27th, the night before the couple's planned departure, Franz insisted Rudolf and Stephanie attend the reception for the German King William.

Rudolf hated the German king and his ties with Bismarck but he wiped it from his mind, turned on his charm and moved about the reception with smiles for all. His world was at peace, his plans laid.

He had invited his hunting buddies, Prince Philipp Coburg and Count Joseph Hoyos, to a hunt on Tuesday in Mayerling. That would remove any suspicion his father might have when he left for Mayerling on Monday. The evening drifted hazily past his eyes. This world seemed a thing of the past.

There were remarks about his starry-eyed, somewhat faraway look. The ladies thought him dazzling. Elisabeth saw his charm and was surprised at the attention he gave to his wife. Perhaps, she hoped, he had regained his senses.

Mary Vetsera was also present with her family. Her eyes met Rudolf's but they didn't speak. Her long slim neck was decked in shining jewels. Her tiara of diamonds brought the royal ladies' greatest gasps.

"Does she think she is an empress?" they sneered. "The emperor should remove her from the empire."

Of course the gentlemen had a different version as they admired her flashing eyes and her seductive figure. No wonder Rudolf had lost his senses.

The night ended with shocked gasps. Everyone was horrified when, as Stephanie passed through the rows of curtseying guests saying goodnight, Mary did not curtsey as protocol demanded. She stood straight and stared Stephanie brazenly in the eyes, her face confident. Her shocked mother pushed her to her knees, almost toppling Mary to the floor. Vienna went into vibration again, this time a stunned vibration. What was going on?

At ten o'clock Monday morning, Countess Larisch drove Mary to the back alley of the Grand Hotel. Mary jumped from that carriage into the one driven by Bratfisch. The countess wished her a great two days at the hunting lodge. She had no idea of the plan. She did think Mary somewhat misty-eyed and vague. Mary departed for Mayerling.

That Monday morning, Rudolf left a letter to Stephanie. 'You are free from my presence and vexation. Be happy in your own way. Be good to the poor little girl who is all that remains of me.'

To his aide-de-camp he wrote: 'I must die. It is the only way to leave this world as a gentleman.'

These letters he left on his dresser.

Rudolf left the Hofburg at twelve noon in a one-horse carriage called a fiacre. He seized the reins from the coachman, drove like a madman, constantly rapping the reins of the galloping horse.

"Faster, faster!" he yelled.

The coachman clung to his seat in panic.

At a crossroad halfway to Mayerling they met Bratfisch and Mary. Rudolf jumped from his coach and jumped in with Mary. Their excited eyes locked and they smiled. They shared quick, irregular breaths. As they settled in the carriage, Rudolf took Mary's hand. It stopped shaking.

Bratfisch drove them through the silent, snow-draped Vienna woods to the lodge. It was dark when they arrived.

Mary glanced quickly at the dark rooms as Rudolf rushed her to his apartment.

"It was a cloister before I turned it into a hunting lodge," Rudolf said, seeing her face.

Mary shivered. *Perhaps that's why it has such a feeling of melancholy*, she thought. She held Rudolf's arm tightly.

That night, their last night, they sat outside on a balcony in the moonlight. The air was still, so still they felt they were the only ones on Earth. In Vienna it was carnival time, Mary's favourite time.

The streets, lively with music and happy voices, floated into her mind. She thought of the waltzes and the frying doughnuts. She could almost smell them. She looked at the trees around them, silent and white with snow. She listened to the silence. She closed her eyes. Vienna was back in her mind. She grasped Rudolf's hand. She was afraid.

He tightened his hand on hers and he tried to soothe her. He pointed to a star with a brilliant light, so close it seemed almost on Earth.

"It is the planet Venus," he said. "And this is the year it comes the closest to the Earth."

He wrapped his arm around her.

"Perhaps it comes to welcome us."

She smiled and nestled closer to him, feeling his warmth. Her fears decreased. They looked up at the sky of stars, they looked into the snow-drenched forest. The quietness and the beauty of the winter night brought a soothing contentment. The carnival festivities faded from Mary's mind and the wonder of the world beyond took its place.

The following morning Franz's hunting buddies Coburg and Hoyos arrived. Rudolf had breakfast with them. Mary ate alone. He didn't hunt with them, blaming the freezing cold and saying he felt unwell. He promised to meet them for dinner. He didn't mention Mary. Only his valet and Bratfisch knew of her presence.

Rudolf met them at dinner that night. Coburg was surprised at his quietness. Usually at Mayerling he was in good humour, ready to party. And there was always a lady or two present. Where were they? Coburg was disappointed — he enjoyed the ladies too, especially Rudolf's choices.

They feasted on roast venison and baked apple dessert. They joked and talked mostly hunting. Rudolf boasted that tomorrow's hunt would make up for what he missed today. At nine, they toasted each other with Baden wine. Rudolf said goodnight and the two men retired to the hunting lodge guest house. Coburg saw a shadow on Rudolf's face.

Mary again dined alone. She wrote letters of farewell.

With Bratfisch, Rudolf and Mary shared their last evening. Rudolf put new candles in the candelabra, filled the fire with logs and ordered champagne from the cellar. Bratfisch was also a singer with the Coachmen Singers. Rudolf had snuck incognito into the small bars where Bratfisch performed many times.

Rudolf gave him a list of songs, including his favourite, "Der Schwalbe Gruss" (The Swallow's Greeting). Bratfisch sang, having as much fun as they did downing champagne. They laughed and they sang and they swayed to the music long into the night until the logs were ashes, the champagne gone and the candles burned down. Mary's eyes were wild with excitement. Bratfisch thought Rudolf's laughter a little forced. He didn't know it was their last night on Earth.

When they were alone, Bratfisch gone, the room was quiet. A small candle flickered on a tiny desk. Rudolf sat quietly watching Mary finish her farewell letters.

To her sister, she wrote: 'We are both going happily to the unknown beyond. Think of me from time to time. Be happy and marry for love. I was unable to do it and since I could not resist love, I am going with him. Do not cry for me. I am going to the other side in peace. It is beautiful out there. Once more, goodbye.'

To her mother, she wrote: 'Pardon me for all I have done. I could not resist love. I am in agreement with him. I want to be buried beside him in the cemetery of Alland. I am happier in death than in life.' Then, as if it were just a short farewell, she expressed a joy of life by adding: 'Bratfisch played the pipes wonderfully for us tonight.'

There were no tears.

In front of the mirror, she undid her hair. It fell to the centre of her back, a lush cascade of soft curls. She saw Rudolf's reflection, smiling as he watched her. He did not move. She smiled, her eyes demure, a tiny sparkle. She felt no fear.

She removed her skirt and jacket, wrinkled from two days' wear. She laid them on a chair. She put her high-heeled shoes beneath the chair. She removed her jewellery and laid it on the tiny table. It flickered in the candlelight. She put on a long white gown, which shimmered down her body. She turned and smiled at him. She was so lovely, Rudolf caught his breath.

He didn't move. He stared at her. His jaw tightened. She was so young, so beautiful. He pushed away that wavering moment.

He jumped to his feet and took her in his arms. He buried his face in her hair. He held her for a moment, his eyes closed. Then he led her to the bed.

She lay on her back, her eyes large and glowing, never leaving his face. Gently, he arranged her hair across her shoulders and down her body. His kisses touched her breasts, her stomach and gently down each leg. His eyes came back to hers. He put the gun to her temple and he pulled the trigger.

The bullet shot through her head and lodged in the wall. Her face became a mess of bloody flesh; blood splattered the wall as high as the bullet hole. He cried out and collapsed to the floor. It was 1 a.m.

Time passed. He didn't know how much. Silence reigned. He struggled to his feet. He paced the room. The candle flickered.

He didn't look at the body. The silence pounded in his ears. He looked at the gun in his hand. His body trembled, his hand trembled. Tears came. Reality came. He sobbed, tormented with pain.

Rudolf struggled to the desk. He sat down. He dropped the gun.

To his mother, he wrote a last farewell. His frustration and his bitter anger for his father rolled over page after page. He blamed him for his feelings of inferiority and incompetence. At 6:30 a.m., he finished with: 'I must die, for I have killed.'

He did not leave a letter for his father.

He heard his valet, Loschek, in the outside hall. He opened the door and went out.

"Please order breakfast. And ask Bratfisch to have the carriage ready. And to call me at seven-thirty."

He returned to his room, whistling. Loschek thought, *He always whistles when he's under stress.*

At seven-thirty, Loschek knocked at his door but there was no answer. He knocked again. Still, there was no answer. He tried to open the door. It was locked. He pounded harder. Still no answer.

He raced down the hall to the dining room where Coburg and Hoyos awaited their breakfast.

"Something is seriously wrong," Loschek announced.

They followed him back. Hoyos pounded on the door, calling Rudolf's name. Still there was nothing.

"I want you to knock down the door," he said to Loschek.

Loschek backed away.

"I cannot, sir. You see . . . the Baroness Vetsera is with him."

"What?" both men asked in shock.

They stared at each other. Then Hoyos turned to Loschek.

"You must break down the door. We will take full responsibility."

They found the bodies.

Mary lay on the bed, her long hair sweeping over her shoulders and across her breasts. A rose was in her hand. Her green dress lay on a chair, the black high heels beneath it.

Rudolf's body lay beside her in a pool of blood, the top of his head blown off and a revolver in his hand. On the table, one tiny candle flickered on the written letters.

The top one to his valet read: 'Dear Loschek. Please fetch a priest and have us buried together in the same grave at Abbey Heiligenkreuz.'

Their wishes were not granted. They were not buried together.

Hundreds of chrysanthemums, roses and orchids covered the coffin where the crown prince lay in state for two days.

The court stated that 'His Royal Highness fired the shot that brought his death, in a mental derangement over a love affair.'

Franz, though stricken with grief, had to safeguard the ancestral prestige of the Habsburgs. He would not permit the announcement that his son had died in a triple catastrophe: adultery, murder and suicide.

Rudolf was buried in the Royal Capuchin Church in Vienna on January 30th, 1889.

Mary's family was informed that her death was a suicide. Franz ordered that she be removed under cover from the lodge so no one would know what had occurred at Mayerling. This would prevent further investigation that could attract attention and suspicion.

Mary's body, dressed in a coat and veil to cover her identity, was smuggled into a carriage. She was placed upright between her two uncles, a broom handle tied to the back of her lifeless body to hide the impression that a dead person was being removed from the lodge. Her suicide, as it was termed, had to be elsewhere.

Her body was carried over an icy, snow-covered road to a small Christian monastery. In a dim and dirty storage room, the body lay in the white gown now streaked with dried blood, covered by her fur coat, on a table so short her bare legs touched the floor.

There were two monks and her two uncles present at her burial. Her mother was not permitted to attend. Not even a single headstone marked the grave. It was not discovered until thirty years later.

Franz choked with agony when he read Rudolf's farewell letter to Elisabeth. At the end of his letter, Rudolf had asked forgiveness of his father, stating: 'I know quite well I am not worthy to be his son.'

Franz collapsed, a broken man. His guilt never left him.

Elisabeth fled Vienna, burying her sorrow in black mourning dress. Her beauty, she never cared about again. Until the day before her death, she wore a high-necked black dress, black laced boots and a black hat with a black veil falling from its brim. A fan and a white umbrella never left her hands. They were her weapons to hide her weatherbeaten face, with its lines that would never be seen.

ℐolace

1

Vienna remained a city draped in black. Elisabeth did not attend the funeral. She couldn't. She huddled in Rudolf's room for hours, at times fearing her sanity was fleeing. Her grief was mingled with guilt, a guilt she could not dislodge from her mind. Had the tainted blood of the Wittelsbachs passed through her to her son?

On a sleepless night in February, when sleet pounded the windows and the wind howled like mad hounds, she threw on her cape, pulled a hat down to protect her identity and fled to the monastery of the Church of the Capuchin.

A monk answered the door.

"I am the empress," she said. "Please take me to my son Rudolf."

They descended down the dark steps into an icy vault. Candles flickered beside the stone casket.

Outside, the monk waited, shivering with uncertainty. Should he have let her in? Twice he heard her loud, anguished wail.

"Rudolf! Rudolf!"

He crossed himself in fear.

The next day, Elisabeth fled Vienna. It was never to be her home again. Her life would become a journey of endless travel.

The court accused her of running like a thoughtless child, leaving behind her dejected husband — who had already found refuge in the arms of his latest amour, Katharina Schratt, an attractive actress from the Burgtheater.

Meaning had left her life. Her mind was a vacuum. Despondency was taking charge. She clung to the small shreds of strength she had left and, with tears running down her cheeks, she prayed that her strength would stay intact.

Elisabeth went to Corfu, to her Villa Achilleion, named after her favourite Greek hero, Achilles. The villa was nestled among olive tree plantations on the plains above the blue-green waters of the Ionian Sea. On her previous visit, she had turned the villa's 129 rooms into a splendour of ancient Greece, portraying her fascination for Achilles.

Achilles was the greatest warrior in Homer's *Iliad* and a hero of the Trojan War. He killed Greece's most dangerous enemy, the Trojan hero Hector, at the gates of Troy. Achilles' father, Peleus, was a mortal. His mother, Thetis, a sea-nymph, attempted to make Achilles immortal by immersing him in the River Styx. The heel she held him by was not immersed in the water, thus leaving him vulnerable to mortal death on a single part of his otherwise invulnerable body. Even today, the phrase 'Achilles' heel' is referred to as a dangerous weakness. The King of Troy shot an arrow into Achilles' heel, killing him.

On the villa's vestibule ceiling, the painter Paliotti had portrayed the four seasons. Paliotti and Pastiglione painted scenes of ancient Greek mythology and romance as described by Homer on the walls of the halls, the salons and the galleries. Magnificent gardens, filled with tropical plants and trees and twenty-five thousand rosebushes of all kinds and colours, descended on sloping terraces to a pink marble seawall.

Despite all this, Elisabeth loved best to walk on a rocky elevation overlooking the sea, through a vined and flowered trellis to her exquisite little Greek temple. For hours that filtered into days, Elisabeth sat gazing out at the sea, her two Great Danes snoring at her side and her books hardly opened.

Not even in this beauty did her sorrow mellow.

"Misery still hangs on my shoulders like a cape," she said to Countess Irma Sztáray one evening when the setting sun was casting its last splendour on the waters below.

Irma was her new companion. Ida had returned to Hungary and married the man who had waited so long for her. Elisabeth missed her desperately. She and the countess were sitting on the balcony of the little temple, cool breezes caressing their arms.

"I must not succumb to misery," she went on. "But this beautiful tranquility is not helping me. It does not blot the pain from my heart. Perhaps travel might mellow the pain of my life and let meaning creep in." Then she added defensively, "I never want to be a burden to my family."

Countess Sztáray couldn't curb her joy. She turned her head to hide her smile. Corfu was just too dull — she loved to travel.

When the royal yacht pulled away from Corfu, tears edged Elisabeth's eyes as she watched the island disappear beneath the horizon. She might never see her beloved Villa Achilleion again.

The imperial yacht became her home. She went anywhere and everywhere: Spain, Morocco, Algeria, Constantinople, Cairo, Jerusalem, Tunisia and Tangier. The sights passed before her eyes as in a dream. The sea was her only solace, a rapture of soothing contentment. She never tired of watching the gentle ripples. Often she closed her eyes, enjoying the soft murmur of the waves and the spray on her face. Often she thought of the writer Heinrich Heine, of his compassion for the misery of the world and human suffering, of his sensitivity to nature and his love of the sea.

At the height of a storm, when the winds drove the waves to tumultuous heights and the boat rocked endlessly, she huddled on the deck, again tied to a chair and wrapped in a blanket up to her neck. The torrent of the sea was like the exciting strains of a concerto taking her from the world, hiding the imperfections of her life.

She abandoned the seas for carriage trips to the lofty summits of the Swiss and the Tyrolean Alps and the mountains of Bohemia. She gazed for hours at the peaks and the breathtaking valleys, lost in their beauty. In the surrounding forests, the melodies of nature took her back to her childhood. Slowly, contentment began to dislodge her despair.

Elisabeth discovered Brittany. She loved the small, quaint towns still enclosed in the same stone walls after hundreds of years. In the ancient moats, wild ducks swam in the muddy waters.

On the Brittany cliffs, she and Countess Sztáray found an old castle that towered high above a violent sea. The castle was mouldy and damp and the sound of the waters crashing against the rocks below penetrated the castle walls with such a roar that the pair struggled to hear their own voices. It was a castle enclosed in the wildness of the sea.

"What a world of glory!" Elisabeth cried.

The balconies became her haven. There, she feasted on her books and let herself drift away into the roar of the wild sea. The pounding waves wrapped her in their arms every night as she fell asleep. The world was left behind.

That is, until a young Polish count, Adam Ubryk, came into her life. He had a desperate plea. He was searching for his sister, Barbara.

For Elisabeth, it was a step back into life and a step forward on her path.

At eighteen, Barbara, spirited and beautiful, had fallen in love with a young officer of the Lancers, a man with no rank, no title and no fortune. Her family, in desperation, forced her into the old Carmelite convent in Kraków. In fury, she refused all contact with her family. That was twenty years before, and there had been no contact since. She was on the list of neither the living nor the dead.

Adam Ubryk had thrown himself at the feet of the abbess of the convent, begging for the truth. She refused to comment. Desperate for help, he turned to Elisabeth.

At once, Elisabeth sent a personal letter to the Archbishop of Kraków asking for his assistance. The abbess of the convent refused to speak to the archbishop on the matter.

There had to be something desperately wrong.

Elisabeth arranged the help of soldiers of the emperor's army stationed in Kraków. They forced their way into the convent in spite of the desperate resistance of the nuns, who were hurling stones and sticks. The soldiers dared not draw their swords.

The searchers found the answer. With torches flaming through dark winding tunnels, they came upon a dungeon, fifteen feet undergound. It was six feet by seven feet, the walls black with leeches and cobwebs. Low moans and groans reached their ears. A naked woman with matted filthy hair, her hands and feet loosely bound by steel chains, was inside. Sister Barbara Ubryk had been found. She clawed at the walls like a terrified animal. Her abilities of speech and reasoning were gone after an incarceration of nineteen years.

The pitiful story came out.

In the first year of her stay in the convent, a nun reported to the abbess that Sister Barbara was planning to escape with her young man. In the dead of night, the abbess, with the help of the nun, forced Sister Barbara into the dungeon and chained her. They blocked the entrance, leaving a small open square for the bread and water that was brought several times a week. No one else knew of the terrible secret.

The abbess and the nun were severely punished by the Pope.

Sister Barbara was placed in an asylum, but her sanity never returned. Still, perhaps she found peace. She would take the flowers Elisabeth brought, her eyes lighting up with their beauty. But she did not recognize her gifter or those around her. The canaries, which Elisabeth also brought, received her biggest smiles as they fluttered and chirped in their cage on her window.

The empress looked up at the stars that night and gave thanks for her life.

Elisabeth returned to Vienna occasionally, but she was not ready to make it a permanent home agian. Her daughter Valerie was now happily married and expecting her first child. Her daughter Gisela had moved on from ponies to horses. Franz still found affection and companionship in the arms of Katharina Schratt. This didn't raise Elisabeth's ire, rather it freed her from guilt.

"Everyone must think me mad, always on the run," Elisabeth said to Countess Sztáray one day. "I'm not mad. I cannot be a burden, wallowing in self-pity. I must find my own way, with more clarity. I must be essentially myself or go mad."

Though she had shelved much of her misery, answers had not come. At times, she thought of death.

"People should not be afraid to die," she said to Countess Sztáray one winter night, when snow lashed the shutters and the fire in the hearth threw little heat. "Death is only an everlasting rest. Perhaps it is happiness." Thinking of Rudolf, she added with gallows humour, "It is also the undiscovered country from which no traveller can return."

2

In 1896, Elisabeth's travels ended. On the shore of Switzerland's Lake Geneva she had found a small, rustic residence that reminded her of Possi. She felt at home again.

It was a time of sorrow and of memories.

Her sister Helene's departure from the Earth in 1890 brought agony, but also memories of two excited young ladies in Bad Ischl and the dashing young emperor who turned their lives upside-down. Tears filled her eyes. It had been a time of innocence and love and the excitement of the unknown.

Her younger sister, Sophie, burned to death in a Paris fire that destroyed the Bazar de la Charité in 1897. She had refused rescue attempts, insisting that the girls working with her at the bazaar be saved first.

Elisabeth's father's death in 1896 had actually brought a kind of solace, rekindling memories of her childhood.

Her sister Maria in England hadn't told her of the death of Bay Middleton in 1892. He was killed riding in the Midland Sportsman's Cup race.

It was Julius Andrássy's death in 1890 that made her raise her eyes and ponder the void in her life. Though agony twisted a knot in her heart, it brought a revelation she could never have foreseen.

She attended the funeral incognito. When the church was empty, the mourners gone, she returned alone. She laid her hands on the casket, gently caressing it. She bowed her head and closed her eyes, remembering. A soft warmth filled her body and cradled her emotions. For a moment, she didn't move. She opened her eyes and raised her head. He was there. She didn't see him, but she knew. Julius was beside her. Her hand warmed. It was in his. She let herself fold into him, their souls entwined. She looked into the darkness.

"I love you, Julius," she whispered with a gentle smile.

They were words she had never dared voice to him.

She walked from the chapel. The evening sky had darkened but the horizon peeked through the mist. A warmth flowed through her. She looked up at the sky, smiling. For the first time, she realized love had been hers in this life. And she had not lost it, though they had both sacrificed their love for their duties to their countries. Love awaited her somewhere, sometime. Peace and solace had enclosed her in their arms.

Franz, however, was concerned. He wrote to her: 'The anarchist movement is growing faster in Switzerland than in any other country in Europe, and royal heads are its goal.'

Elisabeth knew of the anarchists, as all royals did. Most came from the slums. They were against class superiority and hated the rich, especially the royals. They viewed themselves as courageous heroes fighting for the grand cause of the poor, and they desperately searched for notoriety in bloodshed and treachery. That brought them to centre stage and illuminated their courageous dedication.

"I am too unimportant to attract their malevolence," Elisabeth assured Franz.

Two days later, as she walked in her garden, a raven swept down, brushing her with its black feathers and snatching the fruit from her hand. Countess Sztáray let out a cry of horror. Ravens were the most terrifying of bad omens.

"Don't be alarmed," Elisabeth said. "I do not believe ravens are bad omens. Besides, I shall die as my destiny determines."

She quietly watched the raven devour her plum.

"I know," she said rather soberly, "that I am moving towards a terrible end that has been marked out for me by fate, and nothing in this world can prevent me from reaching it."

She remembered the words of the gypsy fortune teller long ago in Munich: "Your hand is written with tragedy. When you least expect it, the tragic end will come."

She remained in Switzerland, walking through the valleys, basking in the pastoral greenery that reached high into the mountains. The loneliness of her life she could not dislodge. She missed her daughters and her grandchildren. In the quiet beauty of the Swiss Alps, melancholy crept in.

A letter from Franz sparked a cry of joy and brought Countess Sztáray flying into her room. Elisabeth's smile was like dancing marigolds. Elisabeth flung the letter into Countess Sztáray's hand.

'Come back. I miss you, and so do your children and your grandchildren.'

A cry of joy flew also from the countess. She wanted to return to Vienna — her young man's patience was running out and life with Elisabeth was dull. She had exhausted all the young men in the area.

Elisabeth gazed out the window, hope racing through her. Could the seams of her life be coming together?

Luigi Lucheni was born in Paris in 1873. His mother, an unmarried laundress, left him on the street. He was raised in an orphanage and by a series of foster families. He foraged a living in subservient jobs. He hated the rich and feasted on the ideals of anarchism.

"I am a glorious anarchist," he bragged to his friends, who also shared his dreams of glory. "And I am long overdue to strike for the cause. When I attain my victory, my name will go down in history and I will be the happiest man on earth. I am no coward and I do not fear death."

Elisabeth and Countess Sztáray arrived at the Hotel Beau Rivage in Geneva on September 9th, 1898. From there they would board the steamer to Vienna. Her identity leaked out.

Lucheni had his victim—an empress, one with no bodyguard. He purchased a sharp knife for twelve francs.

"It's a great deal of money for only one use," his girlfriend grumbled.

Lucheni agreed and returned it for a long, slender file for half the price. He sharpened it like a stiletto and fashioned a wooden handle. He waited for his time.

Masses of white and mauve asters filled Elisabeth's hotel apartment.

"They are pretty, but they are flowers of death," she said jokingly to Countess Sztáray. "Asters are displayed in Vienna's cemeteries on All Souls' Day as a tribute to death."

She quickly dashed that from her mind.

"Let's go shopping!" she exclaimed. "I am going to get rid of all my black clothes and start anew."

And shop they did. Countess Sztáray had never seen her so happy. The black apparel was cast aside. She bought the latest suit in style for her trip to Vienna. It was blue, with a matching hat that sported a soft rose ribbon that hung down her back.

"You are still the most beautiful woman in the world," the countess said.

Elisabeth laughed. Her eyes danced.

"Me? Beautiful? I had almost forgotten the word."

That evening, after a dinner full of amusing chatter, Elisabeth sat alone on the hotel balcony. The moon drifted across the lake, dropping streams of light on its tiny ripples. All around her was silence, comforting and beautiful. She thought of Franz.

There would never be real love in her heart for him, although there would be affection and companionship. He said the hounds were not as demanding and Katharina was only a very good friend. They would have more time together, perhaps travel. And the court ladies? She found a smile. That would never change. Still, a warm contentment filled her and she prayed she would be strong and that her wandering was over.

She rose from her chair to go in when she saw it — a pale white figure hovering in the hotel grounds below her. The white phantom stared up at her intently, then vanished into the trees. *The White Lady*, Elisabeth thought. She was a legend the Habsburgs had believed in for centuries, an apparition of death. There were rumours she had last appeared the day before Rudolf's death. Elisabeth went into her room. She closed her door and told herself she didn't believe in such things.

The two ladies were up early the next morning. The sun was shining and they were excited.

"One more stop before we board the steamer," Elisabeth said.

She bought more gifts for her grandchildren and dashed into her favourite pastry shop.

"These I never get in Vienna," she explained, and then gulped down two sugar-coated buns.

Then they were off, down the path leading to the boat. Elisabeth walked proudly in her new outfit, enjoying its stylishness. She chattered as fast as the fluttering wings of a butterfly sailing from flower to flower. Countess Sztáray was all smiles, wondering if her young man might meet her at the station.

The sunshine was warm, seagulls sailed across the sky and the lake waters sparkled. You would think a case of diamonds had been sprinkled across its surface.

"Look at those beautiful chestnut blossoms still blooming. And autumn is in the air," Elisabeth exclaimed, her smile like the sunshine.

Lucheni lunged from the bushes. Elisabeth screamed and jumped back. She saw the gleaming eyes, the crooked smile, the teeth. Her knees buckled. She went to the ground.

Instantly she was up, back on her feet. The countess caught her, steadying her.

"Stop him! Stop him!" she shouted to the gaping people, pointing at the skinny man charging away.

She brushed the dirt from Elisabeth's cape.

"Are you hurt?" she asked.

"No, I don't think so."

With a firm step, Elisabeth walked towards the steamer and up the gangplank.

On the deck, she collapsed. Countess Sztáray screamed for a doctor. Velvet cushions were quickly brought and placed beneath her head. People milled around, their eyes popping. Smelling salts, cold water and vinegar did nothing to revive her. Neither did Countess Sztáray's terrified cries.

She removed Elisabeth's collar to give her more breathing room. Then a scream of terror fled her mouth. Elisabeth's jacket was wet with blood. It oozed from a small wound just above her left breast.

The steamer's whistle blew as it pulled away from the shore.

"We need a doctor," the countess screamed. "Turn back! Turn back!"

Elisabeth opened her eyes. She saw the bodies hovering around and saw their terrified faces. They were like phantoms. She heard nothing.

Her eyes rose to the azure sky and widened with sudden joy.

Countess Sztáray saw it. She gasped. A rosy hue coloured Elisabeth's face.

The others saw it.

Elisabeth's arms reached up. Her eyes shone.

Countess Sztáray gasped again. What did the empress see?

"Julius!" Elisabeth cried.

A smile filled her face, her eyes. Countess Sztáray saw it, the others saw it. They heard her whisper.

"This time you are taking me with you."

Her arms dropped. Her eyes closed. An expression of peace covered her face. It was soft, gentle and beautiful.

She never opened her eyes again.

3

Luigi Lucheni told the trial judge, "I wanted to kill a person of rank to see my name printed in a paper and to go down in history. But human suffering was the motive of my act."

Switzerland had no death penalty. Lucheni did not hang from the gallows as a glorious hero in front of cheering crowds as he had hoped. He finished his life in solitary confinement deep in the bowels of the l'Evêché (Bishops) prison, down a corridor so dark the guard needed a lantern. There were no windows, only a mattress, a small candle and a chaplain who visited him briefly, once a week. He was Number 1144.

Epilogue

The funeral train carrying Elisabeth's coffin passed slowly through Switzerland and Austria amid muffled tolling bells and sobbing crowds. On September 17th, 1898, it arrived in Vienna, a city deep in mourning.

The streets, the alleys and the railroads were crowded with mourners. A black carriage pulled by black horses, accompanied by the Imperial Austrian Guard and the Royal Hungarian Guard, carried Elisabeth's coffin through the streets and into the Neuer Markt where the Capuchin Church stood. A noble child with a lantern walked before it.

Black-garbed people crowded on to the Graben, the Kärntner Strasse and the Herrengasse, trying to get a glimpse of the Capuchin Church. Citizens were packed in rows so densely they couldn't move and the streets and alleys were like a carpet of black. Many hung on the steeples of the nearby churches of St. Michael and St. Augustine. Moans of sorrow rumbled through the air.

"Thank you. Thank you," shouted a young man, clinging desperately to a steeple.

It was the Polish count, Adam Ubryk, Sister Barbara's brother.

Inside the Church of the Capuchins, draped with white velvet and silver satin, the coffin was laid.

Emperors and empresses, kings and queens, princes and princesses huddled in the narrow pews, remembering the beauty that enhanced the world and the wanderlust of her restless soul.

The royals huddled down in their seats, their faces covered to hide their guilt for their lack of loyalty to their empress and to hide their relief that the threat was gone. There were the Hungarians, whose sobs reverberated against the granite walls — Elisabeth had been their saviour. The Italians bowed their heads, remembering the beautiful lady who had stood up for their freedoms.

Magnificent flower arrangements and wreaths filled the church, their soft fragrance filling the air. In a far corner, overshadowed by the Emperor of Russia's four-metre-wide garland of snowy blossoms, lay tiny bundles of wildflowers wrapped in colourful ribbons. In their midst was a picture of Elisabeth with the words 'Our Queen of Mercy.' The peasants and the poor had brought their love.

When night had fallen and the streets were dark and empty, a lone figure emerged from the church. He walked down the street towards the Hofburg Palace. No one saw the trembling figure, the tear-stained eyes or the tortured face of Franz Joseph, and no one heard his sobs.

A mixture of sentiments has filtered through history. Many have viewed Elisabeth as a woman running from responsibility and displaying her stress like a spoiled child to gain sympathy. Many have viewed her as a martyr. And many have viewed her in a different way, as a woman imprisoned in a society to which she could never belong, seeing a woman with the strength and determination to walk her own path in her own way, with pride in herself.

Are we masters of our fate? Must we take the blame for the paths of our lives? Or do the seeds of our childhood merely nourish our strength as we swirl on preordained paths, an unrelenting chain of events set off at the beginning of humankind?

Elisabeth was buried in the Church of the Capuchins beside her two children, Sophie and Rudolf. Beside her lay an empty crypt for Franz Joseph, who would one day lie beside her.

Franz Joseph died in November 1916.

In November of 1918 the Habsburg Empire collapsed. Countries emerged from World War I with new borders; the map of Europe had changed forever.

Acknowledgements

My story follows very closely the true life of Elisabeth. Most of my research has come from books written in the 19th century that I picked up in England and Europe. I tried to reach into her mind to discover the person she was. I saw her as an extraordinary woman born before her time in a society she could never belong in. Had she lived in our era, not crushed as she was by her society, she might have walked with the greatest of women.

I want to thank my editors, Elspeth Richmond and Sheilagh Simpson, and my copy editors, Renate Preuss and Kyle Hawke, for their help, and also thank Marion Crowhurst for showing me the right path. A great thank you to my readers, Betty and Lauren McKenzie, and Ellen Waites and Sonja Weisenbacher for their encouragement. To my dear granddaughter, Ashley Allan, and her special friend, Doug Colban, thank you for all your time. I also could not have managed without the help of my daughters, Leithea and Janine, and my son, Jim. Thank you so much.

Gloria Allan was educated at the University of British Columbia in Vancouver and the University of Washington in Seattle. Her major was English. She began writing as a cub reporter in Toronto, but gave up that precarious life to become an accountant. She married, raised five children and indulged her love of bridge, golf and travel. Never forgetting her love of writing, over the past several years she has written a novel and several short stories. Then, while browsing in an antiquarian bookstore in London, England, Gloria discovered a small book about Sisi, the beautiful and tragic Empress Elisabeth of Austria and Hungary. She immersed herself in Sisi's story, researching and gathering material for her second novel, *A Walk on Broken Glass*. Gloria currently lives in West Vancouver, BC.

CPSIA information can be obtained
at www.ICGtesting.com
Printed in the USA
LVHW040808030123
736290LV00010B/558